STEPHANIE AMEY has ︙
as chemistry teacher, scienti︙
safety adviser. She worked in ⌐⌐⌐⌐⌐, Kenya and Guatemala before settling in Norfolk. She has previously published two novels, *Holloway 8632* and *An Honourable Man*.

Born in Widnes, Steph lived in Brampton for several years as a child, very close to Hadrian's wall, and this is where her interest in Roman Britain began.

Her first novel in the Aurelius Petrus series was *At the Edge of Empire,* a thriller set on Hadrian's wall during the Roman occupation. The sequel is *The Mithraeum Connection.* Steph is retired and spends her time horse riding, reading thrillers, volunteering as a Magistrate and, of course, writing.

THE MITHRAEUM CONNECTION

Stephanie Amey

NORTHODOX
PRESS

Northodox Press Ltd
Maiden Greve, Malton,
North Yorkshire, YO17 7BE

This edition 2025

1

First published in Great Britain by
Northodox Press Ltd 2025

ISBN: 978-1-915179-53-1

This book is set in Caslon Pro Std

Printed and bound by CPI Group (UK) Ltd,
Croydon, CR0 4YY

This book is dedicated to the memory of my brother Mike George, who bravely fought a long battle against cancer. And to his daughters – Jessica and Emily for whom he kept going.

AD 171 BANNA FORT, HADRIAN'S WALL

DRAMATIS PERSONAE

Silvius Tatius - Prefect in command of Banna Fort

Aurelius Petrus – Centurion at Banna Fort

Ignatius Aquilinus – centurion at Banna Fort

Ruua – a herbalist

Litorius – son of Ruua

Gauori – Petrus' slave

Arsenios – the fort physician

Adrianus – librarius - record keeper for Aquilinus' century

Manius – librarius – record keeper for Petrus' century

Vester, Celsus, Janus, Justus - soldiers in Aquilinus' century

Fabius Ruga – Centurion at Banna fort

Sylva – owner of the brothel in the town

Carantii – the local blacksmith

Lugraca – Carantii's wife

Aurora – Petrus' wife

Augustus Pollux – the Tribune

Faustina – the Tribune's wife

Attia Camilla – new wife of Tatius

Ecdicius – the Signifer at the fort

Aurelius Tatius Felix – former slave to the Prefect at Banna fort

Maximus Petrus Boga – freed former slave

Roburius, Vegetinus, Ferullus – centurions at Banna Fort

Lucullus – retired centurion and merchant in the vicus

Cato – retired centurion

Flaccus – son of a former centurion, working for Lucullus

TERMS

Vicus – the settlement around the fort

Hastile – wooden staff with metal top

Vinestaff – short stick with metal top – symbol of a centurion

Signifer – the Senior record keeper and treasurer at the fort

Librarius – record keeper

Contubernia – a team of eight men, who shared accommodation

Praetorium – the commanding officer's house

Principia – the headquarters building

Pugio – short dagger carried by soldiers

Prologue

He struggled into consciousness and shivered. He lay slumped against a wall, his cheek pressed against the rough stone. His head throbbed and his dry tongue was swollen against the roof of his mouth. An ice-cold breeze caressed his body, kissed his scalp, and numbed his mind. Heavy limbs, arms and legs, wouldn't move. His right hand was balled in a fist, clutching something, something important.

He cried out in a thin weak voice that echoed through the darkness, "Help!"

I

Centurion Aurelius Petrus wanted to go home. He wanted to play with his son, cradle his baby daughter in his arms and then make love to his beautiful wife. Instead, he picked up his cloak from the bed and stepped past his slave, Gauori, who hovered nearby, unsure what to do.

'Good luck, Sir. I'll prepare a good breakfast for your return,' mumbled Gauori.

Petrus grabbed an unlit torch and stepped outside. Calm had settled on the fort as the soldiers went through their evening routines of cleaning armour and preparing food. The distant howl of a wolf pierced the silence. Petrus gasped as the cold air bit his cheeks; he pulled his cloak tighter around his shoulders and walked slowly along the street. A rat scurried across his path. Low voices sneaked out towards him from the barracks as he passed. The gate tower loomed ahead of him in the rapidly fading light. In the shadows, he could just make out a man in a hooded cloak. The man turned and took a lit torch from somewhere behind him, waving it towards Petrus' face. Petrus flinched; his body tensed for attack.

'Petrus,' said Fabius Ruga, his voice instantly recognisable, 'I thought you might have changed your mind.'

Petrus shook his head. The way Ruga had explained things, it hadn't seemed like he'd had much choice. He needed to be successful in his new post, so that he could stay at this fort, near his family. All the centurions and men of power were part of the secretive cult of Mithras. If he wanted to be looked on favourably by the Prefect and accepted by his fellow officers, he had to do this, the first of the initiation ordeals into the cult.

'I hope you've visited the latrines,' Ruga said as he moved towards the door in the gate. 'This will take all night and part of tomorrow and shitting yourself won't help matters.'

Petrus nodded helplessly. His attempts to empty his bowels earlier on had been fairly futile, and his bladder now felt full once again.

'Here, light your torch. I don't want you tripping and twisting an ankle once we leave the road.' Ruga held his torch steady.

Petrus fought to control his trembling arm as he touched his torch to the flame, and it crackled into life. Ruga stepped out of the gate with Petrus alongside him. Behind them, metal scraped and wood creaked as the guards secured the fort. Petrus' feet squelched in the thickening mud as it froze in the cold. Light and noise from the tavern spilled into the street as the taverner threw out two drunk men. They lay on the earth belching and groaning, then fell silent as the two Romans passed them. Smoke from Petrus' home sneaked into the air as they passed; the pull of his family was like a physical pain as he trudged behind Ruga into the merchants' area of the settlement.

The moon fought its way past the clouds and the distant hills were visible against the darkening sky at the edge of the vicus. Ruga led him off the road. The caress of wet grass lingered on Petrus' trouser legs, seeping into the cloth and chilling his skin. He felt the ground rising ahead of him. Ruga swore under his breath as he lost his footing and nearly fell. Petrus reached out to steady him, but the other man pushed him roughly away.

The grass receded and Ruga strode sure-footed up the slope. Petrus was unable to keep up and stifled the urge to cry out. A wolf's howl rang across the night, chased by another's answering call.

Ruga turned and waited for Petrus to reach him. 'Keep up,' he hissed.

Fog drifted towards them, flowing around their ankles and rising softly like smoke. Behind it marched the darkness as night completed its descent. The fort seemed a long way behind them. Petrus shivered as the breeze tore at his face. A pebble slid beneath his foot; he stumbled and swore as hot fat dripped onto his hand.

'Jupiter's sake!' he muttered and wiped his hand on his tunic, smearing grease. The hot cloth clung to his skin.

Ruga's torch had stopped moving as Petrus picked his way carefully past two huge rocks. A building rose out of the ground before them. Ruga beckoned him forward, pointing to a hole at his feet where steps led downwards. He put a hand on Petrus' arm and whispered, 'Careful! Could be slippery.'

Petrus found himself counting the steps as they descended, seven, the lucky number. Light leaked into the night from an ill-fitting door. Ruga drew his pugio and rapped four times on the door with it. At the last blow, he scraped down the wood with the hilt. The door opened. Writhing shadows moved across the ceiling of the nave in the flickering torchlight as Petrus followed him into the temple.

Ruga began to chant, louder and louder. Other deep voices echoed around the chamber. He waved his torch back and forth, revealing men shrouded in cloaks, their faces hidden by dark masks. They began to breathe deeply in unison. Ruga placed his torch into an alcove and put his hand firmly on Petrus' chest, motioning him to stay still. He took Petrus' torch and placed it in a holder on the wall above three carved stone altars, bathing them in light.

'Welcome to the Temple of Mithras.' Ruga waved his hand, taking in the men around him.

A thick oak tree trunk lay on the floor in the centre of the nave.

'Step forward,' commanded Ruga as he drew his sword.

Petrus' stomach turned to ice; he felt the world about him darken and blood roared in his ears.

Ruga tapped the sword with his fingers. 'It's just a symbol.'

Petrus felt himself relax, and the chamber seemed to grow lighter. Two men cast aside their cloaks and move to stand either end of the tree trunk. One of them had pale thin arms, and delicate hands. A strong smell of perfume hung around him; he smelled like the Prefect. The other man had the scarred hands and muscled arms of a fighter.

'This is the first of seven trials you must undergo to become a follower of the great Mithras. You will spend the night in the pit beneath this tree. You must leave your cloak, boots and socks over there,' Ruga pointed.

Petrus slowly folded his cloak and placed it on the floor alongside his boots and socks. He winced as the cold stone floor bit into the soles of his feet. He tried not to shiver.

'We'll return for you at the second hour after sunrise,' Ruga placed a hand on Petrus' shoulder, sensing his reluctance. 'There are holes in the wood to allow air in. You won't suffocate.'

Petrus nodded. The men began to push the trunk aside, revealing a dark pit.

'Mithras' sake!' whispered one of the men, falling to his knees. He began whispering prayers.

The other men moved to stand at the edge of the hole, peering in. They gradually lowered themselves to their knees, joining in the pleas to Mithras.

'What the fu..?' Ruga pushed his way past Petrus, grabbed a torch and held it over the hole, 'For the sake of the Gods, who..?'

Huddled in the corner of the pit, wrapped in a filthy cloak was the body of a man, with his face turned to the wall. The smell of stale urine rose around them.

'Who is it?' Ruga asked.

Petrus moved quickly and slid into the hole. He pulled the rigid body away from the wall and gasped as the dead eyes of Manius, the record keeper, stared up at him. Manius' cracked lips were wide open as if he was shouting. Petrus touched the grey cheek with the back of his hand. It was ice cold. Manius' left hand was raised, the dust peppered fingers clawing at the air with torn fingernails.

'Manius. What's he doing here?' Petrus asked.

Ruga shrugged. 'He's not one of us.'

'Help me lift him out!' Petrus took the body by the arms and dragged him upright. The rigid corpse crouched against the wall, balanced on its toes in an awkward dance of death.

'Grab him! For Jupiter's sake!' gasped Petrus as he struggled to keep the body vertical.

'Within these walls, we only call on Mithras!' muttered Ruga, reaching in and grabbing the body beneath his arms. 'Help me!'

One of the masked men reached in to assist, and they dragged the body onto the temple floor. Another man put his hand out to Petrus who brushed it aside.

'Hold the torch over there. I want to see whether there's anything else in here,' Petrus said.

The light reached into the narrow pit. Petrus looked around. Urine stained the floor where the body had lain. Someone leaned in and pulled him from the pit, releasing him at the last moment so that he collapsed on the floor next to the body. Petrus grunted, pushed himself to his knees, and looked at the dead man.

'How long's he been here?' he asked.

No-one spoke.

'Come on. When did you last use that pit?' he was irritated.

'Watch your tone! We've not opened it for weeks,' snapped Ruga.

'When were you last here? He can't have been missing too long. Someone would've reported it,' said Petrus.

'We were here ten days ago.' Ruga said.

'He was dragged here,' Petrus pointed to the muddy boots, which were scratched and smeared with bits of grass.

The men stepped forward and began to push the tree trunk back into place.

'Stop!' shouted Petrus. 'Leave it uncovered. I may come back to have another look inside it.'

The men stood still, waiting.

'Do as he says,' murmured Ruga.

'Let's carry the body back to the fort,' Petrus said.

No-one moved.

Petrus snapped. 'The man's been murdered!' He took a deep breath. 'I know you want to finish your rituals, but have some respect! I'll go back to the fort while you close up here.' Normally he would have said he'd inform the Prefect, but he was fairly sure the Prefect was the fragrant man with the delicate hands standing beside him. 'Carry the body down using his cloak. Take it to the infirmary and I'll have a look at it in the morning. Make sure the physician doesn't do anything to the body.'

Ruga did not respond.

Petrus sighed, 'I don't know who you all are, although some of you are probably very senior men at the fort. You know that I have experience of investigating murder and I'm sure the Prefect would want the culprit found. Perhaps I can discuss it with him in the morning?' Petrus stared at the man with the fine hands as he spoke. The man did not react.

Ruga handed Petrus a lit torch and said, 'Go back to the fort. Manius' body will be taken to the infirmary, as you suggest. Now leave us.'

The worshippers turned towards the altars and dropped to their knees in silence. Petrus pulled on his socks, boots, and cloak. He walked up the steps; the murmur of praying voices pursued him into the dark night as the door closed behind him. A sea of scattered stars floated across the sky around the waning moon.

The dark outline of the fort welcomed him as he drew nearer. He shivered as the cold wind pushed against him, trying to force him back as he stumbled on rocks hidden in the darkness.

His nose was running by the time he reached the fort. He wiped the snot on his sleeve and banged on the gate. He was immediately asked for the password by the gatekeepers, Rufus and Pius. There had been some issues with them some months earlier. They'd been sleeping on duty. However, following some strict discipline and retraining, they were now diligent and loyal, particularly to Petrus, their centurion. They saluted him as he walked in.

He made his way to his rooms. Gauori stirred as Petrus entered and scrambled to his feet, pushing his bedding out of the way. Silently, he placed a cup of wine on the table and began moving plates around.

'Just bread, Ga,' Petrus mumbled, using a shortened form of the man's name, 'and then you can go back to your bed.'

The slave nodded and passed him some bread on a plate, but remained watching his master as he ate.

'The ordeal didn't take place. We found a body, in the temple,' Petrus said.

'A body?'

'Yes, Manius, the librarius. Go back to bed now. I've no need of you.'

Gauori nodded. Petrus pushed aside the plate and made his way to his room. He lay on his bed and thought about the night's events. He was not a religious man. He followed the rituals and visited temples, going through the motions of honouring the gods, but he had lost faith in most of them. Mithras was a god worshipped by the most senior fighting men; not record keepers like Manius. Why would someone take Manius to the temple and kill him?

II

The Prefect's frozen breath hovered in the air as he addressed the men at parade. He told them that Manius' body had been found and that while Petrus was investigating, he would be relieved from other duties, leaving his optio in charge of the century. Word of the murder had already circulated through the fort, so Tatius was wasting his breath. However, he needed to make the announcement formally, so that it could be officially noted in the fort's records. Tatius waved his hands as he spoke, showing long thin fingers and filed clean fingernails. Petrus noted the brown birth mark on the palm of his hand. Such marks on children could raise fears that they were possessed with evil spirits. Petrus couldn't remember seeing that mark on the perfumed man's hand the night before. The parade ended with Tatius instructing the men to go to the exercise ground at the fifth hour of the day for the annual dedication to Jupiter.

Petrus made his way to the infirmary where the familiar smell of honey and alcohol greeted him. Rows of empty beds had their blankets folded neatly on top, waiting for new occupants. There were only two patients in the building. The physician, Arsenios, was busy dressing their wounds. One had a huge bandage around his head, the skin around his blue eyes was black with bruising and his lips were swollen. The other man had his lower leg missing below the knee. Arsenios would have had to cut this off to save his life. Petrus waited for him to finish.

'Aurelius Petrus, I've been expecting you. Follow me.'

Arsenios led Petrus to a room with shelves weighed down

by bandages, blankets and strange looking equipment. Petrus was a little afraid of Arsenios; the man could save the lives of seriously wounded men, cure illnesses and fix limbs. He was someone with great power, should he wish to use it. Arsenios approached the table in the centre of the room and pulled back the blanket covering the body. The dead man lay on his side; his vacant blue eyes stared ahead. The faint stink of urine hovered around him.

'I can straighten the body for you,' Arsenios spoke quietly. 'The trousers are stained with piss and mud. I'll remove them, along with the boots. His cloak is over there,' he pointed towards a shelf. 'I heard he was in the Mithraeum. What was he doing there?'

'That's what I'm trying to find out,' murmured Petrus, picking up the cloak to examine it. He flinched at the sickening cracks as Arsenios worked behind him. Brown earth and grass stained the cloak and a thin layer of white dust clung to it. He replaced it on the shelf and turned back to the body.

Manius' face was swollen and bruised; a smear of blood had dried on his cheek. The mouth was open. The man's grey skin was stretched over his light frame. Not used to the hard physical training regime of most soldiers, there was little muscle and few scars. His belly was swollen. He had purple bruises at the top of his arms and shoulders. His underpants were tatty and had been repaired many times. His socks had holes in the toes and smelled of stale sweat. The left hand still clawed at the sky. The right arm was straight, its hand was curled in a tight fist.

Arsenios lifted the head, he pointed to the hair which was matted with dried blood. 'He'd been hit on the back of the head with something, probably knocked unconscious. The bruises on his arms and shoulders are from where he was restrained and may be from carrying or dragging him. Dragging probably, you've seen the scratches on his boots?'

Petrus nodded.

'It looks like he's holding something,' Arsenios murmured. 'Shall I open his hand?'

'Yes.'

Arsenios placed a white piece of cloth beneath the hand. He took a deep breath and then forced open each finger. Petrus winced at the sound of each break. Arsenios stepped back. Petrus peered down at the straightened hand with its clean fingernails. Dark hairs lay in the folds of the man's skin and on the cloth. They rose and fell as Petrus breathed.

'Here. Put them in there.' Arsenios handed him a small bottle.

Petrus pressed the hairs into the neck of the bottle and forced the lid into place.

Arsenios pointed at the body's mouth. 'I think he died from lack of water. His lips are cracked and blue. The body's skin is dry and flaky. If I do this,' he pinched the man's arm, 'The skin does not return back the way yours would. His tongue is swollen. That's all from lack of water. Smell that.'

Petrus leaned forward and sniffed at the dead man's mouth. 'Sweet. Like fermenting fruit?'

Arsenios nodded. 'Some sleeping drafts smell that way. He looks a bit fat around the middle, but that's not the case. Something comes from inside a dead person, causing the belly to swell like that. Judging by the smell and the distended belly, I think he's only been dead a couple of days. It's difficult to tell, as it's been quite cold recently. Cold slows the normal processes after death. Do you know when he went missing?'

Petrus shook his head. 'How long could he have lasted with no food or water?'

'It's possible to last weeks without food. But without water? Two to three days at most. Have you noticed the ring marks?'

Petrus looked again at the body's bare hands. The right-hand ring finger bore the marks of a ring, etched into the ashen flesh.

'Where is his ring? He would've worn a signet ring, just as you do,' muttered Arsenios.

Petrus hurried to his office. He locked the bottle of dark hair in his chest, quickly scratched some notes on a tablet and then outlined what further actions he intended to take. He grabbed the tablet and opened the door. A small barefooted boy with straw-coloured hair raced past him and ran in the direction of the barracks.

Petrus cried out, 'Oi! What are you doing?'

The boy stopped and looked over his shoulder at Petrus, a look of horror on his face. He turned and fled. Women and children lived in the barracks, but they were not supposed to move around the administrative buildings. Petrus briefly considered chasing him, but decided against it. He needed to update the Prefect.

Tatius was bent over his work, a half empty wine glass at his side. Petrus waited.

'What can you tell me?' Tatius leaned back in his chair and stretched his arms above his head, sighing deeply.

Petrus pushed his report across the table. Tatius waved it away. 'I'm not going to read it. You're meticulous in your record keeping. I know that from the other business.' *That other business* was how Tatius referred to the previous plot to kill him. 'Give me a summary of what you've found and what you plan to do.'

'Manius had a blow to the back of the head. It would have knocked him unconscious. He smells as if he had taken a sleeping draught. He had some dark hair clutched in his hand when he died. It could be the murderer's – he could've grabbed it when he tried to fight back.'

'The fort and the vicus are full of men with dark hair, so that's not much help. Everyone has access to sleeping draughts. Not just Physicians and herbalists, anyone can buy them.'

Petrus raised an eyebrow, 'I, err, I might make a few enquiries from the women at the market, see if anyone new or unexpected bought sleeping drugs from them.'

Petrus waited. Tatius was quiet. Petrus pointed to his arms,.'He has bruises here and here, from restraint, or maybe where they carried him. His skin is all papery. Arsenios says he died from lack of water. He was certainly dragged part of the way to the temple…'

'How do you know that?' interrupted Tatius.

'The toes of his boots are scratched and muddy.' Petrus replied. He wanted to say, '*as I told you last night when we found him,*' but held his tongue. If Tatius was determined to pretend he'd not been at the temple, then so be it. 'The men in the Mithraeum, well Ruga anyway, said they hadn't been to the temple for ten days. Manius can't have been gone too long, someone would've reported it. The body is not wearing a ring. I can't see why anyone would steal that ring unless it was to use the seal, to fake the mark of the librarius.'

The Prefect frowned. 'Fake records? Surely not. What are you going to do next?'

'Search Manius' rooms. I'll need to go to the records office to see when the other librarii noticed that he had disappeared. I don't remember them reporting him as missing. If any recent documents have his ring mark on them, then that may implicate the librarii. I may need to search their rooms. My informants can try to find out anything they can about Manius amongst the people in the vicus. I also need to find out how many other people knew the whereabouts of the temple and who the members of the Mithraic cult are, so that I can find out if any of them held a grudge against Manius.'

Petrus waited for Tatius to speak, but the prefect grabbed a tablet and began writing. Petrus felt annoyed. They both knew Tatius had been at the temple the previous night and that he could easily list the names of the other members of the cult.

'I'll ask Ruga for the names of the cult members,' Petrus said.

Tatius pushed the tablet across the table, but kept his hand on it. 'These are your orders. You are relieved from your normal duties while you look into the murder. I expect you to be at the temple this afternoon.'

'Of course, Sir. I wouldn't want to miss such an important event. With your leave, I'll just see if I can catch Ruga before the re-dedication.'

Tatius nodded.

Petrus made his way across the fort to Ruga's rooms. He knocked on the door and entered without waiting for Linus, Ruga's slave, to answer.

'He's just got back from the baths. It might be best if you knock first,' grumbled Linus, who was cleaning Ruga's boots.

Petrus did not acknowledge him, but did as he suggested.

'What the fuck!' exclaimed Ruga as Petrus pushed open the door.

Ruga was only half dressed. Petrus put his hand on Ruga's battle-scarred chest and pushed him back into his room.

'Don't touch me!' hissed Ruga as Petrus closed the door. Ruga bunched his fists and stepped towards Petrus, so close that Petrus inhaled his stale breath.

'Quiet!' growled Petrus as he wrinkled his nose. 'You won't want Linus to overhear us talk about last night.'

Ruga pushed past him and pulled open the door.

'Linus! Go and get some meat for later on. I gave you the written orders this morning and you've not been yet, you idle shit!' Ruga roared.

Linus pushed himself to his feet and ambled out of the door.

'Let's talk through here,' Ruga pulled on his tunic and strode into the room. 'Wine?' Without waiting for a response, he grabbed two cups and filled them. He sat down at the table and gestured for Petrus to do the same. 'What do you want to know?'

'Who are the members of the cult of Mithras? Were they all there last night?' Sensing Ruga's reluctance to speak, Petrus took out the tablet and showed him the orders.

Ruga nodded. 'We're sworn to secrecy. He wants me to be the one to tell you,' he paused. 'Well, there are the other centurions from the fort and Tatius. But you recognised him, didn't you?'

Petrus nodded, 'By his hands, and his perfume. Were they the only ones there last night? It seemed like there were more than just six of you.'

Ruga smiled, 'That's the light playing tricks on you.'

'Does anyone else know about the Mithraeum's whereabouts?'

'The Governor, the tribunes, retired centurions, other prefects who've visited the fort. Many powerful people worship Mithras,' said Ruga.

'Do you know if any of them had a grievance against Manius?'

Ruga shook his head. 'I don't think so. Centurions wouldn't bother themselves with the librarius. Most of them deal directly with the Signifer, Ecdicius.'

'Would you know if any of them had been to the temple since you were last there ten days ago?'

Ruga shrugged. 'I am the leader; they would normally check with me first.'

'But they don't have to?'

Ruga shook his head. 'The temple is always open to worshippers.'

'And what about other soldiers, here at the fort? Would they know where the temple was?'

'Doubt it,' mumbled Ruga.

'Local people?'

'No! Definitely not.' Ruga snapped.

'So, Manius and the other librarii wouldn't have known anything about the temple?'

Ruga shrugged, 'They'd have known there is a Mithraeum and there are followers, but they wouldn't have known anything more,' He sighed, 'Different now, of course, everyone will know where it is.'

Petrus grimaced; he was unsure what else to say. Linus burst in through the door carrying a blood-stained sack, which he slung on the table. Ruga glowered at him. Petrus didn't want to watch an altercation between the two men. Linus would get a beating. He returned to his room, where he splashed some water on his face and changed into a clean tunic.

Fog had settled about them like a blanket of smoke. Droplets of water clung like rain to the grey stone temple, feeding the green moss that gripped the outer walls. The waiting soldiers shivered on the parade ground. Petrus pushed open the temple's door and took his place alongside the other centurions. A white goat and a white ram were tethered in front of the altar. The priest stood with his arms raised.

The smell of burning incense hung in the air. Torches cast flickering light across the priest who began to sway and shout, his black robe billowing in the breeze that rushed in through the high windows. He prayed in a strange language, his voice rising to a shout and then falling back to a whisper, rising and falling, again and again, like a wave. The centurions began to stamp their feet and chant. Their voices grew louder; the priest's dance grew frenzied. The soldiers began to step forward and then back in a hypnotic routine. This prayer, this dance, each man knew it by heart. Petrus felt his soul rise up and merge with a sea of army spirits. His body felt light as he filled his lungs with the thick smell of the oils.

The temple seemed to darken around them. The priest

grabbed the ram by the horns and slashed its throat. Blood spurted across the temple, splattering the altar as the ram sank to its knees and rested its head on the floor. As its heart stopped, the blood continued to leak slowly between the flagstones. The metallic stink of death rose around them. The waiting goat bleated and strained at its rope; its eyes wide in fear. The priest pulled it towards him and cut its neck. The goat's back legs gave way, and it fell to the floor, thrashing its legs and slipping in the blood that gushed from the wound in its throat. The priest continued to chant as he knelt in the bloody mess around the animals. He slashed the goat's belly open, dragged out the entrails and lifted them above his head. He called on Jupiter to bless the soldiers of Banna fort as blood and faeces dripped onto his arms and face. He placed the stinking guts on the altar and bowed down before it.

The temple grew lighter. The priest ripped open the belly of the ram and pulled out its stinking innards. He walked out of the temple, struggling with them as they slithered in his hands, like writhing eels. The centurions followed him to stand in front of the waiting men. The priest raised his arms.

'Jupiter the Greatest!' he cried as blood trickled down his face.

The waiting soldiers cheered as the stench of death moved between them.

Cold air forced its way through Petrus' lungs, pushing out the spirits and cleansing his body, lifting him out of the trance. He began to tremble as the priest led the men in prayer, committing the soldiers to Jupiter and imploring the God to protect them. Petrus joined the soldiers intoning the words, even though he didn't believe them. He hated the way he'd lost control of his mind and body during the dedication ceremony. He just wanted it to be over.

Finally, the soldiers were dismissed. A few men remained behind to build the fire needed to cremate the animals' bodies, the last part of the dedication.

'Petrus!' Tatius' voice made him turn. 'Come back inside.'

Two slaves were dragging the carcasses along the floor towards the door, smearing a trail of blood and faeces across the stone slabs. The stink of shit merged with the smell of blood as the animals' perforated bellies spilled their contents across the floor.

'This is for you,' Tatius said, thrusting a squawking chicken into his arms. 'The priest will read them for you,' he smiled at Petrus' confusion, 'About the murder.'

Petrus nodded and smiled briefly, hoping his face didn't show how he felt about the empty ritual. He put the bird on the floor, stood on its wings, took out his pugio and cut off its head. The bird's legs twitched, and a tiny trickle of blood leaked away. He stabbed the body, pulled the flesh open and ripped out the warm slimy entrails, trying not to gag at the foul stink. He handed them to the priest, who gently caressed them with his fingertips. His lips moved, but he made no sound.

'More,' he murmured, 'more. There will be more deaths if you don't act quickly.'

Petrus bit back his retort. It didn't take holy insight to guess that there may be more murders. The priest placed the stinking mess in Petrus' hands and closed his fingers round them. Petrus shuddered.

'Ultimately, you will succeed,' the priest whispered. He turned away, moving back to the newly dedicated altar, his robes smearing a bloody path along the flagstones behind him.

Tatius waved Petrus away. Behind him, the slaves were washing the blood from the floor.

Outside, Petrus dropped the chicken's guts in the fire. The smell of burning meat followed him as he began to walk back towards the fort.

Petrus made his way to Manius' room. The door was ajar, and he pushed it open. The room was spotlessly clean. The pots, pans and weaponry were stacked neatly against the wall and a small fire burned under the chimney. Two pitchers stood in the corner of the room with four cups alongside them. One of the cups lay on its side. A slave was sweeping the floor. He froze, brush in hand, and stared at Petrus as he entered.

'Sir, what can I do for you? My-my master is not here.' He looked around bewildered, as if expecting Manius to return at any moment.

'You know that his body's been found, don't you?' Petrus tried to sound reassuring, as the man was clearly terrified.

The slave nodded.

'Put that down, and sit here for a moment, opposite me.' Petrus lowered himself onto a stool and gestured towards the other side of the table.

The slave let go of the broom, allowing it to fall to the floor. He moved carefully, as if frightened of each step. He lifted the stool with shaking hands and moved it away from the table. He sat down, put his hands in his lap and smoothed the tunic's faded fabric against his legs. His tunic was clean, but had many patches and repairs.

'What's your name?' Petrus asked.

'Docca, Sir.'

'Docca. When you heard your master was dead, what did you do?'

The slave continued to stare at his hands. 'I waited.'

'Waited for what?'

'For someone to come. As you have done.'

Petrus watched him, but he said nothing more. After a moment, Petrus continued, 'When did you last see your master?'

'Seven days ago. He went out for the evening, as he does sometimes. He didn't come back the next morning.'

'Why didn't you report that he was missing?'

Docca's lips trembled, 'He'd instructed me that if he didn't return after a night out, then I should go to the Librarium and tell the others that he had a stomach upset and might be unable to return to work for a couple of days.'

'So, it wasn't unusual for him to stay out overnight and not come back in time for the morning briefing?'

The slave shrugged. 'Every now and then.'

'Was he often gone for several days?'

'Not often, but he has done it in the past,' mumbled Docca.

'Why didn't the librarii report it to the Signifer, or senior officers?'

'I've no idea, Sir. I just told them he was ill, as he had instructed.'

Petrus frowned. 'And what happened when he didn't come back at all that day?'

'Sir, the next morning, I did what I always do and went to look for him.'

'Where did you go to look?'

Docca sighed, 'Firstly, I tried the tavern. He would usually be asleep in a corner. He wasn't there, so I went to look for him in the streets nearby. I'd found him once unconscious in an alleyway a short distance from the tavern, further into the town. He must've been on his way to the woman's then and passed out.'

'Do you know where I can find his woman?'

Docca shook his head.

'Or her name?'

Again, Docca shook his head. Petrus wasn't sure he believed him. Gauori knew all about Aurora. 'And did you find him that day?'

'No, Sir. I did not.'

'What did you do then?'

Docca muttered, 'I just waited here, Sir. I knew, I mean I thought he'd come back, eventually. He usually did.'

'And do you know where Manius' signet ring is?'

Docca rose slowly to his feet and Petrus followed him into Manius' bedroom. Docca opened Manius' chest and reached inside. He turned pale and began using both hands to search the chest. He looked at Petrus.

'It should be here, Sir! I swear! He always took it off and hid it here when he was going to the tavern!' His voice shook as he spoke.

Petrus nodded and put out a hand to steady the trembling slave. 'Go back in there,' he pointed to the other room.

Petrus reached into the chest and pulled out a couple of tunics and a pair of trousers. He laid them on the bed. He searched each item of clothing, shook them, and felt nothing inside them. Frustrated, he put them to one side. In the bottom of the chest were a few sestertii and some fine bronze jewellery, necklaces, and wrist bands. He lifted each one out, placing it on the bed beside the clothes, checking to see whether the signet ring had been caught up in them. It had not. He ran his hands around the bottom of the chest, in case there was a small depression where the ring was hidden. Nothing! He replaced the jewellery, laid the clothes back on top of them, and closed the lid. He lifted the blankets from the bed and felt around the straw mattress. There was no ring. He looked under the bed and lifted the pitcher of stale water. There was nothing beneath them. He walked around, staring at the floor. The ring was not there.

He went back into the other room. Docca sat on a stool with his head in his hands. Petrus thought he could hear the man weeping.

'When did you last see the ring?' Petrus asked.

Docca shrugged, 'I never check that it's there. I just know he takes it off when he's going drinking. He's afraid someone will steal it if he's too drunk to fight them off. Happened once before, nearly had it pulled off his finger in the tavern. He didn't want to risk it again, so hid it there. He told me. Always.'

'When you went out to look for Manius that day, did you lock the door?'

'N-no, I never lock the door.' Tears leaked from the corners of Docca's eyes and slid down his cheeks.

'How long were you out looking for your master?'

'Quite some time, Sir. I came back as it was growing dark.'

Petrus rose. He could check the gates records to confirm some of what the slave had said. He moved towards the door.

'Sir?'

Docca's voice made him turn back towards the slave. 'Yes?'

'What will happen to me now?' The man's voice shook as he spoke. His eyes were wide in fear.

Petrus frowned. He'd not thought about the slave's future. 'I'm not sure. It really depends on whether Manius had a will. If he did, it would say what should happen to you. If not, then you will belong to the army.'

'I have always belonged to the army. I was born at this fort.' Docca's voice was quiet.

'I'll see what I can do.' Petrus hoped that he sounded reassuring.

Docca rose from the stool and picked up the broom.

Petrus looked around. 'When did you last eat?'

'Three days ago, I think,' whispered Docca.

Petrus took a blank tablet from the table and scratched some instructions on it. He passed it to Docca and said, 'here, go to my rooms. This tablet instructs my slave to give you a meal and then enough supplies for the next two days. Come back here then and wait for my instructions,' he paused. 'I may not get an answer as to your future immediately.'

After the slave had gone, Petrus looked around the room. He lifted the pitchers, moved the few bits of weaponry, pots and pans. The ring wasn't there.

The librarii worked with the windows wide open in order to get as much natural light into their room as possible. They never used lit torches as their records, all on wooden tablets, were highly flammable. The entire cohort's history could be lost in a fire. The men did not look up as Petrus entered. They had their thick cloaks pulled tightly round them and wore woollen gloves to keep their fingers warm as cold air flowed in from the open window. The smell of wood and wax hung in the air.

As he began to shiver in the cold, Petrus cleared his throat and said, 'Tell me about Manius.'

Adrianus put down his stylus and ran his fingers through his dark hair. 'Manius? What about him?'

'Why didn't you report him missing?'

Adrianus looked at the other men and then returned his gaze to Petrus. 'We didn't know he was missing, not until last night when we heard he'd been found dead.'

'What about when he didn't turn up here for work? He's been gone for a week!'

'We received a message from his slave saying he'd fallen ill,' Adrianus scowled, 'Manius is, was, occasionally ill, some sort of stomach complaint, so we were used to him being off sick for days at a time.'

'What did Ecdicius say about it?'

Adrianus laughed bitterly, 'Ecdicius? He's not interested in whether we fall sick, or fail to turn up at work. We don't bother to tell him. He's too busy doing other things.'

'What other things?'

The other librarii sniggered, but Adrianus just shrugged.

'Didn't you think to check on him when he hadn't returned after a few days?' frowned Petrus.

Adrianus shrugged.

'What's happened to all his work?' Petrus asked.

'What d'you think happened to his work? We had to pick it up, didn't we?' Adrianus pointed at a pile of tablets to his side. 'I've got to work through those.'

'What was Manius working on before he disappeared?'

'Same as the rest of us, daily records, accounts, that sort of thing.' Adrianus pointed to the stacks of tablets on Manius' table. 'We're busy. The Tribune, Augustus Pollux, is visiting in four days' time.'

Petrus raised an eyebrow. 'Is he? How do you know that?'

'He sent a message saying he would be visiting. Didn't you know?' Adrianus smirked.

'I did not,' Petrus gritted his teeth. As a centurion, he knew he should've been informed. 'Can I look at Manius' work?'

'Help yourself.' Adrianus picked up his stylus and started reading his tablet.

Petrus sat on Manius' chair. He lifted one of the tablets from the pile on the right and peered at it. It was a report from a centurion detailing the training from a week ago; it had the man's signature and ring seal at the bottom. At the bottom of the report was Manius' signature and seal and the word 'Registered'. Petrus looked at a few more tablets. They all had the same signature and seal.

'Those are the ones he'd accounted for,' Adrianus' voice caused Petrus to look up. 'The summaries are in the piles to the left.'

'Thank you,' Petrus lifted one and noted that it was a monthly summary of training. 'What about accounts of purchases and deductions from wages? What about soldiers' wills?'

'Wills're behind you, on the bottom shelf. There's not many in your century that have bothered with 'em. The purchases are on the top shelf over there.' Adrianus indicated a line of shelving in the corner of the room.

Petrus looked at the wills. There were only about twenty. 'Did Manius have a will?'

'I don't know. You'll have to check.'

Petrus sighed and began reading the names on the tablets. He saw his own. It reminded him that he needed to update it following the birth of his daughter. Manius' name was not amongst the tablets. He was surprised. He'd thought Manius, who was so meticulous, would've thought about inheritance.

'Did he have a family in the vicus? Someone to leave his property to?' Petrus asked.

Adrianus looked up and rubbed his chin. 'I think he did.

Sometimes he stayed out overnight. He'd arrive here in the morning looking a bit, well, dishevelled, but pleased with himself. There may not be much property and money to leave, just his slave. He'd taken quite a lot out of his account recently.'

Petrus raised an eyebrow. 'Had he? Show me the records.'

Groaning, Adrianus pushed himself out of his seat and walked slowly to the back of the room, where a separate set of shelves was piled high with tablets. He ran his hand exaggeratedly over them, pulling some out, only to tut loudly and replace them.

'Here it is,' he mumbled and shuffled back towards Petrus, placing the tablet in his outstretched hand. Petrus moved towards the window and peered at the scratchings on the wax. Manius had withdrawn over three hundred denarii in the last six weeks, in amounts of fifty denarii at a time. The balance of his account was only twenty denarii. Each withdrawal record showed Manius' seal and the signature and seal of one of the other librarii. The last withdrawal had been two weeks previously.

'You witnessed these?' he asked Adrianus.

'That's my signature,' muttered Adrianus and returned to his table.

'Do you know why he took out so much money?'

Adrianus shook his head.

'Did he have debts? Did he gamble?'

Adrianus shrugged. 'I don't think so.'

'Didn't you wonder why he needed so much money?' persisted Petrus.

'I didn't care. He was no friend of mine.'

Petrus hesitated. 'You didn't get on?'

Adrianus shrugged.

'Why not?' Petrus asked.

'I didn't like him.'

Petrus waited. Adrianus returned his gaze to his work.

'I'm taking this to the Treasury. I'll return it later,' Petrus said.

Adrianus did not look up.

'What about the Temple of Mithras? Did he ever talk about that?' Petrus asked.

'No one knew anything about that place until last night.'

Petrus moved towards the door.

'You'd better bring that back unaltered,' spat Adrianus.

Petrus did not respond; he slammed the door shut as he left the room. He made his way to the Treasury. Two men stood on guard just inside the door to the building. The Signifer was sitting at his table studying records. Petrus handed him the tablet.

'This is the record of the withdrawals Manius had made from his account over the last year. Can you confirm that he made these withdrawals?' Petrus asked.

Ecdicius peered at the tablet. 'It's a true record. What's this about?'

'Didn't you think it strange that he suddenly started taking out large sums of money? Fifty denarii is more than a year's salary,' Petrus asked, as he replaced the tablet inside his tunic.

'It's not my place to wonder about these things. If I made enquiries about all the withdrawals of any size, I'd never get anything done.' Ecdicius sighed, 'Gambling debts, women, more gambling, who cares?'

'Were you aware that the librarii were covering for Manius whenever he was late back to the fort? Sometimes he was missing from work for several days.'

Ecdicius frowned, 'I was not. All the work got done though, didn't it? I'll look into it.'

'I'm obliged to inform the Prefect that procedures are not being followed,' said Petrus.

'Inform him! Go on then! Do your worst!' He pushed his chair back and stood up. The soldiers standing guard jumped to attention. He didn't look at them as he pushed Petrus towards the door. 'I'm closing the building now,' he mumbled, 'things to do.'

Petrus was shocked and wondered what these 'things' were.

Tatius was feigning interest in some reports as Petrus entered his office.

Petrus began, 'Manius was making large withdrawals from his account. In the last few weeks, he's taken out three hundred denarii. Whenever he left the fort, he would leave his signet ring in the chest in his room, as he was afraid of losing it. The ring is not there or anywhere else in his rooms. It's missing. If Manius didn't return home after a night out, the slave had been instructed to tell the other librarii that his master was ill. This happened about once a month. The other librarii say they thought he was sickly and so they just covered his work. When I asked them what Ecdicius thought about this arrangement, they claim he doesn't check on their attendance.'

Tatius showed no reaction.

Petrus waited.

'I challenged Ecdicius about his failure to monitor the librarii's work and he wasn't concerned. Seemed to think it was alright as long as the work got done and he challenged me to inform you about it!' Petrus said.

Tatius did not respond.

Petrus waited.

Tatius nodded. 'I'll speak with him; this can't be allowed to happen.'

Petrus was surprised at the Prefect's reaction; he'd expected him to be angry. The work of the librarii was key to the functioning of the fort; he had thought Tatius would've been enraged to know that they were not following procedures and missing work when they felt like it. Petrus wondered what else the Prefect overlooked at the fort. The man's reputation and authority had taken a huge knock some months previously and Petrus wondered whether he was so preoccupied with that that he'd let other things slip.

'Manius' slave has been dutifully waiting for Manius' return; I've never seen officers' rooms that clean! He went into the vicus to look for his master after he'd been missing for a day. The signet ring could've been taken while the slave was out.' Petrus said.

'And you believe the slave when he says he was looking for the dead man? And about the signet ring?'

'Yes, yes, I do,' Petrus paused. 'The only reason I can see for stealing the ring is forgery. I'll need to go through some of the records – to see if Manius' ring has been used since he disappeared. Manius started to empty his account about six weeks ago, which is strange. Perhaps he was being threatened or was in debt.'

'Threatened? Who would hold a grudge against a librarius?'

'Someone who's had their pay docked or who was owed a debt of some sort, maybe,' Petrus waited a moment. 'Err, the librarii said they're getting ready for the Tribune's visit in a few days' time.'

'Yes. My new wife will be with them. What of it?' Tatius said.

'I-I was unaware of his visit,' Petrus stammered. Tatius' first wife had taken her own life some months previously following the failed conspiracy to murder the Prefect.

'The other centurions know about it, the followers of Mithras,' mumbled Tatius, finally dropping all pretence about not being a member of the cult. 'You would've been told after your first initiation. You will be required to be present as a witness to our marriage a couple of days after their arrival. And you'll be involved in the preparations beforehand. Speak with Ruga, he's organising the event.'

Petrus took a moment to hide his surprise.

'I'll appoint someone to replace Manius,' said Tatius, 'unless you have anyone in mind?'

Petrus shook his head. 'I guess there are a couple of men who've got good levels of reading and writing.'

'I'll speak with the other centurions; they may have some ideas. What are you planning to do now? With the investigation, I mean.'

Petrus sighed. 'I want to interview the other followers of Mithras. I'll look at the work Manius was doing here at the fort. The new librarius can help me with that. And I'll make some enquiries in the vicus, see if anyone there had a grudge against him. I want to know more about his reputation, both here and in the community.'

'Very well. Keep me informed.' Tatius waved him away.

Petrus hesitated. 'The new librarius must be warned to take care. This work may have cost Manius his life…'

'I'll warn him and tell him to report only to you.'

'Er, one last thing, Sir. Manius didn't leave a will, so all his property reverts to the army. There isn't much money left, but there is the slave, Docca. What will happen to him?'

'Mmm,' Tatius rubbed his chin, 'I hadn't thought of that. He can come into my household to start with. Then we can see if the new librarius wants to buy him. If he doesn't want him, I'll consider buying him myself or the army can sell him to a trader.'

'He was born at the fort. He doesn't know any other life.'

Unmoved, Tatius waved him away. 'A slave is a slave. They're used to being bought and sold. Tell the man, Docca, did you say? Tell him to come to the Praetorium in the morning at the second hour of the day. My slaves will have been briefed by then. Make sure you return all Manius' property to the stores or get someone to do it.'

'Very well.' Petrus bowed his head and left the room.

Docca jumped to his feet as the door opened. The pan he had been holding clattered to the floor. Petrus put out a hand to reassure him, but he flinched, and Petrus let his hand fall to his side.

'I've spoken with the Prefect,' began Petrus, motioning Docca to take a seat.

Docca sank onto a stool and stared at Petrus, his face pale with worry. He clasped his arms around his chest, hugging himself, and rocked gently back and forth.

'Manius didn't leave a will. That means all his property reverts to the army. The Prefect has said you should join his household until the new Librarius has been appointed and settled in. That man will be offered the opportunity to buy you from the army. If he doesn't want a slave, then Tatius has said he may purchase you for himself, or if not, you will be sold to the next slave trader who passes through these parts.'

Docca nodded.

Petrus knew this is what he had been expecting and no doubt fearing. Manius had probably been a good master, certainly one who trusted his slave enough to have him lying to the army. Tatius beat his slaves, and he frequently forced himself on the slave girls. Even so, Petrus thought Docca would probably prefer to have Tatius as a harsh master than risk the unknown beyond the walls of the fort.

'Tatius said you are to report to the Praetorium at the second hour of the day tomorrow. In the meantime, take all of this equipment to the stores. Have them registered as returns from Manius. They're expecting them.' He stopped talking for a moment. 'Leave the pots, pans and crockery. I expect Manius' replacement will have them. It's a shame there was no will.'

Docca rose to his feet and began picking up the pots and pans from the floor and placing them on the table.

'Make sure you eat up all that food before you go,' muttered Petrus, as he left the room. He thought Docca might as well have a couple of good meals before he was once more at the mercy of another man.

Petrus locked the tablet recording Manius' withdrawals from his account in his chest and made some more notes on another tablet, which he also locked away. Night had fallen, and the fort was cloaked in cold darkness as Petrus walked to the gate. Rufus and Pius snapped into a salute.

'Did you notice Manius, the dead man, leaving the fort fairly frequently?'

Rufus nodded, 'Yes, Sir. He was out a lot, a bit, a bit like you, Sir. I think he had family outside, or a woman anyway.'

'And do you keep your records up to date?'

'Yes, of course, Sir.'

'Very well. Then I'll check at the Librarium. Now, let me out.'

'Yes, Sir.' Pius stepped forward and pulled the gate open.

In the moonlight, Petrus picked his way along the muddy road towards the light that sneaked out from the tavern's window shutters. The raucous noise from the drinkers reached out towards him across the darkness.

He pulled open the heavy oak door and was assaulted by the warm stink of ale and unwashed bodies. Some local men were arguing at one table, their shouts and jeers filled the room. The other drinkers were watching them warily, ready to move out of the way if a fight broke out. Petrus sat down and nodded to the taverner who approached and gave him a cup of ale. He had hoped that his informant Carantii might be in the tavern. He waited and drank slowly, asking the taverner for a refill. The men arguing grew louder and Petrus decided to leave. He waved the taverner over and pressed some coins into his hand.

Cold air rushed towards him as he opened the door and stepped into the street. He paused briefly and considered whether to go to see his family. He shook his head and decided to return to the fort. He had a lot of thinking to do about his investigation.

Rufus pulled open the gate as Petrus approached and muttered, 'Not out late tonight.'

Petrus pretended not to hear the comment. He couldn't berate them for noticing his business and then expect them to be able to answer questions about Manius' activities. He walked through the streets towards the barracks. The murmur of voices and muffled cries of children floated into the night as he passed.

Gauori leapt to his feet and began stirring a pot of stew as Petrus entered his rooms. 'It's ready if you are hungry, Sir.'

Petrus sat down at the table as his slave ladled stew into a bowl and placed it in front of him. Gauori took another bowl, gave himself a helping, and then sat opposite his master. Petrus began eating. The hot stew was tasty, the meat was tender, and the gravy was thick and highly spiced. Gauori reached across the table and poured wine into Petrus' cup. He rose, took a cup of water from the pitcher for himself, and returned to the table to resume eating. Petrus smiled; he had no doubt that the slave helped himself to wine when Petrus was not present. Gauori pulled a basket of bread from beneath the table and pushed it towards his master. Petrus took one of the rolls and broke it into chunks, dipping it into the stew.

Sleep eluded him as the distant wail of wolves and cries of owls reached across the night and into his room.

III

The morning rain had drizzled ice-cold water onto the soldiers on parade; the centurions were wet and grumpy as they gathered in Tatius' office for the morning meeting.

Tatius said, 'You will all cooperate with Petrus and answer any questions he has about the Mithraeum, the cult, anything.' He looked at each of them in turn as he spoke.

'Surely you don't think any of us is involved?' spluttered Ruga.

Tatius said, 'It had to be someone who knew where the Mithraeum was.'

'There's more than just us. The Tribune, the Governor, all the previous centurions and prefects who've been stationed here. Some of the retired centurions still live locally,' Ruga said.

Petrus raised an eyebrow.

'That's a good point,' Tatius turned towards Petrus. 'You can get a list of the retired centurions from the librarii and then interview them,' he paused. 'You can also help Ruga with the wedding preparations.'

Tatius dismissed them with a wave of his hand.

Petrus let the door bang behind him in the breeze as he entered the Librarium. Adrianus scowled as he looked up.

'What do you want?'

'Details of the centurions who've retired and settled in the vicus or the countryside near here. I want names and details of where I can find them. I also want the records of when Manius last left the fort, date and time, along with details of all those who were outside the fort on the day that he left.'

The librarius sighed. 'That'll take a while. We'll have to look back at lots of records to confirm his last day here. We'll need to verify with the Treasurer whether the retirees are still drawing their pensions. Some of them may have died. There'll be some widows drawing pensions. Do you want those too?'

Petrus nodded, 'Yes, I do. I'll come and get them in the afternoon, or first thing tomorrow.'

'Well, which is it? This afternoon, or tomorrow?' snapped Adrianus. The other librarii watched this exchange, glancing at each other and smirking.

Petrus raised his voice. 'Watch your tone! I have the authority of the Prefect in this investigation. You're not above a beating. And I'll make sure it's in public!'

Adrianus reddened, 'Apologies Centurion, it's just, we're a bit overwhelmed with all the work. Do you know when Manius will be replaced?'

'In the next day or so.'

Petrus strode quickly out of the room and crossed the fort to the gate.

'Aurelius Petrus!' he heard Ruga come up behind him and turned around.

'Ruga?'

'Are you busy? Meet me at the Tribune's house when you've finished whatever it is you're doing. You know where that is, don't you?'

'I do.'

Petrus tramped through the mud towards the market. Water droplets coated his clothes and hair as he walked. The streets were busy with people. There were a few women in the marketplace, crouched over their produce: withered vegetables, sodden cloth and small animal hides. They chatted quietly to each other as they waited, hoping for customers. As Petrus approached, they looked up warily and fell silent. A beautiful woman with auburn hair and sky-blue eyes crouched over a wooden tray of dried herbs. She smiled fleetingly.

'What kind of herbs do you sell?' Petrus asked.

'What kind are you looking for, Sir?'

'The kind that could be used as a sleeping drug.'

She took a deep breath. 'I haven't got any here today. I could bring some tomorrow, or you could come to my shop.'

'How would I use them?'

'It depends. Most, you boil in water and then drink the water. Others are dried and sprinkled on food. Which do you want?'

'I'm not sure. Do many people buy sleeping herbs from you?'

She nodded.

'Why would they need them?'

She took a deep breath. 'Women who don't want to be pestered by their husbands, or who want their small baby to sleep through the whole night. Men who want to take advantage of women, or of children. I don't ask what they want it for.'

Petrus shuffled his feet, uncomfortable, and glanced down briefly, before once again meeting her gaze. 'Anyone could buy sleeping drugs and know how to use them then?'

She frowned. 'We are people of the earth, Sir. The forests and the fields. Our ancestors have been using the bounty of the land to treat our ailments since the gods put us on the earth. Even children know how to use these herbs.' She waved a hand over her tray of dried leaves and flowers.

'Has anyone new bought them recently?'

'There's always new people.'

Petrus turned away, disappointed. A thin wisp of smoke snaked upwards from the forge, then shot in bursts as it was pumped from below. Petrus smiled, the blacksmith, Carantii, was firing up. He was Petrus' informant. Petrus admired the smith; he worked hard and had put himself in danger while working for Petrus in the past. He quickened his pace.

The door to the forge was closed. Petrus looked about him. there were a couple of women in the street, but they paid him no attention. He rattled the door and said loudly, 'Open up for the Roman army! I have work for your forge!'

He heard the scrape of metal and jangle of keys as Carantii unlocked the door and pulled it open.

'Greetings, Centurion,' Carantii said, his voice overly loud. 'What can I do for the Romans?' He smiled, moved back inside and said over his shoulder, 'Leave the door open.'

Carantii turned to face Petrus, who withdrew his pugio. Carantii stepped back in alarm.

Petrus smiled, 'This is the issue,' he beckoned Carantii closer as he laid his knife on the table.

Carantii moved forward and glanced towards the door. He could not see anyone, so nodded to Petrus.

'Have you heard about Manius, the librarius?' Petrus spoke quietly.

'Everyone has. His body was found in some secret temple of yours.'

'Yes. In the Temple of Mithras. I'm looking into the murder and need your help. Find out as much as you can about the dead man from local people. Did he have a woman and family in the vicus? Did he drink? Did he gamble? Did he have any enemies? He'd withdrawn a lot of money from his savings recently. Where had he been spending it? The location of the temple was meant to be a secret, so was there any talk about it in the area, before this murder?'

Carantii ran his hand through his long straggly brown hair. 'I can tell you that I'd not heard talk of the temple before this murder.'

The door behind Carantii opened and a thin woman walked in. The smith pulled her towards him, his hand around her waist. He placed his other hand on her slightly swollen belly.

She rested her head against his shoulder and brushed her long dark hair away from her face. She smiled at Petrus.

'This is my wife, Lugraca. She knows about my work for you.'

Petrus greeted her, 'Your husband is a good man, and soon to be a father I see.'

'If the gods look kindly on us,' she looked at the floor as she said this.

Petrus wondered if they had already buried dead babies, born before their allotted time. He placed some coins on the table and picked up his pugio, placing it back in its sheath.

'Use the ivy,' he murmured as he left the forge, referring to the ivy that Carantii would tie near the door of Petrus' house as a signal that he had information.

Petrus walked the short distance to his own home and pushed open the door. The warm embrace of the kitchen welcomed him in. Aurora smiled up at him from the stool where she sat chopping vegetables. Their daughter, Antigone, lay against her mother's back, held in place by a shawl. She gurgled and moaned as she slept, dribbling on Aurora's shoulder. Petrus rested a hand on the child's dark hair and felt the warmth of love spread through his whole body. He bent and kissed his wife's cheek.

'I can't stay long,' he whispered. One of the privileges of his rank as Centurion was to be able to come and go as he pleased from the fort. Serving soldiers were not allowed to formally marry, that would have to wait until he retired.

He lowered himself on to a stool as Aurora passed him a cup of watery wine. He lifted it to his lips, gulped it down, and then wiped his hand across his mouth. He settled back and watched Aurora as she worked. He felt himself relax and his eyes began to close as he leant against the wall.

'Are you looking into that murder? Was it one of your men?' Aurora's voice made him jerk fully alert. She offered him a piece of bread.

He began to eat. 'Yes. It was Manius, the librarius from my

century. I've been relieved from my normal duties to investigate the murder and help plan for the Prefect's wedding. His new wife is arriving with the Tribune in a few days.'

'A new wife?' Aurora smiled. 'Well, I suppose a man of his status should have a wife and he does need someone to look after his children and run his household.'

'All the centurions have been told we must attend the wedding. He needs twelve witnesses, so I expect there'll be a few merchants there who do business with the army.'

'I suppose he's hoping people will forget his previous marriage,' said Aurora, brushing a strand of hair from her face.

Petrus grimaced, 'It'll take more than just a wedding for people to forget his wife tried to kill him so that she could return to Rome with her lover. The men at the fort won't forget what happened to their previous centurion either.'

He sighed and took a bite of bread. 'I need to know whether Manius had family here in the vicus and as much as I can about his life outside the fort. Carantii will see what he can find out, but if you hear anything, then get a message to me. Don't make any direct enquiries. I don't want you to put yourself at risk.'

Aurora had got involved in a previous investigation and he was worried for her safety if local people thought she was asking too many questions. Aurora nodded and smiled. He rose from his seat and as he moved towards the door, she took his hand. He turned and pulled her to her feet. Their lips met as lust surged through him. He forced himself to let go of her and stepped back. He kissed the top of Antigone's head and then left the house.

He made his way along the street, deeper into the merchants' area. He'd not been to the Tribune's house before, although he'd been past it many times. It was set back from the road and surrounded by a wall. He approached the thick oak door and knocked. A face appeared behind the grill.

'Aurelius Petrus. I'm expected,' he said.

The key ground in the lock and the door opened. Petrus brushed past the slave and heard the door close behind him. The courtyard had a paved path across the sparse grass leading to the house. A blanket of red and yellow decaying leaves covered two carved stone seats and littered the ground around the small tree from which they'd fallen. The rank odour of urine mixed with the musty dampness. Behind him, Petrus heard the slave peeing against the wall. He frowned; someone would have to sort that man out before the Tribune arrived. The house had been built by the army many years before and as each Tribune came and went, changes were made to the building. The portico was one of Augustus Pollux, the current Tribune's, additions. Four white columns held up the ornate mosaic on the roof. Beneath the roof, four statues of voluptuous goddesses were cemented to the ground, arranged in a way to make it impossible for two people to approach the door side by side, necessitating weaving around the statues. Whilst this was annoying, Petrus had to admire it. It was great defence; it would be impossible for a group of men to charge at the front door. Pollux clearly felt he needed protection from his enemies.

As Petrus slipped past the last statue, the door opened, and a slave bowed towards him.

'Aurelius Petrus, they are expecting you. Please follow me.'

Petrus looked about him as he followed the slave through the atrium. Bright frescoes depicted great gods towering over creatures that Petrus had only ever heard about in tales. The rainwater pool reflected the dull grey morning light and looked uninviting. The ornately carved seats beside it were still damp, the morning not yet warm enough to dry the overnight dew. They passed the dining room where slaves were busy cleaning, replacing cushions and moving empty platters.

In the garden, Ruga walked towards them, accompanied by a woman with long dark hair curling down her back. She arched her eyebrows and licked her lips suggestively as she approached.

Embarrassed, Petrus bowed his head in greeting.

'Madam,' he murmured.

'Aurelius Petrus, this is Faustina, wife of Augustus Pollux,' Ruga waved his arm in her direction. 'She arrived a few days ago, ahead of the main party, to make the preparations for the wedding.'

Hiding his surprise, Petrus bowed again. He had assumed she was a concubine, as the Tribune kept women at several forts.

'Petrus is helping me with the preparations. If you give him a list of all that you need, he'll get it.' Ruga turned towards Petrus. 'We received a message that the Tribune is arriving the day after tomorrow. There will be a few people to a meal when they arrive and then the wedding will be two days after that with a proper celebration. We'll bring the animals here tomorrow. Vegetinus will be going hunting in the morning for boar.'

'The cook has the list on a tablet. I hope the young bride won't be disappointed with the wedding feast I have planned,' Faustina sighed and then took some deep breaths which made her ample breasts rise and fall, showing the outline of her nipples against her robe. She stared at Petrus as she did so. He looked away.

'Is the kitchen this way?' Petrus asked.

He began to walk across the garden, passing plant pots full of brown earth, their flowers not yet growing after the harsh winter. A couple of small evergreen bushes were a splash of colour against the mud-spattered grey flagstones around the garden pool. Wisps of smoke emerged from the roof of the kitchen and disappeared into the morning air. Faustina passed by him. He felt her hesitate as her bare arm brushed against him, her skin soft against his rough hand.

'Perhaps I'll wait here.' He stopped walking, and she continued on into the kitchen. Out of the corner of his eye, he saw Ruga grinning widely.

She came back moments later, 'It's all here, Centurion,' she leant in towards Petrus pressing the tablet into his hand. Her shoulder touched his chest, spreading warmth through his body. He took a deep breath and pulled his belly in so that they were not in contact.

Ruga covered his mouth with his hand, pretending to cough. 'Let's walk back together.'

Relieved, Petrus stepped away from Faustina.

'You'd better watch yourself with that one. Make sure you're not near her at the wedding feast,' Ruga laughed as they left the house and began walking down the street.

Petrus shrugged. 'I'm not interested in her advances. She shames herself behaving that way.'

Ruga grinned, 'She has no shame, that one. She can be very persistent.'

'Speaking from experience, are you?' grunted Petrus.

'Might be,' Ruga mimed thrusting his hips back and forth as he walked, 'As I said, she's very persistent. He wants a big event, doesn't he, the Prefect? Trying to make everyone forget about that mess with his previous wife. Are you worried about how to behave at the feast?'

Petrus did not reply.

Ruga nudged him. 'Just do the same as all the other men. Will you be alright sourcing all that food?'

'Yes. That'll be fine.'

'Good. I've got to concentrate on getting the troops ready and making sure the librarii have all their records up to date. Tatius says Ecdicius hasn't been doing his job properly.'

Petrus nodded. They were approaching the brothel. 'I need to go in here and speak with Sylva.'

'Oh, aye? Speak with Sylva. Can't get enough of it, can you?'

'I'm investigating a murder! Or had you forgotten?' Petrus spat.

Ruga reddened and walked away. Petrus opened the door to the brothel. Riacus, Sylva's huge slave, was guarding the entrance, but stepped aside and Petrus made his way to the salon. A couple of merchants lounged on couches, clutching cups of wine. The young girl who greeted Petrus was the same one who'd been there months previously when he was involved in another murder case. She smiled and beckoned him towards an empty couch. She snapped her fingers and a slave girl stepped forward and placed a cup of sweet wine into his hand.

'You'll want Madam Sylva. I'll fetch her for you. I think she has a guest, err, one of the merchants with her.' She left the room.

Petrus smiled; he knew that Sylva sometimes took lovers. She had worked as a whore in this same brothel for years, but now she owned it and so no longer had to service its customers. He relaxed against the cushions and sipped the wine. The strong smell of incense filled the air. The wine warmed his throat, and he took a large mouthful, draining the cup. The slave immediately stepped forward. He nodded to her, and she refilled his cup. He knew he shouldn't drink too much, but he was annoyed after Ruga's comments, and the sweet drink soothed him. The merchants finished their drinks and walked out of the salon.

'Petrus! What do you want? You've interrupted my afternoon, I was just…' Sylva waved a hand in the air. 'You're not here for one of my girls.' She settled down next to him on the couch. Her perfume forced its way into his nostrils. She clasped her hands between her widespread legs and put her head on one side as she watched him. The loops of her plaited hair dangled in the air. 'Is it about that dead man?'

'You've heard about that, then?'

'Everyone's heard about it. Found him in one of your temples, didn't you? Who was it?'

'Manius, a record keeper,' Petrus replied, 'Dark hair. Was he a customer of yours?'

Sylva looked towards the young girl who was listening to the conversation. She shook her head. 'Not sure I want to help you with your investigation, Petrus. Last time, it cost two of my girls their lives. I have to keep everyone safe.'

'If you don't cooperate, you'll have your license taken away! Won't be able to keep anyone safe then, will you?!' he snapped.

She looked down at her hands and whispered, 'The name is not familiar to me. I can't keep track of everyone who comes here. I'll ask the girls and get a message to you if any of them knows him.'

She got up and swept out of the room. Petrus felt guilty. His previous investigation had led to the gruesome murders of two of the whores. He wondered whether she really would ask her girls about the dead man, or just ignore his request.

Emerging into the weak winter sun, Petrus took some deep breaths of the sharp air, to clear his lungs of the thick fragrance from the brothel. He walked back to the fort and went to see Ruga.

'I'd like to go back to the Temple in daylight, see if there's anything there,' Petrus said.

'Then you'd better give me the list of stuff needed for the wedding. You won't have time to get them. I'll get Vegetinus to show you the way there. Take horses, it'll be quicker.'

Petrus handed the tablet to Ruga and went to the stables to wait for Vegetinus.

They rode in silence. Petrus had tried engaging the other man in conversation, but he hadn't responded. As they arrived at the rocky outcrop near the temple's entrance, they slowed their horses.

Petrus sighed. 'You can leave me now; I'm going to look inside.'

'What about the horse?' Vegetinus ran a hand through his dark hair.

Petrus looked around. A stunted tree cowered beneath the rocks. 'I'll tie him to that.'

Vegetinus rode away.

The temple seemed to grow out of the earth. Its flat roof sloped towards a stream, that pushed past rocks and bent grasses as it flowed down the hillside. Petrus walked around the outside of the building. The coarse stone walls had gaps near the roof to let in light. He tied up his horse, walked down the steps, and pushed at the thick oak door. It creaked in protest.

The nave was dimly lit by the weak light from the windows. The half tree-trunk lay next to the pit. Petrus peered into the hole, but could see nothing of interest. Carved wooden seats worn smooth through years of use, leant against the wall. Three intricately carved altars overlooked the space. One showed Mithras astride a bull, his sword drawn ready to slay it. Another depicted Cautes with his upright torch and Cautopates with his torch inverted, representing the rising and setting of the sun. He walked around the nave, back and forth, staring at the floor. He sighed, realising any traces left by the killers would have been destroyed by the worshippers.

The tree's bare branches bent as the horse strained against its reins, sniffing the ground as it nibbled weak shoots of grass. Petrus mounted and rode towards the fort. Grey clouds raced across the sky, covering the sun; they released their rain, and it pelted the earth. He muttered reassurances to the horse as it shook its head and snorted. The icy rain whipped against his face, numbing the skin as his freezing breath lingered in front of him.

At the fort, he gave his horse to one of the men and made his way to the Librarium. Adrianus made a show of ignoring him as he stood and waited. The other men sneaked quick looks at him but carried on with their work.

Adrianus sighed deeply and pushed two tablets across the table towards him. 'This tablet shows that Manius left the fort eight days ago at the second hour of the night. He did not return. It shows a list of all those who were outside the fort on that day and when they returned. It includes the Prefect, The Signifer, the Physician and four centurions. Rufus has made his mark there,' he pointed to the tablet. 'The other tablet is a list of the retired centurions who chose to stay in the vicus and where they live. Until about a year ago, there were six of them, however, only three continue to draw pension, so I think the others must have died. There's a centurion's widow drawing a monthly widows' allowance, we don't generally keep a record of where widows live, you'll have to ask around in the vicus for that information. You'll have your work cut out interviewing all the army men, let alone those outside the fort.'

Petrus scooped up the tablets. 'If you'd reported that Manius hadn't turned up, he may have been found alive.'

Adrianus picked up his stylus and went back to his work muttering, 'He might have. But men like you stay out all the time.'

Petrus scowled. He did not want a showdown with the librarius, even though he outranked him. He stormed out of the room.

'Adrianus needs a good beating!' spat Petrus as he kicked Ruga's office door closed behind him.

Ruga sighed and rubbed his chin. 'What's he done now?'

'He's unhelpful, rude and ignores me when I enter the room. If the damned librarii had done their jobs properly, we would've known Manius was missing days ago. We might have found him alive!'

Ruga pushed his chair back. 'We would never have thought to look for him in the Mithraeum though, would we?'

'I might have been able to find out about his movements, you never know,' Petrus knew this sounded feeble.

'I'll see to Adrianus in the morning.'

'Four of the centurions were outside the fort when Manius went missing, Roburius, Vegetinus, Ferullus and Aquilinus. I need to question them.'

'Roburius, Vegetinus and Ferullus hang around together a lot. They'll have been drinking and gambling, I expect.

Aquilinus is taking his men out North tomorrow. So, you'd better see him tonight.'

Petrus frowned. 'I wasn't aware there was a problem up North.'

'Tatius mentioned it in the briefing this morning. I expect you weren't listening properly. Probably too busy planning how to question the cult members.' Ruga grinned, 'There's been some breaches and skirmishes at one of the mile castles, and the wall has been damaged. They'll hunt down the tribes and make some examples of them. Your men can help with the wall reconstruction. Your optio is managing them well enough while you're busy with your investigation.' He emphasised the last few words and waggled his head from side to side in mockery.

Petrus pretended not to notice. 'I'll also need to talk to the centurions about the Temple. Maybe we can start now?' He sat down in the chair opposite Ruga. 'How long have you been a follower of Mithras?'

Ruga scowled. 'Since I became a centurion. That's at least ten years. As I told you before, all the centurions and men of power are followers. It helps to smooth things between us. Helps to be in with the big men.'

'How often do you go to the temple? Are you always in groups? I've been there today. It's left open, so anyone can go in.'

'Yes, they could, but you'd need to know about it first. Its whereabouts is not well known, well, it wasn't until now. Why would anyone who is not a follower go there?' Ruga paused. 'After this murder, we'll keep it locked. To answer your question, we normally go as a group, but members can go alone. I've been on my own before planned action. I expect Aquilinus'll be there this evening.'

'What sort of rituals go on there?'

Ruga banged his fist on the table. 'No! I won't tell you about them. They're for initiates to know! You'll have to wait to find out, like everyone else. Anyway, how could that be relevant to the murder?'

Petrus shrugged.

'You'd better hurry if you want to catch Aquilinus,' mumbled Ruga as he turned back to his work.

Petrus made his way to Aquilinus' rooms.

'What do you want?' Aquilinus asked as he shovelled stew into his mouth.

The smell teased Petrus' nostrils and as his stomach rumbled, he realised how hungry he felt. Aquilinus waved Petrus into a seat, turned to his slave, and pointed at the door. The man nodded and left the room.

Aquilinus shoved a cup towards Petrus and poured him some wine. 'Can you be quick? I'm going to the temple tonight as we're leaving in the morning to sort out the northern rabble. And I'm still short of four men thanks to you. Vester and his comrades haven't been on active duty for months.'

'It wasn't me who tortured them! They've got to serve their punishment by doing shitty jobs,' Petrus snapped. 'I want to know more about the cult of Mithras.'

'You know as much as you need to. I won't tell you anymore. You shouldn't even be asking. Secret means we don't talk about it,' mumbled Aquilinus as he slurped his wine.

'I can't see any reason why the murderers would take Manius to the temple, unless it's relevant in some way.'

'Maybe it's a message to cult members, or a specific member?' Aquilinus paused to use a small knife to pick some meat from between his teeth. Petrus fought to remain facing Aquilinus as the centurion's foul breath pushed into his face.

'You were outside the fort eight days ago when Manius went missing,' Petrus said.

Aquilinus put down the knife and looked defiantly at him.

'Men of our rank are often outside the fort,' he said quietly.

'What were you doing?'

Aquilinus waved a hand dismissively. 'I was probably at Sylva's place. About once a week, I go to the tavern, get drunk and then hit the brothel. If I'm a bit lairy, then Sylva gives me two girls for the price of one,' he looked down at his hands, 'To get me out of the way of her other customers. It's a habit I've got into, one the Prefect wouldn't appreciate I'm sure, taking advantage of my position. Last time I had Troucissa and another girl, special they were.' He grinned.

That explained Sylva's attitude thought Petrus. He shrugged. 'I'm not interested in your behaviour at the brothel. Is that the only time you've been out?'

'Yes, but I don't keep a record of my visits. You'll have to check with the librarii.'

'I will. You can be certain of that.'

'Right! That's all you'll get from me. I'm off.' Aquilinus pushed back his stool and stood up.

Loud voices burst into the darkness as Petrus approached Vegetinus' rooms. The smell of alcohol and vomit hit him as he entered. The three centurions, Roburius, Vegetinus and Ferullus were sitting at the table, cradling cups of wine in their hands. A pair of dice sat in the centre of the table, alongside a handful of sestertii. The room was dirty and cluttered. Pots, pans and weaponry lay strewn across the floor and a pitcher lay on its side in a pool of water. A slave hovered nearby, holding a pitcher.

'What d'you want?' Vegetinus slurred belligerently as he rose to his feet.

'Take a seat,' Petrus put out a hand to push the man back down. Vegetinus shook him off and slumped onto his chair.

'I need to ask you some questions, about the dead man,' Petrus began.

The slave dragged a stool over towards the table, but Petrus shook his head, preferring to remain standing. The man poured a cup of wine and held it towards him. Petrus nodded his thanks and drank a mouthful. He winced. The wine was rough and dry against his mouth.

'Ask away,' burbled Roburius.

'You were all outside the fort eight days ago, on the day Manius went missing. What were you doing?'

Vegetinus sniggered. 'Gambling, I expect. That's all we really leave the fort for. Well, that and drinking and the occasional visit to Sylva's place. Last week, mmm. Yes, it was gambling, in the forest.'

Petrus raised an eyebrow. 'In the forest? Do you lose a lot of money?'

'Sometimes. But sometimes we win a lot too.'

'And when you lose, what happens?'

'Not much. We can afford to lose money.'

'Have you ever been involved in betting with Manius?' Petrus asked.

Vegetinus shook his head, 'No, never, not with him.'

'Tell me about the Mithraeum.'

'Nah. You'll have to wait for your ordeals. I know you'll already have asked Ruga and Aquilinus about it, so don't try it with us. Secret is secret.' Vegetinus put his finger to his lips and smiled.

In his office, Petrus reviewed the list of people outside the fort when Manius left for the last time: Arsenios the physician, the Prefect and the Signifer. He struggled to think of a reason why any of these senior officers might want to kill Manius. He glanced down at the list of pensioners and one widow, Honoria.

He walked slowly towards his rooms. The rich aroma of cooking food reached out to draw him in.

Later, he lay in his bed thinking. Was Manius left in the temple as a message to one of the followers of Mithras? If so, who? The most obvious person was himself, as Manius was in his century. Gauori's gentle snores crept into Petrus' room and lulled him into sleep.

IV

'I'll speak with Ecdicius again, to find out what he was doing outside the fort,' Tatius had said when Petrus updated him on his findings from the previous day. 'He was probably just visiting his woman. I was at the brothel and then visited the Temple of Jupiter to pray about my forthcoming wedding. I think we can rule out Arsenios. He wouldn't kill anyone. He's a physician, for Jupiter's sake! You've got plenty of other suspects on your list, haven't you?'

The morning sun peaked out from behind the grey rain-soaked clouds. The damp, muddy streets stank of rubbish and animal faeces. Their stench left a rank taste on the back of Petrus' tongue. The bathhouse opened its sluice and water rushed along the drain, clearing the mess and lessening the smell. Petrus shivered as he made his way to the merchants' area of the vicus and arrived at the house of the retired centurion, Safinius Cato. The door was opened by a slave dressed in tattered clothing. Long, tangled black hair framed his dirty face. He opened his mouth but made no sound as he regarded the centurion.

'I'm here to see your Master,' said Petrus.

The slave looked over his shoulder and then back at Petrus, before stepping aside and allowing him to pass through the door. The interior was dark and musty. The slave moved past Petrus, bumping against his shoulder.

'Watch out!' grumbled Petrus, but the man did not respond.

They emerged into the courtyard area of the house. The stink of rotting food hovered around them as they picked their way across the bare earth. A bald red-faced man stumbled out of one of the rooms. His tunic was stretched tight across the chest; it was stained with food and had sweat marks around the neck. He hitched up his tattered trousers and tightened his belt. His boots were worn and scratched. Behind him, a thin woman in a dirty smock hovered near the door. She pushed a strand of her straw-coloured hair away from her tired face with a hand that was rough with hard work.

'What d'you want?' mumbled the man.

Petrus winced as the man's stale, sweaty smell smothered him. 'Safinius Cato?' he began.

'What d'you want with me, Centurion?' Cato moved to stand up close into Petrus' face.

Petrus wrinkled his nose as Cato breathed warm stale ale over him. He put a hand on Cato's chest and applied gentle pressure, forcing him to take a step back.

'Well?' Cato clenched his fists belligerently.

'Steady, soldier,' Petrus kept his voice even. 'I just wanted to ask you a few questions.'

'Soldier!' spat Cato. 'Cast aside when I retired and given only a pittance to live on! Not enough to feed a wife and family. No recognition for years of service.'

'You draw a monthly pension. That should be plenty if you don't have an extravagant lifestyle.' Petrus glanced around the shabby courtyard. The Roman army was generous to its veterans, and their widows. 'Gamble a lot, do you?' he guessed.

Cato frowned. 'Who've you been talking to? I pay my debts. Are you alone?' He looked past Petrus, towards the door.

Petrus nodded and gestured the man towards a stone seat at the edge of the courtyard, gently pushing him down onto it. 'I want to ask you some questions. Do you still worship at the Mithraeum?'

'The Mithraeum? Why would I do that?' Cato took a deep

breath and shook his head. 'Mithras is worshipped by the army's commanders,' he paused. 'Of course, you know that. As a Centurion, you're no doubt a worshiper yourself. I'm retired. I've no need of his interventions anymore.' He took a deep breath. 'Is this... is this about the dead man? The one found in the temple?'

Petrus nodded, 'His name was Manius.' Petrus watched the old soldier carefully as he said the name, but Cato's veined face showed no recognition. 'What sort of contact do you have with the fort now?'

Cato sniffed and wiped his nose on the sleeve of his tunic; he cleared his throat and spat a thick gob of phlegm on the ground. 'I swear allegiance annually to the Roman Empire, same as everyone else who lives here in the vicus. I pay my ground rent and other taxes. I go once a month to the fort for my pension, little as it is, just like the other retirees.'

'So, you're familiar with the librarii at the fort?'

'Was this Manius one of them? I don't know 'em, not anymore, not like when I was a centurion. I left ten years ago. A lot of men who were serving when I was there are probably gone, retired themselves now. I go straight to the Treasury and pick up my money, sign for it there. The bloody librarii have already accounted for it, including deductions. Well, they have if they do their jobs properly.'

'What do you mean 'If they do their jobs properly'?'

Cato groaned. 'They make mistakes in salary deductions, sometimes deliberately. The illiterate young soldiers don't know enough to argue about it. Historically, it's always the librarii who have their hands in the Emperor's pockets, isn't it? Easy place to make stuff go missing, where the records are kept. I remember a time, mmm, must've been about twenty years ago when the most senior librarius was caught stealing from the army. Maybe this Manius deducted money from the wrong person, or maybe the army caught him stealing and just wanted rid of him. Or maybe someone just wanted to say 'Fuck you' to the army's top men?' Cato smirked.

'Keep those ideas to yourself!' snapped Petrus, embarrassed and angry that he'd not thought of some of them himself. 'Someone might consider them seditious.'

'Sedition? Do your best to prove that one, Centurion!' Cato spat, pushed himself to his feet and stepped close to Petrus. 'Get out!' he sprayed spittle across Petrus' cheeks.

Petrus wiped his hand across his face, turned and walked away. He heard Cato berating the slave who closed the door behind him. He walked to Potitius Aratus' shoe shop. The door stood open and a young man with pale hair sat rubbing wax into a large piece of leather whose smell filled the air. The man looked up and got to his feet as Petrus entered, dropping the leather on the bench in front of him.

'My father is out the back, Sir,' he inclined his head.

'Then bring him, please,' he added, remembering that the young man was probably a Roman citizen.

The door creaked as the man opened it and closed it behind him. The noise made Petrus' teeth hurt, and he shuddered.

The man returned moments later and beckoned to him. 'He said for you to come in here.'

Petrus entered the warm kitchen. It was clean and smelled of bread and animal fat. A thin man with a bald head began to struggle to his feet, leaning on a staff for support.

'Don't get up, Sir,' said Petrus, raising a hand to stop him.

The man nodded and lowered himself carefully back to his seat. His grey-skinned face was pocked with scars and his eyelids hung heavily over his sharp green eyes. He placed one of his out-sized hands across his chest; the fingers, knobbled like tree roots grasped the cloth of his bright blue tunic. He bobbed his head in greeting.

'Centurion,' he murmured.

'Greetings, Aratus.'

'Please take a seat,' Aratus said in a hoarse whisper, waving him towards the table. 'Ale?'

A young woman with chestnut hair put down the wool she was working and lifted a jug. She poured two cups of ale, placing them on the table. In another room, a child squealed and then laughter drowned out the high-pitched noise. A door was thrown open and two small girls ran in, throwing themselves at Aratus. He caught them and grinned, hugging them to his frail body.

'Da, Da,' gurgled one of them.

Aratus released his daughters and said. 'Now, go and play. I've got to talk to this man here. He's a soldier.'

The two girls stared silently at Petrus. One of them stepped forward, put her tiny hand out and touched the belt holding Petrus' pugio. Petrus smiled.

'Wsssht!' Aratus hissed. 'Leave him alone. He's a soldier!'

The woman ushered the two girls outside.

'Sorry, they don't yet know how to behave,' Aratus said.

'That's not a problem. I've children of my own,' said Petrus, wondering how old the man was.

'It's my son who's in the shop, from my first wife,' Aratus nodded towards the door, as if knowing Petrus' thoughts. 'When she died, I was considered good husband material, a pensioner centurion with guaranteed income. Her, over there, she's given me these two girls. They keep me young I suppose, even though my old body is giving up on me,' he sighed. 'Anyway, I don't suppose you want to hear about my ailments. How can I help the Roman army?'

'Have you heard about the murder at the Mithraeum?'

Aratus nodded. 'I think everyone's heard about that. I've not thought about that place since I left the army. Was the dead man a follower?'

Petrus shook his head. 'No. He was one of the librarii at the fort.'

'Strange place to murder him then. I don't know any librarii. I left the army fifteen years ago, haven't had much contact with it since then, apart from the annual dedication, I mean. These days I don't even go to the fort to collect my pension. I send that one with a slave to accompany her.' He inclined his head towards the woman who was working with the wool again.

Petrus noted how Aratus referred to his wife and wondered whether she was the old man's former slave.

'And you haven't heard any rumours about it then?'

Aratus shook his head. 'I barely leave this compound. Can't get about much, as you can see. My son hasn't mentioned anything.'

Petrus got to his feet. 'Thank you for your time.' He passed out through the shop. He nodded to the young man and stepped into the street.

He moved down to the newer part of the vicus where the houses were larger. Calvisius Lucullus' property had once been brightly coloured, but harsh winters and driving rain had dulled the brickwork, pitting the stones and leaving gaps in the lime mortar. Petrus knocked on the door. It was opened by a thin slave whose smock hung loosely from his bony shoulders. Without a word, the slave led him through the dark house; the window shutters had not been opened. Badly aged statues of gods, with dirty cracked faces, littered the rooms, and faded frescoes adorned the walls. They entered an office which contained only a table strewn with tablets and two rough-hewn stools. Behind the table sat a tall broad-chested man with long dark hair. He looked up and frowned.

'Who are you, Centurion and what do you want?'

'I am Aurelius Petrus. I've some questions for you.'

Lucullus sighed and waved him towards the seat. 'Be quick. I've business to attend to.'

'What business are you in?' asked Petrus, thinking he should have found this out in advance.

'Grain, mostly. I'm one of the suppliers to the fort. Have been since I went into business with Sempronius Macro five years ago when we retired. We've expanded since then, of course,.We've plenty of other customers. Just as well, as the fort seems to order less from me than they used to. Only on a monthly basis now instead of fortnightly. Macro passed away two years ago. His wife leaves me to run it and she takes her share of the profits. They live next door,' he paused. 'Aurelius Petrus? Weren't you the one who rode through the streets with Maximus' head dangling from your belt? Bad business that, with Maximus, I mean.'

Petrus nodded. 'Do you still worship at the Mithraeum, or any of the army's temples?'

Lucullus shook his head. 'I worship at some local temples. Their Gods are better suited to my life outside the army.'

'What contact do you have with the fort?'

'As I've said. I fulfil a monthly order. And I collect my pension.'

'Do you know the librarii?'

He shook his head, 'Librarii? No. They monitor the deliveries, but I don't really pay them much attention. I collect my pension and payment for deliveries from the treasury. I might know some of them from my time, if they're still there… err… Adrianus, Manius, Otho. He was my librarius, Otho.'

'Have you heard about the murder of a Roman army officer?'

Lucullus nodded.

Petrus said, 'That was Manius. We found him in the Mithraeum.'

Lucullus raised his eyebrows. 'Why would anyone kill Manius? Why do it in the temple?'

'That's what I'm trying to find out. When did you last see him?'

Lucullus sighed. 'It might've been when I was delivering to the fort. I can look that up.' He began lifting some of the tablets from the table, glancing at them and then tossing them back. 'I don't pay much attention to them, as I've said.'

Petrus waited. Lucullus turned round and began looking through a pile of tablets on the floor.

'Don't worry, I can check at the fort,' sighed Petrus, wondering how Lucullus managed to run a business when he was so disorganised. 'And what about in the tavern, or the brothel, maybe? Did you ever come across him there?'

Lucullus' face coloured. 'I'm not in the tavern as often as I used to be and as for the brothel. Well, I'm married now, and I have slaves for that sort of thing.'

Petrus looked around the bare room. There were cobwebs on the walls and the floor was cracked and dusty. 'Business not as good as it once was, then?'

'We're just… just… Who've you been talking to?' spluttered Lucullus and frowned.

'It's fairly obvious. You're not able to pay for the repairs to the outside of the building.'

Lucullus clenched his fists and snarled, 'I'm prioritising other things.'

'What deductions do you get from your pension?'

'Monthly taxes for this place,' Lucullus waved his arm around the room, 'for connection to the water and sewage systems. In addition, I pay taxes for the business. Nothing out of the ordinary. Why are you asking me these questions? You could check this at the fort without bothering me.'

Petrus acknowledged this with a nod of his head. 'In debt, are you? Your business, I mean.'

Lucullus opened his mouth to speak, but then closed it. He took a deep breath. 'Lots of businesses are in debt.'

'Struggling a bit though, are you?'

Lucullus did not reply. Petrus let the silence hang between them.

'Have you finished your questions? Then you can leave, Centurion.'

Lucullus stood, and Petrus followed him into the street. He heard the slave close the door behind them as Lucullus strode away.

Petrus knocked on the door of the neighbouring house,

which had neat brickwork and freshly applied mortar. The door was answered by a man in a faded tunic. His scarred hands gripped the door frame so hard his fingers were white.

'There's no need to be afraid. I'm here to speak with the widow of Sempronius Macro,' said Petrus.

The man beckoned him in. The interior of the house was brightly decorated, but there were no frescoes on the walls. There were a couple of statues of goddesses, but not as many as he would have expected in the house of a wealthy merchant. In the salon, there were long couches covered with rich cushions. A woman with her blond hair tied in braids walked towards him. She was dressed in a smock and thick trousers.

'How can I help you, Centurion?' she waved him towards a seat.

Petrus bowed his head. 'I'm Aurelius Petrus. I'd like to ask you a few questions Madam.'

'You may call me Honoria,' she fluttered her eyelids and smiled. 'Ask away.'

'What do you know about the temple of Mithras?'

'Mithras?' she paused and raised a hand to her forehead, feigning concentration. 'That was the place where my husband worshipped when he was in the army. It was very secretive. I know he went there, but not much else. Why do you ask?'

'A man from the fort called Manius has been murdered. He worked in the records office. Did you know him?'

'Why would I know him? I don't go to the fort.'

'Then how do you collect your widow's pension?' Petrus asked.

'My oldest son, Flaccus, goes to the fort with one of the slaves for protection.'

'Is he here? May I speak with him?'

She shook her head. 'He's gone to collect grain from nearby villages. He'll be gone a couple more days, I expect. He works with, or I should say for, Lucullus, our neighbour. Recently he's caught the eye of Felix, that freedman from the fort. He'll be going collecting grain and cloth directly for the army soon, I think. After all, that is Felix's business, as you are no doubt aware.'

Petrus raised an eyebrow. He hadn't heard that about Felix. He tried to keep his face passive. 'I've been speaking with Lucullus. He and your late husband were business partners, weren't they?'

She nodded.

'And now, what is your role in the business?'

She smiled, 'My role? I receive a share of the profits and Flaccus works there. That is all. I had hoped Flaccus could be a full partner, but he has no head for business. He just does as he's told.'

'How's the business going?'

'You've spoken with Lucullus, haven't you? It's a struggle right now, judging by his mood, the state of his children, and you've no doubt drawn your own conclusions when you went into his house. It's in a poor state of repair. I get an income each month and I leave the rest to him. I just need enough to feed my family and pay my bills.'

Petrus looked around the room. 'You seem to be doing alright.'

'Macro drew up the partnership in a way that would ensure a steady income for me, his widow.' She watched Petrus for a moment and then continued, 'He wasn't expecting to die, but he had planned for the future, just in case. You see, Lucullus isn't, I mean wasn't, as smart in business as he liked to think. He's learned a lot now, of course, but he's tied into maintaining my lifestyle,' she paused again. 'There are only four of us, me, three children, including Flaccus, and a couple of slaves. Lucullus has six children and a grasping wife.'

'So, you don't get on? Does he resent you?'

She laughed bitterly. 'He's resigned to it. What could he do? He can't get rid of all of us. His wife resents us. Would you like something to drink?' She snapped her fingers, and a slave stepped forward, carrying a jug. The slave poured wine into two cups and handed one to her mistress. Petrus took the other one and drank a mouthful. It was good wine; he swallowed and took another long drink, relishing the rich taste.

'It must be difficult for you, raising your children alone.'

'It was at first, 'specially with all the upset in the vicus, after he died.'

'Upset?'

'He was killed in a brawl in one of the taverns. You must've heard about it. Some of your centurions were there. They saw it all.'

Petrus shook his head.

She frowned. 'Macro was handy with his fists. It was an argument over money.'

'He was owed money?'

'I was told it was something to do with gambling,' she paused. 'He didn't gamble much, not like that other retired centurion who lives over that way.' She waved a hand.

Petrus nodded, 'Cato?'

'Cato, that's it. Occasionally, Marco'd have a drink with him and a bit of a bet. They weren't friends or anything. Just as well. I'd probably have nothing if he'd gone the same way Cato has.'

Petrus waited.

'Happens a lot, doesn't it? Retiring soldiers, don't know what to do with themselves, turn to drink?' she said.

Petrus felt himself redden. 'Thank you for your time.'

The sun was high in the sky, and the clouds were drifting slowly past it. The breeze tingled his face as he walked along the street with his head down, deep in thought. He did not see Carantii walking towards him. Carantii barged into his shoulder, knocking him sideways.

'Oof! What the..?!' Petrus made to grab his pugio.

'Apologies, Centurion,' Carantii backed away and raised his hands as if surrendering.

'Watch where you're going!' snapped Petrus. He marched away. Inside his tunic, his chest tingled as the ivy leaves brushed against his skin. He hid a smile. Carantii had some information.

Petrus made his way to Tatius' office. Tatius barely looked up as Petrus began to outline his interviews with the retired Centurions and the widow.

'I think I need to look into two of the men more closely. Cato is a drunk and a gambler who's in debt. He's very angry, says the pension is not enough to live on and that the Signifer and librarii are taking more deductions than they should. He might have been riled enough to murder Manius. He's bald though, so there would have to be someone else involved, someone with dark hair. He also suggested the librarii might be stealing from the army as well as the men.'

Tatius put his stylus down and sat back in his chair, watching Petrus.

'There's another man who may be of interest. Lucullus, he retired five years ago. His business is not going too well. He's obliged to keep his deceased partner's widow in funds. He said his orders from the fort are half what they were. He might've blamed Manius for that and held a grudge against him. He has dark hair. Perhaps the reason for dropping the orders is somewhere in the records.'

'Maybe Cato's right and Manius was stealing from the army,' said Tatius. He leant forward with his elbows on the table.

'Perhaps. Maybe the Tribune's imminent arrival has spooked someone, who may have acted to get rid of Manius and hoped to cover up his thefts.'

Tatius took a sharp breath in. 'Is Cato spreading that sort of rumour?'

Petrus shook his head. 'No. He didn't mention the Tribune, probably doesn't know anything about his imminent arrival. He still seemed to be fairly drunk when I spoke with him. I warned him of the consequences of such talk.'

'Irregularities in the finances wouldn't reflect very well on us, would it?' Tatius took a deep breath. 'I'm promoting Balbus as Manius' replacement. I've informed Ecdicius of that. I've also had words with him about his duties as Signifer and told him he'll be fined if he fails to carry them out. If he doesn't buck his ideas up, I'll have him replaced.' He held a hand up to silence Petrus. 'I asked him his whereabouts on the day Manius disappeared. He said he was visiting his woman,' he sighed. 'Balbus can start work in the morning. He can take a look at the historical records and see if there are any irregularities. The others can carry on doing Manius' work.'

Balbus was an interesting choice. Physically weak and often ill, he was not someone who Petrus would have relied on in battle. He was timid and not one craving the acknowledgement of officers. However, he had to concede that the young man was very particular about the maintenance and cleanliness of his weapons, armour and other belongings. He always carried out his duties in the workshops and around the fort with meticulous care. This attention to detail could be useful in the investigation.

'He can also check to see if Manius' ring was used after he disappeared. Err,' Petrus stumbled, unsure how to raise the issue, 'if Manius' death is related to the records, and Balbus starts looking into them, then that could put him in danger.'

'Organise a guard for him. He's been told to report directly to you. Keep things confidential.'

'And, erm, it may be an idea to keep the records office under guard as well.'

Tatius leant forward in his chair. 'What do you mean?'

'If there's a discrepancy in the records, the obvious thing to do would be to burn the records office down before Balbus, or someone else, finds it.'

'For Jupiter's sake!' Tatius went pale. 'Sort that out as well, will you? We'll look a right shit show if that happens!'

'I'd like to use those four men of Aquilinus' - Vester, Celsus, Janus and Justus. After that trouble with Maximus, they've turned into very diligent soldiers. Aquilinus speaks very highly of them.' He didn't add that he felt guilty about them being tortured by the previous centurion during the investigation into the murder of two soldiers. 'They're still on light duties and Aquilinus went away to the North this morning, so they've probably not got much to do right now.'

'Yes, use them. They brought that torture on themselves by lying, so don't feel sorry for them. They're still having money deducted from their wages in compensation for the rape of those two local girls last year.' Tatius grabbed a tablet and scribbled an order on it, pressing his ring into the wax.

'And when Balbus has settled into his job and all this is over, I'll discuss with him about moving into Manius' old rooms and possibly buying the slave, Docca. After all, he'll have the salary of a Librarius by then.' Petrus said.

Tatius rubbed his chin. 'Let's focus on the murder first, shall we?'

'Another thing. Macro's son works for Lucullus. He may have felt threatened by Manius if Lucullus was losing business. I'll have a look at him. He's also going to be working alongside Felix who, as you know, has been commissioned to collect taxes for the Army.' Petrus said.

'Felix is a trustworthy man. Is there anything else?'

'Macro's widow said he was killed in a brawl in the tavern and there were some centurions there who witnessed it.'

Tatius frowned. 'I don't remember it. How's it relevant to this murder?'

Petrus shrugged. 'I'm not sure that it is. It was a fight over gambling. She said there was some upset caused.'

Tatius sat back in his chair. "Course there was upset. He was a retired centurion!'

'Maybe the centurions were more than just spectators.'

Tatius sighed. 'Very well, I'll get someone to search the records.'

That night, Petrus fell asleep wondering what news Carantii had for him.

V

Petrus sent for Balbus and the four men from Aquilinus' century. Balbus was breathing heavily when he burst into the room without knocking. Seeing his centurion, he pulled himself upright into a salute.

'You sent for me?' he ran a trembling hand through his curly dark hair. 'The Prefect told me to report directly to you. I-I'm not sure why.'

'Sit down and I'll explain,' Petrus spoke gently, trying to reassure the young man, who looked terrified as he lowered himself onto the stool opposite Petrus.

'You're being promoted to the post of Librarius. That has a lot of responsibilities. It involves the careful recording of the army's work, checking and collating records, dealing with salaries and deductions. It's a crucial role. Librarii are trusted officials, but not always popular, as they deduct fines and costs from men's pay.'

Balbus nodded. 'The Prefect explained that to me yesterday. I went to the Librarium and Adrianus showed me some of the records.' He grinned. 'I've been given a thick cloak and gloves to wear.'

'You'll need them. The windows are always open in the Librarium and the wind can be vicious. That's not why I've called you here. It's about Manius.'

Balbus frowned and opened his mouth slightly, but did not speak.

'I'll be honest with you. It's possible that while he was working in the Librarium, he may have found something wrong with the records. Someone in that office may have been fiddling the figures and pocketing the money themselves. He might have been murdered to prevent him from revealing this to the Signifer. Alternatively, Manius could have been dishonest himself and someone murdered him in revenge, or to keep the matter quiet. The Prefect wants you to look into the records and see what you can find. Manius' behaviour changed about six weeks ago when he started withdrawing money from his wages account. You'll probably have to go back over a couple of months' records.'

'If... if Manius was murdered, then I might be in ...' The young man did not finish his sentence.

'Then you may also be in danger, you mean? Yes, you might. Especially if you do find evidence of falsification of records. I'm arranging a guard for you. They'll be here shortly. You probably know them; Vester, Celsus, Janus and Justus? I won't be telling them the reason you need a guard, and neither will you. One of them will be with you at all times, day or night. You'll sleep in the infirmary while you're doing this work. One of them can watch over you there. We're also going to have a guard in the records office during the night and put extra sand and water in there, in case someone tries to burn the Librarium down.' He stressed the next sentence, 'The reasons for your work must be kept between the three of us, you, me and the Prefect. Report to me every morning immediately after parade.'

Balbus had gone pale. Petrus looked up as there was a knock at the door and Vester entered the room. He saluted, glanced at Balbus and then back at Petrus.

'Are the other three with you?' asked Petrus.

'Yes, Sir.'

'Bring them in.'

Celsus, Janus and Justus crowded into the office. They all looked pale. Some months previously, they'd been in a lot of trouble and were clearly frightened of Petrus.

'Balbus is going to start work in the Librarium as Manius'

replacement. We're concerned about the safety of the record keepers following Manius' death and so we're posting guards in their room. You four are to keep watch over them during the day. I also want one of you in the records' office when the librarii are not working, all through the night. Make sure no-one works outside normal hours or enters the office. You can't take torches in there with you, so I suggest you leave the torch outside and the door open.' He looked at them all for a moment. 'I mean it. No flames in the records room. It's too risky. Everything could be destroyed. You can be on rotation. This will be your only work from now on, until I say so. You are excused from all other duties.'

Vester licked his pale lips, and his translucent skin flushed pink. He opened his mouth to speak. Petrus held up his hand to quieten him.

'I want someone to be with Balbus at all times. He'll be sleeping in the infirmary. So, one of you will be in there with him, as a guard. You must also provide him with his evening meal. Vester, you can organise the shifts.'

'Just guarding Balbus all through the night? Not the other Librarii?' asked Vester.

'Yes, just Balbus at night. There's plenty of space in the infirmary.'

'But…'

'Do your duty here and it will reflect well on all of you.'

Vester grimaced, 'Yes Sir.'

'Very well. Balbus, you can start work in the Librarium right away. One of these men will come there shortly as a guard.'

Balbus rubbed his chin and looked around at the four men who would be protecting him. He got slowly to his feet and left the room.

'Right, who's on duty in the Librarium first?' asked Petrus.

'Celsus,' replied Vester, 'Then Janus can stay overnight in there and Justus can stay with Balbus in the infirmary. I'll take over in the infirmary at the seventh hour of the night and I'll organise food this evening.'

'How come he gets to choose?' muttered Justus, leaning in towards his brother and trying to whisper.

'Because I damn well told him to!' snarled Petrus. 'The Librarium and Balbus' life are in your hands. Now get out, all of you!'

A blanket of cool air coated the fort and Petrus shivered as he walked towards the infirmary. Arsenios held a short log of wood in his hand as he spoke in low tones to the young soldier who'd lost part of his leg. The young man had tears trickling down his cheeks as he listened.

'The carpenter can fashion this into a false leg for you, Aquila. Once your wound is healed, we can fit it and hopefully you can walk again, after a fashion,' Arsenios said.

'And what will happen to me?' Aquila sobbed, unable to keep his voice steady.

'That's in the lap of the Gods,' murmured Arsenios. He squeezed the young man's shoulder and turned to face Petrus, who was marvelling at the physician's skills.

'What can I do for you?' Arsenios asked.

'Can we go through there?' Petrus indicated the room where Manius' body had been stored.

'Of course,' Arsenios led the way.

'You only have two patients at present, don't you?'

Arsenios nodded, 'As we haven't had much conflict with the locals recently, I only have to worry about accidents at work. Of course, when Aquilinus gets back, some of his men are bound to have sustained injuries. They always do.'

'I need Balbus to stay in the infirmary every night until further notice,' Petrus began.

'He's not sick. That would not be appropriate,' Arsenios scowled.

'I can't go into details, but it's necessary for his safety and he will have a soldier guarding him at all times.'

Arsenios opened his mouth to protest, but Petrus cut him off. 'The Prefect has given me authority in this matter.'

'Can you tell me why he's so important?'

'He's replacing Manius.'

'Aah, then he might be in danger. Very well, I shall get a bed made up for him away from the patients and something for the guard.'

'Just a stool for the guard. I don't want him to be too comfortable. Balbus will come straight here after work, and they'll organise food for him.'

'Fine. And are those two out there allowed to talk to him?'

'Of course, he's not in isolation, just here for his protection. He won't be discussing his work with anyone.'

Arsenios nodded.

'I'll leave it to you, then. I'll check on Balbus later this evening.' Petrus said.

The afternoon was dying as the sun slid down towards the horizon. Long shadows danced on the ground as people hurried through the streets anxious to get home before darkness fell. The streets were dangerous at night, particularly for women. Two young girls had been raped the previous year, and many women were still frightened. To Petrus' shame, the rapists had been soldiers.

The mud was thickening in the cold, and it pulled at his feet as he moved. The icy wind dried the drips from his nose onto his top lip. The sound of a horn blasted ahead of him, and local people scattered into the alleyways, leaving him alone in the street. The Tribune, astride a fine black stallion, rode ahead of a carriage and a team of soldiers on horseback. A pale, delicate hand clutched the black curtain obscuring the carriage's window. The Prefect's new bride had arrived. Petrus put his hand to his heart and bowed his head in salute. The Tribune returned the gesture, then slowed his horse and beckoned to him.

Nervously, Petrus stepped forward but kept his distance.

The Tribune bent down and spoke in a low voice, 'I heard about the murder. Update me tomorrow when I'm at the fort.'

Petrus nodded. 'Yes, Sir.'

Aurora watched with a slight smile on her face as Petrus gobbled down his food. The rich meat and thick gravy filled his belly, and the wine soothed him.

'I've heard that Manius had a woman in the vicus,' Aurora said.

Petrus looked up from his food.

'She's a soldier's widow and has two children. Well, one is a grown man now.'

'Can you find out where they live? If necessary, say that there may be an inheritance for them.'

'And is there? Money, I mean?'

He shook his head. 'Manius had withdrawn most of his money and he didn't leave a will. So, his remaining savings will stay with the army.'

'Is it fair to raise her hopes?' she frowned.

'I'm investigating a murder. I need to speak with her.' He grasped her hands and held them to his lips, 'Please don't do or say anything which could put you in danger. I couldn't bear it if anything happened to you.'

She moved into his arms, and they kissed. Petrus felt love rush through his body, and he peeled himself away.

He gasped, 'I can't stay, I really can't. There's so much to do.'

Aurora led him to the door and put her hands to his face. 'Then go. May the Gods be with you, and help you with your work, so that you can come back to us.' She pushed him gently into the street.

Light and laughter spilled invitingly out through the cracks in the tavern's shutters. Petrus pushed open the door and stepped into its warm stinky atmosphere. Most of the tables were occupied by men who clutched their ale and talked in loud, drunken voices. The taverner handed Petrus a drink as he sat down at an empty table. He'd established himself as a regular drinker in the tavern, as this enabled him to easily make contact with Carantii. Whilst he did sometimes go to the forge to speak with the blacksmith, he didn't want that to be a frequent thing. Local people would soon notice and that could raise questions about Carantii and whether he was an informant.

Carantii was having an argument with Felix, the Prefect's former slave.

'You've done well for yourself as a freeman. Able to worm your way into business with the fort, collecting cloth and grain taxes, weren't you?' slurred Carantii.

'I've a good relationship with the Army. A bit like yourself,' replied Felix.

Petrus held his breath, wondering if Carantii was about to be exposed.

Carantii said, 'My business is based on high-quality work, not just sucking up to the Romans.'

'I was not born with your advantages.'

Carantii did not reply immediately, 'You're quite right man, I'm sorry. Fair play to you for making a go of it. Wasn't easy, was it? Let me buy you a drink on my way out.'

Carantii leant forward and offered Felix his hand as the taverner stepped over and poured Felix another drink. The two men shook hands. Carantii handed some coins to the taverner as he left.

Petrus savoured his drink and watched Felix carefully, wondering whether he could use the former slave as an informant. He dismissed the thoughts as he realised that the community would probably always be wary of the former slave and his continued closeness to the army. He moved towards the door.

'So soon?' asked the taverner as he took the coins Petrus gave him.

'Lots to do, I'm afraid,' murmured Petrus.

Carantii's voice emerged from the darkness as Petrus turned towards the fort.

'Greetings, Petrus.'

'Hail, Carantii,' Petrus kept his voice low, and checked that the street was empty. He stepped into the dark alleyway between some of the shops.

'Manius had a woman here in the vicus, a soldier's widow. They say she lives somewhere near the tannery. Has kids, although they're not his. I'll try to find out her name. My guess is that's where his money went. There's not much talk of him gambling or any debts. He visited the tavern occasionally and got quite drunk. His slave would fetch him back to the fort.'

Petrus nodded pointlessly. 'Thank you. I want you to go to the brothel.'

'Always happy to do that sort of work.'

Petrus knew Carantii was smirking. 'Sylva was not very forthcoming when I asked her about Manius, could you see what you can find out?'

'Of course.'

'Aquilinus said he was there the day of Manius' disappearance, with a whore called Troucissa. The Prefect also said he was there on the same day before going to the Temple. Find out about that. Also, find out everything you can about the two retired centurions, Cato and Lucullus. I've interviewed them both. Cato is a drunk and a gambler. What sort of debts has he got? How is Lucullus' business going? Does he have debts? The son of the deceased centurion, Sempronius Macro, is a young man called Flaccus. He works for Lucullus and also Felix, the man you've just been arguing with. Find out anything you can about Flaccus.'

'Is that all? Not much then?'

'I've not finished. Three of the current centurions; Roburius, Vegetinus and Ferullus, are big gamblers. I want to know all about them.'

Petrus held out a handful of coins. A hand gripped his and then the coins slid into the blackness.

'Go well, Centurion.'

'Go well, Carantii.'

The bitter wind blasted his body, and he fought for each breath as he hurried back to the fort. He raised his fist to knock on the gate, but the grill drew back before he made contact with the wood.

'Jupiter,' he mumbled.

The wood creaked as the gate swung open. Rufus and Pius saluted him.

Wavering light and low voices leaked out of the infirmary into the night as he approached. Inside the building, Aquila was sobbing quietly as his friend tried to comfort him. In the far corner, Balbus sat on his bed eating a meal in the candlelight. Justus stood nearby, scooping up mouthfuls of food with his spoon. They both stopped eating as Petrus neared them.

'Everything alright?' Petrus asked.

'Must I even go with him to the shitter?' asked Justus.

'He must never be left alone.'

'Jupiter's sake! I have to watch him pee!' Justus turned away, muttering to himself.

Petrus made his way to the records office. A flickering light sneaked out of the open doorway. He clenched his fists. That stupid bastard! The whole records office could go up in flames if Janus wasn't careful. He barged his way into the room and opened his mouth to shout. He stopped. A single burning candle sat on a plate just inside the door. Next to it were six pails of water and three of sand. Janus was huddled in his cloak in the flickering light, his empty food plate at his side. He began to struggle stiffly to his feet. Petrus waved him back down.

'Just checking on you. I see you've taken the fire risk seriously. That's good,' said Petrus.

Janus muttered something unintelligible and leant back against the wall, pulling his cloak tighter around him. Petrus left him and returned to his barracks.

Gauori stirred in his bed as Petrus brushed past his arm, reaching down for the pitcher of wine. The slave's eyes opened wide, and he scrambled to his feet, head bowed.

He whispered, 'I'm s-sorry, Sir. I fell asleep.'

'That's alright. I just needed a drink.'

'There was a message for you, Sir.' Gauori pushed a tablet across the table. 'It's from centurion Fabius Ruga.'

Petrus peered at the scrawled writing. 'Tomorrow night at the fourth hour. Meet at the Mithraeum for your first ordeal.'

'For fuck's sake!' Petrus threw the tablet across the room. It hit the wall and shattered into pieces. 'That bloody man!'

Gauori scampered about, picking up the shards of wood. Petrus went to his room and laid down.

VI

Augustus Pollux had taken off his helmet and laid it proprietorially on Tatius' table as he sat in the Prefect's chair. He ran his hands through his thick brown hair and pushed it away from his eyes. He really needed a haircut, thought Petrus, as he stood to attention alongside Tatius, whose voice trembled as he spoke.

'Petrus is in charge of the investigation. Currently, we're looking into the record-keeping work that Manius did. We've put a round-the-clock guard on the man checking the records, just in case he turns up something and the murderer tries to kill him too. Manius started taking large sums of money out of his account about six weeks before his death, so something may've happened around then that scared him. It could be someone in the vicus who held a grudge against the man. Petrus can explain more.'

Pollux shifted his gaze to Petrus.

'The person who killed Manius must've known about the Mithraeum. So, I'm making enquiries about the retired centurions who live in the vicus. Two are of interest, in my opinion. Cato, a known drunk and gambler, admitted he is in debt to several people. He's very bitter and says the army pension is not enough to live on. Claims there are too many deductions made by the librarii. He might have blamed Manius for these deductions. The other, Lucullus, runs a grain business that supplies the fort. The business is not going well, and the army buys less from him than we used to. He employs the son of a retired centurion, a young man called Flaccus, who may also be involved. I haven't had a chance to speak to him yet. All of these men may have had reason to kill Manius. Manius definitely had a woman in the vicus. I have feelers out about that, trying to get more information. I don't want to scare her off. She…'

'She'll want her inheritance,' interrupted Pollux.

'There is no will. However, she may not know that. When I find her, she might be able to tell me more about Manius and shed a light on why he suddenly started to withdraw his money.' Petrus said.

Pollux nodded. Petrus could feel Tatius starting to relax alongside him.

'I'm also still checking at the brothel to see if Manius was a regular customer there. Sylva is being a bit difficult right now.' Petrus continued.

Pollux spat, 'Then threaten her. Say we'll introduce a levy for whores or scare her customers away.'

'Are you sure about that old man Aratus?' mumbled the Prefect.

'Yes Sir, I am,' said Petrus. 'He lives modestly, has a good income from his shop and seemed quite content with his lot. And the widow of Sempronius Macro is also well looked after. It is her son who works with Lucullus.'

'But you said you think the son may have had a reason to kill Manius?' frowned Pollux.

'Lucullus might have put pressure on the boy,' Petrus replied.

Pollux said nothing.

Tatius spoke, 'Very well. Unless the Tribune has any more questions for you, you can go. My new wife arrived yesterday evening with the Tribune. I will not be at the Mithraeum tonight.'

Petrus scowled. 'Is it advisable for me to put myself in a pit like that when I'm in the middle of an investigation?'

'It'll give you time to think about it all, Petrus. You might emerge tomorrow and have the whole thing cracked,' grinned Pollux.

'Erm, I meant, someone could take the opportunity to kill me, to stop me from finding Manius' murderers.'

'You're overrating yourself! And your imagination is running away with you. You've already interviewed all the centurions and ruled them out, haven't you?' said Pollux.

'Er, not exactly. Four of them were outside the fort at the same time as Manius, so had the opportunity to kill him, although I can't see their motive,' mumbled Petrus.

Pollux scoffed, 'So was the Prefect and the Signifer. But you've no motive for them either, have you?'

'Err, no, I haven't,' Petrus' voice was barely above a whisper.

'No-one else will know you're in the pit. Here, take this tablet authorising you to take some more money from the Treasury. Sounds like you're going to need it with all these enquiries going on. Your spies must be busy.' Tatius said and pointed to a tablet on the table authorising Petrus to withdraw twenty denarii.

Balbus was hovering near Petrus' office. He had his thick cloak wrapped tightly around him.

'In here,' said Petrus, indicating his office.

'I've not found anything as yet, Sir,' Balbus mumbled as he stood just inside the door. 'I'm being careful, as I don't want the others to grow suspicious. I'm looking back at the old records for the last couple of months, as you suggested.'

'Good. And how is it working out with the bodyguards? And the infirmary?'

'That's all fine, Sir. The infirmary is a good place to sleep, it's quiet. And the injured men are a good laugh sometimes,' smiled Balbus.

'Do the guards stay awake all night?'

'I think so, Sir.'

'Very well then. Come and report again to me tomorrow.' Petrus dismissed him.

Petrus made his way to the Treasury. Ecdicius looked up and scowled.

'Aurelius Petrus, how nice to see you. Here again to point out my further failings as a Signifer, are you?'

Petrus pushed the tablet across the table. 'The Prefect has authorised me to have twenty denarii's worth of coins. I'd like two hundred sestertii, fourteen quinarii and eleven denarii.'

Ecdicius peered at the tablet. He made a show of checking the signature and the ring seal, then rose from his chair and nodded towards one of the guards. The man had a key on a chain at his waist. He placed it in the lock of the gate and turned it, then took a step back. Ecdicius produced a key from his pouch and used it to turn a second lock. The last remaining soldier also used his key. The gate swung open and Ecdicius disappeared inside.

Petrus watched the two soldiers who hovered anxiously near the gate. Perhaps they didn't entirely trust the Signifer. After all, it would be their joint responsibility if money went missing. After what seemed a long time, Ecdicius emerged carrying a pouch bulging with coins. He dropped it on the table.

'Do you wish to count it?' he snarled.

Petrus opened the pouch. He could see the silver quinarii lying on a bunch of sestertii. He shook his head, signed for it, and carried the money back to his rooms. He locked nine of the denarii and most of the sestertii in the chest in his room.

Petrus walked past the market in the winter sun. Two women were arguing. One had a chicken under her arm. It clucked faintly as she waved her free hand about, her bony fingers pointed in the other woman's face. The men in the market watched them, mildly amused, and no doubt hoping there would be a fight. Petrus wondered if he needed to step in, but decided against it. In the past, when he'd got between two women he'd been spat at and scratched. The outcome might be different now that he was a centurion, but he didn't want to run the risk. He made his way to the house of the widow Honoria.

The slave showed him into the salon. Honoria was sprawled on a couch idly playing with her hair as one of her slaves played on a lute and half-heartedly hummed a tune. As Petrus entered, she snapped her fingers, and the slave stopped playing and left the room.

'Aurelius Petrus, what can I do for you? Flaccus arrived back last night if you want to speak with him,' she breathed.

'I'm looking for the freed man, Felix. I know your son works for him, so I thought he could tell me where to find him.'

'And I thought you'd come here for me,' she purred. 'Felix has bought a shop near the tannery, next to the weaver Matugenus. Maybe you know him?'

Petrus nodded. Matugenus regularly supplied the fort with cloth.

'Can I tempt you,' she paused and arched her eyebrows, 'with some wine perhaps?'

Petrus clenched his fists. 'Thank you, but no, Madam, I've a lot to do.'

Petrus approached the tannery whose doors were thrown wide open, releasing the stench of urine and animal fat into the streets. Three men, naked to the waist, plunged their hands into vats of dark liquid and scrubbed at the submerged animal hides. Petrus' eyes smarted, and he felt wet tears on his cheeks as the stink enveloped him. He covered his nose with his hand and hurried past. The smell lingered about him as he pushed towards the edge of the vicus.

Matugenus' door was open. The weaver sat at his loom. Alongside him, two small children were working on a sheep's fleece with metal combs in their hands. Wisps of wool floated in the air like dust. Woven cloth lay stacked against the walls alongside fleeces and a spinning wheel.

The weaver looked up as Petrus approached. 'Greetings,

Centurion,' he returned his gaze to the loom; his fingers worked the thread.

The two children dropped their combs and stared at the Roman soldier. One of them started to whimper. The other turned his head and held a finger to his lips.

'Greetings, Matugenus.'

'The fort's order is not due for another few weeks yet.' The weaver picked up another spool of wool and fixed it to the loom.

'I'm not here about that. I'm looking for the freedman Felix. I've been told he has a place near here.'

Matugenus' fingers stilled, and he looked directly at Petrus for a moment. 'Going to give him some more work, are you? Remind him to put some more my way.'

Petrus didn't answer.

Matugenus waited a moment and then pointed his calloused finger further down the street. 'The shop with the carving of two hands on it. He's adopted that as his symbol. Even had a ring made with it to use as his seal. Fancies himself, doesn't he?'

Petrus did not reply. 'Stay well, Matugenus.'

He'd walked past the shop many times and never registered the finely carved oak sign, depicting two hands clasped together, sealing a deal. It was a fine carving and would have been costly to commission. The door was ajar, and Petrus walked in. The sun's light bounced off the clean lime-washed walls and floor. A brush leaning against the wall was clearly used, as the floor was free of dust and there were no cobwebs beneath the roof. Shelves along the back wall were stacked with tablets.

Felix was reading at a table. He rose as Petrus entered.

'Aurelius Petrus, Greetings,' Felix spoke in Latin and smiled as he spread his arms wide in friendship, then put his hand to his heart and bowed.

'Greetings, Felix,' Petrus nodded his head.

Felix had put on some weight since he had left the fort as a freedman. His cheeks were flushed, his arms were thicker, and the shape of the bones around his neck and shoulders was no longer visibly straining against his skin. He wore a thick woollen tunic.

'You're looking well, and business is good I hear,' said Petrus.

'I'm making my way. I've been fortunate to be able to use contacts at the fort. Won't you sit down for a moment?'

Petrus lowered himself onto the stool opposite Felix.

'How can I help the army?' Felix asked.

'You act as a go between for the army and some of the merchants, don't you?'

'Yes, I do. You'll also have heard that I collect the grain and cloth taxes as well. What of it?'

'Who do you work with apart from Matugenus and Flaccus?'

Felix looked surprised. 'You're remarkably well-informed ,Petrus. I don't work with Flaccus; he works for me. A small point, I know, but an important one. Why are you interested? Centurions don't normally get involved with these issues.'

'I'm investigating a murder.'

'Let's hope it doesn't…' the words died on Felix's lips.

Doesn't end with the murder of innocent women, was what he'd been going to say, thought Petrus. 'So, who else?' he asked Felix.

'Lucullus and I did a bit of business a while back. Mainly I work with Matugenus and Riderua.'

'What can you tell me about Lucullus?'

'Mmm. Rumour is he's not doing too well right now. His suppliers seem to be coming up short and he's having difficulty fulfilling his orders for the fort.' Felix looked around furtively and lowered his voice even though they were alone in the shop. 'The suppliers're selling to other people, like Riderua, for instance. Maybe Lucullus short-changed them.'

'Why did you stop working with him?'

'He didn't pay me what we'd agreed. I was just setting up back then. We didn't have a written contract, and he thought he could underpay me, as I wouldn't know any better, being a former slave.'

'What did you do about it?'

Felix shrugged. 'Put it down to experience and made sure I got written contracts from then on.' He grinned, 'Might've mentioned it to Ecdicius when I was at the fort. I think they've cut his order to the minimum. They keep him on the list of course, just in case there's a problem, poor harvest or something.' He frowned. 'You won't tell him that will you? I don't want to make enemies. It's better that he thinks he got one over on me.'

'Does he have debts?'

Felix's eyes widened. 'You really don't know about business, do you? Most merchants have debts at one time or another. Usually at the beginning they're indebted to some of their suppliers, then after they've been paid, they're back in profit. Word is Lucullus is not always in profit. You've seen the state of his house. Doesn't look like a wealthy merchant's place, does it?'

The door to the rooms behind opened and a young red-haired woman, her belly swollen in pregnancy, walked in carrying a pitcher and a plate of bread. She placed the pitcher on the table and poured two cups of ale, cautiously placing one of them in front of Petrus. She turned to leave, but Felix grabbed her hand, and she stood still, looking from Felix to Petrus and back again.

'My wife Achai,' Felix said.

'Madam,' Petrus nodded his head in greeting.

Felix released his wife's hand, and she left the room. He broke off a chunk of bread and stuffed it into his mouth as he pushed the plate towards Petrus, indicating he should help himself.

Petrus was trying to hide his surprise and lowered his head as he busied himself with a piece of bread. 'I didn't think you'd be married,' he mumbled.

'Why not? Slaves are people too.'

Petrus felt himself redden in shame. His mouth bulged with the soft dough. 'Is there anything else you can tell me about Lucullus or anyone else supplying the fort?'

Felix shook his head. 'Only that he has to support the widow of his former partner, Macro. That's quite a big drain on his finances, I would think.'

'And do you know anything about Cato?'

Felix grinned. 'Cato? You mean the drunk centurion, in debt to everyone due to his gambling? What's there to say about him?'

A thought occurred to Petrus. 'Do you remember when Macro was killed?'

Felix's eyes widened. 'Y-yes I do.'

'His widow says there was some upset and there were centurions in the tavern. They saw the fight. It was about gambling debts.'

'Yes, those three centurions, Roburius, Vegetinus and Ferullus were in the tavern at the time. The former Prefect said they should've stopped the fight. There was some rumour that they weren't just observers, but were involved as well. The Prefect ordered Maximus to investigate. Nothing came of it.'

Petrus knew the investigation would not have been thorough if it was conducted by Maximus. He swallowed the bread and took a huge gulp of ale from his cup. He rose and offered his hand to Felix who shook it. 'Thank you, Felix. Will you contact me if you hear anything else that you think would be of help to me?'

Petrus put some coins on the table.

Felix pushed the money back towards him. 'I will gladly help you out in this matter, Petrus, and in any future matters. I owe you my life and my freedom, despite anything the Prefect might say to the contrary. But we must keep it confidential, just between you and me. The community must know that my dealings with the fort are purely commercial.'

Petrus scooped the coins back up and put them in his pouch.

'Stay well, Aurelius Silvanus Felix.' Petrus watched as Felix drew himself up and stood proudly at the use of his full name.

'Go well, Petrus.'

The winter sun had breathed life into the streets, and people were moving around. Petrus realised he was approaching Lucullus' house. He paused, briefly wondering whether he should go in and talk to the man about his debts. The sound of raised voices reached him. The door to Lucullus' house opened and Adrianus stumbled into the street, 'Don't come back, you arsehole!' a man shouted and the door slammed behind him. There was the screech of metal as the bolts were drawn across. The librarius pulled his hood over his head and ran towards the fort. Lucullus had lied!

Inside the fort gates, it was chaos. The men ran around gathering weapons and securing their families inside the buildings. There was a low hum of excitement and trepidation. Petrus saw Pollux leave the Records office and make his way towards the barracks for an inspection. Petrus walked to the Treasury.

Ecdicius groaned when he walked in. 'Petrus, what now? I've just been told by the Tribune that he's not happy about the way I supervise the librarii. You dropped me in it, didn't you? Not happy just snitching to the Prefect, were you?'

Petrus was filled with hope. The Tribune would make things right. He'd get the librarii working properly again. He said, 'Then be cooperative and I'll leave you alone. Which merchants supply grain to the fort?'

'There's three or four of them,' Ecdicius turned, drew a tablet from a pile behind him, and ran his finger down the list as he spoke, 'Riderua, Cola, Dudda and sometimes Lucullus.'

'Why only use Lucullus sometimes? He's a former centurion. Don't we owe him some loyalty?'

'He doesn't always pay his debts to the farmers who sell to him. We can't be associated with that, and…' Ecdicius didn't finish.

'And Felix told you what Lucullus did to him?'

'Yes. He deserved a break after all those years working for the Prefects. Lucullus was just taking advantage. We have to keep him on our books for security of supply, which I do. Keep him dangling.'

'And when did Felix start collecting the grain and cloth taxes?'

'He's only done it once – at the back end of the summer. The Prefect's authorised it. I'll be sending him round again in the Spring – that'll be for just cloth and maybe a few hides. We don't take grain as a rule until the summer. We don't want the peasants to starve. That breeds resentment.'

'Have you had any trouble directly with Lucullus? Not providing what's asked for, or not paying his taxes?'

The Signifer hesitated and then shook his head. 'Nothing directly. He wouldn't be so stupid.'

'Is Lucullus friendly with the librarii?'

'I doubt it. They dock his pension and count his deliveries. He probably resents them. Wouldn't be good for them to associate with him, might smack of corruption. Why?'

Petrus shrugged, deciding to confront Adrianus and Lucullus himself.

At his rooms, Petrus instructed Gauori to wake him at the end of the second hour of the night. He was hungry, but thought it was better to undertake the ordeal on an empty stomach. He lay on his bed and thought about Lucullus and Felix. His eyes closed.

VII

Carantii kissed Lugraca and then slipped out of the kitchen into the night. He relished the sting of the winter air in his lungs as he took some deep breaths. He hurried towards the brothel, conscious of the weight of Petrus' money in his pocket. Riacus stood aside as he entered, and Carantii made his way to the salon. He threw himself onto one of the couches. The cushions squeezed around him, taking the weight of his body and relaxing his muscles. The thick aroma of smoking oils wafted around him. It was still early, and he was the only customer. He sighed and looked at the young girl behind the table. She ignored him as a slave stepped forward and poured him a drink. He gulped it down and held out the cup for another.

The girl looked up. 'And what would you like tonight? One of the girls, the more experienced women, or one of the boys ,perhaps?' she purred and licked her lips.

Carantii felt uncomfortable. She was only a child. She shouldn't be behaving that way. What did he expect? She'd probably been born here and knew no other life. 'I'd like one of the more experienced women. Someone who's been here a good number of years. I've heard good things about Troucissa.'

She nodded, 'The older ones are cheaper of course. I'm afraid Troucissa is with a client. You'll have to wait.' She held out her hand.

'I don't want to wait. I'll have one of the others.'

He pressed some coins onto her palm, and she left the room. He lay back against the cushions and closed his eyes as he lifted the cup to his lips and savoured more wine. Aware of the slave stepping forward, he placed his spare hand over the cup and gently shook his head.

Three tired looking women entered the room. Each one had a full figure and the holly tattoo branding that Sylva used was visible on their pale necks. They didn't smile as they paraded in front of him, swinging their hips and wetting their lips with tongues that darted out from their slack mouths. They had once been attractive, but now they were worn down by years of hard work. They just looked sad.

Carantii pointed his finger. 'That one.'

'Ovinca,' said the girl. 'A good choice.'

Ovinca looked past him as she took his hand. She led him down the corridor where two feeble candles cast weak light on scratched doors and faded fabrics. He'd been in the more expensive end of the building months before when helping Petrus. In the expensive part, there were rich drapes, plush cushions and young-looking women with fresh skin and tight bodies. The grunts and sighs of sex reached out to him as he passed by doors left ajar.

The bed looked clean, but the cushions bore the stray hairs and imprints of previous customers. Ovinca fluffed the cushions and then drew him onto the bed. He lay down, and she began to lift his smock. She leant forward and placed her lips on his, forcing them apart. She placed her tongue in his mouth. She moved to take down his trousers.

'Not ready for me, then?' she whispered as she looked down at his nakedness. She leant down with her mouth open.

Carantii pulled up his trousers, lay back on the bed and hugged Ovinca close. She sighed and snuggled in towards him. He kissed the top of her head, breathing in the oils she used on her hair. She probably didn't get much tenderness these days. He gently stroked her upper arm with his thumb. Her pale skin was cool. Her hot breath tingled against his face.

'I was a bit worried about coming here. People keep getting murdered, don't they?' He felt her body tighten against him.

'That was all that centurion's doing. He killed the soldiers and those girls.' Her voice was muffled against his chest.

'What about the latest murder? I heard that the dead man was a customer here too.'

She sighed. 'He was one of my regulars, but he stopped coming here two or three years ago, after he took up with Ruua, the soldier's widow. My daughter still lived here with me then. She was a small child, and I didn't like the way men were beginning to look at her. Some men hurt children that way. I sent her to the countryside. She's safe now.'

'Having a woman doesn't stop men coming here though, does it?'

'No,' she paused, 'Ruua must be special for Manius to stop visiting us like that. She used to work here; you know? That's where she met her soldier. She had her boy living here with her; he used to run errands for Sylva. After she fell pregnant again, the soldier took her away, built her a place to live on the edge of the town, I think. I heard he took both children as his. After he died, Manius took up with her. The boy must be a grown man by now. Her daughter is probably now about the same age as my girl was when I sent her away.'

'You must miss your daughter,' Carantii mumbled.

'She has a better life now. She's with her cousins in the countryside. She doesn't have men prowling about her. She's safe, and she's free of the stigma of being born here in this place.'

Carantii pulled her closer and closed his eyes. Her breathing slowed.

Loud banging dragged Carantii into consciousness. Ovinca rolled away and pulled up her robe, scrambling off the bed as he sat up.

The door burst open. Riacus' huge body filled the doorway. 'Time's up, Blacksmith,' he grumbled.

Carantii passed Riacus and went back to the salon. Two men lounged on the couches and the young girl loitered nearby. He left without further comment and made his way to the tavern.

The familiar stink of ale and sweat surrounded him as he entered the warm room. He slid onto a bench alongside one of the merchants and nodded to him. Spilled drink pooled on the scarred table and seeped into his sleeves as he leant his arms on it. The taverner poured him a cup of ale, and he gulped down a mouthful.

'Greetings, Carantii,' slurred the man next to him.

'Greetings, Burcterda.'

They drank in silence for a while. Carantii occasionally glanced around him. There were a few men he recognised. On his second cup of ale, he decided to start talking.

'Thought I was going to come to blows last time I was in here, arguing with that freedman Felix,' he muttered.

'Yes, he made you look a bit of a fool, didn't he? You shouldn't 'ave criticised him for using his contacts at the fort. We'd all do that if we could,' mumbled Burcterda.

'Mmm, I know. Drink got the better of me. I guess I was a bit jealous. It's been a while since the army asked me to do any metalwork for their horses or make any weapons, apart from that centurion, Petrus. He came into the forge about his pugio and didn't want to pay me enough for the work,' he sighed. 'Felix's done well for himself. Not like some of them from the fort. Lucullus for one.'

'Lucullus is still in there with the fort, providing grain, but not so often as the others. He's in debt, as I heard. Maybe he had a falling out with the record keepers,' Burcterda said.

'What difference would that make?'

'They're the ones that place the orders, aren't they?'

'Suppose they are. Still, he can't be doing too badly. He employs that young lad, son of Macro, doesn't he?'

'That's because the old man wrote the contract like that. He must've known the boy's a bit soft, not cut out for business, so tied things up in case he died, to make sure his widow was provided for, and the boy had a job. Otherwise, the lad'd be labouring or something, not swanning around like he does,' Burcterda grumbled bitterly.

Carantii raised an eyebrow. 'Sounds like the lad's not the only one with no head for business.'

The other man laughed. 'Then there's that drunk Cato. He's fallen a long way. Owes a lot of money, gambling debts.'

Carantii took a few more mouthfuls of ale and thought about what to say next. 'Most of them manage well enough though, don't they? Plenty leave enough for their families if they pass on. Like the widow, whatshername? Ruua is it? Used to be a whore 'til a soldier married her? He built her a house, didn't he?'

'Mmm, yes. She married that man, Tarpeus, I think his name was. He fell in love with her at the brothel and claimed her kids as his when he retired. They got citizenship and everything. Like a dream come true for a whore, I guess. There's not many that happens to. He built her a house on the edge of town. Then he died. She's an herbalist now, has her own shop. I heard she took up with that other Roman, the one who was killed. Wonder if he left her anything. He was in here occasionally, couldn't hold his ale. Sometimes his slave had to come and find him, take him back to the fort.'

Carantii nodded and drank some more. He bought Burcterda a drink, and the two sat in companionable silence.

Carantii pushed himself to his feet. 'Go well, Burcterda.'

'Go well, Blacksmith.'

He picked his way carefully along the muddy street and pulled some ivy out of his pocket ready to leave as a sign at Petrus' house.

VIII

It was approaching the end of the second hour of the night. Petrus waved away Gauori's offer of wine. He'd spent some time sitting in the stinking latrine and had exchanged a few words with some of his men as they sat there straining, but he hadn't been in the mood for chatting. He didn't want this initiation. When he became a full member of the Mithraic cult, he'd have even more rituals to observe and sacrifices to make.

'Good luck, Sir,' whispered Gauori, as he opened the door for Petrus to leave.

In the torchlight, he could see rats scurrying across the streets in front of him as he walked to the East Gate. The Gatekeepers saluted as they unlocked and banged the gate closed behind him. The wind and sun had dried the mud, and he was able to walk quickly down the dark street. As he passed deeper into the vicus, faint lights crept out of the merchants' houses and rooms behind shops. The occasional dog barked. He walked on.

At the edge of the vicus, he took the path up the slope towards the temple. The wind bit into his face and snot dripped from his nose as he picked his way carefully along the rough path towards the two tall stones near the temple. Quickly, he relieved himself next to the rocks. He walked slowly down the seven steps, rapped four times and then scraped the hilt of his pugio along the wooden door.

The door swung open and dark figures drew him inside as they chanted. The torch was snatched from his hand, and someone pushed him towards the black hole in the centre of the nave.

'Remove your cloak, socks and boots, and get in,' hissed a voice.

Reluctantly, Petrus did as he was told. An outstretched hand took the clothes from him. The ice-cold stone numbed his feet. He moved to stand near the pit. A raised torch illuminated the space, barely more than three feet wide and just longer than a soldier was tall. Petrus lowered himself down into the pit. He winced as he landed on the frozen floor, still bearing the stains left by Manius.

'Until the morning,' a voice floated down to him.

Tiny splinters of wood rained down on him as the tree trunk slid across the mouth of the hole. He brushed ineffectually at his tunic. He thought he could just hear the scrape of the temple door as they left. He reached up, stood on his toes, and touched the rough underside of the trunk with his fingertips. A slight breeze tickled his hands. Reassured that there was still air entering the space, he relaxed and leant against one of the walls. He slid slowly to the floor, put his head back, and began to go over everything he'd learned since the killing. These thoughts took him nowhere.

Frustrated, he closed his eyes in the darkness. Knowing what he faced, he had wrapped a fleece around his chest to keep warm. However, his arms and face were growing numb, and he rubbed them hard with his hands, creating a fleeting heat. The cold was beginning to penetrate his woollen trousers. He wriggled his buttocks to try to wake them up. He pushed himself to his feet and tried to walk around in the confined darkness, his arms stretched out ahead of him. He had only managed two paces when his hands hit the wall. Frustrated, he turned and took one step, turned sideways, and waved his arms about as he lifted his legs one after the other, marching on the spot. The cold breeze fell into the pit and rustled his hair.

His shoulders began to ache, and he yawned, pulling chilly air into his lungs. He moved back to the wall and slid to the floor, hugging his knees to his chest. He leant his head back and tried to imagine his family at home, his son Titus playing in the yard, and his baby daughter Antigone gurgling in her mother's arms. He smiled in the darkness.

IX

Voices dragged him awake as the moving tree trunk above his head showered him with specks of dust and wood. Petrus raised his arm to shield his eyes from the light that rushed into the pit. Hands reached in, grabbed him by the shoulders and dragged him out, letting him fall to the floor. He lay there blinking as relief washed over him. It was over. His frozen hands and feet tingled. He tried in vain to flex his fingers and toes, but they were unresponsive. He crawled towards his boots. The men around him, their faces shielded by their masks, grumbled and jeered as his thick fingers fumbled with his socks. Frustrated ,he grappled with his cloak, pulled it around his shoulders, and stumbled to his feet.

Ruga, not bothering to hide his face, clapped Petrus on the back and grinned, 'One down, six more to go to become a full member. The next one will be in a few days' time.'

Hands guided him to the door; he leant against the wall to stop himself from falling. 'The password is Cerebrus,' someone murmured. They pushed him up the steps into the wintry morning. His toes screamed in pain and his fingers throbbed as feeling forced its way back into his hands and feet. He picked his way carefully down the slope, stumbling as each leaden foot slipped on the ground. He clapped his hands, interlocked his fingers, and stretched them. The vicus had never looked so inviting.

As he came level with his own house, he noticed the ivy tied around the boot scraper. Carantii had information for him. He paused momentarily, before deciding not to return to the fort. He pushed open the door and stepped into the warmth. The kitchen was empty. He removed his cloak and moved to stand near the fire, leaning against the wall. He breathed deeply, inhaling the smell of fermenting milk, and closed his eyes.

Antigone's feeble cries made him open his eyes and turn around. Aurora was placing the baby in a basket; she gurgled and fell silent. Petrus kissed Aurora's cheek and lowered himself onto a stool.

'You look tired,' Aurora said.

'I've been in a pit at the Mithraeum all night. It was bloody freezing. The first of the initiations. There's six more of these damned rituals before I become a full member of the temple.'

'When did you last eat?'

'Yesterday morning,' he took the bowl of fermented porridge she offered him.

He ate quickly, barely tasting the food. His stomach rumbled appreciatively, as she handed him a cup of wine.

'I would've thought they'd give you some leeway as you're looking into that man's death,' Aurora said.

He laughed bitterly and stood up. 'Some chance. The army marches on.'

'I've heard that Manius' woman is an herbalist. That's all I've managed to find out so far. I didn't want to ask too many questions. Maybe Carantii has more for you. Have you seen the ivy outside?'

He nodded. 'I hope he's got something to help me. I'm a

bit stuck for ideas. I've identified a few people who might've had a motive to kill Manius, some retired centurions with grudges against the fort and perhaps Manius in particular. His signet ring is missing, and I've got someone going through the records to see if it's been used to forge documents. One of the retirees lied to me about knowing the librarii.' He sighed, 'I wish I could stay here. I'm tired and stiff from last night, but I've a lot to do. After the re-dedication at the Temple of Jupiter, the Prefect asked the priest to read the entrails and he said I would be successful in finding the murderer, but there'd be more deaths if I didn't act quickly.'

'But you don't believe that, do you?'

He shrugged, 'It's not important what I believe. It's what the Prefect believes that counts and he'll believe the priest. He wants someone to blame.'

Aurora nodded. She moved into Petrus' embrace and placed her head against his chest, breathing deeply. He kissed the top of her head and rested his cheek against her hair. He whispered words of love into her ear and felt her relax against him. He closed his eyes.

Reluctantly, he pulled himself away, grabbed his cloak and opened the door. He stepped into the street. Water hung in the air, like fog, settling tiny droplets on his face and clothes. He turned towards the Blacksmith's forge. His legs felt heavy as he walked, each step a huge effort. The street was empty, so he stepped to the side of the forge and knocked on the door. It opened a fraction; Lugraca's face appeared, and she looked him up and down. She pulled the door wide open and let him in, indicating a stool near the fire. He shook his head, afraid that if he sat down, he'd fall asleep. He leant against the wall. The heat from the forge's fire spread through the bricks against his back.

'I'll get him,' Lugraca said and left the room.

'Petrus! So early?' Carantii bellowed.

'I'm on my way back from a night in that damned Mithraeum.

I saw your sign. What have you got to tell me?'

Carantii took a seat at the table and poured some ale. He waved the pitcher at Petrus, who shook his head.

Carantii began, 'Manius' woman is called Ruua. She's a former whore from Sylva's place. When she was there, she had a son. The women who have daughters tend to send them away, to keep them safe from the men who could hurt them. Ruua fell pregnant again, and a soldier called Tarpeus married her when he retired and adopted her son. He took the daughter as his own when she was born. So, both the children have got citizenship. Tarpeus built them a house. Manius had been a frequent visitor to the brothel. But after old Tarpeus died, he started up with Ruua and stopped visiting Sylva's. The daughter is still a child, but the son will be a grown man. Seems Ruua is now an herbalist. She's moved to a shop. Manius only drank occasionally, but when he did, he got really drunk and sometimes his slave would come to fetch him back to the fort.'

Petrus nodded. 'Where is her shop?'

Carantii shrugged. 'Should be easy enough to find. There's not that many herbalists in town. You could also try the market. I've been told Lucullus is in a lot of debt. Business is not too good. He has to employ that Flaccus. That's the way Macro set up the contract, to provide for his widow and the boy in the event of his death. The other man, Cato, is a drunk and is in debt due to gambling.'

Petrus placed some coins on the table and rose to his feet. 'Thank you, Carantii. Don't forget the other things I asked you to look in to.'

Carantii grinned and moved the coins around the table with his forefinger. 'I won't forget, but I may need more funds. If Cato is a big gambler, I may need to have a few bets to find out what's going on. I can't just ask questions without arousing suspicion.'

Behind him, Petrus heard Lugraca take a sharp intake of

breath.

He nodded. 'I'll bring you some quinarii, or maybe a denarii or two.'

Lugraca opened the door, Petrus stepped out and trudged up the street towards the fort.

He rapped on the gate.

'Password?' a muffled voice said.

'I can't remember. It's me, Aurelius Petrus, centurion,' Petrus snarled. He'd been so cold that morning and so focussed on getting warm, he'd completely forgotten those murmured words.

'No password, no admittance,' mumbled the voice.

'Climb up the steps and look over the wall, for fuck's sake! You'll recognise me!' shouted Petrus. 'Go on! Do it!'

He thought for a moment that they were ignoring him. Then he heard the scrabble of feet on stone and two heads peered over the parapet.

Petrus waved his arm, 'For Jupiter's sake! Let me in!'

They disappeared. There was a scraping sound, and the door swung open. Petrus glared at the two men as he passed. He knew he shouldn't be annoyed; they were just obeying orders, but he was a centurion!

Gauori grinned widely when Petrus burst into the room. Petrus waved away the plate of bread Gauori pushed across the table towards him. He grabbed the cup of wine and gulped it down as he took off his tunic, unwrapping the fleece he'd placed round his chest. He pulled on a clean tunic. He just wanted to sleep, but there was so much to do.

'I'll be back later,' he told Gauori and left the room.

In his office, he began making some notes about what

Carantii had told him and also his plans to find Ruua and interview her.

There was a knock at the door. Boga, the former slave, walked in. He was dressed in a thick smock and trousers, with a rich green cape around his shoulders.

Boga smiled and bowed his head in greeting. 'Aurelius Petrus! I was just collecting some of my money and thought I might know something of interest to you.'

'Come in Boga, take a seat,' Petrus sat back and poured him a cup of wine.

Boga raised an eyebrow as he took the cup and put it to his lips. He had been the slave of a former centurion and had gained his freedom and inherited a large amount of money the previous year, when Petrus had killed his master.

Boga took several sips of the wine and then put the cup on the table. 'I owe you my freedom, Aurelius Petrus, and shall always feel indebted to you.'

Petrus nodded.

'I assume you're investigating Manius' death? He had a woman in the vicus. I expect you'd like to speak with her. She lives near me.'

Petrus felt a surge of hope rush through him.

Boga smiled. 'I'm now with Maximus' widow, Dagvaldia. I'd been going to her house for many years with Maximus and well, you know… Anyway, we'd noticed Manius was a frequent visitor to the area. I followed him once. He is, was, not the type to notice a man like me. He went to the Herbalist Ruua's place. It seems he's been going there for a couple of years, took up with her when the old soldier Tarpeus died. I thought I could show you where it is.'

'Are you sure it won't cause you any difficulty, locally I mean, if you're seen helping the Romans?'

Boga laughed. 'It's always assumed I'm helping, due to my background,' he stood up, bowing his head and placing his hand across his heart. 'Might as well be true.'

'Thank you, Boga. I'll come to your place tomorrow morning.' Petrus reached into his pouch and pushed some coins across the table.

Boga made no attempt to take the money. 'I will never take payment from you.' He bowed again and left the room.

Petrus desperately hoped Ruua would tell him something useful. He thought about Boga for a moment. The former slave had done well for himself, married a wealthy widow, and set up in business. He began to write about this encounter in his notes.

Balbus burst into the room carrying a small sack over his shoulder. He leant against the door to keep it closed and raised a hand to silence Petrus, who frowned at the man's rudeness.

'Sir,' Balbus began, his eyes wide in excitement, 'I've come now while the others have gone for a break. I've found something!' He turned the sack upside down and tablets cascaded across the table. He scrambled to catch them and put them into some sort of order.

'Look,' he was breathless, as he pushed two of the tablets towards Petrus who glanced down at them.

It was an inventory of deliveries from Lucullus, dated two months previously. The corresponding entry to stores was also there. Petrus checked quickly – grain, animal hides, live sheep. He pushed it back towards Balbus.

'It all looks in order to me,' he sighed.

'But look carefully at the numbers,' Balbus pointed. 'There, grain… XXXVIII delivered, then look at the number entered to stores XXXVII. This receipt tablet,' he tapped on it with his finger, 'is an authorisation for payment signed by Manius for thirty-eight sacks of corn and Lucullus has accepted payment. It's Manius' mark and seal here, look!' He pointed at the wax seal and the scrawled marks. 'And this is the storeman's mark here. And Lucullus' here.'

Petrus checked again. He was right. 'So, Manius and Lucullus were stealing from the army.'

'It looks that way.'

Petrus looked at the remaining tablets. 'And those?'

'These are deliveries with mistakes in the receipts, going back about six months. Look at this one,' he pushed a tablet towards Petrus, 'Delivered and paid for LXXXIII sacks of grain, moved to stores LXXIII. And there's more here,' he pointed at the tablets.

'Is it always Lucullus who makes these deliveries?'

'Yes, it is. There's a summary that I've made, here,' Balbus withdrew a tablet from his tunic and handed it to Petrus.

Petrus looked down the list. 'That's over a hundred sacks of grain paid for that didn't arrive at stores.'

'Yes it is,' Balbus voice trembled slightly.

'You've done well, Balbus. I'll keep these,' Petrus began scooping them back into the sack. 'Carry on looking at Manius' work. Has anyone queried what you are doing?'

'A couple of them asked what I was doing and why I needed a guard. I just said I'd been instructed to look into Manius' work in the last six weeks of his life. I always keep a few of those tablets nearby, so that it looks like I'm working with them. I've already checked, there's nothing amiss in that six-week period. As to the guard, I just said that until his murder was solved, I'd been informed I would have a guard. I've told them it wasn't my doing.'

Petrus thought for a moment and then asked, 'Was it always Manius who recorded deliveries from our suppliers?'

Balbus shook his head. 'Manius was the most senior librarius, and would normally delegate the task to others. I've checked other merchants' records, and that was the case. Adrianus or one of the others monitored deliveries, so I'm not sure why he started signing for these deliveries from Lucullus. Unless...' his voice trailed off.

'Unless Manius had decided to go into business with Lucullus, the business of stealing from the army,' said Petrus.

Balbus nodded. 'I haven't checked the other librarii's receipts, as you only told me to look at the dead man's. Should I be checking those as well?'

'Yes, you should,' Petrus paused, 'Who monitored the work of the librarii?'

'Er, the Signifer and of course the Prefect occasionally as well.'

Petrus' guts clenched. A sudden jolt of excitement and fear hit his brain. Was this it? Had the Signifer failed to complete checks because he was involved as well? It still didn't explain why Manius was killed, unless he wanted to stop his involvement. Adrianus may have been part of it. After all, he knew Lucullus, who had lied about it. Or Adrianus could be blackmailing the merchant.

He fought to keep his voice steady. 'Good work, Balbus. Carry on and take care. Speak to no-one else about it.'

The look of pleasure left Balbus' face and was replaced by one of fear. He nodded solemnly and left the room.

Petrus pushed his chair back. He thought for a moment, then rose to his feet and opened the chest in the corner of the room. It contained the evidence and reports from the previous murder investigation. Beneath the blood-stained cloak of the Prefect's former wife, were the reports he had written. They were stacked in neat piles, alongside the tablets containing lists that Manius had made for him. Each list was neatly written, signed by the dead librarius, and bearing his seal. Petrus took out two of the lists and moved back to his table. He examined the seal and signature on one of the tablets that Balbus had given him and compared them to those on one of the lists. He moved towards the window, hoping to get more light.

A loud knock at the door startled him, and Arsenios strode into the office.

'Petrus I really must… What are you doing?'

Petrus put the two tablets together. 'Nothing, I'm just trying to make out something on one of these tablets. It's not easy to see.'

'I've got just the thing to help you with that. Come on, it's in the infirmary,' Arsenios moved towards the door, 'and that's what I wanted to see you about, the infirmary. Those lads of yours are making a mess and disturbing my patients. I can't have them sleeping there if they behave like animals.' Sensing Petrus' reluctance, he pointed to the tablets on the table. 'Do you need to look at those ones as well?' he picked up the sack from the floor. 'Let me help you put them in here. Might as well look at them all. Come on!'

Petrus hesitated momentarily, reluctant to involve Arsenios. He sighed, and they scooped the tablets into the sack. He locked the chest and followed the physician out of the door just as a small boy with light yellow hair darted past them and disappeared around the corner of the building. It was the same little boy he'd seen a few days previously. He didn't know which barracks the boy lived in. If the child persisted in playing near the Principia, then he would be made to leave the fort, along with his mother. Petrus didn't like the idea of families living inside the fort, but it had become fairly common across the empire. He knew he was very lucky to have his own house in the vicus.

He hurried to catch up with Arsenios. 'What exactly is the problem with Balbus and the others?' he asked breathlessly.

'You'll see for yourself,' Arsenios flung open the door to the infirmary.

The smell hit him first, urine and decaying food. The two injured soldiers were feigning sleep as Petrus walked over to the bed assigned to Balbus. A pot of urine sat under the bed. Plates with the remains of meals lay strewn across the floor; the food was dried and rotting. A cup lay on its side; a stain on the flagstones marked where the spilled wine had seeped away.

'I see what you mean.'

'And they were up gambling late into the night. I can't have them disturbing my patients, they need their rest,' Arsenios lowered his voice, 'especially the lad who lost his leg.'

'I'll get it sorted.'

'What about your tablets?' Arsenios nodded at the sack Petrus was carrying.

Petrus hesitated.

'Come with me.' Arsenios led him into the back room and closed the door behind them. He sat at the table. 'Tell me what you're looking for. Is it related to Manius' death?'

Petrus nodded. He decided to trust the physician, who was not officially an army officer, and he could see no reason why Arsenios would be involved in the murder. His whole purpose for being in the army was to sustain life, not take it. Petrus took out the two tablets he'd been looking at – the one with the deliveries and the list of soldiers Manius had given him previously.

'I want to check that Manius signed for these deliveries,' he pointed at the sack of tablets and then handed the two in his hand to the physician, 'These two are lists he made for me last year, so I know they are definitely his seal. If you could look at them while I see to Balbus and his companions, I'd be grateful,' he paused. 'You must swear to the God Jupiter that you will not speak of this to anyone else. Your life, and mine, may depend on it.'

Arsenios nodded gravely, 'As you know, I am a man of science. So, for what it's worth, I swear before Jupiter to keep this matter between us, along with anything else you wish to share with me.'

Petrus accepted that Arsenios was taking an oath before a God he didn't believe in, much as Petrus had often done himself. He passed the sack to him and left the room.

'Balbus! Come with me.' He said as soon as he entered the records office.

The young soldier went pale as he put down his stylus and stood up. 'What about Justus?'

'No!' Petrus put up his hand, as the soldier rose to his feet and walked towards the door. 'Stay here. I'll bring him back.'

Balbus walked in silence beside Petrus as he strode back to the infirmary. The young soldier was breathless with fear as they walked up to his bed.

'I'm disappointed in you. I put you in here for your safety, not so that you could live like a pig and stay up all night gambling!' Petrus hissed, 'Get this cleaned up! Now!'

Balbus trembled as he picked up the pot of urine and carried it towards the door with shaking hands.

'Don't spill it!' snapped Petrus as he walked behind him.

He watched in disgust as Balbus emptied the pot into one of the drains that ran beneath the fort. Balbus straightened the blanket on his bed and quickly gathered up the bowls and plates.

'What shall I do with these?' he mumbled.

'I should make you wash them, but I haven't got the time to waste supervising you. Leave them outside. You and Justus can clean them at the end of the day.'

'What if they get stolen while we're at work?'

'That'll serve you right. You'll just have to buy some new ones. Now come on, let's get back to the records office.' Petrus grabbed Balbus by the collar and propelled him out of the infirmary.

Behind them, he heard the two wounded soldiers giggling.

'You've just been promoted, damn you! Behave like an officer and not the son of a pig! If I get any more complaints from the physician, I'll dock your pay and reconsider your position.'

He marched Balbus towards the Librarium and sighed. 'You were doing such good work, and then you let yourself down like this. What got into you?'

Balbus shrugged. 'I didn't think about cleaning up the plates. My life is so strange at the moment, being guarded night and day and working in secret. It's so boring sleeping in the infirmary with just one of those lads to talk to, and I can't tell him what I'm doing, or why he's guarding me! Gambling just passed the time.'

Petrus nodded. 'Yes, I see that, but try to stay on the right side of Arsenios, won't you? Otherwise, I don't know where I could move you that would be safe.'

Petrus entered the back room in the infirmary. Arsenios had lit a candle. He held one of the tablets in his hand and was peering at it through a glass sphere filled with water. Rainbows of light danced on the table in front of him. Petrus whispered a prayer of thanks to Bacchus for the beautiful display.

Hearing him, Arsenios turned and said, 'The rainbows are caused by the sunlight falling on the glass. Look, if I hold my hand here to block out the sunlight, the rainbows disappear.' He held his hand up and cast a shadow across the table.

Petrus began another prayer.

'Any god responsible for this would want us to use it to help us, just as they would allow us to use the wind and the rain.' Arsenios' voice was calm and reassuring.

Petrus nodded his head and moved closer to the table.

'Take a look at this through the glass.' Arsenios held the glass over the tablet.

Reluctantly, Petrus did as the physician suggested. The writing appeared huge, as if it had jumped off the tablet. Petrus recoiled in fright, his hands out in front of him, ready to defend himself.

'Don't be afraid Petrus! It's science, not sorcery!' Arsenios clapped him on the shoulder and smiled. 'The shape of the water distorts what our eyes see, making it bigger and clearer. It's called magnification.'

Arsenios pushed Petrus gently forward. Petrus placed his shaking hands on the table and peered through the glass. The tablet was the record of one of the deliveries that Balbus had shown him.

'This was not signed by Manius,' declared Arsenios, pointing at the writing.

'How can you tell?'

'Look at this list, the one Manius gave you when you investigated the last murder,' Arsenios held the tablet under the glass and pointed, 'Look at the seal and signature.'

Petrus peered at the marks in the wax.

'Now look again at the deliveries' tablet.' Arsenios brought the other tablet alongside the first. 'What do you see? Round the signature and the seal? Look carefully.'

'This seal and signature are clear around the edges,' Petrus pointed to the list Manius had given him, 'The seal mark on the delivery is in a kind of pool with a ridge round it, and the signature is slightly different – it's more slanted and the letter 's' has a tail. It's as if, as if…'

'Go on, as if?'

'As if the wax has been melted and then the signature written by someone else, not Manius,' murmured Petrus.

'Exactly! And look at this,' Arsenios held another delivery receipt under the glass.

'That's the same, the same pool of wax, the same slanting. A forgery,' finished Petrus. His heart beat faster and he caught his breath.

'That's my belief, yes.'

'Who could have done that?'

Arsenios shook his head. 'I can tell you what's there. I can't tell you who did it, or why. That's for you to find out.'

'Have you checked the other deliveries?'

'Yes, and they are all the same, the signatures have been forged on all the deliveries for about six months before Manius' death, but then it stops about a month ago.'

'Adrianus and the other librarii are the most obvious suspects. They're the ones with the most opportunity to change the records,' Petrus murmured, thinking aloud. 'And Adrianus was arguing with Lucullus just yesterday… I need to find the signet ring,' Petrus breathed deeply, then realising Arsenios was watching him, he scooped up the tablets and put them in the sack. 'Thank you. I should not have told you my ideas. Tell no one about this, or anything I've just said. If necessary, will you come with me and speak to the Prefect about this, this, magnification,' he pointed at the glass, 'and how we used it?'

'I will.'

Petrus smiled briefly. He picked up the sack and strode out of the infirmary, heading for the Prefect's office.

The Prefect was nowhere to be seen in the headquarters buildings. He made his way to the Praetorium. The soldiers on patrol there walked away from its steps as he approached. The door was opened by a slave girl in a faded tunic barely covering her shoulders. Black and blue bruised finger-marks ran round her neck and her hand shook as she gripped the doorframe.

'I need to see the Prefect,' said Petrus.

She nodded wordlessly and stepped back, opening the door wide to let him in. She flinched as he entered, afraid he might touch her. She led him through the house, walking stiffly and slowly as if each step caused her pain. Petrus had no doubt that Tatius had caused the girl's injuries. They passed through the elaborately decorated rooms; he barely noticed the statues and frescoes that had once held him in awe. They entered the salon where torches cast flickering light across the empty couches. The lingering smell of the freshly painted walls overpowered the aroma of the oils smoking in pots around the room.

The girl turned to face him, her voice barely above a whisper, 'The Prefect will be with you shortly, Sir.'

Petrus put some of the tablets on a table and waited.

The door opened, and the Prefect entered in a haze of perfume. His skin was freshly scrubbed, and he wore a rough smock over his trousers.

'Petrus! What is it? It had better be important. I've just come from the baths. I'm preparing for the wedding.'

'Balbus has found some discrepancies in the records. At first glance, it looks as if Manius was stealing grain from the army. Look here,' he pointed at the figures on the tablets. 'He signed for more grain deliveries than entered stores, sometimes it was only one or two sacks, sometimes it was ten or more. This tablet is a summary of the amounts taken over a six-month period.' He pointed to another tablet. 'It stops about six weeks ago, which is when Manius started taking money out of his savings account. The deliveries are always made by the retired centurion Lucullus…'

'There's a motive for killing him!' interrupted Tatius. 'Lucullus could've been working with him.'

Petrus did not speak for a moment and then asked, 'Why would Lucullus kill the man he was working with?'

Tatius opened his mouth to speak, but Petrus hurried on. 'Manius might have decided to stop doing it about six weeks ago and as you say, Lucullus could've killed him to keep him quiet. Or anyone wanting to cover this up to protect themselves. Like, Ecdicius, or the other librarii perhaps.'

Petrus suddenly realised that the Prefect had the most to lose if the Tribune found out that the Librarius was stealing from the army. Tatius stared at him.

'I examined the records more closely and compared them with the lists which Manius made for me last year. The signatures on the deliveries are slightly different and the area around the seal looks as if it has been remelted. I think these are forged signatures and seals. Whoever has Manius' ring has changed the records.'

Tatius' picked one of the tablets up and held it close to his face with trembling hands. 'How can you see that?'

'Arsenios has a glass object that makes the writing bigger and clearer. I can bring him if you wish.'

Tatius shook his head.

'We should inform the Tribune,' said Petrus.

'No! Keep it between the two of us. The thefts appear to have stopped. Informing the Tribune can wait 'til after the wedding.'

He stared defiantly at Petrus. 'I'll find out who's behind this. I suppose the physician knows about the thefts. But you'll have told him to keep it to himself. What are you going to do next?'

Petrus watched the Prefect carefully as he said, 'The most obvious people to have forged these documents are the other librarii. They know their way round the records, they sign off deliveries and payments. I want to search their rooms to see if one of them has Manius' missing ring. Adrianus is the one who normally checks the deliveries; he is the most likely person. Yesterday I witnessed him arguing with Lucullus in the vicus. Yet Lucullus had told me he didn't know any of the librarii, so he lied. I want to start by searching Adrianus' rooms.'

Tatius lowered himself onto a couch. His voice shook as he spoke. 'Get some more soldiers to stay on guard outside the records office, to keep the librarii inside while you and Fabius Ruga search their belongings. I want a witness if anything is found and each librarius should be there to watch his room being searched. That way he cannot claim you planted the ring. Do it now!'

Petrus nodded and scooped the tablets into his sack.

'You've done well Petrus. I always had faith in you,' Tatius' voice followed him out of the door.

The slave girl led Petrus back through the house. As he reached the front door, he saw Docca walking towards him, carrying a large basket of vegetables. The slave had a dark blue bruise on the side of his face. When he saw Petrus, he looked away.

Ruga was in his office and looked surprised when Petrus explained what they were going to do.

'Very well. I'll send five of my men to the records office. You've already got one man there, haven't you? They can escort the librarii back to their rooms and wait with them, watch 'em, make sure they don't try to hide anything.'

'My man must not leave the Librarium. He must remain on guard there. You'll need to send an extra man.'

Ruga nodded. 'Fine. I'll get Adrianus brought to his room.'

'What the fuck are you doing?' growled Adrianus as he walked towards them.

Petrus replied, 'We've reason to believe you, or one of your fellow librarii has Manius' ring. The Prefect has given us authority to search all the librarii's rooms. We wanted you here while we did it.'

Adrianus went pale and clenched his fists. 'Do your worst. You won't find anything.'

Petrus pushed open the door, and they went through to the room where the librarius slept.

Adrianus followed them and stood in the doorway, arms folded across his chest. A pitcher of water was covered with a cloth in the corner of the room. Petrus lifted it. There was nothing underneath. He lifted the blanket from the bed and shook it out. He folded it and placed it on top of the locked chest. He lifted the mattress and squeezed it all round the edges, examined the seams for any small holes where a ring might be hidden. He did the same with the small cushion Adrianus used as a pillow. Nothing. He replaced the blanket on the bed. Ruga grabbed Adrianus roughly by the arm, pulling him across the room.

'Open it!' instructed Ruga, pointing at the chest.

Adrianus sighed, reached into his pouch, and withdrew a small key. He unlocked the chest and threw the lid open, banging it against the wall. Ruga began searching the chest, lifting items out, examining them and then placing them back inside, shaking his head. Petrus got down on his haunches and looked under the bed. A layer of dust coated the floor, but there was no ring. He lifted the bed and felt under each foot, in case it was hollow. On the floor was a pile of clothes. Petrus lifted a tunic; it stank of stale sweat. He ran his hands down the tunic, checking for hidden pockets. There were none. He searched the other clothes, finding nothing.

'You need to do some washing, or get a slave,' Petrus murmured. Adrianus grunted.

The two centurions entered the other room, with Adrianus behind them. The room was fairly empty. A table, a chair, crockery, a pitcher of water, some armour and weapons were stacked against one wall. The floor had been swept clean and there was a faint smell of perfume. Petrus checked under the legs of the table and chair; they were solid. He opened the window shutters and ran his hands around the wood. Nothing. Behind him, Ruga was lifting the crockery and banging it down in frustration. Petrus heard him moving on to the armour and weapons, clattering them together as he searched. Petrus lifted the pitcher of water. There was nothing beneath it. As he banged it down in frustration, some of the fetid water slopped over his hand. He wrinkled his nose in disgust and wiped his hand on his tunic.

'You should change that water. It'll make you ill,' he murmured, curling his lip.

Adrianus did not respond. A sudden thought struck Petrus. He lifted the cloth and plunged his hand into the stale water.

'What are you doing?' Adrianus took a step forward but was held back by the soldier.

Petrus' fingers closed round a small metal object, and he pulled out a ring, holding it up to show the other men. He examined the seal and felt a surge of excitement.

'This is Manius' ring.'

Ruga's mouth fell open. Adrianus began to turn away. The

soldier tightened his grip on his shoulder, preventing him from moving.

'You're going nowhere!' hissed the soldier.

'Well Petrus, I never would've…' whispered Ruga, then gathered himself together. 'Right! Take him to the cells and lock him up.'

The soldier twisted Adrianus' arm behind his back and shoved him out of the door.

'Well done, Petrus!' Ruga clapped him hard on the back.

Petrus placed the ring in the pouch at his belt and headed for the door. 'I'll go and tell the Prefect while you organise the guards for the cells.'

There was a sudden commotion outside. A soldier ran past shouting 'Fire! Fire! The records office! Fire!'

Petrus ran. Men were running towards the Librarium, carrying buckets of water. Ruga and Aquilinus began shouting orders.

Justus' voice emerged from the records office as he directed the other men. A line had formed. Men passed containers of water from one to the next. As Petrus reached the Librarium door, the line stopped moving. Justus emerged, coughing, and gasping for air.

He croaked, 'It's out. The fire is out.' He leant against the door frame. 'Get in there!' he pointed at the man next to him. 'Take that bucket with you, in case he comes back.'

'Who comes back?' Petrus took Justus by the shoulders and pulled him upright, searching his face for meaning.

'The boy, the boy who started it,' whispered Justus.

A child!

Water leaked out of the office, carrying the blackened remnants of the destroyed records. Petrus entered the room. The acrid smell of smoke, burnt wood, and wax filled his lungs. The fire had engulfed the three rows of records closest to the window. Black soot coated the shelves and grains of sand peppered the scorched tablets, as the charred roof dripped water onto the floor.

Beneath the window lay a small torch; its fat smeared rainbows across the floor. Petrus felt Justus move behind him.

'You did well. Your quick reactions have saved most of it,' Petrus said.

Justus walked past him and put out his hand to touch the window shutters, smearing soot across his fingers. He regarded them for a moment and said, 'I was going to close the shutters when a child appeared at the window. A boy, I think. He had that straw-coloured hair that these local people have. He saw me, panicked, and must've dripped oil or something on his hand as his sleeve caught fire. He screamed and dropped the torch just inside the window before he ran off. Lucky you'd placed the pails of water and sand near the door, Sir, otherwise the whole place would've gone up in flames.'

'Would you recognise the boy?'

Justus shrugged, 'Maybe. It all happened so fast.'

'Come with me.' Petrus led him outside where a group of men lingered, keen to see what had happened.

'Get a broom and sweep up this mess!' Petrus ordered one of them, whom he vaguely recognised as one from Ruga's century.

The man froze for a moment, then moved away. Ruga walked toward them; Petrus held up a hand to silence him.

'It was a child who threw a torch into the room. We need to get all the women and children out onto the parade ground and look for him. He's small with yellow hair.'

'That's not much of a description. There're loads of 'em look like that,' grumbled Ruga.

'We'll find him. Get some men to clear the barracks. Room by room. Don't tell them what it's about. Make sure we get everyone out onto the parade area. But first, make sure there's at least two men guarding this office, at all times. Get the buckets refilled with sand and water.'

For a moment, it looked as if Ruga was going to argue with the more junior centurion. Then he turned and began barking orders. Janus ran up to them.

'Aurelius Petrus. I'm supposed to be taking over the guard duty at the office. What shall I do now?' he panted; his eyes wide with excitement.

'Take over. Make sure there are filled buckets just inside the door. Some men should be doing that now. Make sure that man there,' he pointed, 'sweeps up properly. Don't touch anything that's burned. I want the librarii to see what can be saved.'

Shouts filled the air as women and children began to emerge from the barracks, some wrapped in blankets to shield themselves from the cold. One or two of the women had babies at their breasts or wrapped tightly against their backs. Older children ran out and raced down the street towards the parade ground, younger ones clutched at their mothers' clothes as they walked.

The soldiers herded the last of the women and children forward onto the parade ground. The women trembled in fear as they waited in the cold breeze. The children whimpered and moaned, hiding their faces in the women's trousers, dribbling snot onto them.

'Is that all the barracks clear?' Petrus asked Ruga's optio.

The man nodded.

Petrus began to walk amongst the families. He spoke quietly to most of the women, who gathered their children about them and then hurried away. Twenty women remained on the yard. They placed their children protectively behind them as Petrus moved around. He beckoned Justus forward.

'Can you recognise the one who threw the torch?'

Justus walked around, sometimes he grabbed a child pulling them forward and peering down at their faces.

'This one, I'm fairly sure it was him,' Justus held the shoulder of a child aged about six who struggled in his grip. The boy wore a huge smock that reached down to his knees; the sleeves hung down over his hands. It was the boy Petrus had seen running around the Principia.

'Roll up your sleeves, Son,' Petrus said, trying to soften his voice as the boy whimpered and shook his head. Petrus turned to his mother. 'Roll up his sleeves!' he said more firmly.

The woman's hands shook as she began rolling the sleeves back. The child winced and moaned in pain as she exposed a blistered red burn extending past the wrist on the back of his right hand.

'You need to stay here,' said Petrus, as he placed a hand on the woman's arm. 'Keep hold of the boy,' he told Justus. 'The rest of you can go,' he said, turning back towards the women.

They dispersed rapidly, some making their way back to the barracks, others fled towards the gates and the safety of the vicus.

Petrus squatted down, so that he was at the boy's eye level. The boy trembled.

'You've been running around the offices quite a lot recently, haven't you?' Petrus spoke in the Carvetti language.

The boy didn't respond.

'How'd you get that burn?'

'He fell in a fire,' muttered the woman, tears running down her cheeks.

'Is that what he told you?' Petrus looked at the woman.

She nodded.

'And you believed him?'

She did not answer.

Petrus looked back at the boy. 'I think you got that throwing a lit torch into the records building.'

The boy turned away. Petrus put a hand on his shoulder. The boy flinched. A wet patch appeared on the ground by the boy's feet and the stink of urine rose about them.

'Let's get your father, shall we?' Petrus tried to keep his voice soft. 'Who is your man? Here in the fort, who are you with?' he asked the woman.

'Ennius. He's one of Aquilinus' men,' she snivelled as tears ran down her face.

Petrus realised that a group of soldiers were watching him. He turned to one of them and said, 'Fetch Ennius.'

The man ran off. The boy's mother knelt down in the dirt and hugged her son who rested his face against her shoulder. She whispered in his ear, but he shook his head and whimpered.

A short dark man raced towards them. He put his arm protectively around the woman and child. 'What's going on? What are you doing to my family?'

'Watch yourself, soldier! Remember who you're talking to!' snapped Petrus.

The man released his family and saluted. 'Apologies, Aurelius Petrus.'

'Justus saw your boy throw a lit torch into the Librarium. That's how he got his burn. The fire could've burned the whole place down. I want to know why he did it. I want to know what he's been doing running around the Principia these last few days, when he knows children are not allowed around there. I will get him to tell me. Whatever it takes!'

Ennius knelt down next to the boy and pulled him into his arms, talking quietly to him. Petrus did not try to listen to what he was saying. The woman was glaring at Petrus. The boy began whispering in his father's ear. Ennius nodded and murmured encouragement. The boy moaned and showed Ennius his hand. Ennius ran his fingers gently over the undamaged flesh surrounding the weeping wounds as he muttered reassurances to the child. Finally, the boy went quiet and Ennius moved him to stand next to his mother. He rose to his feet.

'One of the men who said he works in the Librarium dared him to run around the Principia every afternoon a few days ago. He said it was a test of security, as children weren't allowed around there. He said it was a very important job and if he helped out, he would get a reward of some sweet fruit and his father would get good reports that might help him get promoted to become a centurion.'

'And did he give him the fruit?'

'Yes, he did. Kandianus says it was rich and full of honey.'

'Which librarius was it?'

Ennius shrugged. 'The description sounds a bit like Adrianus. He told the boy he was in charge, so that fits, doesn't it?'

'The person might've said he was in charge to make himself sound more important,' Petrus thought aloud. 'And what about burning down the Librarium?'

'The man told him to do that today. He said he was testing to see how quickly the soldiers responded to a fire. He told Kandi it was an important secret, and he wasn't to tell anyone about it. He said there wouldn't be much damage. When Kandi, Kandianus said he didn't want to do it, the man said it was a very important test and that I would be punished for having a disobedient son who wouldn't follow the army's orders. He said Kandi and his mother would be made to leave the fort and I would be dismissed and maybe even killed if he didn't set fire to the Librarium, or if he told anyone about these tests. He frightened the boy.'

'Send your woman back to the barracks. Come with me and bring him with you,' said Petrus.

Ennius mumbled to the woman and then took Kandianus by his left hand and followed Petrus across the parade ground. Justus trailed along behind them. The boy began to slow, dragging his feet. Ennius scooped him up into his arms and carried him. The sunlight was fading fast as they reached the Principia.

'Right, get in there,' Petrus opened the door to his office, 'I'm going to stand him beside the window, so that he can see out, but no one can see him.'

Petrus manoeuvred the boy so that he was standing sideways in the shade of the shutters. He was just tall enough to see out of the window. He would be able to see the Librarium and some of the other buildings.

Petrus spoke to Justus. 'Get all the librarii and tell them to stand outside the Librarium. Also, get Centurion Fabius Ruga to meet me at the cells. Now!'

Justus hurried away.

'Wait here with your father. Shortly some men are going to come to stand over there,' he pointed, 'Kandianus, I want you to tell me whether any of them is the man who dared you to do these things. Nothing is going to happen to you or your father if you tell me the truth. Do you understand?' He tried to sound kind, but the boy was clearly terrified.

'It'll be alright, Son. Just do as the centurion says,' Ennius murmured.

'Stay out of sight, both of you,' Petrus ordered.

Petrus made his way to the cells. Two soldiers stood on duty inside the building. Adrianus sat slumped on the dusty straw. He looked up when Petrus entered.

'How long are you going to keep me locked up in here? What're you charging me with?' snarled Adrianus.

'I want you to come and look at the Librarium.' Petrus motioned one of the guards to open the cell.

'The Librarium? Why?'

'You'll see.' He dragged Adrianus to his feet and walked him outside.

Fabius Ruga walked quickly up to them, 'Petrus, what's going on?'

'Help me out here, would you? Take Adrianus and show him what happened with the fire.' Petrus winked at Ruga.

Ruga took Adrianus by the arm and marched him towards the Librarium. Petrus returned to his office. Out of the corner of his eye, he could see the other librarii gathering nearby. He moved to stand near the boy.

'Look over there. Is any of those men the one who's been talking to you?'

The boy maintained his grip on his father's hand as he stood on tiptoes and peered out. His eyes widened, and he stepped back into the shadows.

'It's that one there, just going into the room, alongside that centurion. See, he is important. That's why he's with the centurion,' Kandianus whispered.

Ruga and Adrianus were entering the Librarium.

Petrus spoke in Latin to Ennius, 'Go to the infirmary. Tell Arsenios I sent you to get the boy's hand dressed, then go back to your barracks and stay there with your boy until you hear from me. Do not let the boy out of your sight, I mean it. His life could be in danger. Keep your woman with you.'

Ennius nodded and took the child away. Petrus strode over to the Librarium and dismissed the librarii waiting near the door. Inside the building, Adrianus had gone pale as his gaze rested on the shelves behind the table where Manius had sat.

'Fortunately, the fire didn't take hold. I think some of the burned tablets may be salvageable too,' murmured Petrus.

Adrianus didn't respond.

'Take him back to the cells and then meet me at the Praetorium. We need to tell Tatius what's been going on,' Petrus said to Ruga.

The slave girl had fresh marks on her neck, and she trembled as she held open the door for them to enter the Praetorium. Petrus was filled with disgust and shame knowing how the Prefect had been abusing her. They followed her through to the salon. All through the house, slaves were busy cleaning, straightening drapes and preparing the house for their new mistress' arrival.

Ruga looked around as they waited in the salon. 'He's made some changes since I was last here, ready for his new bride I imagine.'

Tatius rushed in, pulling a thick cloak around his uncovered shoulders. 'What is it now, Petrus? Ruga? You know how much I've got to do tonight before my wedding? Sacrifices to the Gods and the other normal rituals. You do know that.'

'There've been some dangerous developments that we felt you should know about, and I wanted to confirm with you the next steps to take tomorrow,' Petrus said.

'Tomorrow, after my wedding,' Tatius corrected him.

Petrus took a deep breath and withdrew the signet ring from the pouch at his belt, handing it to Tatius. 'This is Manius' signet ring. We found it in a covered jug of water in Adrianus' rooms. He's now in the cells.'

'What does he say about the ring?' Tatius asked.

'We haven't had a chance to interrogate him yet,' Petrus held up a hand to stop Tatius from interrupting, then realised how rude that might seem as Tatius raised an eyebrow, and he quickly put his hand down again. He waited for Tatius to speak.

'Is it because of the fire?'

'Yes, a small child was seen throwing a lit torch in through the window of the Librarium. Fortunately, we were able to extinguish the fire before it really took hold. We'd been prepared,' Petrus said.

'You foresaw that Petrus, well done. Is there still a guard on the building and fresh buckets of water and sand there too? In case someone tries again.'

Petrus nodded, 'All taken care of, Sir.'

'Well done. What else?'

'Justus, one of the soldiers guarding Balbus, saw the boy who threw the torch; the boy's hand was burned, and his sleeve had caught fire, so he was easy to identify. He is Kandianus, the son of Ennius, a man in Aquilinus' century. He admitted he'd been dared by one of the librarii to run around near the Principia over the last few days; he'd been told it was a security test. I'd seen him twice myself as he ran past the office. The librarius gave Kandianus some food as a reward and told him it would help his father become a centurion if he helped with these security tests. Today he was told to throw the torch into the Librarium, to see how quickly the army would react to fire. The librarius told him that if he didn't do it, then he and his family would be made to leave the fort and his father would be demoted and possibly killed.'

'Do you believe his story?'

Petrus nodded. 'I took him to my office and arranged for all the librarii, including Adrianus, to wait outside the Librarium. When Kandianus saw Adrianus, he identified him as the man who'd told him to do these things and start the fire.'

'Where is the boy now?' asked Tatius.

'I told Ennius to take him back to the barracks and to keep him there with his mother. The boy's life might be in danger.'

'That's good work. Get Ennius excused from duties for the next few days to keep an eye on his son. Adrianus can wait in the cells for a while, I think. It might make him more amenable to answering some questions. And now what?' asked Tatius.

'I want to get Lucullus in. He lied when he told me he didn't know the librarii. I'm sure he's involved in the thefts.'

Tatius did not respond.

'It may be that Manius found out about the thefts and he was killed to silence him.' Petrus watched Tatius carefully.

'Mmm. Let's see what the interrogations come up with. What else are you doing?'

'I'm still making enquiries in the vicus,' said Petrus.

'You keep saying, 'I'm making enquiries in the vicus.' They'd better come to something!' snapped Tatius.

'Did you manage to find the records concerning Macro's death, Sir? I've heard Maximus conducted an investigation.'

'Macro's death? Oh, yes, he did. Roburius, Vegetinus and Ferullus were present; they were exonerated. They'd been there cheering Macro on and hadn't realised how badly injured he was. The centurions were docked their pay for six months and had to stay within the walls for the same period for bringing the army into disrepute.'

Petrus raised an eyebrow, 'Might be worth questioning them again over Manius' death.'

Tatius sighed. 'You can do that, but I don't think you'll get anywhere with it. Manius wasn't a gambler, you've said that yourself. Do as you see fit. But I want you two to sort this mess out with Adrianus first.' He paused. 'There's nothing there that can't wait 'til after tomorrow. Make sure you're both clean and presentable at the wedding, for Jupiter's sake. The ceremony will be at the third hour of the morning.' He looked the two men up and down and then left the room.

'That's us told then,' muttered Ruga as they walked out of the Praetorium. 'Right, I'll speak to Aquilinus about Ennius. Then I'll see that the guards keep Adrianus isolated but fed and watered. You take your time getting beautiful, won't you?' Ruga laughed.

X

Petrus took a clean cloak and hung it around his shoulders. Gauori was grinning inanely, pleased that his master was looking so fine in his clean tunic and shiny boots. He'd massaged some perfumed oil into Petrus' back and shoulders, which were still a bit stiff from the night in the Mithraeum; the smell made Petrus feel like a rich man. He mumbled some thanks.

He fought against the strong icy wind as he made his way along the streets. The thick tunic clung to the oils on his back and rubbed his skin as he moved, an unpleasant feeling, as if his skin was wet. There were only a few people battling their way through the vicus. The familiar smoke snaked up from the forge's roof. Carantii was working. Petrus checked around him. No-one was paying him any attention. He rapped on the door.

'Open up! For the Imperial Army. Open up!' he growled.

The door creaked as it swung open, and he stepped inside.

'Have you finished that work for me?' Petrus demanded in a loud voice.

'Yes, Sir, I have it here,' Carantii grinned.

Petrus took a few steps towards him and banged his fist on the table, leaving six denarii and six quinarii on the table. Carantii scooped up the coins, pushing them into the pocket of his trousers.

'About time,' Petrus muttered and strode away.

He began walking in the direction of the Tribune's house. A figure he recognised approached him.

'Boga, I was just coming to find you,' Petrus said, as the former slave drew level with him.

'And I you, Petrus. Come, I will take you to the herbalist's place.'

After a few minutes, they turned off the main street and into an alleyway of small crooked buildings. Rotting food and rubbish littered the ground, their stench hanging in the air. A couple of small children dressed in ragged clothes ran towards them and then disappeared into a side street, squealing in delight. Ahead of them a sign dangled from a building, leaves and flowers carved into it. Boga stopped.

'This is Ruua's place.' He bowed and left Petrus in front of the building.

The door was wide open. The cold air followed him inside and lifted the dust from the floor, pushing it gently round his legs. Bunches of dried herbs and grasses hung from the walls, their delicate aroma drifted around the room. A woman with thick auburn hair stood at a table grinding herbs with a pestle and mortar. She looked up and smiled, her sky-blue eyes widened in surprise. Petrus recognised her as the woman he'd spoken with in the marketplace a couple of days before. She laid down her equipment and wiped her hands on the apron that covered her smock.

'You,' he began, 'Are you Ruua?'

'Yes. I've been expecting the army,' she spoke in Latin.

'Why didn't you tell me who you were when I came to the market?'

'Would you have believed me if I'd said I was the dead man's woman? Or would you have thought I was trying to get his belongings and money? Everyone knows the Romans leave wills.'

Petrus did not reply. She had a fair point.

'Follow me,' she beckoned to him.

The stench of death, blood, and guts assaulted him as he stepped into the warm room. Petrus' stomach heaved, and he tried to breathe through his mouth as the rank odour of flesh and entrails surrounded him. A man with a knife in his hand was working on two carcasses dangling from hooks fixed to a beam in one corner of the kitchen. A bowl of feathers and perforated innards lay at his feet. He did not turn round as the woman ushered Petrus through the door and then shut out the vicious cold of the afternoon.

'Please take a seat, Centurion,' the woman said, pointing towards a stool near a table. 'Ale?' she did not wait for a reply and poured him a cup.

She moved to sit on a stool in the far corner of the room, leaning against the wall, as if trying to get further away from him. She lifted the cup of ale to her lips, her hands trembling.

Petrus spoke in the local language, 'When did you learn of Manius' death?'

'That morning, after his body had been brought back from your temple. Word spread quickly in the vicus.'

'Tell me about your relationship with him.'

'Relationship!' exploded the man, turning round and stepping towards the table, looming over Petrus.

Petrus got to his feet, his hand on his pugio.

'Hush, Litorius!' The woman rose and placed her hand on the man's arm, pushing him gently onto a stool facing Petrus. He was broad shouldered with thick scarred fingers and long dark hair covering most of his face. Petrus sat back down on the stool and picked up his ale.

'After my father died, it didn't take long for Manius to start sniffing around when he saw a woman alone,' spat Litorius, his face red with anger; his blood-stained fingers tightened around the knife.

Ruua remained standing and stared at a point on the wall above Petrus' head as she spoke. 'As you know, I used to work in the brothel. Litorius was born there. When I fell pregnant with my daughter, Tarpeus, one of my customers, built me a house and took my children as his own. When he retired, we married. That's why my children are Roman citizens, yet I am not,' she paused. 'I was a whore, then a wife, and now a widow. After Tarpeus' death, I moved from the house to this, this place.' She took a deep breath. 'Manius, well, he knew me from that other life. He started visiting. He was… he provided for us.'

Petrus nodded. It was a common enough story, soldiers taking up with women. She was lucky Tarpeus had gone as far as marrying her.

'And you collect your widow's pension every month?' he asked.

She shook her head. 'Litorius goes to the fort and collects it. It covers the taxes and keeps us in food. I sell herbs here, as you can see. We're hoping to start to make and sell leather goods.'

Petrus nodded, 'And how will you pay the tanner? Do you work?' he addressed his question to Litorius.

'Apprenticed to the leatherworker, aren't I? What's it got to do with you?'

Petrus slammed his fist on the table, the cup wobbled, and ale slopped onto the scarred wood. 'I'm investigating a murder. Watch your mouth!'

Litorius looked away.

The door burst open.

'Mama!' a young girl ran in, shrieking in delight. She threw herself at her mother, hugging her waist and forcing her to stagger backwards.

Ruua hugged her, then turned her round to face Petrus. 'We've a visitor, Tarpi. A friend of Manius.'

The girl opened her mouth wordlessly. She turned back to her mother, burying her face in the woman's belly. Her tiny hands clutched the smock, the fingers turned white. Ruua stroked her hair, smoothing down the wild black curls. She whispered reassurances as the girl wept. Ruua picked her up; she hung in her mother's arms, weeping, her face against the woman's shoulder. Ruua staggered out of the room and closed the door behind her.

Litorius pushed himself up. 'Now, if you've got what you came for, Centurion…'

Petrus rose and stepped towards him. 'I haven't finished. Ask your mother to come back in.' He moved his hand to his pugio.

Litorius backed down. He flung the door open and shouted, 'Ma! Ma! He's still got stuff to ask you. Get back here.'

Petrus raised an eyebrow at the young man's rudeness. Litorius went back to his butchery, ignoring Petrus, who settled back on his stool to wait.

Ruua closed the door behind her. 'Tarpi's frightened of soldiers. She hasn't always been. When I first took up with Manius, she used to play games with him, sing to him and was always climbing into his lap for a hug. Then she changed and was frightened, of him and all soldiers.' She paused. 'What else did you want to ask?'

'Did Manius talk about his work?' Petrus noted that Litorius was standing still, listening.

'Not really, no.'

'Did he have any enemies you were aware of? Had he fallen out with anyone?'

'No.'

'Did he seem different in those last few weeks he was here?'

'Different?' she asked.

'Worried or frightened.'

'No. He was just the same as always.'

'Did he go to the tavern a lot?'

'Only occasionally, and then he would drink to excess. I heard his slave had to fetch him from there and take him back to the fort. He never came here after visiting the tavern.'

'What about gambling?' asked Petrus.

'Gambling? No. He didn't do that.'

'And when was he last here?'

'About two weeks ago.'

'Anything unusual happen then?'

'No. He came here. We ate our meal and went to bed. He'd gone when I woke up the next morning,' she said.

'Was that unusual? Him leaving so early?'

'Sometimes he didn't stay the whole night. Just visited,' she shrugged, 'and then, after, he went straight back to the fort. I assumed that's what happened, anyway.'

'Manius began taking money out of his savings account about six weeks ago. Do you know what he was doing with the money?'

Litorius turned round and stared at his mother.

'He-he gave it to me. I have it here. Please don't tell anyone. I don't want to be robbed.'

'It was a lot of money. Why would he do that?'

She shrugged. 'He said he didn't trust the army to look after it.'

'He could've left a will.'

She shook her head. 'He said he didn't trust the record keepers,' she paused. 'Perhaps he thought I, we, deserved it.'

'You didn't think to ask why suddenly he didn't trust his fellow record keepers?'

'It's not my place.'

'Three hundred denarii is a lot of money. You…'

'Three hundred denarii. Did he give you that much?' spluttered Litorius.

'Yes, yes he did,' her voice was barely audible.

'And still you didn't think to ask why he was giving it to you?' Petrus persisted.

He waited.

'You told me about sleeping draughts when I spoke with you before,' he continued.

She nodded.

'And do you use them yourself? To make Manius more… compliant, if you didn't want him to… to pester you?'

'I have never used them with any men. I've never had the need.'

'But you have them here, don't you? In your shop?'

She nodded.

'Then get some for me.'

Ruua left the room. She returned with a small bunch of dried roots and handed them to him. He turned them over in his hands, rubbing his fingers along the rough woody twigs. He sniffed at them. The sweet smell tickled his nostrils. He wrinkled his nose.

'How would I use them?' he asked.

'They're roots. Boil them and then drink the liquor.'

'Is this just one dose?' he looked dubiously at the brittle leaves.

'That's enough for two doses for an adult, I would say. Depends on the size of the adult.'

'How long would a man be asleep for?'

'It's generally enough to keep him asleep from nightfall to sunrise. 'Depends, if he uses them a lot. The body becomes accustomed to it and then you need stronger doses.'

'And would Manius have needed a stronger dose?'

She shrugged and turned to look into the fire. 'I wouldn't know. I've never given them to him. He never had any problem sleeping here.'

'If a man drank two doses, would it kill him?'

She shook her head. 'No, but it could kill a small child. The plant relaxes the body and slows breathing. In our histories, they tell of children dying like that.'

'Did Manius ever talk about the Mithraeum?'

'The Mithraeum? The temple? No.'

'You know about it, then?'

'My husband Tarpeus, was a soldier, he mentioned it, said it was a place for senior officers to worship.'

Petrus waited for her to say more.

'Out of questions now, are you?' Litorius snapped, 'Time for you to go then, isn't it?'

Petrus placed some coins on the table and stood up, putting the herbs inside his pouch. He pushed roughly past Litorius, knocking him against the wall. The stink of the dead birds clung to his clothes as he walked back towards the main street. Ruua had not told her son about the money. That had been clear from his reaction. Petrus wondered what the young man would be saying to his mother now that they were alone.

The gate to the Tribune's home was opened by a slave in a clean tunic who bowed to Petrus as he stepped through into the courtyard. The yard was clear of fallen leaves and the limestone seats had been cleaned. Branches of yew trees and trails of ivy lay in the corners of the yard. The smell of damp greenery filled the space, obscuring the pervasive stink of pee he'd noticed on his previous visit. The ground was wet, and he trod carefully along the slippery stone path leading to the door. He weaved between the statues holding up the portico, noting that they too had been scrubbed clean. The door was opened by a slave dressed in a white robe who beckoned him forward. He scraped his boots against the metal bar at the foot of one of the statues and stepped inside. The frescoes' colours were clear and bright; the animals leapt off the walls towards him as he followed the slave past the pool. They moved into the garden and entered the crowded salon, which was heavy with incense. The slave melted away.

Fabius Ruga turned towards Petrus and smiled, a cup of wine in his hand. The other four centurions lurked behind him.

'Ah, Petrus! Just in time,' Ruga nodded to a slave who handed Petrus a goblet of wine.

He took a sip. It was rich, expensive, fruity wine, not the stuff he was used to. It tingled his lips and caressed his mouth as he drank, warming his throat as he swallowed. He gulped it down.

'Steady! It's strong stuff,' whispered Ruga.

Petrus nodded and looked about him. The goddesses Juno and Minerva stared down at him from the walls. A couple of merchants he recognised from the vicus stood together in a corner, looking awkward; they held their wine carefully as if it might be fragile. A priest in white robes lurked nearby, casting a dark shadow against the brightly painted walls.

'Petrus! You made it!' Faustina touched his arm, making him flinch.

He forced a smile onto his face and bowed his head. 'Madam.'

She raised a hand to her hair, which was coiled like that of a bride. She smiled. 'Such an auspicious occasion.' she paused and licked her lips. 'The entrails were read by the priest this morning. It is a lucky day to be married, even though the bride has no maids to attend her.' She brushed a hand down her white gown, and then casually loosened the woven belt at her waist. 'It will just have to be me, as matron, who shields her from the evil spirits that always lurk on a wedding day.'

Petrus thought she would be too busy flirting to protect the bride.

A flurry of activity behind him heralded the entry of the Prefect with Pollux at his side. Tatius was dressed in a deep purple robe, and he carried a sword at his side. Faustina moved away. The men all cheered as Tatius moved to stand in front of an altar to Jupiter at one end of the room. A bowl of incense burned in front of it.

Faustina led a small woman into the salon. The bride clutched Faustina's arm for support; the hem of her white dress brushed along the floor. Her head was covered with a flame red veil, as was traditional in senatorial families. They moved to stand alongside Tatius. The priest seemed to glide across the room to hover beside the altar.

Tatius handed the priest some coins. The man nodded and began muttering prayers. Tatius turned towards his bride and drew back her veil. She was beautiful and very young. Her coiled jet-black hair, held in place with a bronze comb, highlighted her pale skin. Her tiny breasts pushed against her white robe and a tightly woven belt gripped her waist. Tears glistened on her cheeks as Faustina lifted her right hand and placed it in Tatius' right palm.

'Where you are Gaius, I am Gaia,' the girl managed to say.

Petrus did not hear Tatius' words of response; he was distracted by a rustling behind him as a slave stepped forward and placed a yellow cake in Faustina's hands. Faustina broke the cake above the head of the bride and prayed aloud to Jupiter to bless the marriage as cake crumbs rained down on the girl. Tatius smiled and plucked crumbs from her hair, placing them in his mouth. He brushed his fingers across the hair on the top of her head and crumbs rained down past her tear-stained face and onto her shoulders. She caught some of them and pushed them between her lips with trembling hands.

Pollux unrolled a sheet of vellum and the guests watched as the couple signed the marriage contract. He handed Tatius a bulging green pouch, containing part of the bride's dowry. Tatius bowed to him and fastened the jangling pouch to his belt.

'Behold, Attia Camilla, my wife!' grinned Tatius and led her past the guests and out into the garden.

The guests cheered and Petrus found himself joining in as they wished the couple luck and followed them through the garden. Behind them, Faustina gathered up the crumbs of the cake from the floor and placed them in a pouch, to bring her luck. In the garden, the evergreen bushes had been tidied up and ribbons of purple and white trailed around them, leading the guests across the cleaned flagstones to the dining room.

The enormous room had high ceilings, and the lit torches illuminated frescoes painted in bright colours. Three large couches had plush cushions ready to receive the guests. Faustina fussed around them, positioning Tatius in the middle of the central couch with Camilla to his right and Pollux to his left. 'I shall be here next to you, my husband,' she said. She positioned Ruga, Aquilinus and three of the centurions on another couch and indicated to the remaining guests, including Petrus, to take the last one, with Petrus at the end that was closest to where she would be reclining.

Petrus wriggled into place on his stomach, his elbows on the cushion in front of him. He disliked this style of eating, which the richest Romans favoured. He found it difficult to eat food lying down, and he invariably got stomach-ache. Fortunately, he was not invited to such lavish feasts very often, although he feared that might change if he was admitted to the Mithraic cult. Slave girls stepped forward and poured them all drinks. Petrus drank slowly. It was going to be a long afternoon. More slaves arrived with platters of salted fish and strange pickled vegetables that tasted like earth. Wine flowed and there was a course of wild boar with apples, spiced with garlic and pepper. The men's voices grew louder as they drank more and more wine.

Attia Camilla drank very little and only nibbled at her food. She answered her husband's questions in a quiet voice, inaudible to the rest of the guests. Tatius appeared to grow tired of her and turned to speak with Pollux. Ruga was also watching the bride and when Petrus glanced at him, he raised his eyebrows and made a sexual gesture with his left hand. Petrus scowled. He placed his goblet on a side table and took a deep breath. His head was starting to feel heavy.

'Petrus?' Faustina purred, and he turned to look at her. 'Tell me about the murder.' Her eyes sparkled in delight as she rolled towards him on her couch. Her robe fell open to show her bulging breasts.

Embarrassed, Petrus turned his head quickly to watch the slaves removing the platters of half-eaten food. He looked back at Faustina and said, 'Madam, I am not at liberty to discuss my work on the murder. I have various avenues to explore. Several people had reason to hold grudges against Manius. But whether they would have killed him is another matter.'

'But why in the Mithraeum? That's supposed to be a secret place. Or was. Now everyone knows about it,' she laughed.

Petrus tried to shrug his shoulders, but this was impossible, as he was supporting himself with his elbows.

'Do you think Tatius and the girl make a good couple? She's only a few years older than his children. How's she supposed to control a household?'

Petrus remained silent.

'And do you have a woman, Petrus?' she ran her tongue across her lips and leant forward, allowing her robe to open again, enjoying his discomfort.

'I have a wife and children in the vicus.'

'Unofficial wife, of course,' she fluttered her eyelids.

'Only unofficial in the eyes of the army. She is a Roman citizen and I have made provision for them all in my will,' he snapped.

'So proper, Petrus... Don't you just want to have fun sometimes?'

Petrus was annoyed. Why did she persist in this behaviour? He decided to take advantage of the rich wine he'd had. He belched loudly, smiled and rubbed his belly. He slowly closed his eyes and then opened them wide and slurred, 'S-sorry Madam, too much wine, I think.'

Faustina turned her back on him. He let his eyes close again, but kept his elbows locked, so that his head remained above the cushion.

'Had enough, have you?' The merchant next to him nudged his arm so hard that Petrus fell forward, landing with his face in the cushion, amongst the fragments of food and smears of grease.

He quickly pushed himself upright, wiped his face with his sleeve, and looked to his left. 'Probably,' he mumbled.

The merchant's ginger beard had remnants of food clinging to the hair. It turned Petrus' stomach.

'Bad thing, the murder, wasn't it?' grumbled the merchant. 'That Manius was a strange one, drank occasionally to excess. Slave had to fetch him from the tavern sometimes. Who's going to take over? The Signifiera, I suppose. 'Til they find someone else amongst the rabble sufficiently educated to do the job.'

Petrus noted his mispronunciation of Signifer. The man's Latin was poor. Maybe he felt he didn't need to learn Latin very well, as the army needed him. Petrus spoke in the local language, 'The Roman army is not a rabble.'

The merchant glanced away. 'Of course not, I didn't mean…'

'Yes, yes, you did mean it. Manius will be replaced. There will be no interruption to your business with the fort. How often was Manius in the tavern? How often did his slave have to fetch him?'

The merchant paused. 'Less so now than a couple of years ago. Back then he used to fall asleep in the tavern. Nearly got his signet ring stolen once, as I remember. Then he stopped wearing it.'

Petrus studied the man's face. His nose had the broken veins of a hardened drinker. 'What was your name again?' Petrus asked.

'I'm not…'

'I can always ask Augustus Pollux the Tribune, and he'll wonder why you wouldn't tell me yourself.'

'It's Diatoua,' the man took a deep breath. 'I am sorry Sir; I really meant no offence.'

Petrus smiled and picked up his goblet. 'You've been very helpful, Diatoua. Now let's drink to the bride and groom.' He clinked his cup against the other man's, noting that the merchant's hand was shaking as he lifted his drink to his lips.

Sweet dishes arrived; figs, pomegranates, and pears dripping with sweet honey. Petrus munched on the pears and delighted in their taste.

Eventually, Tatius pushed himself to his feet and held out a hand to his wife. He led the party outside. The late afternoon light was fading. Delicate flakes of snow danced in the breeze that tugged at the bride's veil and ruffled the hair of the centurions who gathered round the carriage. The driver sat huddled beneath his cloak. The carriage rocked as Tatius helped his bride inside and then climbed in beside her. The Tribune carried a lit torch as he walked at the head of the procession along the street. The Centurions marched with their hands on their swords, ever watchful. The mud sucked at their feet.

Petrus cried out as he lost his footing and nearly fell. 'For fuck's sake!' he mumbled.

The fort gate opened, and the carriage proceeded along the deserted streets. Women and children peered out of the windows of the barracks, watching the spectacle. At the Praetorium, a slave girl opened the door clutching some sheep's wool greased with oil and fat. Attia Camilla descended from the carriage, took the wool and smeared the grease across the door frame. Without looking back, she entered the building. Tatius climbed out of the carriage and followed her inside. The Tribune handed the torch to Ruga and then got into the carriage, which turned round and headed for the gate.

Petrus yawned; his head was starting to throb. He walked slowly towards the infirmary. It had its familiar smell of honey. The injured soldiers were chatting quietly. At the other end of the room, Balbus lay on his bed with his eyes closed. The floor was clean and there were no used bowls or rotting food lying about. Petrus watched Balbus' chest rise and fall; it was not the deep breathing of a man asleep. He nudged Balbus' leg. The man's eyes shot open in alarm, and he began to push himself off his bed.

'Steady! Don't get up. Where's your guard?' whispered Petrus.

'Gone to get me some food, Sir.'

'Anything else to report?'

'The librarii are rescuing some of the burned tablets. I've just carried on looking at records. I haven't found anything else yet. Do you think they'll try to burn the Librarium again?'

'They? Who's they?'

'Well, whoever did it the first time.'

'I don't think it'll happen again, but there are pails of water and sand in the room, aren't there? And there's always someone in their guarding it.'

Balbus nodded.

'Well then, we're as ready as we can be.'

Petrus knocked on the door to the next room. It was opened

by Arsenios, who smiled and stepped back to let him in, closing the door behind him.

'Just wanted to ask about that little boy I sent to you yesterday,' said Petrus.

'Ah, yes, a bad burn. He said his sleeve caught fire.'

'Yes, it did. He's the one who set fire to the Librarium.'

Arsenios whistled in surprise. 'Did someone put him up to it?'

Petrus hesitated, but then decided as he'd already told the physician most of what was going on, he might as well tell him everything. 'Yes. Adrianus, the senior librarius. I think he did it to destroy the evidence of his theft from the army. It was he who used Manius' ring on the forged tablets. I found the ring in his room.'

He paused and then removed the twigs from his pouch. 'See these? An herbalist gave them to me, said they're a sleeping draught.' He put them into Arsenios' outstretched hand. 'She said boil 'em up and then drink the liquor. She said that's enough for two doses.'

Arsenios nodded. 'Looks like a type of valerian root.'

'She said people's bodies become used to it if they take it for long periods.'

'Yes, yes, they would.' Arsenios gave the roots back to him.

'Right. I'll give it a go.' Petrus yawned. 'I need a rest.'

Arsenios smiled. 'Been at the Prefect's wedding celebrations, have you?'

Petrus nodded. He left the room and passed by Balbus and Vester, who were busy tucking into their food. There were two men leaning against the Librarium door, talking quietly to whoever was inside. He walked towards the cells but saw that Ruga was just emerging from the building.

'Adrianus is a little less cocky after a night in there,' murmured Ruga as Petrus caught up with him. 'I don't think he's too keen on the food either.'

'Let's discuss how to handle the arrest and interrogation of Lucullus with the Prefect in the morning,' said Petrus, who did not like the rough treatment meted out during questioning of prisoners.

Petrus waved Gauori away and climbed onto his bed. He closed his eyes and let the wine take over.

XI

The air was thick with the stink of sweaty bodies and stale ale as Carantii pushed his way into the tavern and onto a bench at a table where three men were slurring at each other as they argued. They nodded a greeting to him as he gulped down his drink and held out more coins so that the taverner refilled his cup. Behind him, two men crouched rolling dice and betting on the outcome. They had placed their money on the floor. Carantii rose from his seat and moved to watch them.

He recognised one of the men, a labourer. The man grabbed the dice in a bunched fist, kissed his knuckles, and then threw them to the floor. The dice skitted and jerked as they span across the uneven earth floor. The man groaned at the low score. The second man laughed, a guttural noise, deep in his throat. He took the dice and threw them into the corner. An even lower score faced upwards. The labourer laughed and grabbed the money. The loser punched his shoulder, forcing him to stagger sideways. Carantii put out a hand to steady the man as the loser rose and stepped towards them. Carantii drew himself up to his full height, and the loser paused, stood still for a moment, and then backed down before slamming out of the tavern.

'A sore loser, that one. Is he always like that?' mumbled Carantii.

'Yeah, pretty much. Lots of men are you know, especially when they lose big time,' replied the man.

'Who bets big time?'

'The big money men don't often bet on dice. Hand-to-hand fights are where the money is.'

'Fights? So, could I earn some big money betting on two men fighting?'

'Aye. But you could lose big money too, Blacksmith. I didn't think you'd got much spare. Not now you've got a wife.' He grinned lecherously.

Carantii did not reply.

The man continued, 'Sometimes they have two women fighting. I hear they're vicious, tearing each other's hair out.'

'Isn't fighting for money and betting on it outlawed by the army?'

'Lots of stuff happens that's outlawed. Army overlooks most of it. Some army men bet on the fights.' He paused, 'Is that whose money you're flush with? The army's?'

Carantii felt his insides turn to ice, and he struggled to hold the other man's gaze and keep his voice steady. 'Well, I do overcharge them, don't I?' he forced himself to laugh, 'and they keep coming back. Their own smiths clearly aren't up to much,' he spat on the floor.

'Dead right,' muttered the man.

'So, these fights..?'

'You'd need a fair bit o' money to even get there. Only a few merchants and them army officers ever have enough.'

'Do the army men lose a lot of money?'

'Sometimes. They sometimes start fights of their own with the other gamblers when they lose, that Roburius and his fellow centurions, I mean. One of the retired centurions was killed in a brawl a while back, wasn't he?'

Carantii nodded, 'Yes, but that was a long time ago.' He waved the taverner over. 'Join me in a drink.'

The man grinned. 'There's no point getting close to me. I can't get you into one of the fights.'

'No. But you could tell me who to approach, couldn't you? Might see if I could take some more money off Roman soldiers. I don't want to get into a fight, though.'

'Senna, he's the one who organises everything,' he nodded in the direction of a large man with a mass of tangled brown hair who was just finishing his drink.

Carantii walked over to the big man who looked him up and down and said, 'I heard you. Want to watch one of the fights, do you? I hope you've got plenty of money. You must bet on each fight, it's a minimum of two denarii.'

'I've got that much.'

Senna grinned; his mouth was full of crooked black teeth. 'Why the sudden interest? I've not seen you gambling before.'

'I've not been flush with the Romans' cash before. I want to make some more.'

Senna laughed. 'I'm always happy to separate a fool from his money. Meet me outside here tomorrow when the sun is at its highest. I'll take you.'

Carantii settled on the bench opposite Senna and bought another drink. He sipped it slowly, thinking about what he'd heard.

Senna gulped down the ale, wiped his mouth with the back of his sleeve, and then left the tavern. Carantii waved to the taverner.

'Best be careful. You've not been gambling much before, have you?' mumbled the taverner as he poured another drink.

Carantii smiled. 'I won't get in to trouble, I know what I'm doing.'

'Everyone thinks that at the start. Even Cato probably thought that once. Look at him now! That idiot even lost bets with that boy of Ruua's a couple of weeks ago, and that boy is hardly ever in here.'

'I guess the boy just got lucky then.'

'Lucky? He was cheating. And Cato was too drunk to notice. Served him right, I reckon. The boy's due a bit o' slack, lost his father and then that Roman, Manius, muscled in on Ruua. He and the boy don't, I mean didn't, get on.'

Carantii nodded. He waited, but the taverner had no more to say. He drained his drink, put some coins on the table, and muttered his goodbyes. He rose unsteadily to his feet and stepped into the dark night.

Lugraca stirred as he slipped into bed. She wrapped her arms around him and breathed her sleepiness into his face. 'Good night?' she murmured.

'Interesting,' he lay back and stared into the darkness, 'I'm going to have to bet a lot of money tomorrow.'

She mumbled, 'We don't have a lot of money to lose.'

He laughed. 'No, we don't. I'll be using Petrus' money, at an illegal fight.'

'Illegal? You'll be careful, won't you?'

'Always,' he pulled her closer. 'There's something you could help me with.'

'Anything,' she whispered as she climbed on top of him.

XII

Petrus' head throbbed. He dragged himself up off the bed and scooped some water out of the pail in the corner of his room. He pulled on his clothes and walked slowly into the kitchen. Gauori was sweeping the floor. The sounds of the bristles against the stones made Petrus want to cry out. He lowered himself onto a stool and slowly pulled his plate across the table. The shriek of the plate as it ground against the wood made his teeth hurt. He sighed and took a mouthful of bread. The squelch and click of his jaw pounded inside his forehead as he chewed.

'Here, drink this,' whispered Gauori, placing a cup of warm liquid at his elbow.

Petrus took a mouthful. It was sweet, fruity and full of honey. He felt the pores in his mouth open and relax. It slid down his throat, and he took another drink. It felt like it was reaching his head, dulling the pain. He opened his pouch and took out the roots that Ruua had given him.

'Here, take these. They're a sleeping drug. I want you to boil them up and then keep the liquor from them. Cover it over and we'll look at it later. Keep the roots aside. I'm not sure what to do with them.'

Gauori's eyes widened. He took the roots, placed them in a pot, and poured water over them to the depth of his thumb. He placed the pot on the fire.

During parade, the winter air forced its way into Petrus' lungs and he breathed out the white mist of wine fumes. He followed Ruga to the office where Tatius sat at his desk, looking satisfied with himself.

Tatius said, 'You two look a bit rough. Drank too much of my fine wine yesterday, did you?'

'Perhaps we did Sir, but it was a joyous occasion,' replied Ruga.

Petrus updated Tatius on his investigation.

Tatius said, 'To summarise, you think that Adrianus has been working with Lucullus to steal from the army. You saw them arguing. After Manius' death, Adrianus stole his ring and used it to make it look as if it was Manius doing the stealing. Adrianus forced the young lad to set fire to the Librarium to destroy the records. Why set the fire now?'

'He had probably planned to set fire to the Librarium when Manius discovered the thefts, but then after Manius was killed, he felt safe. However, when Balbus began looking at the records, he may've started to worry again,' replied Petrus.

'Did Adrianus or Lucullus kill Manius because he found out about the thefts?'

'I'm not sure, Sir, they might have. That might be why Adrianus didn't report him missing. However, Adrianus did not leave the fort that last day. So, he would've needed an accomplice. Someone who knew where the Mithraeum was.'

'Lucullus used to worship at the Mithraeum. I'm sure Ruga will get the truth from Adrianus.' Tatius looked in Ruga's direction.

Ruga clasped his hands together, stretched his arms out, and cracked his knuckles. Petrus winced. Ruga enjoyed brutal interrogations.

Petrus said, 'I spoke with Manius' woman. She's an herbalist;

she told me about sleeping draughts made from plants. She sells them to lots of people. I suppose she could've sold them to Adrianus or Lucullus. I want to arrest Lucullus and to continue with my other investigations.'

Tatius sighed. 'You're never satisfied, are you? Sometimes the simplest solutions are the correct ones. Still, you were right last time. I shouldn't forget that. Right, Ruga, you interrogate Adrianus. Petrus can give you the summary tablets showing the thefts and any other background information that you need. Petrus, go and arrest Lucullus. Let's see what he has to say. Then we'll know what steps you need to take.'

'Where shall I put Lucullus? Do we want him next to Adrianus? They could agree their stories,' asked Petrus.

Tatius steepled his fingers, rested his chin on his fingertips and thought for a moment, 'A good point. But there is nowhere else to put him. We only have the one jail. Put him in the cells and make sure there's someone guarding them at all times, day and night, monitoring any communication between them. Someone you can trust.'

Petrus nodded. 'And what about the boy, Kandianus? He's in the barracks with Ennius and his mother right now. I'm worried someone might try to harm him. He's a witness.'

'Keep them in the barracks for now, until this matter is concluded. When this theft is resolved, I'm going to give all the men instructions to clear their families out of here. The fire could've been catastrophic. Tell Ecdicius to fine Ennius three months' pay. I want an example made of him.'

'Moving the women out will cause resentment,' muttered Ruga.

'I don't care. I want them gone. The men can find them places in the vicus or send them to the countryside.'

Petrus unlocked the chest in his office and pulled out the tablet, summarising the grain thefts. He handed it to Ruga.

'It was Adrianus' job to check the deliveries. He forged Manius' signature on the records, after he stole the ring. Lucullus did not deliver anywhere near as much as was recorded.' A sudden thought occurred to him, 'If Adrianus was stealing grain at the point of delivery, then he would have needed help from someone inside the fort, and a place to store it. Ask him about that. I'll ask Aquilinus how Vester and those other lads managed to divert grain from stores that time a few months back.'

Petrus went to the workshops and collected Germanus, Flavius, Corvinus, and five other soldiers from his century. He knew that was more men than he needed, but he wanted a show of strength. They gathered their equipment and stood to attention while he briefed them.

'We're going to arrest Lucullus, the retired centurion, at his home. Two of you will enter his compound with me while the others wait outside. Some of you may remember him from his time at the fort. Do not acknowledge him. Do not engage him in conversation. He is suspected of various crimes, and I do not want him to feel he is amongst friends. Is that clear?'

The men chorused, 'Yes, Sir!'

They headed out of the gate. The bloody stink from the butchery raced towards them on the wintry breeze. A couple of women emerged from a shop, and Petrus recognised Aurora, deep in conversation with the other woman. At the marketplace, there were a couple of women selling withered vegetables. He saw Ruua squatting in the dirt with her bunches of dried herbs spread out on a sack in front of her. Ruua glanced at him and nodded her head in greeting. Beside her, the girl, Tarpi, poked at a dead mouse with a stick. She looked up. Seeing Petrus, she scrambled to her feet and darted away.

They passed deep into the vicus and arrived at Lucullus' house. Petrus instructed six of the soldiers to wait outside. He knocked on the door. It was opened by the same thin creature as before. Petrus pushed past him, and the man cried out. 'Master!'

Lucullus stormed out of his office and shouted, 'What the fuck do you want?'

Seeing the soldiers, Lucullus reached for a sword hung on the wall, his hand groping the air. Corvinus stepped forward and knocked his arm aside, twisting his hand behind his back. He pulled him round to face Petrus. Flavius took his other arm.

'Calvisius Lucullus, you are under arrest on suspicion of theft,' said Petrus.

Lucullus went pale, 'In the name of the Gods, what are you on about?'

He began to struggle against the two soldiers and cried out in pain as his arm was twisted harder. Petrus strode into Lucullus' office and looked around. On the shelf behind the desk were a stack of tablets. He took the door key, stepped outside, and locked the door.

'What are you doing? You've no right!' cried Lucullus.

'I have every right if you've been stealing from the army,' he dropped the key into his pouch.

Lucullus opened his mouth to argue, but Corvinus jerked his arm, and he squealed. They moved towards the door with Lucullus dragging his feet and trying to pull away from the soldiers. As they stepped into the street, Lucullus quietened down, shocked to see six more soldiers waiting outside. A small crowd had gathered nearby, watching.

Lucullus stopped thrashing against the soldiers, stood upright, and shouted, 'Nothing to see here! They just want a word with me, that's all.'

Petrus had a sudden thought, 'Keep him here! You two, come with me,' he pointed at two of the men.

The men followed Petrus to the neighbouring property. A timid slave girl opened the door and let them in, taking them through to the salon without a word. Honoria was having her long blond hair styled by a young slave. A young man with broad shoulders and thick dark hair was lounging on a couch nearby; he leapt to his feet when the soldiers entered.

'What can we do for you?' the young man's voice was high

and shrill. He clenched his fists as he spoke.

'Are you Flaccus?' asked Petrus.

The young man bowed his head in acknowledgement. 'What brings the Roman army to our home at this early hour?'

'You're in business with your neighbour, Lucullus, I believe.'

'That's correct, we're part... well I work for him. He was my deceased father's business partner.'

'Do you help him with deliveries to the fort?'

Flaccus puffed his chest out and stood a bit taller. 'I help him with all his business dealings, and I am involved with the free man Felix as well.'

'Then I must ask you to accompany us to the fort to answer some questions.'

'But, but, I...'

Petrus interrupted him, 'We've just arrested Lucullus. It would help our enquiries if you came with us now, rather than me having to come back to talk to you later,' he paused, 'If I wasn't able to find you, I might think you'd run away, which could be taken as a sign of guilt. You'd also face the embarrassment of being dragged through the streets.'

Flaccus opened his mouth and closed it again.

'Is he under arrest, Aurelius Petrus?' Honoria asked.

Petrus looked towards her. 'He is not. However, as I've said, his cooperation would be looked on favourably. I need to ask him questions about his business with Lucullus.'

'Can't you do that here?'

'Madam, I've arrested Lucullus. I don't know what information he'll give me, but I've no doubt I'll have to speak with your son. With a bit of luck, he could be back before nightfall.'

Honoria sighed, 'You'd better go with them, Flaccus. If he's not back before it's dark, I'll send someone to the fort to speak with your commander.'

This was an empty threat, and they all knew it.

Flaccus followed them through the house. As they reached the door, Petrus turned to him and said, 'Do not speak with Lucullus.'

Flaccus nodded.

Outside, Lucullus was quiet. He stood with his head bowed, encircled by the soldiers. He looked up as Petrus returned and stared sullenly at Flaccus. Petrus motioned the young man to join him, and they walked ahead of the group, with one soldier beside them.

'Look here, Clemens, Leo, you must remember me. This is all a mistake, isn't it? No need for this. Come on, I'm coming quietly. Does it really take so many of you and a centurion to bring me in?' Lucullus said in low tones.

The soldiers did not acknowledge him. He tried to speak with them a couple more times, but in the end fell silent. It began to drizzle; ice cold water dripped onto their heads, seeped into their clothes and spattered the earth with dark spots. Petrus was relieved when they arrived at the fort. He whispered the password, and the gate swung open. Petrus glanced behind him and saw one of the soldiers take Lucullus' arm and propel him forward.

At the Principia, he told two soldiers to wait with Flaccus and the rest marched Lucullus towards the cells. Lucullus stopped walking when he realised where he was being taken. He waved his arms and fought off Corvinus and Flavius as they made to grab him. Two more soldiers stepped in; the four of them subdued Lucullus and dragged him after Petrus.

Ruga flexed his fingers as he emerged from the jail building. He raised a hand to bring the group to a halt and then beckoned Petrus forward.

He said in a low voice, 'Adrianus is still saying it was Manius who falsified the records. He says he can't explain how the signet ring came to be hidden in that pot of stale water in his kitchen. About the fire, he said 'The boy is obviously out of control. Why would you believe the word of a snivelling child of a Carvetti whore over that of an officer of the Roman Army?' I'm going to leave him there for a bit. He's in pain. I'll have another go later.'

Petrus replied, 'Let's take Lucullus into the building, so that they see each other. That may encourage one of them to open up, to be the first man to tell his story, so that he gets more leniency by throwing the other under a horse.'

Ruga patted him on the back. 'Great idea Petrus. I hadn't realised you were so devious.'

Petrus led them into the jail and flung open the door to the empty cell next to Adrianus. The four soldiers carried Lucullus in and dumped him in the dusty straw. Adrianus was slumped in a corner. His face was bruised and puffy with one eye swollen closed. Blood dribbled from the corner of his mouth. He watched as Petrus locked the door to the cell and then began to crawl towards the bars separating the two cells.

Ruga burst into the building and yelled, 'No, Petrus!'

Petrus turned towards Ruga and stood with his hand still on the cell door. Behind him Lucullus had moved towards Adrianus who was mumbling.

Ruga said, 'We'll keep them separated. Take him outside.'

Petrus unlocked the cell, and the four soldiers entered. Lucullus leapt to his feet and began throwing punches. The soldiers moved in, and Flavius punched him twice in the stomach. Lucullus fell to the floor, curling his knees up towards his chest. Corvinus kicked his back. He groaned and lay still. The four men grabbed him and dragged him out of the cell. Behind them, Adrianus closed his eyes and muttered prayers.

Lucullus sank to his knees outside the building. He held his body rigid. The four soldiers picked him up and dragged him after Petrus, who strode towards the parade ground.

'Tie him to that stake,' said Petrus.

The rain was now falling steadily as they bound Lucullus' hands and tied him to the wooden stake.

'Leave him there, but keep an eye on him. I don't want anyone talking to him,' he instructed the soldiers, who nodded and moved to stand under the eaves of a building, sheltering from the rain.

Flaccus was leaning against the wall to Petrus' office with his eyes closed. One of the soldiers with him nudged his foot; his eyes flew open, and he looked about him wildly.

'Come into my office,' Petrus tried to sound friendly as he unlocked the door and murmured to the two soldiers, telling them to wait outside.

'Take a seat,' he pointed to a stool and Flaccus sank down onto it. 'Would you like a drink?' Without waiting for a response, he grabbed two cups and poured out some watery wine, pushing one cup towards the young man who frantically looked around him, as if searching for a way to escape.

'How long have you been working with Lucullus? Have a drink, the wine is sweet.' Petrus sipped from his cup.

Flaccus gulped down the wine. 'I began working in the business when I turned sixteen, then continued after my father died, so a little more than four years.'

'And do you enjoy it?'

Flaccus frowned. 'Not as much as when Father was alive. I had more responsibility then. Now I have to do pretty much, as Lucullus says. Sometimes I'm away for a few days at a time buying stock. Then I get to make my own decisions.'

'Do you always go away on your own?'

Flaccus shook his head and took another mouthful of wine. 'No, only when it's small collections, like when you visited our house the other day. If it's big, or multiple suppliers, then Lucullus likes to supervise. The time before, we went out to Coria together and were gone for around two weeks. It was a huge opportunity, but he doesn't really trust me to negotiate.'

'Two weeks? Can you tell me the exact dates you were away?'

'I can't remember the dates, but I have it written down at home. Father encouraged me to record what I did in business each day and what I'd learned. I have continued that practice since his death.'

'Did you always accompany Lucullus when he made deliveries to the fort?'

'I started to a few months ago. Lucullus said some grain had gone missing off the back of the cart and he'd not been paid for it. I think some soldiers eventually admitted to stealing it. My job is to keep an eye out while it's being unloaded here in the fort.'

Petrus nodded, 'And did you watch it being loaded on to the cart from wherever Lucullus had it stored?'

Flaccus shook his head. 'No, I didn't. It was always done before I got there.'

'Was it always the same librarius who signed for your deliveries, or did it change at all?'

'It was always the same man, brown hair, not too tall.'

'Adrianus,' murmured Petrus.

'If that was his name.'

'The description fits him. You never saw a librarius with curly dark hair then?'

'No. Never.'

'Right, that's it. Thank you for answering my questions.' Petrus pushed his stool back and stood up. 'You're free to go now. But I would like one of my men to go back to your house with you and collect the records you mentioned, the ones that you keep about the business. I need the records for the last, err, let's say six months.'

Flaccus looked relieved. He smiled and got to his feet. 'Yes, yes, of course.'

Petrus assigned Corvinus to escort Flaccus home and collect the records he needed. Petrus trusted Corvinus; he was thorough and had helped save the Prefect's life the previous year.

Petrus watched them walk away. Flaccus was talking

animatedly, still terrified. Petrus went into Aquilinus' room, where the centurion was busy at his table.

'Petrus?' Aquilinus did not smile.

'Last year, when we discovered that Vester and those other lads had stolen some grain when they were unloading a delivery, how did they manage to do it?'

Aquilinus frowned. 'Why are you bringing all that up again? They were given barley rations for two months and their pay was docked for six months, which was about ten times the value of the grain they stole. Being on barley really put them in their place. To this day some of the other men still give them food meant for the pigs as a way of rubbing it in.'

'Did they explain how they managed it and where they stored the grain?' sighed Petrus.

'They were working unloading a delivery. Adrianus was checking as always and as the sacks had been counted by the storeman, one of them dropped a sack on his foot and created a commotion after managing to spill some of it. This distracted both the librarius and the storeman and they sneaked a sack away, hiding it behind a barrel. They went back for it after dark and took it back to their room, where they stored it.'

'Didn't their immune Argentus see it?'

'Apparently not. They split the sack into smaller portions and kept it in their chests and under their mattresses. They used the grain to get sex from the local women, as you know.'

'And did you speak with Adrianus about it?'

'Of course I did! He wouldn't take any responsibility, said once stores had signed for it, it was the storeman's lookout, although he did say he would monitor more carefully going forward. Why all these questions, Petrus?'

'We think Adrianus has been stealing from stores. Ruga's interrogating him now.'

Aquilinus raised an eyebrow. 'I pity Adrianus then.'

Petrus made his way to the prison. Two of Ruga's men leant against the bars of Adrianus' cell, watching him. He lay curled up on the bloody straw, whimpering incoherently. The hard taste of blood settled in the back of Petrus' throat.

'Where's Ruga?' he asked.

'You've just missed him. He's gone to talk to the other man, the one tied up on the parade yard,' replied one of the soldiers as he straightened his tunic and stood to attention.

Petrus hurried across the fort. It had stopped raining. Water dripped from the rooves and plopped into the puddles on the soggy ground. At the parade area, Lucullus was slumped, half-lying in a puddle of water, his hands pinned behind his back. His hair was plastered across his forehead and his clothes were darkened where the rain had soaked through. The four soldiers guarding him lingered nearby, laughing and joking amongst themselves and occasionally glancing at their captive.

Ruga walked up to Lucullus, deliberately dragging his feet. He splashed water and grit into the other man's face. Lucullus swore, wiped his cheek ineffectually on his shoulder, and snarled at the centurion.

'Let me get that grit off,' snarled Ruga as he leant forward and wiped the man's cheek with his blood-stained hand, smearing blood and grit across his face. Ruga laughed as he untied the rope and pulled him to his feet. Lucullus staggered a couple of steps and gripped onto Ruga for support.

'I can barely feel my legs, you sh…' he gasped as Ruga shook him off.

Petrus stepped forward and said, 'I can take it from here, Ruga. Can I get one of these men to take the prisoner to my office? I'll question him there. I'd like a word with you first.'

Ruga nodded and pushed Lucullus towards Flavius, 'Take him and wait outside Petrus' office.'

'Not so arrogant now, are you?' mumbled Flavius as they led Lucullus away.

'I just missed you at the cells. Did Adrianus say anything?' asked Petrus.

Ruga replied, 'You were right. Once he saw we had Lucullus, he couldn't wait to tell his side of the story and drop Lucullus in it. He says it was Lucullus' idea. He claims Lucullus threatened him to make him get involved. Said he was frightened of the man. They would agree in advance how many sacks of grain the merchant could provide. Then they'd agree a different number to actually be delivered. Lucullus retained the excess grain for sale elsewhere. Lucullus would be paid for what was ordered and then they'd split the profits, equal shares. Manius started asking questions about six weeks ago, when he'd covered the deliveries once and he thought Lucullus' behaviour was a bit suspicious. He began searching the old records for evidence. When Lucullus heard about that, he threatened Manius one night in the vicus. Must've really scared Manius, as that's about the time he started withdrawing money from his account. When Manius went missing and the slave couldn't find him, Adrianus got that small boy you'd seen running about in the fort to steal his ring from his rooms. Adrianus began changing the records and forging Manius' signature. Didn't think anyone would spot the differences, even when you sent Balbus to check his work. He panicked when he saw Balbus taking a sack full of tablets to you. That's when he decided to get the boy to burn the Librarium down.'

'Why didn't Manius tell the Signifer, the Prefect, or anyone else about his suspicions?'

Ruga shrugged, 'We'll never know. Maybe he wanted all the evidence first, so that there could be no doubt about it. Maybe he was going to blackmail Adrianus, or he wanted a cut of the profits.'

'I wouldn't have said Manius was like that, but then I wouldn't have said Adrianus was either, I suppose. Err, when you say Lucullus threatened Manius, was that a death threat?'

'I should think so. Adrianus says he thinks Lucullus killed Manius.'

'Wasn't Lucullus worried Flaccus would find out, or is he involved as well?' Petrus asked.

'Adrianus says the boy's a fool. Wouldn't notice anything amiss. Lucullus only keeps him on because he must. That's the way old Macro set up their partnership. Wily old boy he was.'

'Let me speak with Lucullus. Hopefully, we can get him to confess without having to beat him at all,' Petrus glanced down at Ruga's blood-stained fists.

Ruga nodded. 'I think the two lads on guard in the cells would like a break from it, too. It gets you down after a while if you haven't got the nerve for it.'

Petrus knew how that felt.

He left Ruga and returned to his office. Lucullus was leaning against the wall, shivering. Flavius and his companions were clustered round him in silence.

'I'm sorry about all this, leaving you out there in the rain. I had to follow orders. You know how it is,' Petrus sighed theatrically, 'Come with me now,' he put his arm round the man's shoulders and helped him into the office, lowering him onto a stool.

Flavius had followed them in.

Petrus waved him away. 'Fetch him a blanket and then wait outside.'

Lucullus was shaking with cold; his face was pale, and he hugged his arms tight to his chest.

'Wine?' Petrus asked, as he poured two cups and pushed one across the table towards him.

Lucullus picked up the cup. His hand trembled as he raised it to his lips and the wine slopped onto his hands, dripping down his fingers like blood.

Petrus took out a clear tablet and sat with his stylus poised. 'I saw you and Adrianus arguing at your house. Why did you lie to me about not knowing the librarii?'

'I didn't want you to suspect me of the murder.'

Petrus frowned. 'Adrianus has started talking. He says the

pair of you have been stealing from the army for months. Says it was all your idea.'

Lucullus was silent for a moment, clearly thinking what his options might be. 'It wasn't my idea. He came to me last year, around the time you put that other centurion's head outside the fort. He knew my business wasn't going too well, and he suggested this might be profitable to both of us.'

Petrus nodded. 'Go on,' he said, scratching some notes.

Lucullus sighed, 'We did a trial run, just one sack less than was recorded. That all went well, so we started doing it on a regular basis. Then Manius started asking questions about six weeks ago. Adrianus said he might be suspicious, but not to worry. After Manius' body was found, Adrianus said we should stop in case anyone else started looking at the records. He said he'd make sure Manius got the blame for the previous thefts. Dead men can't talk.'

'What about the ring?' asked Petrus.

'What ring? I don't know anything about a ring.'

'Manius' signet ring was used to forge the records; make it look like he was stealing. We found it in Adrianus' room.'

Lucullus put his hands together, his fingers linked with each other in an effort to stop them shaking. 'I didn't know what he was doing.'

'You expect me to believe that? Weren't you worried? If Adrianus thought you were going to be discovered, I'm sure you would've wanted to know what he was going to do.'

Lucullus shook his head. Flavius burst into the room with a blanket. He flung it at Lucullus, who caught it, wrapped it round his shoulders and covered his head.

'Pull that back, will you? I want to see your face while you talk to me, see if you're lying,' snapped Petrus.

Lucullus regarded him for a moment, then with a trembling hand pulled the blanket back, uncovering his pale face. He hugged the blanket around him. Petrus silently poured two more cups of wine and took a long drink.

'What about Flaccus? Is he involved?' Petrus asked.

Lucullus laughed bitterly, 'Flaccus? No. I wouldn't trust him with something like this. He might've blabbed to his friends. He doesn't have a head for business, not really. I just give him simple tasks to carry out, collecting orders and so on.'

Petrus nodded and made some more notes. 'When did the two of you decide to burn down the Records Office?'

Lucullus cried in alarm, 'The Records Office! No, no!'

Petrus snarled, 'Really? That would've been a way to ensure your thefts weren't discovered, wouldn't it? All Adrianus had to do was scare some poor half-wit of a child to make him throw a burning torch into the Librarium and Claudius is your uncle. Job done.'

'I - I swear I knew nothing about it,' whispered Lucullus.

'Knew nothing about it,' repeated Petrus, as he scratched the words onto the tablet. 'Right, then answer me this, when did you decide to kill Manius?'

Lucullus looked at his hands. 'I threatened to kill him one night when I saw him on his way back from the tavern. I just wanted to scare him, make sure he didn't tell anyone until Adrianus had got rid of the evidence. I'd never have killed him. Never.'

'He clearly thought you might kill him; he started taking his savings out of his account,' persisted Petrus.

'But I didn't do it. I know nothing about his death,' Lucullus' voice shook.

Petrus made a huge gesture with his stylus, 'I'm just writing "The suspect denies knowing anything about the murder of librarius Manius. The centurion, however, is not sure he believes him".'

'I swear on the lives of my children. I didn't do it. I don't know anything about the murder,' Lucullus gasped.

Petrus sighed and pushed the tablet and stylus across the table. 'Read it and sign as your statement.'

Lucullus' lips moved as he read the tablet. He signed at the bottom and pushed his own signet ring into the wax. Petrus stood up and grabbed him by the arm, hauling him to his feet. 'Come on.'

They walked towards the cells. Lucullus offered no resistance, but Flavius and the other soldier fell in behind them, keen for another chance to rough up their prisoner. They entered the prison building. Lucullus took a sharp intake of breath when he caught sight of the man curled up in the straw.

One of the guards opened the adjacent cell and Petrus pushed Lucullus inside. He walked behind him and moved him over to the corner where he closed a metal ring round his ankle, securing him to the wall.

'I want you to listen carefully to anything they say to each other and report back to me or Fabius Ruga,' Petrus hissed at the two guards as he moved towards the door. The men nodded.

Petrus made his way to Ruga's office, 'Lucullus says he didn't know how Adrianus was forging the records, or that he'd got the boy to set fire to the Librarium. He admits threatening Manius, but he claims he didn't kill him. Well, the threats worked. Manius began withdrawing his money. Lucullus was very cooperative. I would've said too cooperative, except that his story matches Adrianus.'

'So far. Let's go and ask Adrianus some more questions,' Ruga said, getting up from his chair.

Reluctantly, Petrus followed Ruga across the fort to the cells.

XIII

Carantii followed Senna into the forest clearing. A crowd of men stood to one side, jostling a small dark man who was busy taking bets, making marks on a slate with a charcoal stick as he did so. Several of the men were merchants, dressed in rich clothes. Others were men Carantii recognised from the town. To one side stood three centurions, instantly recognisable by their uniform.

'It's a minimum bet of two denarii,' the small man nudged Carantii's arm, 'which one are you going to bet on? Belicianus, the small one, or the large man, Scoruilos?' he pointed towards two men who were pacing aggressively nearby. Scoruilos' tattooed face had angry red scars down the cheeks. The fingers of his huge hands were gnarled and crooked, as if they'd been broken many times. Belicianus paced around with his bald head down, muttering to himself.

'The little man,' said Carantii, pressing coins into the man's hand and watching him mark his slate.

'Ready!' yelled Senna.

The two men strode to the centre of the clearing and began circling each other. The crowd moved closer, urging the men forward.

'Fight!' cried Senna.

Scoruilos stepped forward and began swinging punches. Belicianus ducked and weaved, dodging each attempted strike, circling his opponent, and then dashing in to hit his face hard before ducking away quickly. Scoruilos snarled and twisted round. Belicianus' foot caught on a pebble. He lost his balance and Scoruilos grabbed him, but he slipped through the big man's grasp and ran round him, kicking his legs from beneath him. Scoruilos fell on his back and Belicianus leapt onto his chest, sitting astride him, raining punches onto his head, bursting his lip and smearing blood across his face. The big man bucked, rolled and threw Belicianus aside. They both scrambled to their feet. Belicianus raced towards Scoruilos and head butted him in the chin, making him groan and stagger backwards. Caught by the crowd, he was thrown forward again and grabbed Belicianus by the neck, choking him. Belicianus swung his arms, punching the big man in the ribs and chest, to no avail. His flails grew weaker. Scoruilos took a step back, lifting Belicianus off his feet. Belicianus went limp and Scoruilos released his grip, letting him fall to the ground. Senna grabbed Scoruilos' hand and raised his arm.

Senna shouted, 'The winner! Settle your bets.'

Men moved towards the man who'd taken their money, pushing and swearing as they tried to get his attention. Carantii watched as the man drew a handful of coins from the pouch at his belt and began handing them out. The three centurions remained standing at the side, muttering to each other. A man knelt next to Belicianus and slapped his cheeks.

'Is he dead?' Carantii asked the man standing next to him.

'Doubt it, although I wish he was, I just lost five denarii on him. Normally, he's a sure bet. He's beaten dozens of men much bigger than that fat lump over there.'

'Maybe he's…' Carantii began.

'Maybe he's ill. Were you going to say?' The man interrupted, 'Or maybe he took some money to deliberately throw the fight.'

'Does that happen?' Carantii raised an eyebrow.

'Sometimes, not often, especially if the army lot are here,' the man nodded towards the centurions, 'Vegetinus and his two friends have just lost their money. Best hope they get some back on the next fight, otherwise there'll be trouble.'

'Do they often lose?'

'A fair bit, yes. They sometimes cause a problem if they lose big time. That's always the way with the centurions. Like that one who got killed a few years ago, Macro. He wasn't in debt, just didn't like losing, so started a fight in the tavern and it cost him his life in the end. That one's in a lot of debt, though.' The man nodded towards a bald red-faced man in a stained smock and tattered trousers lurking at the edge of the crowd.

'Is that Cato?' Carantii asked. The man looked vaguely familiar. Carantii thought he'd probably seen him drinking in the tavern.

'Yes, it is.'

'Heard a lot about him. First time I've really noticed him,' Carantii lied.

The man nodded. 'Heard bad things, I expect, eh? He often loses, he's in debt to lots of people. Very handy with his fists, though. He hires himself out to merchants who want debts collected. Threatens and then beats the poor sods. He does, that makes 'em pay up.'

'Really? Who would hire someone like him?' Carantii tried not to sound too interested.

The man gave a deep throaty laugh. 'Lots of people. Analeugus, Netacius, others too.' The man paused. 'I've not seen you here before.'

'It's my first time. It may be my last. I've already lost,' Carantii went as if to move away.

'Hold on!' The man cried, 'Wait for the next fight. It's two women. That's always a spectacle. One of 'em is Senna's slave; he's often puts her in the ring. She's a proper scrapper.'

Belicianus had woken up and was helped to his feet and taken away as Senna dragged a woman forward. Her hair was a tangled mass of red curls, her smock was stained and dirty. Senna threw her to the ground. A tall woman made her way forward. Her beautiful face had a scar running from her right eyebrow up across her forehead and underneath her raven black hair. Senna's slave scrambled to her feet.

Carantii shook his head when asked if he wanted to place a bet. The man muttered, 'You're supposed to bet on every fight. That's the deal.'

Carantii sighed and reached into his pouch. 'The raven-haired one,' he said.

'That's Gleva, she's one hell of a fighter,' mumbled the man next to Carantii.

'Fight!' bellowed Senna.

The crowd cheered. The two women rushed forward. Each one grabbed the other by the hair and began pulling, while she scratched and clawed at her opponent's face with her free hand. The watching men jeered. The slave began kicking Gleva, who responded by pulling her head down, raising a knee and smashing it into the slave's face. There was a sickening crack as the slave's nose broke and blood gushed down her face. She began to choke and let go of Gleva as she bent forward, gasping for breath. Gleva punched her head repeatedly, and the slave sank to her knees. Gleva leapt on her, knocking her back, her arms flailing. She lay there for a moment, making gurgling noises. Gleva sat astride her, took hold of her hair and lifted her head off the ground, then slammed it on the earth. The slave moaned. Gleva slammed her head onto the ground again and again. The crowd had gone quiet. Senna grabbed Gleva and pulled her to her feet.

'The winner!' he shouted, raising her arm up.

Behind Senna, the slave rolled on her side, choked and vomited blood. Carantii stared as she pushed herself onto her knees and leant forward with her hands to her face, trying to stop the bleeding.

'Your winnings,' the small man pressed six denarii into Carantii's hand and drew a line through the scratchings on his slate.

Carantii continued to watch the slave as she stood upright,

choking blood, tears and snot. 'Isn't someone going to help her?' he murmured.

'She's just a slave,' someone behind him muttered.

A man stepped from the crowd and grabbed the slave by the arm, roughly dragging her away.

'You're a fucking thieving bastard!' the cry made Carantii turn. One of the centurions had his arm round Senna's neck. Another had wrestled the man, taking bets to the ground.

'Give us our money back!' the man holding Senna shouted.

'You lost. It was a fair fi…' Senna gasped as the third centurion punched him in the stomach.

A group of rough looking local men charged towards the centurions, their arms flailing. Cato screamed and jumped into the fray. Carantii walked quickly into the woods, following those men who didn't want to become embroiled in the fight.

The sound of the fighting faded as the men pushed their way through the forest. Soon, the only sounds they could hear above their own breathing were the snap of branches beneath their feet. They emerged onto the road and turned towards the vicus.

'That was a lucky escape. I thought I was going to get caught up in that ruckus,' mumbled Carantii.

'Those army men are often like that.' The merchant beside him sighed. 'They've lost a lot of money recently. I can't remember the last time they won. They even managed to lose on the dog fights as well. They're all going to end up like that idiot Cato if they carry on like that. And they're still serving officers. At least Cato didn't get into real trouble until he left the army.'

Carantii nodded, and they trudged on in silence.

XIV

Adrianus opened his eyes as Petrus and Ruga entered the building. He crawled into the corner of his cell, watching them warily.

'A few more questions, Adrianus,' Ruga said in a harsh whisper, approaching the man who cowered beneath his gaze.

'No more. No more. I've told you everything,' begged Adrianus.

'Have you? Have you really? Get him up,' said Ruga, nodding to the two guards who'd followed them in.

The two men dragged Adrianus to his feet. He hung limply in their grip, his knees buckling beneath him. Ruga grabbed his hair and pulled it back so that he looked into Adrianus' wild eyes.

'When did you decide to follow through on Lucullus' threats to kill Manius?' Ruga said, looking beyond Adrianus to Lucullus who was scrambling over to the bars, his face against them, watching, listening.

'Keep that one quiet,' Ruga nodded towards Lucullus and Petrus stepped towards the bars, blocking Lucullus' view.

'Well?' Ruga said.

Behind him, Petrus heard a grunt as Ruga punched Adrianus in the stomach. There was the sound of retching.

'I… we didn't. I've not left the fort for weeks. I didn't kill him!' snivelled Adrianus.

Adrianus' scream turned Petrus' stomach. His own blood pounded in his ears, as there were more gasps and moans. He did not turn to watch.

'I didn't kill him. I didn't,' whimpered Adrianus.

Petrus suddenly span around. 'Wait! I think he's telling the truth!' His voice sounded shrill and desperate to his own ears.

Ruga glared at him. Petrus grabbed the summary tablets from the table near the door, put them inside his tunic, and stepped outside. Ruga followed him.

'We can check the gate records to see if it's true that he didn't leave the fort. He wouldn't have known where the Mithraeum was. I know he's got dark hair, but he would've needed help to move Manius. He couldn't have done it himself. He's not a strong man,' said Petrus.

'What's dark hair got to do with it?'

'We... I think the murderer has dark hair.' Petrus was annoyed with himself that he'd let that piece of information slip.

Ruga laughed and mimicked, "I think the murderer has dark hair'. Who told you that? The priest when he read the entrails? Some crazed local mystic? Are you losing your mind? Anyway, dark hair, that's not much help, is it? Half the fort's got dark hair, yourself included. I agree that Adrianus is too weak to move a dead body. Could be Lucullus though, with his luscious locks.' He paused, 'Fine. Go and check your records. We'll leave those two in there. We can update the Prefect tomorrow.'

Petrus went back to his office. He picked up the list of people who'd left the fort the day Manius disappeared. Adrianus' name wasn't on the list. He was telling the truth, about that bit at least.

Petrus took Flavius and Helvius with him to Lucullus' house. The slave who answered the door immediately tried to close it when he saw them. Petrus stepped forward and rammed into the door with his shoulder, pushing the slave backwards and marching into the house.

'What is this?' cried a woman with two young children hanging onto her smock.

Petrus ran his eyes over the woman, taking in her fading beauty. He looked away dismissively. 'I'm Aurelius Petrus of the Roman Army. I'm going to look in your husband's study.' He took a step forward.

'Where is Lucullus? You can't just…' her voice faded as Petrus unlocked the door and walked into the sparsely furnished room.

'Flavius, wait outside,' he said. 'Don't let her disturb me.' He closed the door behind him.

Petrus sat at Lucullus' table and began to search through the room. The dusty records were haphazardly stacked on the floor and shelves. He was surprised to see how detailed they were, not only accounting for items bought and sold, but also summaries of conversations Lucullus had had. Eventually, he found the ones covering the last few months and cross-checked them with the dates on the tablets which he'd brought with him. The amounts recorded as sold and paid for matched the ones on his summaries. They also recorded the running totals of grain he had in stock. The stolen grain was unaccounted for. Maybe it had never existed and was just numbers scratched on tablets. Petrus shrugged; finding the stolen grain wasn't his concern. He gathered all the relevant records covering the preceding six months and went to the door, where he spoke to Flavius.

'Get a sack from the kitchen and bring it here.'

He heard Flavius speaking with Lucullus' wife as he went back inside. Moments later Flavius reappeared with Lucullus' wife just behind him. Petrus began shovelling the tablets into the sack.

'What are you doing? You can't just take my husband's things,' the woman snapped.

'I'm investigating a crime. I can take whatever I deem necessary.'

He picked up the sack and tried to move past her. She grabbed his arm, which he shook off. He took a deep breath, hating himself for what he was about to say next. 'I'll arrest you and you can spend some time in the cells with your husband. You know how we interrogate women, don't you?'

Tears began to roll down her cheeks at the threat of rape. She let her hands fall to her sides. Petrus turned away, attempting to push aside the feeling of shame.

He thrust the sack at Flavius mumbling, 'Carry this,' and

ushered the woman out of the door.

'When will he be back?' she asked, her voice quiet.

'When we've finished with him.'

As they left the house, he saw Flaccus standing with the crowd that had gathered outside. He beckoned to the young man.

'Walk with me,' Petrus said.

Flaccus did as he was told and began walking alongside Petrus.

'Where does Lucullus store his grain?' Petrus asked.

'He's got a couple of buildings on the edge of the vicus. Pays some locals to guard them. One of my jobs is to regularly check there's been no thefts from them. They're guarded day and night, as he's always worried about fire.'

'Have you ever found any grain or anything missing?'

'No, never. It's an easy job counting grain sacks, apart from the rats, that is. They're everywhere.'

'Could there be another store? One you've never been to?'

Flaccus shook his head. 'No. And why would he need another..? Oh, for the stolen grain. I swear Sir, he never told me.'

Petrus believed him. Lucullus wouldn't have trusted the young man with anything important, he was too naive. They walked on in silence for a while as Petrus tried to think of more questions to ask Flaccus. Rain began to pour ice-cold water onto them and by the time they reached the fort they were drenched.

At the fort gate he said, 'You can leave now, Flaccus. I'll be sure to get a message to you to come and collect your belongings, or I may send one of these men here to bring them back to you.'

Flaccus looked relieved as he pulled his cloak tighter around his shoulders and strode away. Petrus whispered the password in the ear of the guard and the gates swung open.

At his office, Petrus took off his cloak and used it to wipe his face and hair, then he hung it on a hook on the door where it dripped steadily onto the floor. He waved his arms back and forth a few times to try to warm himself, and then sat down. His wet clothes clung to his skin, sucking out the warmth from his body. He emptied the sack of Lucullus' tablets onto the table. He arranged them in date order, took the oldest one and began to read.

He was soon immersed in Lucullus' life. The tablets were not just a record of his business, but also contained details of his private life. *Argued with Hersilia again today, she wants to spend more money on fine clothes for the children. I explained it was a waste as they'd grow out of them so quickly and need more, but she moaned on and on. I relented in the case of Theophilia. She's of marriageable age now and we need her to look the part so that we can get a good match. But not the boys. They can make do with cheaper clothes.*

Outside his office, he heard Flavius talking in low tones to someone. He quickly scribbled some orders and opened the door. 'Flavius! Go to my rooms and tell Gauori to bring me a pitcher of wine.'

Flavius set off at a trot towards the barracks. Petrus resumed his seat. He picked up some more tablets. He saw that on the days that the thefts occurred, Lucullus had written *diverted to store* and the amount of grain stolen. However, Petrus could not find any details of where this store of diverted food was kept.

He paused when there was a knock at the door and Gauori entered with a pitcher of wine and a clean cup. Grinning, the slave poured the wine and scooped up the older cups, which had dried with sticky stains. Petrus continued to read the tablets, smiling occasionally at the trivial conversations that had been recorded.

Suddenly, he saw it. Dated seven weeks previously, *Adrianus came to the office this morning. That bastard Manius has found some errors in the delivery records. My deliveries. If he informs the Prefect, we're done for.*

Then two days later, *Saw Manius leaving the tavern tonight. We had words, in a dark alleyway. I thought he was going to shit himself. I don't think he'll cause any more problems.* There it was, in Lucullus' own records! Petrus felt a rush of excitement as he continued reading.

Two weeks previously, Lucullus had written that he had visited Coria where he traded with other merchants, exchanging hides for barley corn. It had taken him four days to reach Coria, as he'd gone via several farms. He'd spent three days in Coria itself and then returned to Banna. He'd got back five days before Petrus had visited him. Damn him! If these were true records, then he was away when Manius went missing.

Petrus sighed and opened the sack of Flaccus' tablets. Flaccus had recorded even the smallest interactions with people concerning the business along with his own comments and thoughts. *I can't believe it! Lucullus is going to take me with him to Coria! I'll watch him negotiate. I have so much to learn. We'll be staying away.* The dates of his entries matched Lucullus' notes. *Lucullus took me to visit the brothel! What an experience! One I may repeat when we return to Banna. Dated fourteen days ago, We've driven hard bargains in Coria and Lucullus is really pleased. We are to return to Banna and will be home the day after tomorrow.* He detailed plans to return to some of the villages a couple of days after they got back to Banna.

Petrus grabbed an empty tablet and scribbled the details of the dates of the trips and the house where they'd stayed in Coria. He then wrote his report, stating that Adrianus and Lucullus had come up with a plan to defraud the army. When Manius discovered their crime, Lucullus had threatened him. Adrianus had not left the fort for more than five weeks, so could not have killed him. The records of Lucullus and Flaccus indicated that they were away at the time of the murder, although Lucullus could have paid someone else to do it. His two suspects seemed to be in the clear. If necessary, he could send someone to check in Coria at the house where they'd stayed, and the brothel. He locked the summaries and report in his chest. His initial excitement had faded and been replaced by disappointment.

He scooped the tablets into a sack and left the room. He

crossed the fort to the infirmary and approached Arsenios' room. The door was open. Arsenios was studying something beneath the glass bowl. He put it down as he heard Petrus approach.

'Cast your eye over these. Check for forgeries, would you? Let me know if you find anything. Keep the tablets safe. They're evidence.' Petrus emptied the sack on to the table.

He did not notice how Arsenios' eyes widened when he saw how many there were.

Petrus pushed open the door to his rooms as Gauori scrambled to his feet and began reaching for the meal he'd prepared.

'Where are the roots I gave you earlier? And the boiled liquid?' asked Petrus between mouthfuls of food.

'Here, Sir,' Gauori pushed towards him a plate containing the drying roots, and a bowl of brown liquid across the table.

Petrus bent forward; the dark liquor smelled of earth. 'It's a sleeping draught Gauori. Something like this was given to Manius to make him easier to control.' He sat up straight and looked directly at his slave. 'I need to know how it affects a man. I want you to drink it.' He pushed the bowl back towards Gauori.

Gauori's eyes filled with tears and his lips moved, but he made no sound.

'Go on. Drink.' Petrus kept his voice low.

Gauori whispered, 'What have I done wrong, Sir? I don't want to die.'

Petrus rose from his seat and placed a hand on Gauori's arm. He hated doing this, but he had to know what the roots' effects were. 'I wouldn't harm you. I've been assured it just sends you to sleep.' He lifted the bowl up towards the slave's lips. 'Drink.'

Gauori took the bowl with shaking hands. He closed his eyes and began to gulp it down.

'Go on, all of it,' urged Petrus, tipping up the edge of the bowl.

Gauori took a huge gulp, put the empty bowl down, and frowned.

'Sit down,' Petrus guided him on to a stool. 'Eat this while we wait.' He gave him a hunk of bread.

Petrus continued eating his meal. Gauori chewed slowly, with his eyes downcast, tears still running down his cheeks. Petrus poured some wine and pushed a cup towards him. He waited.

Gauori took a couple of sips of wine, rubbed his belly, and rested his forearms on the table.

Petrus watched him.

Gauori's eyelids closed, and he jerked his head up, forcing his eyes wide. He took some deep breaths as his eyelids drooped and his shoulders sagged. Petrus rose from his seat. He felt guilty at forcing his slave to drink the liquid, but he'd needed to understand whether Manius could have been subdued in that way. He put an arm around Gauori's waist and lifted him to his feet. The slave moaned and leant his head against Petrus' shoulder, dribbling on his tunic. Petrus guided him to his mattress and laid him down.

Gauori took deep slow breaths and mumbled, 'Don't let me die, Sir. Don't let me.'

'I won't let you die.' Petrus placed a hand on the slave's shoulder.

Petrus watched him for a few moments and then began clearing the table. He banged pots and pans and grumbled to himself, taking quick glances at the sleeping man. Gauori didn't stir. Petrus scooped some water from the pitcher, dipped his fingers into it, and flicked droplets onto Gauori's face. There was no reaction. Satisfied that he was deeply asleep, Petrus moved into his own room and laid down on the bed.

XV

Gauori was still asleep when Petrus readied himself for parade. He bent down and shook the slave hard. His head wobbled from side to side, but he did not wake up.

After parade, Petrus sent for Balbus.

'Sir, I...' he began.

'Have you found any further errors in the work?' asked Petrus.

'No, Sir. I have checked many, many records and found nothing.'

'Very well then. You should now start work as a proper Librarius. Gratianus can tell you what the duties involve. Tell him it's under my orders and that of the Prefect.'

'Really? And what about my bodyguards?' gasped Balbus.

'We'll leave your bodyguards in place at present. I don't want you in danger. You may need to be a witness at the trial. Just start the normal Librarius' work. Come and see me later if you have any difficulties.'

Petrus dismissed him and made his way to Tatius' office. The other centurions turned towards him as he entered. They'd obviously finished their reports. Petrus felt himself shrink slightly under their gaze. He waited, but Tatius did not dismiss the other men. He opened his mouth to speak just as the door crashed open, raining splinters of wood onto the floor.

'Get out!' screamed Augustus Pollux, the Tribune, as he stormed into the room. 'Not you, Petrus! Stay right where you are!' bellowed Pollux as he flung himself onto a stool and leant forward, placing his fists on the table.

The other centurions saluted him and filed quickly out of the office.

'What a shit shower you've got here, Tatius! What the fuck is going on?' spat Pollux.

Tatius opened his mouth, but no words emerged.

'Last year, one of your own centurions tried to kill you. Today, those idiots on the gate wouldn't let me in, even though I'm carrying the Tribune's insignia. Are those the two who kept falling asleep last year? Why are they still here? The disciplinary code is clear, or haven't you read it?'

'I, err, I was advised by Julius Maximus that it could be dealt with locally. And… and it has been, hasn't it Petrus? They're two of our best now, eh?'

Petrus nodded.

'You often followed Maximus' advice, Tatius. That turned out well, didn't it?'

'The gatekeepers are following procedure by not letting you in,' mumbled Tatius.

'Get me some wine before I smash your face in!' bellowed Pollux.

Tatius scrambled to his feet and walked to the door, where he spoke. 'Hey. Go to my house and get one of the slaves to bring some wine.'

They heard running footsteps as Tatius pushed the door closed and sat back in his seat, not raising his head to look at Pollux.

'What's happening about the murder?'

Tatius pointed at Petrus. 'He was just about to update me.'

Petrus took a deep breath and watched Pollux closely as he spoke, 'The killer or killers has dark hair, they forced Manius to drink a sleeping draft and then took him to the Mithraeum where he died of lack of water. Prior to this murder, not many people knew of the location of the temple, which means it had to be a senior officer, of centurion rank, or above. According…'

Tatius interrupted, 'Above centurion rank, are you suggesting a Prefect, or even a Tribune?' he glanced at Pollux as he said this.

'Don't interrupt, you idiot! It's a fact, only centurions or more senior men would've known about the temple. Carry on, Petrus,' snapped Pollux.

Tatius' face reddened, and he looked down at his lap.

Petrus continued, 'According to my inquiries, Manius visited the tavern occasionally, where he would drink to excess. He did not have gambling or other debts. At the beginning, I couldn't really find anyone in the vicus with a grudge against him. Apart from the retired centurion Lucullus who resented having his orders of grain cut, and another retired centurion called Cato who blames all the librarii for his pension being inadequate. Years ago, Manius used to visit the brothel, but since he took up with a soldier's widow, he stopped going there.' He shrugged, 'Why pay for it when it's free at home, I guess. Whenever Manius left the fort to go to the tavern, he always took off his signet ring and left it in his chest. When his body was found, the signet ring was missing, and we later found it in Adrianus' room. He's another librarius.

'So, Manius originally intended to go to the tavern that day. But I don't think he did. I think he went straight to his woman's place. I've… we've, been able to prove that after Manius' body was found, Adrianus used the ring to forge records to make it look like Manius had been stealing from the army. It appears that Manius had found a discrepancy in the grain delivery records and started asking questions. All the thefts occurred when Lucullus made deliveries. Under interrogation, both Adrianus and Lucullus admit the thefts, but they deny murdering Manius, although Lucullus admits he threatened him. I have records to show that Adrianus didn't leave the fort during the period when Manius was missing, and Lucullus was out of the area.'

'But the records could've been forged,' murmured Tatius.

'The Physician is helping me check the records for forgeries. I'm confident neither man was involved in the murder.'

'How can the physician know which are forgeries and which are not?' Pollux didn't wait for a response. 'How long was

Manius missing before his body was found?'

'Around seven days,' replied Petrus.

'Seven days! What the fuck?'

'There'd been some sort of cover up going on amongst the librarii. They never reported each other being sick,' murmured Tatius.

'We'll get to that later. Carry on Petrus, what are you doing now about the murders?'

'I've got my informants out in the vicus. I'll see what they come up with.'

Pollux sighed, 'I want a result Petrus. And quickly!' Then he turned back to Tatius. 'You've lost control here. What's going on with the librarii? Why wasn't this theft found earlier? Isn't the Signifer checking inventories? Aren't you checking? It's your responsibility.'

'I, err, I do make checks. So does the Signifer.'

'How often?'

There was no response.

'Damn you Tatius! I can't, no, I won't protect you from this shambles when the Governor hears about it.'

Tatius' eyes grew wide, and he glanced at Petrus who moved towards the door.

'Don't move, Soldier!' bellowed Pollux.

Petrus paused.

'Take me to the physician. I want to see how he checks for forgeries. No! Tatius, don't move,' he bellowed, pointing at the Prefect who had begun to rise from his chair. 'You stay here and think about how to get this place in order. It's all on you!'

Tatius lowered himself back onto his seat and pulled some reports across the table. He did not look up.

Petrus collected two tablets from his office, a forgery and one with Manius' original signature.

In the infirmary, Arsenios had his arm around the young soldier Aquila who hobbled beside him, groaning. Petrus stared. Below the man's left knee was part of a tree trunk, thick as his leg at the top and then tapering down to a thin pole at the end. Arsenios had made the man a false limb! The leg was tied on with a leather harness and the tap-tap of wood on stone rang across the empty infirmary. Petrus coughed. Arsenios looked up and nodded in greeting. Aquila grimaced, removed his arm from Arsenios' shoulder, and saluted Petrus.

'This is Augustus Pollux, the Tribune,' began Petrus, searching Arsenios' face for signs of recognition. Arsenios was unmoved. 'He's come to see the tablets.'

Aquila began to tremble. Arsenios held him steady and gently guided him back to his bed as he waved a hand towards his workroom. Petrus led the way, with Pollux stamping along behind him.

Arsenios seated himself at the bench, and Petrus handed him the two tablets from his office. Arsenios gave Pollux Manius' original tablet. The winter sun sneaked in through the window and Arsenios' shadow hovered above Pollux's like a demon above its victim.

'This is a tablet we know was signed by Manius. Look at it through this glass.' He handed the glass to Pollux.

The water inside sloshed around and Pollux struggled to hold it steady as he placed it above the tablet. Pollux's hand trembled slightly as he peered at the writing. He whispered to himself, words Petrus couldn't quite hear, but he guessed the Tribune was praying. He'd gone pale.

'And?' Pollux whispered.

'Now look at this one, allegedly written by Manius, when he signed for goods delivered.' Arsenios held the tablet beneath the glass. 'Can you see here? It looks like the wax was remelted and the signature is slightly different. Manius' marks were consistent. I've checked a lot of his documents. This is a forgery.'

'Manius did not take charge of deliveries,' Petrus' voice made Pollux jump round in fright to face him. 'That wasn't his role as the most Senior Librarius.'

Arsenios was nodding. 'I've also been checking the tablets from Lucullus' study that Petrus gave me. They have not been altered in the way of re-melting the wax. Same goes for that lad Flaccus' tablets.'

'Follow me, Petrus!' bellowed Pollux and walked out of the room.

Petrus mouthed 'thank you' to the Physician and hurried after the Tribune. Pollux marched into Tatius' office and sat back on the stool facing Tatius who was writing something and sipping from a cup of wine. He put down his stylus and poured Pollux a drink, pushing it across the table towards him. Pollux swept his arm across the table, knocking the cup to the floor. It shattered, spraying wine across the wall and leaving fragments of clay in a sea of red near Petrus' feet.

'When did you find out about the thefts?' Pollux spoke through gritted teeth and didn't wait for a reply. 'Was it a couple of weeks ago? Or a couple of days? Either way, why didn't you report it?' He held up his hand. 'Don't you dare say it's because I was away collecting your bride.'

'I only found out a couple of days ago, when Petrus reported it,' Tatius was looking down as he spoke, but then raised his head defiantly to stare at the Tribune.

'Assuming I believe you, why didn't you tell me?' Pollux said.

Tatius didn't reply.

'Too busy planning your wedding, eh? Couldn't wait to get your end away with that new bit of flesh?' Pollux sneered.

Tatius looked down and did not respond.

Pollux sighed, 'We all have needs Tatius, you fool! You'd better get this matter sorted and quickly. I want an example made of Adrianus and Lucullus. People must see that theft cannot be tolerated. I'll be making a report to the Governor. It's a matter for him what happens to you.'

Pollux rose and moved to the door. 'Is there anything else, Petrus?'

Petrus shook his head.

'Walk with me, Petrus,' Pollux said as he left Tatius.

They headed for the gate.

'Not sure I believe Tatius about all this, are you?' Pollux kept his voice low.

Petrus shrugged awkwardly. Rufus and Pius scrambled down to the gate and pulled it open, saluting the Tribune.

'Keep me informed of progress. I want you to come to my house at least once every two days, if not daily. I want to know where your murder investigation is at. Suspect everyone,' he paused, 'even those at the highest level, like me.'

As Petrus watched Pollux walk away, he realised that Pollux suspected Tatius might be involved. He could have killed Manius to keep the thefts a secret while he covered them up, desperate to maintain his reputation. Dangerous thoughts! As he walked back towards his office, a group of soldiers passed him. He beckoned one of them over. The man went pale with worry as he approached and saluted.

'Hail, Centurion,' the man said.

Petrus returned the gesture. 'Go to my rooms and ask the slave to bring some wine to my office.' He frowned as the man didn't move. 'Well? Is that a problem, soldier?'

'No Sir, is that all?'

Petrus smiled, 'You're not in trouble lad. Not with me, anyway. If you've got a guilty conscience over something, then I suggest you own up to your superior officer right away, 'cos if he finds out later, you'll be in the shit, won't you? Go, now!' he waved a hand in the direction of the barracks.

Petrus collected the sack of tablets from the infirmary and then settled himself in his office. He began to try to organise his thoughts and make some notes. Perhaps Manius had told Tatius about the thefts of grain. Realising how serious this was and how it would look to the Governor, Tatius may have decided to get rid of Manius. If word ever reached Rome about his incompetence, it would damage his future prospects and he would never reach Senatorial status, or any other position of authority on his return to the Homeland. Petrus didn't think for a moment that Tatius would have dirtied his own hands with the murder. He could have hired someone to kill the man. There were probably plenty of men both inside and outside the fort who would have been happy to do this work for the Prefect in order to further their own ends. The use of the temple by any co-conspirators could just have been to cast suspicion on a wider group of people. Using this logic, the Signifer was also a suspect, as he was supposed to monitor the work done by the librarii. Petrus knew how dangerous these ideas were, as he locked the tablet in his chest and put the key in his pouch.

There was a loud knock at the door. Gauori staggered in, carrying a jug, a cup and a plate with a thick pile of almond nuts and honey on it. He moved slowly as he placed the items on the table and withdrew a spoon from inside his tunic. He lifted the jug and poured the wine; his hand shook as he lowered it to the table.

'I'm sorry, Sir. I'm still not properly awake yet. That sleeping thing you gave me was very strong,' he said.

'Yes, it was. Were you still asleep when the soldier came to my room?'

Gauori blushed and rubbed his side as he spoke. 'Err yes, I was. He woke me up with a few sharp kicks. I'm sorry, Sir.'

'It's my fault, Gauori. Don't apologise, you've done nothing wrong. I forced you to drink it. I felt I had no other option. Go back now and rest. Go on.' Petrus smiled, stood and shepherded Gauori from the room.

Petrus scooped a spoonful of honey into his mouth. The thick dessert coated his tongue and his mouth filled with saliva. He crunched the nuts and swallowed, washing it down with wine. He returned his attention to his investigation. He decided to re-interview everyone.

Ruga frowned as Petrus entered his office. He sighed, 'What now Petrus? What did Pollux want?'

Petrus shrugged. 'Just an update on the murder and thefts.' He was reluctant to be drawn into a discussion about the Tribune. Army politics were difficult to navigate at the best of times, and he didn't want to be associated with gossip.

He sat down opposite Ruga, placed a blank tablet on the table and took out a stylus. 'I just needed to check a few things with you. How often have you been outside the fort in the last three weeks?'

'Think I may've murdered Manius, do you? What would I have against him? He was never involved in docking my pay. The only time I've been out was a couple of times to visit the brothel. You can check the dates with the gatekeepers' records, and cross-check with Sylva if you don't believe me.'

'How long have you been a follower of Mithras?'

'I've already told you that, ever since I became a Centurion, just over ten years.'

Petrus sighed and made a couple of meaningless squiggles on his tablet.

Ruga grinned. 'You'll probably find the others say the same. What need does a centurion have to leave the fort, apart from to see women? Unless we're on a special investigation like you, eh? Got everything else we need right here. Well, pretty much everything else.'

Petrus waited.

'The gamblers, like Roburius, Vegetinus and Ferullus leave to go gambling. They like to risk larger amounts of money than are available amongst the soldiers here at the fort. Ask them.' Ruga said.

Petrus stood to leave. 'I already have. But I will speak to them again.'

'A moment, Petrus,' Ruga's voice made him turn.

'Tonight – at the temple. Time for your next ordeal.'

'Must I? I'm in the middle of this...' sighed Petrus.

'Yes, you must. Life moves on, even in the middle of this... thing.' Ruga waved his arm around.

Petrus trudged out of the office towards Aquilinus' room. It was empty.

'He's drilling his men,' murmured a soldier who was passing.

'Then go and get him,' said Petrus.

The man hesitated for a moment and then trotted away. Petrus entered the office, sat down on a stool, and tried to gather his thoughts.

'What now?!' Aquilinus bellowed as he threw himself onto his chair and glared at Petrus. 'Who do you think you are, summoning me?'

'I'm working on the Tribune's behalf.' Petrus leant his forearms on the table and bunched his fists. He felt a small sense of satisfaction as Aquilinus flinched and leant away from him.

'How can I help, Petrus?' Aquilinus' voice was barely audible. He had been in trouble with the Prefect some months previously when four of his men had raped some local women and been suspected of involvement in previous murders. He remained nervous of Petrus.

'How long have you been a follower of Mithras?'

'Since just after I became a centurion. Went through the same initiations as you will be doing, only without the body in the temple.' A brief smile passed his lips.

Petrus did not return his smile. 'How often have you left the fort in the last three weeks?' Petrus took out his tablet and sat with his stylus ready to write.

Aquilinus opened his mouth and then closed it again. He was still for a moment. 'I told you last time, I was at Sylva's place. With a whore called Troucissa and another one whose name I didn't ask. You can check that, if you'll take the word of a whore, that is. You should spend some time at the brothel yourself Petrus, might make you a bit less uptight.'

Petrus ignored the comment. 'Have you heard about Adrianus?'

Aquilinus looked directly at Petrus and spoke quickly. 'Before you begin, he's only notionally under my command. He reports to Ecdicius, the Signifer. I have very little to do with him.'

'You had no idea what he was doing, stealing grain?'

Aquilinus shook his head. He clasped his hands together in his lap. Petrus thought that was to stop them shaking.

'Why is it always my men?' Aquilinus murmured.

Petrus changed the subject, 'Are you aware of any centurions who gamble?'

'Roburius and his two friends, you mean? Everyone knows about them. Quite high stakes with some of the merchants, I heard.'

'Are they ever in debt? Do they get in fights?'

Aquilinus shrugged. 'Maybe.'

Silence settled between them.

Petrus sighed and got to his feet. 'I'll go and ask them.'

'Those three have gone to some of the milecastles to supervise reconstruction work. You can send for them, if you're prepared to wait. Or you can speak with them this evening,' He snorted, 'Oh no! You can't do that; you've got your next ordeal tonight. I'll see you there.'

Petrus left the office, slamming the door behind him.

He looked at the list of men who'd been outside the fort at the same time as Manius. Tatius had returned just before daylight the following day. Ecdicius was only out for a few hours. He was back before nightfall and passed through the gates at the same time as a local man whose name Petrus could not make out. He'd have to remind the gatekeepers to write more clearly. Petrus swore under his breath, knowing he would have to interview both the prefect and the signifer. They both had reason to kill Manius if he'd told them about the thefts of grain, and they wanted to protect themselves from the Tribune's wrath. He rubbed his face with his hands and suddenly felt tired.

He walked over to the Treasury. Ecdicius was busy looking at his records. He did not look up as Petrus entered the room.

'Signifer, I need to ask you some questions,' Petrus began.

Ecdicius frowned, 'Questions?'

'In relation to my murder investigation. Do you want these men present?' Petrus waved his hand in the direction of the soldiers guarding the vaults.

Ecdicius ordered the men to wait outside and closed the door behind them.

'Not going well, is it, your investigation? Can't be if you've come looking for me,' sneered Ecdicius.

Petrus felt himself redden, 'What do you know about the Mithraeum, the temple where Manius' body was found?'

'Prior to that event, nothing. I'd heard rumours of course, but not being a fighting man, I was never going to be part of that cult, was I? Now, I know as much as everyone else, where it is, and I can take a guess at who worships there. You, for one.'

'Perhaps you could explain what you were doing when you left the fort on Manius' last day, err, just over two weeks ago. On the date of...' He glanced down at his tablet.

'There's no need to tell me the date. I can tell you where I went. I only leave the fort to see my companion in the vicus. You're not the only one with people outside, you know.'

Petrus nodded, 'Of course not. What's her name? Where can I find her?'

Ecdicius did not reply.

'I need to verify your whereabouts.'

'Am I a suspect? Really? What reason would I have to kill Manius?'

'He found out that one of your librarii was working with a merchant to steal from the army. You would've wanted that to be kept quiet, so that you didn't lose your job.'

'Stealing? I don't know anything about any thefts. What thefts?' Ecdicius got to his feet and stepped towards the door.

Petrus moved to block his exit.

'Get out of my way! I'm going to the Librarium right now to talk to them!' barked Ecdicius.

Petrus put a hand on his chest and pushed him backwards. Ecdicius rocked on his heels and clenched his fists.

'I wouldn't do that if I were you. Striking a centurion would be bad enough, but one who's investigating a murder that you could be implicated in, that would be much worse. Sure sign of guilt, I'd say. Sit back down!' Petrus snarled and pushed him again.

Ecdicius slid back onto his chair and glared at Petrus.

'Do you make regular checks on the librarii's work?'

Ecdicius turned his head away and did not reply.

'It's part of your duties as Signifer, isn't it?'

Petrus waited.

'And the Prefect is also supposed to check occasionally, isn't he?' Petrus leant towards the Signifer, resting his bunched fists on the table.

Ecdicius stared straight ahead in silence.

'So you don't do it regularly. When did you last make checks?'

Ecdicius shrugged.

'You lazy, incompetent piece of shit! Sitting there lording it over the rest of us as you count out our salaries.' He paused. 'Manius discovered that Adrianus has been working with Lucullus to steal grain. Did you know what they were doing? Did Manius tell you about his suspicions?'

Ecdicius shook his head.

'I don't believe you. Manius was a diligent librarius and stuck to the rules. Did you kill him to stop him from informing the Prefect and the Tribune?'

The Signifer went pale, 'No! Of course I didn't!'

Petrus wasn't sure he believed him. 'It would've been easy to overpower Manius. He wasn't a big man. Are you a murderer as well as incompetent?'

Ecdicius' eyes were wide in fear. He spoke in a barely audible voice, 'I didn't kill him. I left the fort and went straight home. Then we came back here for the night.'

Petrus noted he used the word home, so he must love the woman. He spoke in a low growl, 'Then give me her name and whereabouts, so that I can check!'

Ecdicius looked up at him and murmured, 'His name is Andecarus. He has a room near Aledus the carpenter. We came back here. I go to the vicus to collect him and bring him back here. That's what we always do, go to my rooms. I try not to get noticed.'

He'd been discrete. Petrus had not heard any gossip about the Signifer. He took a deep breath and spoke in low tones. 'I had no idea. There is no shame in being with a man. I must go to the vicus to check your story with him. You understand that, don't you?'

Ecdicius nodded.

'Did you see anyone else when you were in the vicus? Any of the centurions, or the Prefect?'

'The Prefect was walking ahead of me as I left the fort. Brothel-bound I should imagine.'

'Keep the information about the thefts to yourself.' Petrus raised a hand as Ecdicius opened his mouth to protest. 'The Prefect and Tribune are already aware. I have their authority.'

The Signifer nodded and turned away. Petrus returned to his office, collected the tablet with the gate records for Manius' last day and strode towards the gate.

'Rufus, Pius, listen to me,' he snapped as they held the gate open for him.

The two men froze, their eyes wide in alarm.

Petrus sighed. 'I've been looking at some of your records and your writing is difficult to read sometimes.'

He pointed to the name below Ecdicius' on the tablet. 'What does that say?'

Rufus screwed his eyes up and peered at the scratching on the wax. 'Err, Ande. Ande.'

'Pius? Any idea?' Petrus asked.

Pius shook his head.

'This is an important piece of evidence for my investigation, and we can't read it, can we? Fortunately for you, I've found out what it says. Another time, we may not be so lucky. Consider this a warning. I'll record it in my notes.'

The two men nodded. Petrus brushed past them and walked through the gate.

A steady drizzle soaked into his clothes, washing over his skin. He turned off the main street and approached a shop with a carpenter's sign outside. The door was open. An elderly grey-haired man was working with a piece of wood. He caressed it with his fingertips as he slid a metal tool across the surface, removing a thin sliver of wood.

'What can I do for you, Centurion?' his voice was barely a whisper.

'I'm looking for a man called Andecarus. I've been told he lives near here.'

'Ah, the soldier's boy? Yes. I rent him the place next door, or rather I rent it to the Roman. What do you want with him? Not in trouble, is he?'

'No, he's not in trouble. I just wanted to ask him about the Roman soldier. Is he round here often, the Roman, I mean?'

'Depends what you mean by often, I suppose. A couple of times a month, I reckon.' He inclined his head towards the neighbouring building. 'The boy never smells of drink. Polite enough, to me that is, but then, of course, I'm the landlord, so he would be.'

'When was the soldier last here?'

'About three weeks ago.'

'Is Andecarus there now?'

'He's always there these days. He works occasionally for me, but he doesn't need the money. He's a weaver too, I think, so could have his own income. That soldier keeps him well enough and often takes him back to the fort.'

'Thank you.' Petrus reached into his pouch for a coin.

The old man shook his head. 'Keep your money. I don't work for the army. Go well, Centurion.'

The walls to the neighbouring building looked freshly painted. Petrus knocked on the door. A tall young man opened it. A mass of dark hair framed a handsome face, with large brown eyes and long eyelashes. He was broad shouldered; his arm and chest muscles strained against his smock. Petrus could see why some men might find him attractive.

'Yes?' the man asked, looking up and down the street as he spoke.

'Andecarus?' Petrus asked.

The man nodded.

'I'm investigating the murder of an army officer. I need to talk to you about Ecdicius. Let me in.'

Andecarus stepped back, allowing Petrus to enter. The room contained only a stool, and a loom laden with dark blue wool whose thick animal smell tickled Petrus' nostrils. Dust danced in the light of the open windows as the man led Petrus through into the kitchen and pointed to a stool. Petrus shook his head and moved to stand near the door. Crockery was stacked against one wall, a piece of dried meat hung on a hook near the fire. The room was clean, and a brush lay next to the gently crackling fire. Andecarus sank onto a stool and held his hands near the flames to warm them.

'Ecdicius looks after you, doesn't he?' Petrus began.

Andecarus nodded.

'How long has he been doing that?'

'Months, well, a couple of years,' mumbled Andecarus.

Petrus raised an eyebrow. 'Does he come round here often? Do you know in advance when he's coming?'

He shrugged, 'Often enough and no, I never know when he will arrive.'

'What if you weren't at home when he came?'

'Ecdicius knows where to look for me.'

'Where might that be? The tavern? The brothel?'

Andecarus sighed, 'I don't have to work at the brothel! I have enough to live on, from what Ecdicius gives me. I can earn more with my weaving, as you saw in the next room, and I can also work for Aledus. I don't go to the tavern. That might cause an upset.'

'What sort of upset?'

'Just like you did, some men assume I'm from the brothel. Not everyone is as accepting of two men as the Romans are.'

'Where did you first meet?'

'What has this to do with your investigation?'

'Maybe nothing,' Petrus snapped and decided to take a risk. 'Who was your Master when you were a slave?'

Andecarus reddened and tears came into his eyes. 'His name was Caesonius Decimus, formerly a centurion of the Roman Army. My mother was in his household. I was freed when he died.'

Petrus felt ashamed. He'd been bullying the man.

'Does he stay the night when he visits you?' Petrus tried to make his voice softer.

'No. We usually spend some time here and then go to his rooms at the fort. You can check that with your gatekeepers.' Andecarus' voice was barely above a whisper.

'And what do you do at the fort?'

'I help him keep the place clean and we... we spend time together.'

'When was he last here?'

'About three weeks ago. It was no different to usual.'

'Did he seem agitated at all, or different in any way?'

'No. He was just his usual self.'

'Did he say if anything was bothering him at the fort?'

'No.'

Petrus felt ashamed of his own behaviour, taking out his frustrations with Ecdicius on the Signifer's companion. He left the building. As he made his way back to the fort, he noted the ivy tied to the boot scraper at his home.

Petrus pushed his plate aside; his stomach was full. He took a long gulp of wine and wiped his hand across his face. Gauori was beaming as he finished his own meal. He seemed to have made a full recovery from the sleeping drug. Petrus pushed himself to his feet, grabbed his cloak and a lit torch, and stepped into the darkness. He gasped as the icy air entered his lungs. His cheeks tingled as the warmth was dragged from his skin. The dank smell of decay hung in the street and his feet scuffed against rubbish dropped by the soldiers. He reminded himself to get a squad of men to clean up the streets.

As the fort gate closed behind him, worry began to creep into his mind. He had no idea what the second ordeal at the Mithraeum would be. He hurried through the vicus. Smoke snaked into the darkness from the forge, then belched dust into the weak moonlight as someone used the bellows. Carantii was still at work. Petrus rattled the door.

'Open up you drunken sod,' he whispered.

Metal grated on metal, and the door swung open a crack. Petrus squeezed inside. Carantii grinned at him in the shimmering candlelight.

'Had an interesting time in the forest yesterday. I bet on a couple of fights – one of them between two women. That was vicious, that was. Cato was there and so were three centurions. One of their names is Vegetinus. I didn't get the other two. They all lost money, on both fights, from what I could tell. They weren't very happy and attacked the organiser and his betting man. It ended up with loads of men scrapping. I didn't stay around to see what the outcome was, but I'm told your three centurions have lost a lot of money recently and on dog fights as well. Cato is in debt to lots of people for gambling and he works off some of his debts by squeezing other people.'

'Squeezing other people?'

'Merchants who are owed money pay Cato to beat their debtors up. They soon pay once Cato has got a bit physical with them.'

'Do you know the names of these merchants?'

'Analeugus and Netacius were mentioned.'

'Do you think they'd give evidence if it comes to it?'

Carantii shrugged.

'This is good work, very useful information. See if you can find any other names. Did you lose some money on the fights?' Petrus opened his pouch and took out some quinarii and a denarius. 'Don't forget those other matters I asked you, will you? Aquilinus and the Prefect at the brothel I mean.'

Carantii shook his head as he gathered the coins and put them in his pocket. 'I'll see what I can do.'

'The Signifer Ecdicius has a man in the vicus called...'

'Andecarus. Works for the carpenter Aledus and lives in one of his rooms. Ecdicius visits there a lot. What of it?'

'Nothing, you've just confirmed it for me. So, it's common knowledge here in the vicus?'

'You Romans can't keep your families secret, you know?' grinned Carantii.

'I do now,' murmured Petrus, somewhat surprised.

Petrus slipped out of the door and heard it being locked behind him. He hurried through the dark streets.

He left the road and headed up the hillside. Dancing tongues of distant light guided him towards the temple. The worshippers stood in a row, barring his way, not allowing him to enter. The men were wearing the same helmets, but the veils of skin were tucked away, revealing their faces in the flickering light. He was not surprised to see all the fort's centurions and the Prefect. He turned as a man stepped behind him. It was Ruga. Petrus caught his breath.

'Take off your clothes. All of them,' Ruga's voice was harsh.

Petrus groaned inwardly and began to undress, shivering as the cold air bit into his flesh. He handed his clothes to Aquilinus. He took off his underwear and boots and stood naked in front of the men. Ruga stepped forward and placed a piece of cloth around Petrus' head, covering his eyes. Petrus felt fear rush through his body. His heart pounded in his chest and he clenched his fists.

'Steady,' murmured Ruga in his ear and then began pushing him forward.

Petrus stumbled, raising his hands and groping the air ahead of him. A hand prodded the base of his back, driving him on. He stepped slowly, placing each foot carefully, as the cold earth's sharp stones scratched at his feet, bruising the flesh. Icy water sucked at his toes as he entered the small spring. Another step and his feet sank into mud, a brief warm embrace before cold water flowed over them.

'Kneel down,' Ruga said.

Petrus lowered himself to the ground, plunging his hand into the water to steady himself against the spring's stony bottom. He winced as the rough pebbles poked into his knees and feet. He pushed himself upright, his arms by his sides and tried to control his breathing. He waited.

He started to shiver. Chants rose through the air, the deep voices rising and falling in rhythm as the other men moved around him. He waited.

Suddenly, men were splashing in the stream; ice-cold water was hitting him from all sides, cascading over his head and shoulders. He groaned as he fought to remain upright and keep his hands at his sides. Cold seeped into his body; his teeth began to chatter uncontrollably and pain shot through his jaw. He struggled to keep his mouth still, but his teeth chattered on. His hands went numb. He couldn't feel his knees. The chanting grew louder as the water continued to assault him.

The water stopped. The chanting ceased. He raised his arms and clasped them around his trembling body. Hands lifted him to his feet and guided him, stumbling across the earth. He couldn't feel the ground beneath him. They dragged him down the steps and into the Mithraeum, forcing him to his knees again. The cloth was ripped from his eyes. In the gloom, he could make out the men, their faces now covered. One stepped forward and drew a sword. Petrus felt his guts clench but could not raise his arms to defend himself.

The man touched the flat blade of the sword on each of Petrus' shoulders; then placed the tip against his chest and said, 'You have been cleansed in the holy spring and you have now passed the second initiation. You are now a nymphus, a bridegroom. Rise, rise.'

Petrus had recognised the man's voice, but his numbed mind could not summon his name. He was hauled to his feet. Hands vigorously rubbed rough cloths against his arms and body, drying his skin. Someone ruffled his dripping hair, then massaged his scalp. Inside Petrus' head, he screamed. Dull pain caressed his muscles as the feeling began to return. He flexed his fingers and hissed.

'Get dressed. Wear this beneath your tunic and sleep in it tonight,' The man thrust a short smock of fine cloth into his hands.

Petrus pulled the smock over his head and fumbled with his clothes. His fingers throbbed as he felt them return to life. The smock inside his tunic caressed his skin as he moved, warming his body. He struggled to pull on his boots and stood up straight.

The chanting began, the men's voices rising and falling in the slow rhythm. He was handed a lit torch and then guided to the door. He put his free hand out to touch the worn stone steps as he moved slowly into the night.

'Go now, brother. Rest in your smock. Keep it safe as a sign of belonging.' Petrus knew the voice now. It was Aquilinus.

He felt weak as he picked his way carefully down the sloping ground and onto the road. His limbs were stiff and heavy as he trudged through the darkness and into the vicus' empty streets. The noise from the tavern reached towards him across the darkness as he passed.

He waved Gauori away as he entered his rooms. He pulled off his boots and collapsed into bed, fully clothed. His last thought as he fell asleep was how much he hated the Mithraeum.

XVI

Petrus woke bathed in sweat. The thin Mithraeum smock clung to him in a hot embrace. His muscles ached from the previous night's cold, and every movement roused the dull pain that had spread through his body. He swore and undressed, folded the smock neatly and placed it in his chest.

Petrus noticed Felix lurking near the administrative buildings as he made his way across the fort. The winter sun forced its way through the thin clouds and kissed the translucent ice covering the parade ground, melting it into a slippery sheet. Adrianus stood between two soldiers in front of the whole fort, gripped by two soldiers who held him upright. His face was a mess of swollen bruises and thick lips. Lucullus stood erect beside two more men. Ecdicius and the librarii had been told to stand alongside them. The watching soldiers stared at them in silence.

Tatius took a step forward. The Tribune grabbed his arm and pushed him aside.

Pollux said, 'Aurelius Petrus' investigation has uncovered Adrianus' abuse of his position as a Librarius. He has been working with Lucullus to steal from the army. Both men have confessed to these crimes. The murdered man, Manius, had discovered the thefts. Lucullus, the disgraced former centurion, will be ostracised and stripped of his pension. His business will be sold to Aurelius Tatius Felix, a true and faithful Roman citizen.

'Adrianus forged records to make it look as if Manius was the thief. When these forgeries were discovered, he forced a small boy to set fire to the Librarium, putting the whole fort at risk. He has admitted his crimes and will face the death penalty.'

Adrianus cried out and began struggling against the two soldiers holding him. They dragged him forward and threw him on the ground in front of Pollux. Aquilinus bellowed orders and six of his men raced forward, carrying hastiles. They began beating Adrianus. He screamed and curled himself into a ball, his arms raised in a vain effort to protect his head. The frantic slap of wood on flesh merged with the crack of bones. Petrus felt his guts clench.

Adrianus' whimpers and groans spread across the parade ground as the beating continued. The spectators were frozen in place.

A hollow crack landed against Adrianus' skull.

He fell silent.

The men continued to strike his motionless body. Their quick breaths were a white mist in the cold air.

'Enough!' cried Pollux.

The soldiers stepped back. Their clothes, hands, and faces were spattered with blood. The metallic tang of butchery surrounded them. Arsenios stepped forward and rolled Adrianus onto his back. He placed a hand flat on his chest and then held his fingers below Adrianus' broken nose. He wiped his hand on his trousers, smearing the man's life across the cloth.

Arsenios did not look at Pollux as he said, 'He's dead.'

Petrus felt a huge blackness descend on him. He was unable to move. All the soldiers stood in stunned silence. Tatius' lips were moving, but he made no sound. The men wearing Adrianus' blood on their clothes lifted the dead man up and dragged him like an animal towards the infirmary. Ecdicius was pale and shaking as he turned aside and vomited. The silence was broken and the men around Ecdicius jeered; two stepped forward and guided him away towards the Treasury. Lucullus was on his knees, snivelling.

'Banish him!' Pollux instructed the soldiers as he pointed at Lucullus.

Pollux walked away. Behind him, two soldiers forced Lucullus towards the fort gate. Tatius stepped forward and raised a shaking hand. The men fell silent.

Tatius cleared his throat and fought to control his voice. 'A child living in the barracks was forced by Adrianus to set fire to the Librarium. All women and children are to leave the barracks immediately. I want everyone gone by the end of the day. You can send them home to the countryside or find them places to stay in the vicus. I don't care. This is for their own protection and the security of the fort. If you wish to be released from duty today to sort out their arrangements, then speak with your officers.'

A murmur of discontent rippled through the men. Tatius raised his hand to silence them.

'Any family found inside the fort from tomorrow will be treated as Roman army property!'

Petrus raised his eyebrows. Tatius was threatening them with enslavement!

Lucullus wept as he was dragged towards the fort gate. 'Can I at least say goodbye to my wife?'

The soldiers ignored him as they tied his hands together and handed the rope to a mounted soldier who set off with Lucullus staggering along behind him.

Felix appeared beside Petrus. 'Would you come with me to Lucullus' place? I'm to take control of the house and the business.'

Petrus nodded. He ordered four men to accompany them.

'We may need them if his wife puts up a fight,' Felix mumbled, clearly relieved.

They walked through the vicus which was alive with people. Men stood in groups with their heads bent, deep in conversation. As the soldiers approached them, they stepped back, fear in their eyes. News of the death, the banishment and the clearing of families from the fort had spread quickly. A restless crowd had gathered near Lucullus' house. One of the soldiers pushed them aside to clear a path to the door.

Petrus told three of the soldiers to stand guard at the gate. The door opened before he had raised his hand to knock. The skeletally thin slave led them through the house to the atrium. Lucullus' wife entered the room, her chestnut hair straggled over her face and shoulders. Her robe was smeared with dirt and a thin odour of sweat and dust hung around her. She put a hand to her face and pushed the hair from her eyes, leaving a smear of dust across her forehead.

She whispered, 'Aurelius Petrus. I'm, I'm…' she lowered herself to a couch and looked up at him, her lips trembling. She clasped her hands together and held them in her lap.

'You're Hersilia, aren't you?' He tried to sound gentle.

'Yes, yes, I am.'

'Have you heard about your husband?'

She nodded.

'He admitted stealing from the army and has been ostracised. His business and this home will be taken over by the army and sold to this man here. He will continue to support Macro's widow.'

'And what of me, and my children? What are we to do? Where are we to go?' Tears trickled from her eyes, forming black streaks down her cheeks as her make-up ran. 'My daughter, Theophilia ,is ready for marriage.' Her voice faded.

Petrus did not respond.

Felix stepped forward. 'If I may?' he paused briefly, and then continued, 'My wife Achai is now the lady of this house. You are welcome to stay here, as an employee,' he stressed the last three words. 'You can help with the running of the house and assist once our baby is born. My wife may also need instruction, in, in the ways of a lady. It's up to you. If you want to stay, I'll find a room for you and your children near the slaves' area. You'll all be fed and sheltered there, and I'll give you a small wage. Your children will be expected to work as well, for their keep.'

She let out a loud sob, nodded her head and mumbled, 'I'll

gather our things.'

Felix's voice was harsh. 'Be careful what you gather, lady! Everything in this house is now mine.'

'I… I only meant my clothes and, and the children's…' her voice trailed off.

'Get the things you want to keep and take them to your chamber. I shall come there when the sun reaches its highest point, and I'll decide what you can keep.' He made a shooing motion with his hands, dismissing her.

The woman rose from her chair and ran from the room.

'Harsh that, Felix. Some of the belongings are probably her dowry,' murmured Petrus.

The former slave nodded and sighed, 'And the dowry is the possession of the groom unless he divorces his wife, so those are now my things. I had to make my mark, assert my authority. Meeting her in her chamber is also shaming for her, I know that. I expect I'll go easier on her as time goes on and she may become a kind of friend to my wife. She has a lot of adjusting to do. They both do, Achai and her. Achai will be moving in here this afternoon. Thank you for accompanying me Petrus. Fortunately, there was no unpleasantness. Now, if you'll excuse me, I have a stock-take to organise. And I'll see if I can find this missing grain.'

'Stay well, Felix.'

'Go well.'

Petrus made his way through the vicus, followed by a gaggle of small children, excited by all the activity involving soldiers. He arrived at Pollux's property and was beckoned through the gate by the ever-watchful slave. The yard had been swept and smelled of fresh earth. He slipped between the gleaming, white statues and knocked on the thick, oak door.

'You know where you're going now, don't you, Sir?' the slave said as he let him in.

Petrus nodded and made his way to the atrium, where he stood and waited.

'Petrus! What do you want?' Pollux strode towards him.

'You asked for regular reports Sir, and I need your help.'

'Help, eh? Well, let's hear your report and then I'll see about helping you.'

'I've learned that three centurions from the fort; Vegetinus, Roburius and Ferullus are heavy gamblers and have lost a lot of money betting on men fighting and also on dog fights. When they lose, they often get violent to try to get their money back. They were also present a few years ago when that retiree Macro was killed in a brawl over money in the tavern. There were rumours in the community that the three men had been involved in his death. Centurion Julius Maximus investigated, and they were exonerated. However, as you know, Maximus was corrupt, so there may have been more to it than he reported,' he sighed. 'We'll never know, but it does raise some questions about their conduct. I don't know if they're in debt. I can check with the Signifer what their balances are, but they may be in need of money. That could mean they blamed Manius for some reason, if he docked their pay. It would've taken just one of them to subdue Manius. The retired centurion Cato is heavily in debt and hires himself out as muscle to recover money owed to merchants in the vicus. He could've been hired to kill Manius, as could any one of the three centurions.

'I'm still waiting for confirmation that Aquilinus was at the brothel. Ecdicius, the Signifer, was outside the fort for a while at the same time as Manius. He was reluctant at first to explain what he was doing. Seems he has a man called Andecarus in the community. The man works for a carpenter called Aledus who rents him a room. That is the only reason Ecdicius says he ever leaves the fort, which he does quite frequently. I've spoken with his boyfriend. The two of them were back in the fort before nightfall the day Manius left. The gatekeepers records confirm this. I think he was ashamed to admit it, but...'

'No shame there,' interrupted Pollux, 'Even Emperors have boyfriends. And it's no different to the men who bring their women back, is it?'

Petrus nodded and then continued, 'If Manius informed the Signifer about the thefts, then he might have had a reason to kill Manius, to cover that up. Ecdicius claims he didn't know anything about it, but I'm not sure I believe him. He may have wanted to try to sort it out quietly before anyone senior found out.'

'The same motive applies to the Prefect, and he was also outside the fort during the time that Manius disappeared.' Petrus' voice was barely a whisper. It was dangerous to suggest the fort commander might be a criminal.

Pollux grimaced, 'It's all if's and maybe's. Why didn't you look at the centurions and Prefect at the start, if they were outside the fort?'

'I... I thought I could discount the senior officers.'

Pollux grunted, 'You of all people should've learned that not all senior officers can be trusted. What do you want from me?'

Petrus looked down at his boots. 'I need to ask the Prefect some questions about when he became aware of the thefts of the grain. I also want to know more about what he was doing outside the fort when Manius went missing.'

The Tribune nodded, a smile forming on his lips. 'He's already said he found out about the thefts when your man Balbus discovered them. But you don't believe him, do you?'

Petrus remained silent.

'Neither do I. The execution this morning will have rattled him. I think he thought I was going to let Adrianus off with dismissal from the army. He's more likely to tell the truth today.'

Petrus didn't feel it was safe to make a comment about Tatius

'I don't feel I can ask him those questions. He's my senior officer.'

'You want me to question him?'

Petrus nodded.

'And would you want to listen in?'

Petrus reddened and shuffled his feet. 'I… yes, but I wouldn't want him to know I'd asked you to interrogate him.'

'Interrogation? Are you suggesting I rough him up a bit?'

'Not at all, Sir. Just ask him some questions. When did he find out about the thefts? Was Ecdicius aware? If he did know about them before Balbus informed me, what did he propose to do? Did he challenge Adrianus, or Lucullus? What was he doing outside the fort when Manius went missing? He mentioned being at the brothel and the temple. The records show he was gone until shortly before daybreak. How could he have spent that much time in the temple?' Seeing Pollux roll his eyes, Petrus stopped. 'Sorry Sir, of course you are experienced in these matters. You don't need me to tell you what to do.'

'No, indeed. Very well, I'll send a message to Tatius to be here at the last hour of the day today. You should arrive well before that and stand in the shade behind that door,' he pointed. 'I will question him. He's in trouble whether he's involved in this or not. The thefts are his responsibility. He'll probably be recalled to Rome and dismissed. He knows that, so it's in his interests to cooperate.'

'Thank you, Sir.'

The door to the herbalist's shop was open. Ruua was seated at her table, grinding shells with her pestle and mortar. The harsh crunch made Petrus wince. She looked up and frowned.

'Aurelius Petrus, what can I do for you?'

'Have you, or your boy, had any more thoughts about Manius? Did he mention anything that was worrying him? Did he behave differently that last time?'

She put down her work. 'As I've already said, he was just the same. Seems to me you've got the two killers already. You executed one of them.'

'They didn't do it.'

'If you say so. What about those who didn't want the thefts to be public knowledge? They could've killed Manius to keep it quiet.'

So, she was clever too, thought Petrus. 'Careful. You don't want to be talking against the army like that. What about your son, can I speak with him?'

The door flew open and Tarpi hurtled in. Seeing Petrus, she froze, then turned on her heels to run, but Ruua was too quick and grabbed her daughter's arm, preventing her from fleeing. Tarpi struggled in her mother's grip, tears rolling down her cheeks.

'Steady, Tarpi,' Ruua said, in a gentle voice. 'This man means you no harm.'

Tarpi stood still, watching Petrus with fear in her eyes.

'Go get your brother,' Ruua said. 'He's with the tanner.'

She pushed Tarpi towards the front door, forcing her to pass Petrus. Tarpi took a deep breath and edged past him, drawing her arms in, fearful of any contact.

'Why is she so frightened?' asked Petrus.

Ruua looked at him for a moment. 'You're intimidating with your uniform and weapons. You're meant to be frightening, aren't you? You rode through the streets with your enemies' heads dangling from your saddle just a few months ago. Perhaps you should be asking yourself why some children aren't afraid of you.'

'What d'you want now, Centurion?' Litorius pushed past Petrus and stood next to his mother.

Tarpi did not come back into the shop. Petrus could just see her out of the corner of his eye, trying to stay out of sight, but close enough to listen to the adults talking.

'Tell me about the last time you saw Manius,' said Petrus.

'It was here. He came to stay as always,' Litorius said.

'Was he wearing his ring?'

Litorius frowned as if he deep in thought. 'I don't remember.'

Ruua said, 'No, no, he wasn't. He must've thought about going to the tavern and then changed his mind. He always took it off if he was going to the tavern.'

'And what about the next morning? How was he then?'

Litorius looked at his mother and then shook his head. 'Gone before I got up.'

'Can you think of anyone who had a grudge against Manius, or who would've wanted to harm him?'

'He wouldn't have told me anything like that. He wasn't my friend. I was just her son, a nuisance that had to be tolerated. I imagine there's plenty had a grudge against him for docking their pay. You'd be able to find that out up at the fort, wouldn't you?' sneered Litorius.

'And was your pension ever docked?' Petrus addressed his question to Ruua.

She raised an eyebrow. 'I have my taxes and ground rent taken out each month, but nothing else. Why would my pension be docked?'

'Why did Manius start giving you so much money, the three hundred denarii?'

Ruua raised her finger to her lips and murmured, 'People might overhear you.'

Petrus lowered his voice. 'Why didn't you tell your son about the money?'

Ruua and Litorius exchanged glances.

'It's none of my son's business. Manius gave the money to me.'

Petrus watched Litorius. His lips were moving, but he made no sound as he stormed out of the shop.

'You weren't at all curious as to why he suddenly started giving you money?' Petrus persisted.

Ruua turned back to her herbs and muttered, 'Go well, Centurion.'

Petrus was irritated by her attitude, but could think of nothing else to ask.

XVII

The sunlight was fading as he entered the brothel and collapsed onto a couch. The girl who normally welcomed customers ignored him even though he was the only one there. He didn't mind. They both knew he wasn't a big spender, so she had no need to make him feel special. A slave stepped forward and poured him some wine. He sat back against the cushions, happy to wait.

'Carantii? What can we do for you?' the girl stood in front of him.

He pushed himself upright. 'I'd like Troucissa, I think.'

The girl held out her hand, and he pressed some coins into her palm. 'You know the way.'

Carantii walked down the corridor where dying candles flickered weakly, and shadows danced on the walls. He opened a door and walked into the room. Troucissa was seated on a couch, brushing her thick brown hair. She rose and took his hand, guiding him towards the bed. She pushed him backwards, sat astride him, and began to work.

Carantii woke with a start, wondering how long he'd been asleep. Troucissa was lying awake next to him, staring up at the roof. He took her hand, felt her flinch, and let it go.

'Sorry,' he murmured.

She grasped his hand, forced a smile onto her face and whispered, 'Don't be sorry.'

Carantii smiled and rummaged in his pocket. He handed her a coin. 'You're great.'

She hid the coin somewhere inside her clothing and leant

into his body, sighing.

'I heard sometimes you serve clients with another girl,' Carantii began.

'Fancy a threesome, do you? That's double the cost.'

'Oh right, I heard some men get a pair for the price of one,' he winked.

'Only that creepy centurion, Aquilinus. He gets special rates if he comes in drunk and starts causing trouble. It's Sylva's way of dealing with him. She needs to keep the army on side.'

'Does that happen often?'

She shook her head. 'Not so often. The last time was a couple of weeks ago.'

'Weren't there any other army men here to stop him causing trouble? There's normally plenty of them in here.'

'No. The Prefect had been here earlier in the afternoon, but by the time Aquilinus got here, he'd gone.'

Carantii sighed and pulled her close. They lay there for a while and Troucissa began to snore softly against his chest. He gently moved away from her embrace and stood up. He closed the door gently behind him. Troucissa deserved some rest.

The salon was empty. He made his way quickly out of the brothel, carrying his cloak over his arm. He walked down the street and stepped into the alleyway beside Petrus' house. The streets around him were still busy, and he didn't want to be seen. He checked around him. There was no one in sight. He lifted his cloak to put it round his shoulders and dropped a coin on the ground.

'For the sake of the Gods!' he mumbled and bent over to pick up the coin. As he did so, he quickly placed ivy around the boot scraper.

He straightened up and carried on walking down the alleyway. He had not seen Aurora enter the alleyway behind him. Seeing him there, she had turned back into the main street and spoken to the woman she was with, whispering 'There's a man there, the Smith, I think. Let's just walk. I don't know him. It might not be safe.'

XVIII

The damp streets were full of women, walking slowly with stunned looks on their faces. Some had small children clutching to their clothes or babies suckling at their breasts. Some would find accommodation in the vicus, paid for by soldiers. Others would have been cast adrift and would walk away towards the villages nearby. One or two, in desperation, might approach Sylva and start working at the brothel. A few men in uniform scowled as they walked alongside their families, searching for places for them to live.

Pollux ushered Petrus out of the salon and told him to stand behind the door. He moved into the shadows and tried to still his breathing. This was dangerous, both physically and politically. If the prefect found out about it, then Petrus was afraid of what might happen.

He heard a slave show Tatius into the salon.

Pollux grunted, 'Take a seat. Don't get too comfortable!'

Petrus imagined Tatius sitting down with a puzzled look on his face.

'You wanted to see me, Sir?' began Tatius.

'Your librarii have been covering up for each other when they're off sick, or even missing from the fort.'

Tatius mumbled a response, but Petrus couldn't make out the words.

'How long's that been going on?'

There was no answer.

'What was your Signifer doing? Doesn't he make checks on them?'

There was silence.

'And what about the grain thefts? When did you really find out about them?' Pollux snapped.

Tatius sighed loudly. 'A couple of days before Manius went missing. I was going to investigate.'

'Changed your story since we last spoke, haven't you? Last time you said you only found out when Petrus told you. You're a bloody liar!'

Petrus heard shuffling feet, and a chair crashed to the floor.

'I will hit you, you idiot. Tell me the truth!' shouted Pollux.

'I'm sorry, Sir. Manius and Ecdicius came together to see me a couple of days before he disappeared. I... aaah!'

Petrus assumed that Pollux had struck the Prefect as the noise of scuffling reached him.

'Why didn't you report it?'

'You were away, travelling with my bride,' the Prefect gasped.

'That's a feeble excuse. You could've sent a messenger. Even so, why didn't you report it immediately, when I got back, eh? Were you trying to cover it up?'

'Not exactly, Sir. I wanted to investigate.'

'Did you question your Signifer?'

'Yes. He was as shocked as I was.'

'You wanted to cover it up, didn't you? Sounds like a good motive for murder to me.'

'I didn't kill him.'

'Both you and Ecdicius were outside the fort the last time Manius left there. What were you doing?'

There was a long pause. Petrus imagined Tatius was considering lying to Pollux.

'I cannot speak for Ecdicius, Sir.'

'Don't get smart with me. What were you doing?'

'I started at the brothel.'

'And after that?'

'I was there a long time,' he paused, 'and then I went to the Temple of Jupiter, to pray for guidance on my forthcoming marriage and what to do about the thefts.'

'And after that?'

'I was there the whole night Sir, making sacrifices and praying. The thefts are a big stain on my record. It could be the end of my career.'

Silence.

'I returned to the fort just before daylight,' Tatius said.

'Can anyone verify your presence at the Temple? The priest perhaps?'

'I was alone.'

'Your story is barely believable. You wouldn't accept it from one of your men, would you?'

There was a long pause.

'As far as I'm concerned, you and that useless Signifer Ecdicius are suspects in this murder. And I'm going to instruct Petrus to treat you as such. You are to cooperate with him and answer any questions he poses. Is that understood?' Pollux said.

Silence.

'Is that understood?'

'Yes, Sir.'

'Now get out of my sight.'

Petrus heard nothing more. He waited.

'You can come out now,' Pollux said.

Petrus walked into the Salon. There were cushions and drapes on the floor, and one of the couches had moved. Petrus bent to pick up the cushions.

'Leave that! I've slaves to tidy up. Did you hear him?' Pollux asked.

'Yes, Sir.'

'You can check out whether he was at the brothel easily enough.'

'I've already got someone looking into that.'

'Be careful around Tatius. He knows that he'll be recalled to Rome shortly. As a failure. He is a man with little to lose.'

Petrus had thought the same, but was surprised that Pollux would share his concerns with a man ranked much lower than himself.

'Very well then, don't let me keep you,' Pollux dismissed him.

Petrus walked slowly along the street. Darkness fell quickly at this time of year and the streets were now deserted. It was that brief period before the few nighttime people like thieves, drinkers and night soil men emerged from their homes. He reached his own house, put his hand on the door, and pushed it open. Light spilled into the darkness, revealing the ivy tied round the boot scraper.

Petrus stepped into the room. Aurora rose from her stool and wrapped her arms around him, burying her face in his chest. He breathed in the smell of her.

'Carantii,' she mumbled into his tunic.

He put his hands on her shoulders and held her gently at arm's length. 'What did he say?'

She shook her head. 'I just happened to turn into the alleyway here and see him as he left the ivy. He would've been on his way home. I told Audaga I'd seen him and we just walked away, as it wouldn't be safe for a woman to enter her house with a man so close by like that.'

'He's getting careless again, if you saw him,' mumbled Petrus.

Aurora sighed. 'Are you going to eat before you go round and disturb him and his lovely wife?'

He smiled. 'Yes, that would be nice.' He sat down on a stool.

Aurora turned to the fire, stirring the pot of food. The door burst open, and Titus raced in, hurling himself at his father, almost knocking him off his perch.

'Hey! Steady!' Petrus hugged the boy to him and tousled his hair.

'There's a rat in my room,' said Titus as he snuggled into his father's embrace.

'Well, we'd better go and see to it, hadn't we?' Petrus set the boy on his feet and stood up, grabbing his hastile. He walked out of the kitchen with his son walking behind him carrying a broom.

He opened the door. A candle flickered on a table near the bed. Two red eyes looked back at him from a dark corner.

'Ready?' whispered Petrus.

Titus nodded and closed the door behind them. He walked forward with the broom swishing it across the floor. The rat began to move, and he whipped the broom sideways, catching it and propelling it across the room. Petrus raised his hastile and brought it down on the rat's body. There was a sickening crack, and the animal lay on its side. Its belly had burst open, spilling its guts onto the floor in a tiny pool of dark blood. The rat's legs flailed helplessly. The stink turned Petrus' stomach as he scooped up the body. The innards leaked between his fingers. Titus opened the window shutters and Petrus hurled the dead animal into the dark night. Titus reached a hand towards the remnants of guts where the rat had lain.

'No. I'll do it,' said Petrus.

He swept up the mess with his hand, trying not to flinch at the smell and the slime as they slid on his palm. He reached out through the window and let them fall into the darkness. Titus closed the shutters and wrinkled his nose in disgust. Petrus took a cloth from inside his tunic, wiped his hands on it, and then wiped it across the stone floor.

'Now, are you going to bed?' Petrus asked.

Titus nodded and climbed onto his mattress. Petrus began a tale about a brave centurion who fought mythical creatures.

As he spoke, he watched his son's eyes begin to close. The boy's breathing grew deeper, and he drifted into sleep. Petrus leant forward, kissed his son's head and pulled the blanket up around his shoulders. Titus had had frequent fits when he was younger, and they'd feared for his life. Aurora and Petrus had prayed to various gods to help him, and Petrus had taken advice from Arsenios. He'd not had a fit for a while. Perhaps their prayers had been answered, or maybe the physician had been correct, and he had simply grown out of them. Either way, they were no longer so afraid that he would die.

Antigone lay on her mattress, snoring gently. Petrus and his wife ate in silence, and then he began to talk. He told her everything that he had found out over the last few days and then began to explain what had happened that morning.

'Under Pollux's orders, Adrianus was beaten to death in front of the entire fort. Some of the men were sick at the sight of it. Tatius was terrified. He was trembling so much afterwards, he could barely speak.

'Lucullus has been banished. All his property has been sold to Felix who will have moved his pregnant wife in there by now. Lucullus' wife has agreed to stay there as a servant. That's a come down for her. I don't know how long she'll actually stay, but at least she has a roof over her head.

'Tatius and Ecdicius, the Signifer, were both outside at the time Manius left the fort. Ecdicius was with his man, Andecarus. They've been together for years and he often brings him back to the fort. I had no knowledge of it. I don't think anyone at the fort did. He's kept it a secret. I think he was a bit ashamed. I've spoken with Andecarus and he backs up Ecdicius' story, as do the fort's records. The Prefect is more difficult.'

'Yes, I imagine he wouldn't take kindly to you challenging him,' Aurora nodded.

'Fortunately, the Tribune was prepared to ask the Prefect questions on my behalf. Tatius claims he went to the brothel and then spent the night making sacrifices in the Temple of Jupiter, but no-one saw him there. Tatius has been really careless at the fort, not noticing the thefts, or that the Librarii were not reporting each other's absences. He has a strong motive for killing Manius, wanting to cover it up while he sorted it out. He'll be removed from his post and returned to Rome. He knows that. Pollux ordered him to co-operate with my investigation and told him he's a suspect. Pollux warned me to be careful, as Tatius has nothing to lose. He could be very dangerous.'

He paused and then continued, 'I can't really see Tatius murdering a man.'

'Fear and shame can be big motivators though, can't they? Tatius could lose everything. Ecdicius could lose his job,' murmured Aurora.

Petrus nodded. He rose and pulled Aurora close to him, kissing her passionately.

'Careful,' she giggled, stroking his face with the back of her hand, 'otherwise you'll get distracted and not get to see Carantii after all.'

He smiled and kissed the top of her head. He opened the door and stepped outside into the enveloping night. He made his way quickly to the forge. He stepped to the side of the dark building and knocked on the door. It was opened by Carantii who stood aside and beckoned him into the warm room. Lugraca looked up from the loom where she was working and smiled. She rose to her feet and pulled a stool across the room, beckoning Petrus to sit opposite her husband. She handed him a cup of ale.

'You were seen leaving the ivy at my house today,' Petrus began.

Carantii whistled in surprise.

Lugraca dropped her wool and hissed, 'That's dangerous.'

'Yes, it is. Luckily, it was only Aurora who saw you. She turned into the alleyway just as you were leaving it. She told the woman she was with that she'd seen you and they moved on. It's normal for women to think of their own safety first when men are near their homes. You need to take more care, my friend.'

They all knew that informants were despised by their communities. In some areas, they'd been murdered when they were exposed. Petrus didn't want the Blacksmith's death on his conscience, and he didn't want to lose a valuable source of local information.

'I'll be more careful,' said Carantii, looking at Lugraca as he spoke.

'You've got something to tell me?' Petrus slurped his ale.

'I need to go to the forest again, so that Senna thinks I'm really interested in gambling. Otherwise, it'll seem odd.'

Petrus grimaced, reached into his pouch and withdrew four denarii. Placing them on the table, he mumbled, 'I hadn't thought about that.'

'Tatius was at the brothel on the same day that Aquilinus last went. But he'd left by the time Aquilinus got there,' Carantii watched Lugraca out of the corner of his eye as he spoke, gauging her reaction to his visit to the brothel, 'It's true Aquilinus kicks off in there and Sylva placates him with two women at the standard price for one. Otherwise, he'd upset the customers.'

A tear rolled down Lugraca's cheek. She wiped it away and picked up her work.

'Why hasn't Sylva reported him to the army?'

Carantii shrugged.

Petrus thought for a while. He drained his ale and stood up. 'Thank you Carantii. That's been very helpful. As I've said, I'd like you to spend more time finding out about Cato. Speak to the merchants you say hired him. Did anyone see Tatius that last night after the brothel?'

Lugraca opened the door, and Petrus stepped into the alleyway. As the door closed, he did not see Lugraca push Carantii away as he tried to embrace her.

Petrus made his way back to the fort. He had a lot to think about.

XIX

The centurions stood dripping wet in Tatius' office after morning parade. The relentless rain rattled the roof as each man gave his report from the day before. When everyone except Petrus had spoken, Tatius made to dismiss them.

'Excuse me, Sir. I would like Vegetinus, Roburius and Ferullus to come to my office. There are some questions I need answering, after I've spoken to the Signifer,' said Petrus.

Tatius frowned. He opened his mouth and then closed it again. He looked down at his hands. 'Very well. You three. Wait outside Petrus' office and answer his questions when he's ready for you.'

'How long's that supposed to be?' muttered Roburius.

'It'll be as long as it is necessary,' snapped Tatius. He raised his voice. 'Get out! Now! All of you!'

'Well?' Tatius said tetchily, when they were alone. 'What have you to tell me?' He didn't wait for a response. 'I was summoned to Pollux's place yesterday. He damn near accused me of murdering Manius! Jupiter's sake! I told him! I've told you too. I was at the brothel and then the Temple. I was there the whole night. He got me to admit I knew about the thefts of the grain before your man Balbus found them. I knew because Manius and Ecdicius came to see me, a week or so before he went missing. I was going to investigate. I was! Then the bloody man was killed!' He groaned. 'If I don't get this thing sorted, I'll be sent back to Rome in disgrace.'

Petrus kept his face still and stared straight ahead, not looking at Tatius. It was too late for Tatius to save himself. An example would have to be made.

'Tell me about your investigation. You're not making much progress, are you?'

'There's illegal fighting going on in the forest. Organised by a man called...'

'Senna! Yes, yes, I know about that,' Tatius interrupted him. 'It's going on at lots of places. We don't waste resources chasing them. That's been decided at the highest level.'

Petrus hid his surprise. 'Roburius, Vegetinus and Ferullus are at a lot of these fights, betting and losing money. They bet on dog fights as well.'

Tatius nodded, 'I guessed as much. They're not in debt to anyone though, are they?'

Petrus shook his head. 'Not as far as I know. That's what I want to check with Ecdicius. Cato, that retired centurion, is often there too, arguing and fighting when he loses. I've heard that he hires himself out as muscle to collect other people's debts. I'm trying to get more information about the people who hired him. Could be that he was roughing up Manius and overdid it.'

Tatius was silent. He picked up his stylus with a shaking hand. Exasperated, he swore and slammed it back on the table. He glared at Petrus.

'I thought you said previously that Manius didn't gamble. How could he owe money then?'

'Maybe it wasn't money. Maybe someone had a grudge against him for something else.'

'You've not had much luck finding out who or what that might be, have you?'

'Ecdicius has a man in the vicus. He was with him the day Manius was last at the fort.'

'The man might lie to cover for Ecdicius. People in love, or lust, do that. They lie,' murmured Tatius.

Petrus shook his head. 'The gatekeepers' records show the two of them were back here at the fort when Manius went missing.'

'Anything else?'

'Aquilinus often has a lot to drink and then causes a scene at the brothel. Sylva gives him two girls for the price of one to get him to quieten down.'

Tatius didn't say anything.

Petrus waited.

'Unless she makes a complaint, we can't act. And anyway, being randy doesn't mean he's a murderer! What would be his motive?'

'I'm not sure about motive, but he was outside when Manius went missing.'

'A lot of supposition there, Petrus, and not much evidence,' snapped Tatius. He lifted a shaking hand to smooth his hair.

'I think I should bring Cato in for questioning.'

'Can't see what good that'll do you. You'd do better to interview that widow and her son again, find out what Manius was really like. Push her, them, really hard.' Tatius waved Petrus away.

Petrus made his way to the Treasury.

'Petrus! What the fuck do you want now!' Ecdicius rose from his seat and waved the guards away. 'Go and stand outside! I want to speak to this centurion alone!'

'Well?' Ecdicius threw himself back onto his seat.

'You knew about the thefts, didn't you? Manius told you about them and the two of you went to see the Prefect.'

'Yes, yes, we did. He told us to leave it to him, that he would sort it out. I said that such things should be reported to the Tribune.'

'And?'

'Tatius told us he would report it. He told us not to say anything to anyone about it, he would tell the Tribune and act against the thieves. I, we, did as we were ordered.'

'What about when Manius' body was found?'

'I went back to the Prefect and said we must go to the Tribune.'

'But you didn't, did you? Neither did Tatius.'

'Tatius threatened me. Well, he threatened me about Andecarus, said he would find some charge against him, which meant he would lose his freedom. Said he'd sell him to the next slave trader who passed by. I... I couldn't lose him.'

Ecdicius' cheeks were wet with tears as he turned and picked up a tablet from the shelf behind him. He pushed it across the table. 'Here, I got Tatius to sign this document to say he'd been informed.'

Petrus glanced at it. It looked like Tatius' signature and ring seal. He nodded.

'And I wrote these notes on the same day, in case anyone ever asked about it.' Ecdicius pushed another tablet across the table. His hand was shaking.

'Covering yourself, eh?' murmured Petrus as he scooped up the tablets.

'He can't come to the fort anymore, not after Tatius made families leave the fort,' Ecdicius' voice was a whisper. 'I'm glad he still has a place in the vicus. I can't live without him.'

Petrus nodded, recognising the other man's pain. He thought for a moment and then said, 'The three centurions, Ferullus, Vegetinus and Roburius, have they been making big withdrawals from their savings?'

Ecdicius nodded. 'Most months. They take out quite a bit, usually around fifty, sometimes a hundred denarii a month. I've heard they're big gamblers, betting on all sorts of fights, dogs and men. They're not bothered.'

'Does that mean they don't have much saved up?'

'Usually a centurion with several years' experience like them, would have a few hundred, maybe a thousand or so denarii of saved salary,' Ecdicius paused, 'I can't remember the exact figures, you'll have to check with the librarii, but each of them has less than a hundred denarii. They'll soon run out of money completely.'

Petrus raised an eyebrow. There was a motive.

The three centurions were leaning against the wall, trying to keep out of the drizzle as Petrus approached.

'What the fuck is this all about?' Vegetinus said as he stepped into Petrus' face.

Petrus put out a hand to stop him from getting any closer. 'I have a few questions to ask you, that's all. The Prefect has instructed you to cooperate with me. It would be best for everyone if you do as he said.'

Vegetinus shrank back, deflated.

'Right, you first then,' Petrus pointed at Roburius.

Roburius followed him into the office.

'Take a seat,' Petrus waved towards a stool and poured him a drink of wine.

'Tell me about the fights in the forest,' Petrus began.

Roburius shrugged. 'Not much to tell. We turn up when Senna lets us know they're taking place. We bet.'

'And the dog fights?'

'Same sort of thing.'

'Do you lose much?'

'Sometimes. Win sometimes, too.'

'How do you feel when you lose? Angry?'

'Sometimes. If I think there's been some cheating. Like throwing the fight.'

'And what do you do then?'

Roburius shrugged.

'Cause fights, don't you? Try to get your money back by force.'

Roburius did not respond.

'A couple of days ago, the three of you lost twice and took on nearly the entire community in a fight. Doesn't paint the army in a good light, does it?'

Roburius scowled, 'Got a spy there have you Petrus? One of the merchants I suppose. Bastard's telling tales! Yes, we did get into a scrap. We'd lost quite big; I'd bet five denarii and the others a bit more. Senna put that slave of his in and she didn't put up much of a show, so we didn't think it was fair.'

'Tell me about Cato.'

'Cato! That drunk. He'll bet on anything. Talk about fighting. Every time he loses.'

'Got involved with you three the other day, didn't he?'

Roburius nodded.

'You withdraw money from your salary regularly, don't you? Is it all for gambling?' asked Petrus.

'What's it to do with you?'

'Just answer the question.'

'Yes, yes, I do. I'm a free man. I've earned it. So, I can spend it on whatever I like.'

'What'll happen when you run out of money? Which you will. What happens then?'

'I won't run out of money. Centurions are well-paid.'

'You've less than a hundred denarii in your account.'

'What the fuck? How do you know that?' Roburius went pale.

'I've checked with the Signifer.'

Roburius took a long drink of the wine. His hand trembled as he held the cup. 'I didn't realise it was that low.'

'Ever been tempted to hire yourself out to some of the merchants to help them collect their debts? Earn a bit of money on the side?'

Roburius lowered the cup to the table and sniggered, 'What? Like Cato, you mean? No. It's against army regulations.'

'Suddenly concerned about army regulations? You're not so bothered when it comes to gambling though, are you?'

Roburius looked down at his hands and did not reply. Petrus let the silence hang between them.

'Is that it?' Roburius asked.

'Yes, you can go.'

Petrus followed him to the door and beckoned Vegetinus inside. Roburius strode away without a backward glance.

The interviews with Vegetinus and Ferullus were similar and did not provide him with any more information. Both men were shocked to learn how little money was left in their accounts.

Petrus gathered together all of Flaccus' tablets and put them in a sack. He put all Lucullus' tablets in another and sent two soldiers to take them back to the vicus. He rubbed his eyes and sighed. He took a few deep breaths, hoping inspiration would come to him. It didn't. He ordered six soldiers to accompany him, and they headed for the fort gate. He was surprised to see Felix loitering nearby.

'Felix! What are you doing here?' Petrus asked.

'I was just about to send a message to you with one of the gatekeepers.'

'What did you want?'

Felix drew himself upright. 'I think I've located the missing grain.'

'Really? How? Where?'

'I went through the records and found details of a storage building at the edge of the vicus. Would you like to come with me?'

'You've not been there yet?'

'No. I wanted you to come, as a witness and...' Felix's voice trailed off.

And for protection, thought Petrus. 'Lead the way, Felix.'

The rain had stopped; the sun cast weak light across the street, but failed to warm their wet backs as they trudged through the mud. They entered a maze of alleyways where the buildings were made of mud bricks and had thatched roofs. The stink of decaying food and human waste filled the air. This was 'unauthorised inhabitation', part of the vicus the army didn't tax or even acknowledge. A stone building rose up from the sea of brown. Two men stood nearby, watching the soldiers approach. They walked stiffly forward; the outline of their hidden weapons was clearly visible through their clothes.

'Stand aside! I'm the new owner of this premises.' Felix withdrew a large key from inside his tunic.

One of the men stepped up to him and shoved him hard. Felix staggered backwards, sliding in the mud. He was steadied by one of the soldiers. Petrus grabbed the man and pushed him up against the building.

'Want to fight?' snarled Petrus.

The man went limp in his arms. 'I'm only doing my job,' he muttered.

'Lucullus has gone. I know you'll already have heard about that. I'll continue to pay you, but only if you let me in to check the stock,' said Felix.

Petrus released the man who grunted and then moved to stand with his companion away from the door. Felix bent to the lock and turned the key. The door swung inwards. In the sunlight, dust danced across sacks of grain as two huge rats scuttled past.

'Your stolen grain, Petrus,' murmured Felix looking satisfied. 'I imagine he would have sold it back to the fort at some point in the future.'

Petrus guessed there were over a hundred sacks in the store. He said 'Good work, Felix. Arrangements will be made to collect it. I'll see to it that you are rewarded for this. Make sure those two men stay here and guard it. On second thoughts, you stay here too with one of my men. I'll send a cart.'

They moved quickly through the vicus.

The door to Cato's house was opened by the same scruffy slave. 'He's not here, Sir,' the man said.

Petrus pushed him out of the way, and the soldiers piled in behind him.

'Search the place. He might be hiding,' Petrus ordered.

The soldiers began moving through the building. The sound of opening doors and chests reached Petrus where he waited near the trembling slave. Cushions and drapes were thrown from rooms into the hallways. There was a shout from deep within the house, and the sounds of a scuffle. Three soldiers emerged with Cato struggling between them. Cato dragged his feet as they pulled him forward; his face was bleeding, and his tunic was torn.

'He was hiding in the wash house,' said one of the soldiers.

'What the fuck?!' Cato mumbled and dribbled blood onto the floor. He reeked of stale alcohol.

'I want to question you about your work as a debt collector,' Petrus said.

'I don't collect debts!' spat Cato.

'No, but you rough people up to encourage them to pay the merchants.'

Cato shook the men off and attempted to stand up straight. He wiped his mouth on the back of his sleeve and slurred, 'What of it? I've done nothing illegal.'

'Then why were you hiding?'

Cato stared at him, belligerently. 'It's my fucking house! I wasn't hiding.'

'If you've done nothing wrong, then you won't mind coming to the fort to answer some questions.' Out of the corner of his eye, Petrus saw the thin woman with tired eyes watching them;

she shielded two toddlers who clutched at her smock.

Cato's eyes flicked towards the woman and then back to Petrus. His rank hot breath pushed into Petrus' nose as he said, 'Caussa, my wife, and my children might be in danger if I'm not here.'

Petrus resisted the urge to cover his face with his hand. 'You've not been bothered about their safety these past weeks while you've been out drinking and gambling.'

'But now I'm being taken in for questioning. People will think I know something.'

'And do you know something about the murders?'

'I don't know anything. But people will talk. Please! I'll come with you but bring my wife and children. Keep them safe, out of sight. No-one must know where they are. Please. I'll come quietly.' Cato's voice shook.

Petrus considered this for a moment. Cato began to sink to his knees, his hands raised in supplication. It was pitiful.

Petrus turned towards Caussa, 'Get a cloak to cover your head. Wrap up your children. These men will carry them.'

Caussa took her children into another room. Cato had tears running down his face. He wiped snot from his nose with his sleeve.

'Can your slave read?' Petrus asked.

'Wh-what? Yes, yes, he can read. Why d'you ask?'

Petrus did not reply. Caussa returned with the children wrapped in tatty blankets. She wore a faded brown cloak. As she approached him, she pulled up the hood to cover her face.

'Pick up the children!' ordered Petrus.

The two soldiers scooped the children into their arms and followed Petrus out of the house.

'Lock the door. Do not let anyone in here apart from your Master, his wife and any soldier carrying written orders from me, Aurelius Petrus!' Petrus instructed the slave.

The bewildered man looked at Cato.

Cato mumbled, 'Do as he says.'

The door closed, and they heard the key rattle in the lock.

'Are you going to walk quietly?' murmured Petrus.

Cato pulled back his shoulders and began walking slowly, flanked by the soldiers. Petrus led them through the streets where people stood aside to let them pass. Caussa wept as she hurried along behind them. The children moaned and dribbled as they clung to the soldiers carrying them. It seemed a long way back to the fort.

Petrus told the soldiers to take Cato to the cells. 'Give him something to eat and drink. I'll be along shortly. Then send a cart to collect that grain.'

Cato began to protest, 'Hey…'

'Go with these men. I'll look after your wife,' Petrus said.

The soldiers let go of the children and they ran to their mother, who hugged them to her. Petrus led them across the fort to the infirmary.

Arsenios turned away from Aquila's bedside and approached Petrus, glancing at the woman. 'What can I do for you?'

'This is, err, Cato's wife, Caussa, and her children.'

Arsenios nodded. 'Are they ill?'

Petrus frowned, 'No. But they may be in danger. Take care of them, please.'

Arsenios sighed. 'This is the second time you've asked me to take care of people who are perfectly well! This is an infirmary. I'm a physician, not a bodyguard. I still have your two lads in here at night.'

'I'm sorry Arsenios, but this is the safest place for them. Please, do as I ask. Once the murder is solved, everything will go back to normal.'

'I not sure our lives will go back to normal, Petrus. But I will do as you ask. This way, Caussa,' Arsenios waved an arm in the direction of his back room.

Petrus made his way to the Prefect's office.

Tatius looked up. 'Petrus, I hear you've found our grain. That's great work.'

'It was Felix, Sir, not me.'

'Well, we'll take the credit for it,' mumbled Tatius.

Petrus did not think there was much credit to be gained from finding grain, which shouldn't have gone missing in the first place. The Prefect had dark circles under his bloodshot eyes, and he smelled strongly of alcohol. Tatius picked up a cup of wine and took some huge gulps.

'I spoke with Ecdicius about the centurions' salaries. He says they each have less than a hundred denarii in their accounts. They take out a large amount each month. I've interviewed them and they say they bet regularly. They admit to losing large amounts of money and causing fights with the organisers, but say they have never worked as debt collectors like Cato does. I'm going to pursue this further with my informants. Desperate men do desperate things,' said Petrus.

'But they're not completely broke, are they?' muttered Tatius,. 'Still worth pursuing, I suppose.'

'I've arrested Cato. He's in the cells and smells strongly of drink. I'll let him sleep it off before I question him.'

'Cato? You still haven't explained why you think he would be hired to rough up Manius. Let me speak with him.' Tatius pushed back his chair and stood up.

Petrus started to protest, but Tatius waved him aside and strode out of his office. Petrus followed him across the fort. Tatius barged his way into the prison building. Two young soldiers were leaning on the bars staring at Cato who was sat slumped against the wall, his head in his hands. The straw around him was wet and the stench of urine made Petrus' eyes water. Cato looked up as Tatius entered. He started to tremble and shuffled back into the corner of the cell. He gasped as Tatius bent towards him and gripped his shoulder.

'Collect debts, do you?' snarled Tatius.

Cato moved his head a fraction to the left, winced in pain, and mumbled, 'I frighten people. I get a bit rough sometimes.

That usually encourages them to pay up to whoever they owe money to.'

'What about gambling debts? Do you help with them too?'

Cato raised an eyebrow. 'A debt's a debt. I don't ask what it's for.'

'Who've you frightened or beaten up in the last few weeks?'

'I... I don't remember all their names. I've got them written down at home somewhere, or I had before your soldiers came and turned my house over. My wife keeps the records.'

'Did you overdo it sometimes with your victims? Ever go a bit far, did you?' Tatius sneered.

'N-n-no! I swear,' slurred Cato.

'Do you do work for anyone from the fort?'

Cato looked away and was silent for a few moments. He mumbled, 'No.'

Tatius turned to Petrus. 'Better get someone over there to his house to look at the records if you think it's relevant.'

Petrus nodded.

'Well, what are you waiting for?' snapped Tatius.

'I'm just listening to your questions.'

'Go now. There might be vital information there.'

Petrus didn't like being dismissed. He walked slowly from the building and moved to stand near the window, straining to hear Tatius' next questions. Tatius kept his voice so low that Petrus was unable to make out the words. Cato made no sound at all that Petrus could hear. Frustrated, he made his way to his office and sent for Balbus and the four soldiers who'd been to Cato's house with him. He scribbled orders on a tablet.

'Balbus, I want you to go with these men to Cato's house. Take this tablet with my orders and seal to show to the slave there. Somewhere, Cato's got records of the people who paid him to beat up their debtors, and who those debtors were. I need the details for the last two months.'

Balbus nodded, and the men went away. Petrus returned to the cells. Tatius was just handing the keys back to the guards.

The interrogation had not lasted very long. Cato lay on his side, mumbling to himself. Petrus wondered how thorough Tatius had been.

'I've given him a tablet and stylus; he's making a list of the men he beat up or frightened and those who have employed him, the ones he can remember, anyway. We can check that against the records you've sent for. Don't think it'll help us much.'

Petrus nodded distractedly, then said to the guards, 'Get clean straw for him.'

The two men nodded, and Tatius shepherded Petrus out of the door, closing it behind him. They walked across the fort together.

'He doesn't know anything about the murders. He's not really in a fit state to do anyone much harm, is he? No-one else is to question him. I've given orders to the guards to that effect. I don't believe any of the merchants would've asked him to kill Manius. Not even for a big debt. Killing an army officer is a serious matter, not one you'd give to that drunk. Let him sleep it off and release him in the morning when he's sobered up. There must be something else going on here. What are you going to do next?' asked Tatius.

'Let's see what Cato's list turns up. There may be a link to Manius after all.'

'I doubt it Petrus. I think you're wasting your time. You'd better have something else in mind, or this investigation will grind to a halt. None of us wants that to happen.' Tatius entered his office and closed the door behind him.

'Sir, sir?' A young soldier approached Petrus. 'Arsenios, the physician has sent for you. He wants you to come to the infirmary.'

'Oh, does he? Why?'

'He didn't say.' The young soldier turned on his heel and trotted away.

Arsenios was with Aquila in the infirmary. The injured man was hobbling down the room on his wooden leg. He gasped with each step and his face twisted in pain. Arsenios was murmuring encouragement.

'Ah, Petrus. Come with me,' Arsenios waved in the direction of his room.

Petrus took the seat offered him, opposite the physician.

'Where's Cato's wife?' he asked.

'I've sent them to my room at the brothel. They'll be safe there.'

'You've a room at the brothel?'

Arsenios nodded. 'I treat some of Sylva's girls there. They get illnesses, it's a common thing for whores. I also see to local people, about once a week.'

'I didn't know you worked outside the fort,' Petrus noted, as if for the first time, that Arsenios had dark hair.

'I am not directly under the Prefect's command, as you know. I've discussed it with the Tribune, and he has authorised it. I can come and go as I please. I earn a little money from the local people who come to me when their traditional remedies have failed. It helps them to be more positive towards the fort. It's very common at forts for physicians to do that sort of work. Is Cato in the cells?'

'Yes. He's been beating people to get them to pay their debts.'

'And is that important for your investigation?'

'It might be. He might have been asked to beat Manius and went a bit too far.'

'Have you questioned him?'

'No. The Prefect spoke with him. Why do you want to know?'

'Cato is very ill. He needs ale or wine to survive. He must drink regularly or he will be in a lot of pain. If he does not get a drink, he will die. I've seen people like him before, they cannot be cured. The inside of their bodies are diseased. I've seen inside the corpses. Before he dies from lack of ale, he will wet himself and lose control of his bowels. It is a dreadful way to die.'

Arsenios waited. Petrus did not respond.

'It's a very serious thing if someone dies while being questioned.' Arsenios said.

Petrus nodded. 'Is he more likely to tell the truth when he's suffering without ale?'

'He'll probably tell you anything you want to know.'

'How do you know he's so ill?' Petrus was suspicious.

'Caussa came to see me at the clinic at Sylva's.'

'Why wasn't I aware that you had a place at the brothel?'

'Why should you be made aware? You're just a centurion. As I've said, it's been authorised by the Tribune.' Arsenios laughed, 'Perhaps you should suspect me, Petrus. I think I was outside the fort at the same time as Manius, that last day. After all, I have dark hair, the know-how to forge documents and I understand how to use sleeping drugs.'

Petrus frowned. He'd never considered Arsenios as a suspect. He saved lives, he didn't take them. 'Why would you have wanted Manius dead?'

Arsenios shrugged, 'Money, sex. The usual things, perhaps. Seriously Petrus, you had better make sure you can discount people like me before you start accusing others. You could be on dangerous ground.'

Petrus nodded. He knew that. 'How much ale would I need to give Cato, to keep him alive?'

'Enough to control his symptoms, the shaking. A lot more than you or I could drink.'

'Thank you, Arsenios. Stay well.'

'Go well, Petrus, and take great care.'

In his office, Petrus began reviewing his notes. Who would have hired Cato to beat up or kill Manius? The librarius had docked the pay of some people, retirees and soldiers, but would that have been a reason to kill him and take him to the Mithraeum, or hire Cato to do so? Petrus didn't think so. Manius had been found with dark hair in his hands, presumably torn from the head of his assailant. Cato was bald. So did that rule him out as the murderer? He could have had an accomplice. Ecdicius and the Prefect both had dark hair, and a reason to kill Manius if he was about to expose their failures. Arsenios had been outside the fort the afternoon that Manius left the fort for the last time. The three betting centurions and Aquilinus had also been outside the fort that day. Petrus put his head in his hands and sighed.

Petrus entered the brothel, walking past Riacus without acknowledging him. The huge slave followed Petrus into the empty salon. The young girl leapt to her feet.

'Centurion, how can I help you?' She indicated for him to take a seat.

'Bring Sylva,' he eased himself on to a couch and took the drink handed to him.

'Petrus?' Sylva scowled as she sank down next to him and breathed deeply.

Petrus' eyes were drawn to her ample bosom as it rose and fell with each breath. She had clearly wanted him to do that, to demonstrate that she had some control over him, and so with a look of satisfaction, she pulled a shawl around herself. Petrus lifted his eyes to her face.

'What is it this time?' she purred.

'Does the Fort physician work out of here sometimes?'

'Yes, yes, he does, at least once a week. He has my slave's room at the back.'

'How do local people know when he's there?'

She shrugged, 'They just do. Shortly after he arrives, they start trickling in. They come through the back yard. I put a slave on the gate.'

'How do you know when he's coming?'

'I don't. But this establishment never closes, so he knows he can just turn up. He gives priority to my girls. After all, they can't work if they're ill, especially down there.' She pointed between her legs. 'He treats the kids too and the slaves.'

'Why didn't I know about this arrangement?'

She raised her eyebrows. 'Since when was I obliged to share everything with you?'

Petrus sighed. 'Was Arsenios here that time when the Prefect came? That date I asked about.'

'Yes, yes, he was. He worked late and stayed the whole night, as he does sometimes. He left just before light the next day.'

She waited.

'Is that everything?' She rose to leave.

'Is Caussa there? In Arsenios' room, now?' Petrus asked.

Sylva nodded. 'Arsenios sent a message, saying she should stay here.'

Petrus paused for a moment but decided not to ask to see Caussa or the room. After all, he'd been in there during the previous murder investigation when they found the bodies of two of Sylva's whores. He rose to his feet, nodded to the girl, and left.

In the street, the sun was sliding towards the horizon as the night advanced, dragging colder air behind it. Petrus' feet slid in the thickening mud, and he struggled to maintain his balance. As he stepped into the Tribune's courtyard, he wondered idly whether it would stay clean once the Tribune went away again. The slave led him to the salon. Petrus settled himself on a couch; a bowl of oil smouldered on a nearby table. The statues had been moved around the room since his last visit. He struggled to think of the right words to use with Pollux.

'Petrus!' Faustina wafted through the room in a haze of

perfume. Her long chestnut hair was coiled tightly into a bun. She had applied a lot of make-up, and her lips were bright red. She licked them suggestively.

He got to his feet and forced a smile onto his face. 'Madam.'

She waved her hand. A slave offered her a cup of wine and carried another towards Petrus. He took it and sipped the rich liquid.

'What brings you here?' Faustina put her hand on his arm and pushed him gently back onto the couch. She settled beside him, her hand resting on his thigh.

Instinctively, he shrank from her touch and slid away along the seat. 'I'm here to brief your husband. It's not a matter you should be concerned about.'

'Murder at the Mithraeum? The secret cult! Of course I should be concerned. My husband might be in danger!' she fluttered her eyelids and moved her hand to rest on her ample cleavage as she breathed. She watched him carefully.

Petrus held her gaze.

'You uncovered the thefts. How clever!'

Petrus wondered how long he would have to endure this awful woman before Pollux put in an appearance.

'Petrus!' Pollux entered the room, pulling his robe more tightly around him. He flung himself onto a couch. 'Update me.'

Petrus jumped to his feet. Faustina giggled behind him and shuffled along the sofa away from him.

Petrus began, 'Three centurions are heavy gamblers, they have spent almost all of their wages on betting, and each have less than one hundred denarii in their accounts. They fight a lot when they lose money. They might be getting desperate, but they all deny working as debt collectors like Cato. I need to check on that. My informants are working on it. Ecdicius was outside the fort for a brief period on that last day collecting his man, but fort records show they were both inside the fort before nightfall. He does have a motive for the murder, as the librarii report to him, and he might've wanted to cover it up. However, when I interviewed him, he said that he and Manius reported the thefts to Tatius who told them not to take any action, while he made further enquiries. After Manius was killed, Ecdicius says he went to Tatius again and said he must report the matter to you. Tatius told him not to, again saying that he would investigate the matter. Tatius threatened to bring charges against Ecdicius' boyfriend. He's a former slave, so he would be enslaved again and sold to the next trader who passes through.'

Pollux's face reddened in anger, and he muttered, 'That bloody fool!'

'As you know, there is no-one who can verify the Prefect's visit to the temple that night. Both Ecdicius and Tatius have dark hair, which is significant as Manius was clutching dark hair in his fist.'

Pollux nodded, 'There's a strong motive for Tatius, undoubtedly. His whole reputation and future career were threatened if the thefts were exposed.' He waved a hand at a slave, who brought him some wine. The slave topped up Petrus' cup.

'The only way to get him to confess to that would be pressure from someone like yourself,' mumbled Petrus.

'Pressure?' squealed Faustina. 'Are you suggesting my husband should torture the Prefect?'

Pollux and Petrus turned to look at Faustina, who covered her mouth with her hand to stifle a giggle.

'My darling, I had almost forgotten you were there. I think you would be better leaving us to discuss this alone. Such matters are not for a woman of your sensibilities to hear.' Pollux lifted her to her feet and propelled her from the room, closing the door behind her.

'If it comes to pressing the Prefect, then I will do so,' said Pollux.

'It's possible that two men were involved in the deaths. It's quite a way to the Mithraeum, a long way to drag or carry a man, even one who was unconscious through drugs. Cato has admitted to hiring himself out as a sort of debt collector.

Could be one of his beatings went too far and Manius died. But I'm still not sure why someone would want to harm Manius. Cato is in the cells at the fort and is supposed to be making a list of people who employed him and his victims. I also have my men at his house where he says there is a written record of who he's worked for.'

'That's remarkably cooperative of Cato. Perhaps he really does have nothing to hide. What else did he tell you?'

'It wasn't me who questioned him. The Prefect insisted on doing it. He would not allow me to listen to the interrogation.'

'That's suspicious,' mumbled Pollux.

Petrus continued, 'He gave Cato a tablet and stylus to write down the names of people he'd worked for. Tatius has instructed me to release Cato in the morning.'

Pollux frowned.

'Arsenios has told me that Cato has an illness and if he does not get ale or wine every day, then his body will start to tremble. He will lose control of it and eventually die.'

Pollux nodded. 'I've seen such men before.'

'Arsenios says Cato is likely to give me the complete truth when he is desperate for a drink.'

Pollux nodded.

Petrus waited.

'And?' Pollux asked.

'I thought I might question him further in the morning when I give him some wine.' Petrus paused. 'You might want to be there to question him yourself or to listen to his answers.' He tried to keep his voice steady. 'I think we need to ask him if he was ever approached by Tatius.'

Petrus tried to hold Pollux's gaze as he said this. He knew that his suggestion was very dangerous. He held his body rigid, to stop it from shaking.

Pollux took a couple of deep breaths. 'Very well. I'll send for Tatius in the morning. I won't be here when he arrives and will leave orders for him to wait here. I'll be at the fort, and we'll see what Cato has to say for himself. Wait until my arrival before you speak to him. Is there anything else?'

'Arsenios, the physician works out of the brothel on a frequent basis, treating Sylva's girls and the local people.'

'Yes, yes, I know. What of it?'

'He was there on the day Manius disappeared. And he has dark hair, although I can't see a reason for him to murder Manius. Sylva says on that day, he worked late with local people and stayed the night, until just before daybreak.'

'I don't see the physician as the murderer, do you?' Pollux began to usher Petrus towards the door, 'Well done. You've certainly raised some interesting points that need resolving. Now, if there's nothing else?'

As Petrus made his way through the villa, he noticed Faustina watching him through an open door, clearly unhappy at being excluded.

XX

Carantii had been in the tavern since mid-morning. He'd been drinking slowly but was starting to develop a headache. He'd been chatting amiably with the other customers, but apart from moaning a bit about the army in general, he'd not learned much that was useful, and was wondering whether to walk home while he still could. He sipped at his drink and nodded as one of the merchants, Cunovindus, moaned about one of his suppliers.

'We'd agreed three bullocks this month, but when I got there, there were only two.' He moved his forefinger back and forth across the table, agitatedly, as he spoke.

'What are you going to do about it?' asked Carantii, feigning interest.

'I'll look for alternative suppliers, won't I? I'd promised them to Belligedo, the butcher. Now he's on my back and I may lose his custom.'

Carantii waved the taverner over and paid for another drink.

'You've been in here a long time,' commented Cunovindus.

'A man needs a break from his wife sometimes.' There was some truth in this. Lugraca had been very quiet since the night before, pushing him away if he approached her. She always seemed to have tears in her eyes.

'Especially a pregnant one, eh? Finish the day off at the brothel, will you?' Cunovindus smirked.

Carantii shrugged, 'Might do.'

Out of the corner of his eye, he noticed Analeugus enter the tavern. Analeugus was one of those strange pale-skinned people with white hair and blue eyes, who were often ostracised by communities. He looked like an old man and moved stiffly, dragging one of his legs as he walked. The room fell silent as the drinkers watched him.

'Analeugus! Take a seat here. Have a drink on me!' shouted Carantii, waving his arm in the man's direction. 'I'm spending some of the money I won.'

Cunovindus' eyes widened, and he stood up and moved to a different table, muttering, 'I don't want him near me.'

'You're not afraid of me, then?' asked Analeugus, settling onto the bench. His skin was cracked and thin. Carantii could see the blue and green streaks inside his body. The noise level rose as the tavern's customers resumed their conversations.

'Me? No. I had a cousin like you when I was a child. He never made it to adulthood. You're one of the lucky ones.' Carantii waved at the taverner and pressed coins into his hand as he poured the merchant a drink.

Analeugus raised his cup to his lips. 'How can I help you, Carantii?'

Carantii smiled, 'I'm owed some money, and the man is refusing to pay up. I heard that you hired Cato to help you when you had a similar problem. Did it work?'

Analeugus nodded. 'When Cato's sober, he's pretty good at scaring people and roughing them up a bit if necessary. I've used him a couple of times. People think that because of my condition, they can cheat me out of my money. Well, they're wrong. Cato's done work for Netacius and a couple of other merchants as well in the past. Do you know him?'

Carantii shook his head. 'I've only seen him at a distance.'

'Well, he's in here quite a bit. He gambles and drinks, owes money all over the place. He does some of his persuasion work to pay off those debts. Last time I saw him, he was with the son of that herbalist Ruua, betting on the dice. Ruua was with that dead man, Manius, wasn't she? The boy and Manius didn't get on from what I heard. The boy probably resented him, and

Manius probably just thought that the boy was in the way. Lost a lot of money to the boy that night, Cato did.'

Carantii nodded. 'I saw Cato at one of Senna's fights. He lost his bets and joined in with the centurions who began to beat Senna up.'

'I heard you lost some money too.'

'Aye, I did, but I won it back.'

'Be careful, Carantii. There's many men been involved with betting and lost everything.'

Carantii looked at him sideways. 'Thanks for the warning. I know what I'm doing.'

Analeugus looked at him for a moment, then sighed, 'If you promise to pay Cato well, then he'll get people to pay you your money. He can handle himself. Well, he was a soldier, wasn't he? Stands to reason. He'd be handy in a scrap. But make sure you pay him promptly. He may be a drunk, but he doesn't forget if you've hired him. And he'll certainly beat you up if you don't pay him. I think that wife of his keeps records.'

'Where can I find him?'

Analeugus grinned, 'Hang around here long enough and he's sure to turn up.' He waved a hand at the taverner, who refilled their cups. 'Mind you, I heard the soldiers took him to the fort this afternoon. So, you may have missed your chance with him for a while.' He sighed and lowered his voice. 'Them other centurions who were at Senna's fight, they may do a bit of threatening for you. It's been suggested that they're available to do the same work, but be careful, it'd be different employing serving soldiers. I've not heard that anyone has used 'em yet. But they're definitely available.' He leaned forward and poked a finger towards Carantii. 'Make sure you get your money, Carantii. If word gets round that you overlook debts, it'll be the end of your business. And it will encourage people to behave that way with the rest of us.'

The two men continued to drink in silence.

Carantii pushed himself to his feet. He felt the room tip sideways as he staggered towards the door. Behind him, Analeugus jeered. He stepped outside. The cold wind rushed to meet him, making him gasp. The moon's weak light barely reached the street as he placed each foot carefully onto the ground, feeling the mud shift slightly beneath him. As he reached the forge, he staggered and leant against the door. He vomited in the alleyway beside his home, splashing his boots. He cursed as he wiped his mouth with the back of his hand and pushed open the door. The warmth hit him as he stepped inside, and he swayed in the candlelight.

'Woah! Steady there!' Petrus murmured in his ear as he put out his hand to steady the drunk man.

Alarmed, Carantii whirled round, swinging his arms wildly. He'd not been aware that he was being followed. Petrus laughed as he grabbed the blacksmith and guided him to a stool.

'You'd better take more care Carantii. I could've robbed you.' Petrus' eyes sparkled in delight.

'Almost anyone could've robbed me, except I've drunk all my money,' mumbled Carantii, taking the cup of water Petrus pressed into his hand. 'I've been in the tavern all day collecting information for you.' He gulped down the water and banged the empty cup on the table.

Petrus poured some more water into the cup and put some coins beside it. 'That should cover it.'

'Analeugus told me he has hired Cato as muscle to recover money from his debtors. Says he's very effective when he's sober, threatens and beats people up if necessary. Quite a few merchants use him. Cato's wife keeps the records in case the merchants are late paying Cato for his services. He said he's heard that those three centurions are available to do the same kind of work. But he warned me to be very careful as they're serving soldiers. He…'

'Did he say who he'd heard that from, or who employed them?' interrupted Petrus.

Carantii shook his head. 'No, he didn't. He did say that one evening Ruua's son played dice with Cato and took a lot of money from the old drunk. You've got Cato in custody now, haven't you?'

'Will Analeugus give evidence against Cato if needed?' Petrus asked.

Carantii shrugged. 'Maybe. Maybe not. He's already treated as an outcast, as he has that thing, that makes their skin pale and see through, strange blue eyes. So, being a witness won't do him any more harm.'

'Thank you. You've done well. Do you need any help? More water perhaps?' Petrus refilled the cup again.

Carantii shook his head, 'I'm in my own house.'

Carantii's stomach heaved as he watched Petrus leave.

XXI

'Balbus left these tablets,' Gauori handed him a sack and pushed a plate of cold food across the table towards Petrus.

Petrus grabbed a slice of the meat, stuffing it into his mouth. He chewed enthusiastically, wiped his hands on his tunic and tipped the tablets onto the table. They had lists of names and dates scratched into the wax, along with the amounts owed to Cato for his services and the names of the merchants who employed him. Alongside each name was a signature – he guessed that was Caussa signing to say that Cato had been paid. Most of the merchants' names were familiar to him; Belligedo, Gamigoni, Netacius, Analeugus.

Later Petrus lay on his bed wondering what Cato might tell him the next day.

XXII

A thin sheet of ice covered the ground, and the men slipped and cursed as they trudged across the fort to the morning parade. Tatius looked pale and his voice shook as he gave a short briefing and then dismissed the men.

In his office, Tatius barely listened to the centurions' reports. He seemed distracted. When it was Petrus' turn, he opened his mouth to speak, but Tatius held up his hand to quieten him.

'Release Cato this morning if he's sobered up. I've been summoned to the Tribune's house,' Tatius said. He stood up and hurried away.

The centurions looked at one another, shrugged and moved towards their own offices. As Petrus entered his office, he was surprised to see the Tribune sitting at his table.

'Sir. I am just collecting my notes on my way to the cells. Can I suggest that you stand outside, at one of the windows? You'll be able to hear everything that's said. I think if you come with me to see him, he may be too frightened to speak.'

Pollux nodded and rose to his feet. They took their time walking to the cells. Petrus felt a sense of excitement tinged with fear. Was he about to solve the murder?

Petrus watched Pollux walk around the prison building and stand close to one of the windows. Petrus pulled open the door and walked into the building. The sharp stink of urine and faeces hung heavily in the air. Two soldiers, whom he recognised as Crispus and Vitus, sprang to their feet and saluted him.

Cato lay on the floor, clutching his belly. His trousers were wet.

'He's been lying like that most of the night. Pissed himself.

He just got to the bucket in time when he needed a shit,' sneered Vitus.

'Why've you left him lying there like that? He's not an animal!' Petrus snarled.

The two men looked at each other.

Petrus shook his head. 'He's a former centurion. Show some respect! He needs a drink. Go and get a pitcher of wine and two cups. Don't water the wine down! I want it strong. Bring him some more clothes,' Petrus ordered Vitus, who headed outside.

'Let's take his clothes off and cover him with a blanket while we wait for Vitus to return. Put him in the next cell with some fresh straw. Then clean out this one. It stinks!' Petrus snarled.

He snatched the keys from Crispus, opened the cell, and knelt down next to Cato. He put a hand on his back. Cato looked at him with watery eyes, his lips trembling. Beads of sweat clung to his forehead.

'Let's get you changed eh, Cato,' Petrus murmured, lifting the man gently to his feet. The smell made Petrus' eyes water.

Cato lifted his arms above his head like a child and let Petrus peel his tunic off. Cato trembled as Petrus pulled down his soaking trousers, exposing his shrivelled genitals. He stumbled forward and Petrus caught him, guiding him out of the gate and into the neighbouring cell, with its clean straw. Crispus wrapped a blanket around the man's shaking body. Petrus lowered Cato onto a stool. He took a cup from a nail on the wall, dipped it into the pail of water, and held it to Cato's lips. Cato's crooked fingers closed around Petrus' hands as he gulped it down.

'More,' whispered Cato.

Petrus refilled the cup and gave it to him. Cato's hands shook as he bent forward to take a drink.

Crispus carried the shit-filled pail out of the building, his head turned to the side as he walked, trying not to inhale the stink. Vitus hurried in, carrying a bundle of clothes. A wide-eyed slave followed him, carrying a pitcher of wine and two cups. They entered the cell.

'Help him dress. Put that wine on the floor over there, near the water. Then take those clothes and wash them. Pass me that tablet and stylus.' Petrus pointed at the tablet lying on the floor in the neighbouring cell.

The slave put the wine on the floor. He reluctantly entered the other cell and gathered up the tunic and trousers, grimacing at the stink. He passed the stylus and tablet through the bars to Petrus and then left the building. Vitus snatched Cato's blanket from him and grumbled as he helped him dress. In the neighbouring cell, Crispus began shovelling the stinking straw into a sack.

'Go and help Crispus,' ordered Petrus, locking the cell door behind Vitus as he left. Petrus pulled over a stool and sat opposite his prisoner.

'Petrus?' whispered Cato. 'What's this about?' He stank of stale sweat and alcohol. His foul breath forced its way into Petrus' body. Petrus recoiled and then forced himself to lean in towards the man. He poured a cup of wine and held it towards Cato, who reached out with a shaking hand. He took the cup and raised it to his mouth, spilling wine onto his tunic and dribbling it down his chin.

'Owe a lot of people money, do you?' asked Petrus, glancing at the tablet. The illegible scrawl was of no use to him.

'We've spoken about this. I pay people, eventually,' mumbled Cato.

'You're a debt collector, aren't you?'

Cato gave a bitter laugh. 'Ironic, isn't it? A man in debt hires himself out to collect debts.' He held his cup out for more wine.

Petrus shook his head. 'Who've you worked for in the last three months?'

Cato let the cup fall to the floor, hugged his arms around his belly and croaked, 'The odd merchant here and there. Netacius is one, there are others. I tried to write their names down.' He nodded at the tablet.

Petrus shoved the tablet into Cato's face. 'What the fuck is that supposed to say?'

Cato was silent.

'I want names.'

Cato frowned, as if struggling to remember. 'Why?'

'Just tell me their names.'

'Would think better if I had a drink. My head is beginning to ache.' He put his hand to his head and groaned.

'Names first.'

Petrus poured himself a cup of wine and began to drink. Cato's lips trembled as he drooled onto his lap. He lurched to his feet and moved to lean against the wall, turned towards the empty pail and began peeing. His body was shaking so much, he splashed urine on the floor. When he'd finished, he remained slumped against the wall, sagging at the knees. Petrus rose and picked up the blanket from the floor. He wrapped it round Cato's shoulders. Cato nodded his thanks and drew it tighter round his body as Petrus moved him back to the stool and remained standing next to him.

The two soldiers had finished cleaning the other cell. 'Go and wait outside. Stand away from the building. I want to talk to the prisoner in private,' Petrus said.

Crispus and Vitus left. Petrus knew the Tribune would ensure they were not standing within earshot. He waited until he heard the Tribune shuffling his feet outside. Cato began to groan. Arsenios' warning came back to Petrus.

'I'll give you the names. Help me,' Moaned Cato. 'Analeugus,' He took a deep breath, 'Exuperatus, Gamigoni.' He held his hand out, groping the air.

Petrus held a full cup of wine just out of his reach.

'Gamigoni? Really?' Petrus was surprised to hear the merchant was involved with debt collectors. He had helped Petrus out during a previous investigation.

'And others. Catus, Lanuccus, Belligedo, Netacius,' Cato

began slurring his words.

Petrus held the cup of wine to Cato's lips. Cato wrapped his trembling hands around Petrus' as he drank. Petrus quickly poured him another, but placed it on the ground just out of Cato's reach. He grabbed the fresh tablet and quickly scratched the names Cato had revealed.

'Have you ever worked for anyone who is in the Army?' he asked.

Cato's eyes widened, and he stammered, 'N-n-n-No. He asked me yesterday. No, no, I won't tell anyone.'

Petrus poured himself another drink and slowly lifted it to his mouth, smiling. The strong wine was starting to affect him. He felt warm and his head was heavy. Cato's eyes began to water, and his lips moved. Petrus leant forward to try to hear the words.

'No, no, I can't say,' whispered Cato.

'The physician has told me how ill you are. Without ale or wine, you'll get a headache so bad you'll think your head will explode, every limb in your body will cry out in pain, you'll piss and shit yourself. Then you will die a horrible death.' Petrus hated himself for saying these words. He picked up his cup of wine and pretended to drink some more, watching the pathetic former soldier.

'T-T-Tatius,' murmured Cato.

'Speak up, can you?' snapped Petrus, conscious that he wanted Pollux to hear what was being said.

'Tatius! Tatius, the Prefect. He threatened me again yesterday.'

'What do you mean, again?'

'He came to my house some weeks ago and said he'd been having some trouble with Manius, one of the librarii. Offered me five hundred denarii if I'd get rid of him. Kill him. I knew Manius, he's with that herbalist, the former whore… Tatius didn't say why he wanted him got rid of, said they'd tried threatening him, but the man persisted in his accusations. I wasn't keen. Killing someone is a big step. Then Tatius told me he'd bring some trumped-up charges against me, take my home, our citizenship and hound us out of the vicus, if I didn't do as he asked. He f-forced me. Gave me a hundred denarii there and then and said I'd get the rest later.'

Petrus picked up the cup and handed it to Cato. 'Why didn't you report it?'

'Report it?' Cato began to cry, wailing like an infant. 'Report to who? You? One of the other centurions? The Tribune? Who would've believed me? I'm a drunk.' He gulped down some more wine and held out the empty cup.

Petrus waited. The man had a fair point. Who would believe a known drunkard's word against that of the Prefect?

'And-and I needed the money. One hundred denarii in my hand. It cleared a lot of my debts,' Cato mumbled.

'So, the two of you, drugged Manius and dragged him to the Mithraeum, where you left him to die?'

'No. No. I was drunk. I found him unconscious in the street. I saw it as an opportunity, dragged him into the alleyway and took him to the Mithraeum. I meant to go back for him, but I just got drunk and forgot. First, I remembered about it was when you found his body.'

'You dragged him all the way to the Mithraeum on your own? I don't believe it.'

Cato's whole body was shaking. The cup slipped from his hand. Petrus surged forward and caught it. He immediately refilled it and gave it back to Cato.

'Go on,' encouraged Petrus.

Cato gulped more of the wine. It ran down his chin. 'I don't remember.'

'I don't believe you. Someone with dark hair was involved. You couldn't have covered the pit over by yourself, either. That's a big tree trunk.'

Cato shook his head and began to cry. He rocked back and forth on his chair. Petrus waited as the wretched man drooled like a baby. He could hear the gravel crunching outside. Pollux was growing restless.

'Tell me again. Where did you find Manius? I want to write it down, so that you can sign the statement.'

'I was on my way home from the tavern. I'd lost a lot of money betting. I found him in an alleyway. I thought he was asleep at first.' Cato mumbled between sobs.

Petrus wrote down the words, 'And then?'

'Well, I was afraid of the Prefect. He'd threatened my family.'

'Tell me again what he had asked you to do, so that I can write it down.'

'T-Tatius had said he'd pay me five hundred denarii to get rid of Manius. When I was reluctant, he threatened to make up some false charges against me and have us thrown out of our home and the vicus. He said we would lose our citizenship.'

Petrus waited. Cato groaned.

'Why go to the Mithraeum?'

Cato shrugged. 'I wanted to cast blame on the cult, I suppose. I… I don't remember much about carrying him up there,' he paused and bent his head to look at the floor. Drool fell onto his boots. 'There-there was someone helping me. He wore a dark hooded cloak. He didn't speak.'

'Who did you think it was?'

Petrus waited.

'Did the Prefect pay you the remaining four hundred denarii? After the body was found?' Petrus asked.

Cato did not respond.

'Did he?'

Cato nodded. 'I needed the money.'

Petrus scribbled this onto the tablet.

There was silence.

'What happens to me now?' Cato mumbled.

'Read this.' Petrus showed him the tablet and gave him a stylus. 'If it is a true record of what you've said, sign it.'

Cato peered at the writing. He grabbed the stylus and

scribbled a signature, handing it back. Petrus rose and picked up the pitcher of wine, taking it to Cato and placing it near the man's feet. The cup shook in Cato's hands as he held it in his lap, slopping red wine, like blood, across his tunic.

'What will happen to my wife, my children?' whispered Cato.

'I will take care of them,' Petrus wasn't sure he'd be able to do that, but the man needed to believe it.

Petrus felt elated and sad. 'I'll see that you get more wine.' He locked the cell and walked outside.

'Do you think he's telling the truth?' asked Pollux as they walked together towards Petrus' office.

'I think so. He was frightened to tell me, but the need for more wine was greater than his fear. I need to speak to Cato's wife, see if she can confirm what he says.'

'We can't give much credence to the wife. She's not a Roman citizen, and it's in her interests to lie for her husband,' said Pollux.

Petrus raised his eyebrows, 'But if she confirms his story, he will still be held responsible for Manius' death and most probably will lose his life as a result. She can't save him. She'd implicate herself as well. She should've informed...' he stopped talking. Who would've believed a local woman over the Prefect's word? 'I'm going to go and see her.' He put the signed confession inside his tunic.

'I'll send Ruga to arrest Tatius and bring him back here. I'll have him held in his house and I'll question him later. I want to speak to Ecdicius as well,' said Pollux.

'I'll leave that with you then, Sir.' Petrus made to leave.

'I want you to listen in to the interrogation when I speak to Tatius.'

'Yes, Sir.'

As Petrus headed across the fort, Pollux's voice followed him as he shouted orders for Ruga to come to his office. Petrus increased his speed.

The ice had melted, and the cool breeze lifted the moisture from the ground, hardening the mud beneath his feet. He was grateful the brothel was not far away. He pushed past Riacus and walked into the empty salon. The girl leapt to her feet and rushed over to him. Brushing a wisp of hair away from her face, she fluttered her eyelids and smiled shyly.

'Aurelius Petrus?' her child's high voice rang out in the still room. 'What can we do for you today?'

'I'd like to see Sylva.'

She rushed out of the room. A slave appeared at his elbow, a glass of wine in her hand. He waved her away and sat down on a couch, leant forward, and rested his elbows on his knees. He was tired. He fought to keep his eyes open as the effects of all the wine he'd drunk spread through his body.

'Petrus! What is it now?' Sylva snapped, then forced a smile onto her face.

'You still have the wife of the retired Centurion Cato here with her children, don't you? I have authorisation from the Tribune to speak with her.'

Sylva breathed deeply for a few moments, watching Petrus face as her breasts rose and fell. He glanced away, not wanting to give her that power over him.

'Follow me then,' she rose from her seat and walked towards the door.

In the private part of the brothel, small rooms led off the open courtyard. She beckoned him to one corner and knocked on the door. A child cried out inside and the lock rattled. The door cracked open, and a face appeared.

'Caussa, I'd like a word with you about your husband,' Petrus said.

Her hand flew to her mouth, and tears filled her eyes. She stepped back from the door, Petrus entered the room. He looked over his shoulder at Sylva who hovered nearby.

'Thank you, Sylva. That will be all.'

'Go easy, Petrus. She's an innocent woman,' muttered Sylva, turning away.

The window was open, and light filled the room. In his

mind's eye, he could still see the bodies of the two whores he'd brought to a room here some months previously for Arsenios to examine. He felt he could still smell the stink of the sewer where they'd been found. Caussa's two children were lying in bed, clutching the blankets around their thin bodies and peeking out at him with wild eyes.

'Cato has confessed to taking Manius to the Mithraeum and leaving him in the pit where he died of thirst.'

'I have something to show you. It's my written witness statement,' Caussa said.

She moved over to the bed and withdrew something wrapped in a cloth. She gave it to him. He unravelled the cloth. It was a tablet. He moved over to the window to read it. It was dated about six weeks previously.

A soldier arrived at the house today, a senior officer. Cato was terrified. The man asked Cato to kill someone from the fort called Manius. The soldier offered to pay Cato five hundred denarii. Cato refused. The man threatened to charge him with some made up crimes, drum us out of the vicus and strip Cato and our children of citizenship. He gave Cato one hundred denarii and said the rest would be paid when the man was dead. I listened from behind the door as they spoke. The soldier did not know I was there. Cato told me to write this down. Protection, he called it. My name is Caussa. I am the wife of Cato.

Caussa's signature was at the bottom of the tablet.

She whispered, 'That is why he took Manius to the temple. That soldier forced my Cato to kill the man. I swear on my children's lives.'

It may well be on your children's lives, thought Petrus as he put the tablet inside his tunic. 'Who was the soldier?'

'I don't know. He had the uniform of an officer, but I didn't recognise him. I swear, on...'

'On your children's lives, I know.' Petrus snapped, then said more gently, 'Would you recognise him if you saw him again?'

She went pale, but nodded. Behind them, the children began

to snivel and moan. Caussa moved to sit on the bed with them, muttering words of comfort in a strange language and hugging them to her.

'If you come with me to the fort, I'll make sure you're not seen by any of the men we suspect may have done this.' Petrus tried to sound reassuring. 'If you can identify the soldier who threatened Cato, it could help his case.' he winced as he said this. Not much could really help Cato.

'Can I see my husband afterwards?' she asked.

'Perhaps, for a short while. He may not be sober, though.'

She sighed, 'He hasn't been sober for years, Sir. He's not well.' She pulled the blankets further round her children and got up from the bed, grabbing her cloak as she did so.

Petrus stepped out into the courtyard, where one of Sylva's slaves was loitering. 'Fetch your mistress.'

The girl ran away.

Sylva emerged after a short while.

'What now, Petrus?'

'Caussa is accompanying me to the fort. Take care of her children.'

Sylva looked as if she was about to argue, then thought better of it, scowled and nodded. She clicked her fingers, and a slave stepped forward. Sylva spoke to her in low tones. The slave went into Caussa's room and began singing to the children.

Caussa pulled the hood of her cloak up to cover most of her face and followed Petrus into the street. He looked around. No-one seemed to be paying them much attention. After all, he was a familiar face about the vicus, and he'd visited the brothel frequently during recent months. He took Caussa's arm and guided her towards the fort.

Rufus grinned and winked at Pius when he saw Petrus entering the fort with a woman. He did not say anything as he closed the gate behind his centurion, but Petrus had no doubt that gossip would spread through the fort and beyond very quickly. He hoped Aurora would know that he would not betray her with another woman. They walked through the fort to Petrus' office. He moved a stool to the side of the window. Caussa would have a clear view of the Librarium from there without being seen.

'Sit here, Caussa, I'll get someone to guard the door outside. Do not let them see your face and do not speak to anyone apart from me.'

She nodded and sat down.

Petrus closed his office door behind him. 'You!' he shouted at a young soldier walking past. 'Come here and stand guard. Do not let anyone into or out of my room.'

'Y-yes, Sir,' the man saluted and did as he was told.

Pollux was walking away from the Treasury towards Petrus and stopped when the two men were level. 'I've just been interviewing Ecdicius. He has repeated exactly what he told you yesterday. He told Tatius about the thefts and after Manius' death, Tatius threatened to enslave that boy Andecarus if Ecdicius reported the matter. The things we do for love, eh?'

Petrus said, 'I've got Cato's wife in my office. She showed me a witness statement she'd written on a tablet about six weeks ago. It details how a soldier, an officer, came to her house and asked Cato to kill Manius. It backs up what Cato said yesterday. She said she didn't know the man's name but might be able to recognise him. I suggest Ruga should walk with Tatius across the fort near the Librarium and we get Ecdicius and the other centurions to walk in the opposite direction. We can watch the reactions of the Prefect and Signifer as they pass each other. That may loosen Tatius' tongue, if he thinks Ecdicius is talking. I'll be with the woman in my office to see if she can point out the man who threatened Cato.'

Pollux nodded his agreement. 'That's a good plan. After that, come back to the house and listen to me questioning that fool Tatius.'

Petrus was surprised that the Tribune openly criticised Tatius like that. Maybe Tatius had fallen so low in the man's estimation that he didn't merit loyalty from the Tribune. Perhaps Pollux was setting a trap for Petrus, trying to get him to deride Tatius so that he could hold it against Petrus in the future.

Petrus said, 'Instruct the soldiers guarding Tatius to walk alongside him so that it doesn't look like he's a prisoner. I… we don't want any of them to be able to say we highlighted them to the woman.' He held his breath for a moment. Was Pollux about to berate him for giving orders?

'Very well.'

Caussa was sitting quietly in his office, looking at her hands. Petrus sat down near her.

'In a short while, you'll see some men walking past that building over there,' he pointed to the Librarium. 'If you see the man who came to your house, tell me. Don't be afraid. You cannot be seen from outside if you stay seated there. The man will not be able to see you. You are safe here with me.'

Caussa nodded. Petrus poured a cup of wine from his pitcher and passed it to her. She took a small sip and smiled briefly. Petrus could think of nothing to say to her, so they sat quietly, waiting.

Shouts and the sound of marching feet reached across the fort. They watched as Tatius, dressed in blue tunic and trousers followed two soldiers across the fort. He marched alongside Ruga and had four more soldiers close behind him. They headed past the Librarium and turned towards the cells. Roburius, Vegetinus, Ferullus and Aquilinus marched with Ecdicius towards them from the direction of the cells. The Signifer did not look at Tatius as they approached him. Tatius stopped walking and said something to Ruga who shook his head and prodded him in the back, moving him forward.

Petrus watched Caussa. The cup wobbled and wine spilled onto her hands, seeping like blood between her fingers.

'The one with the plain blue tunic walking alongside the man wearing the same uniform as you,' Caussa spoke quietly.

'Are you sure it was him? Is there anyone else there you

recognise? Anyone who has been to your house?'

'I've seen those three, the centurions walking in the opposite direction with that man not in centurion's uniform,' she pointed towards Roburius, Vegetinus and Ferullus. 'Not at our house. They're often in the town. They're quite well known, I think.' She looked at Petrus out of the corner of her eye. 'Not in a good way.'

Petrus nodded. They watched Ruga march Tatius in a circle back to his house and the three centurions took Ecdicius back to the Treasury.

'If you come with me, I can let you see your husband briefly.'

A smile lit up her face, and she looked fleetingly beautiful beneath tired eyes as she pulled up the hood of her cloak. Petrus took her arm and led her towards the cells. He told the two men guarding Cato to wait outside the building.

Cato was seated on the floor with his back against the wall, his legs bent up and his forearms resting on his knees. He had his head against his arms and a cup dangled loosely from one of his hands. He was snoring, a gurgling, choking noise. He jerked awake and raised his head as he heard the key in the lock. He mumbled something incoherent as his wife entered the cell and dropped to her knees beside him. Petrus didn't bother to lock the gate; Cato was too drunk to try anything like escape. He sat down on a stool at the guards' table and tried to listen to the conversation.

Caussa wrapped her arms around Cato's shoulders and hugged his head to her breast. He blubed like a baby as she whispered to him. Petrus realised she was singing a lullaby. Cato groaned and wailed. He buried his face in his wife's clothes and clung to her.

Petrus waited.

After some time, Caussa got to her feet and walked out of the cell.

'Can I go home now?' She asked.

'I want you to stay at Sylva's place for now. You may be called as a witness.'

'A witness?'

'Cato has admitted to causing the death of a member of the Roman army. He says he didn't mean the man to die. There will be a trial to determine if it was murder. The other man will also be tried for the same offence and for conspiracy.'

Seeing Caussa's puzzled look he continued, 'Conspiracy means plotting with another person. The other man may deny that he ever came to your home. That is when you would be called as a witness. Put up your hood now and I'll take you back to Sylva.'

She did as he said, but paused. 'Will we be banished?'

Petrus thought for a moment. He didn't want her to flee. 'You cannot be held responsible for your husband's actions. Stay at the brothel. You'll be safe there. I will do my best to look after you.'

They walked across the fort and out of the front gate.

Petrus was relieved to see the brothel's courtyard gate close behind Caussa and he dashed back to the fort. He ignored Rufus' questioning glance and made his way to the Praetorium.

Two guards barred his way into Tatius' residence.

He growled, 'Stand aside. I am on the Tribune's business.'

The men were unmoved. Ruga appeared in the doorway.

'Let him in you idiots! He's a bloody Centurion for Jupiter's sake!' Ruga shouted.

The two men lowered their weapons and allowed Petrus to go up the steps and into the building. He followed Ruga towards the salon.

'You've really done it now Petrus. You'd better be right about this, or we're all in deep shit,' muttered Ruga.

Pollux stood near the salon; his arms folded across his chest. He beckoned to the two men.

'Well?' asked Pollux.

'She identified the Prefect,' Petrus replied.

Pollux nodded. 'I'm going to leave the door ajar so that you can both hear the interrogation. I'll have Tatius facing away from you, but stay out of sight just in case he does turn his head. And it goes without saying, don't make a sound.'

Both men took up their positions either side of the door.

'You've had a difficult year all in all, haven't you?' Pollux began.

There was no reply.

'Your wife conspired with your senior centurion to kill you. The centurion whom you relied heavily on. They killed two whores as well. It took Petrus to work out what was going on. I'd hoped you'd got a grip on things since then.'

'I do, I mean, did,' mumbled Tatius.

'I don't think allowing your own Librarius to steal from the army is being on top of things. When did you really find out about the thefts?'

There was silence for a while, and then Tatius spoke.

'Several weeks ago. Manius and Ecdicius came to see me. They showed me their records, and I asked Ecdicius why he hadn't noticed these errors. He… he said that he had been so busy renegotiating prices with merchants he hadn't had time to do as many checks as normal.'

'Changed your story since the last time we spoke of this, haven't you? You miserable piece of shit!'

There was silence.

'Ecdicius was renegotiating? Doesn't the Roman Army dictate terms?' spat Pollux.

'Not around here, Sir. The weather is always so bad, it's not a place to guarantee good crop yields. The people go hungry themselves and do not often have surplus to sell. We don't take taxes if the crops fail, as we don't want to breed resentment, it just causes more problems. Then we have to purchase food. I…

well things have been a bit difficult since my first wife, Prima, did what she did, and I've spent a lot of time and effort trying to... there was a significant loss of respect, and authority,' he paused. 'Shock and embarrassment affected my performance, I admit that. I had to train up Petrus as well when he replaced Maximus and he's not been a quick learner. It's been a big step up for him. Perhaps too big. Centurion is a critical role, and I've been thinking about replacing him.'

Petrus bridled when he heard this. Ruga smirked and raised a hand to his mouth as if to stifle a laugh.

'That's not what I've observed. He seems to be doing a good job to me,' Pollux said.

'Puts on a good show when you're around,' mumbled Tatius.

'It still doesn't excuse what's been allowed to happen!'

There was a long silence.

'I may've been distracted by the forthcoming arrival of my new wife,' Tatius said.

'What did you do after Manius alerted you to the thefts?'

'You were not resident here at the time and I... undertook further investigation to determine the exact nature of the problem.'

Petrus shifted his feet. The sound pierced the silence, and he froze for a moment, wondering whether he'd been heard in the room beyond.

'What sort of investigation?'

'I checked all the records myself to confirm what Manius was saying.'

'And was he correct?'

'Yes. Yes, he was.'

'And what did you do?'

'I... I was planning a trial.'

'And later, what did do when Manius said he was going to inform me, or the governor?'

'I... he didn't say he would do that.'

'I've been told that is exactly what he said he would do. That is what is expected of any man in the employ of the army. Did you threaten him in any way?'

'No.'

'Perhaps you'd like to think about that answer for a moment. I've been directing an investigation of my own, you know. We've spoken with a lot of people in the vicus and the fort.'

'I… I mean, I told him not to inform you. I said I would do it.'

'We have Cato in custody. He's been talking.'

'You can't trust a word that drunkard says,' Tatius laughed bitterly.

'There's more than just his word. We've written evidence and an eyewitness who says a soldier visited Cato and offered to pay him five hundred denarii to kill Manius. When he wasn't keen, the soldier said he'd charge him with crimes, strip him and his family of citizenship and drum them out of the area.'

'What witness? How does the man know it was me? Could've been any soldier.'

'The witness was brought to the fort and identified you when they saw you walking across the yard earlier today.'

There was no response from Tatius.

'Are you saying the witness is lying?' Pollux asked.

A slave approached the salon, carrying a pitcher of wine and some cups. Petrus waved him away and slowed his breath in concentration.

'Cato has admitted that he found Manius drunk in the street, and with your help carried him to the Mithraeum. He states he'd intended to return for the man to release him, but he was drunk and forgot.'

'No! I didn't help him!' Tatius cried out. 'I admit I went to see Cato and said I'd pay him fifty denarii to threaten Manius, to make him keep quiet about the thefts. I swear before all the gods.'

A scuffling noise and some groans reached out of the room ,and furniture crashed to the ground as Pollux struck Tatius.

'You've changed your story for the third time. Which version of events am I supposed to believe is true? You cannot account for your whereabouts at the time Manius went missing,' Pollux said.

'I-I was in the temple the whole night, praying for guidance and luck in my forthcoming marriage.'

'You've no witnesses who can support that.'

'I give you my word as a Prefect.'

'The word of a man who's already lied to me on several occasions and admits to paying someone to threaten one of his own people! Such a man could easily be involved in murder.'

There was silence.

'Cato's confession is probably enough to convict you,' Pollux sighed.

Petrus thought he could hear Tatius weeping.

'What about Ecdicius? After Manius' body was found, he came to you again and told you to report the thefts, didn't he? What did you do then?' Tatius snarled.

'I told him I would do it and he should keep quiet and leave it to me, as the Prefect.'

'And when he insisted? You threatened him, didn't you?'

There was no response.

Tatius cried out, 'Don't hurt me again!'

'Then answer me! What did you say to Ecdicius?'

Tatius sobbed, 'I... I threatened to enslave his lover. He thought he'd kept it all quiet, that he kept a man in the vicus. He's a former slave. I said I'd charge the lover with an offence and then sell him to the next passing slave trader.' He laughed derisively, 'That got him to back down alright.'

There was no sound from the room.

'What will happen to me now?' Tatius' voice was weak.

'The Governor will decide. There'll be a trial. Murderers are normally put to death. However, you and Cato are Roman citizens, so more likely is enslavement. You'll already have guessed as much.'

'And if I'm found not guilty?'

Pollux gave a harsh laugh. 'In that unlikely event, you'll be recalled to Rome in disgrace.'

'And my family?'

'Your sudden concern for your family is touching. Their fate will be decided later.'

Nothing else was said. Petrus looked at Ruga, who was pale in shock.

'Is there anything else you want to say?' There was a brief pause. 'Read through this and sign here.'

Pollux's footsteps rang across the room. He flung the door open and told the two centurions to enter the room.

Tatius leapt up from his chair, 'W-w-what is …?'

Tatius began to struggle against the soldiers guarding him, grunting with the effort. They restrained him and pinned his arms to his sides.

'Empty his room here, Ruga. Leave just a mattress a blanket and a bucket. We'll keep him under arrest. I don't want him talking to anyone else. But take care. I don't want him to harm himself, either. Put two guards outside at all times. And do not let him have contact with his family!'

Ruga nodded. Tatius began to struggle again. Ruga grabbed his pugio and jabbed it against Tatius' stomach.

Ruga hissed, 'We can do this however you like. You can come quietly, or I'll have you roughed up a bit first and you can lie there in pain for a few days while we wait for the Governor. What's it to be?'

Tatius face reddened, but he stopped fighting and began walking towards the door. Petrus turned to leave.

'A moment, Petrus,' Pollux said.

Petrus paused and turned back to face the Tribune.

'I don't believe what Tatius said about you not being up to the role of centurion. You've done well here. Solved a murder and identified people stealing from the army. I will tell the Governor all about it when he arrives and make sure it's mentioned in reports. After the Governor's visit and the trial, you can have some leave, spend time with that family of yours in the vicus.'

'Thank you, Sir.' Petrus felt himself fill with pride. 'Has a message already been sent to the Governor?'

'I did it yesterday. I was confident you had the right man, men. I expect he'll be here in a couple of days. In the meantime, Ecdicius must be punished. He should've raised the alarm, even though he was being threatened by Tatius. He should also have known his men weren't following orders.' He sighed. 'I'll fine him six months wages. I want your man Balbus to be Manius' permanent replacement. He's earned that. You can stand down his bodyguard now. Get him to move into Manius' rooms. And tell him that amongst his duties is a regular check on the delivery records,'

'Yes, Sir. Also, Manius had a slave who's been transferred to the Prefect's household. The idea was to see if Manius' replacement wanted to buy him. Should I offer him to Balbus?'

'Good idea. Can he afford it?'

'I doubt it, Sir, but he could pay a bit each month, and he'll get a pay rise with the promotion.'

Pollux nodded. 'Sounds like a good idea. Offer the slave to him, see what he says. I'll instruct Ecdicius to monitor his work for the couple of months. I would normally speak to Balbus myself, but there's a lot to do here, trying to sort out this mess. Like getting Tatius' wife to start packing, and those children of his.'

'And Sir, I, don't wish to add to your burden, but the three centurions, the gamblers...'

'Yes, I know. They've spent almost all their savings. So?'

'There is talk in the community that they're available for hire, in the same way as Cato is. Although I don't have any witnesses.'

'For fuck's sake! Bloody idiots! That's something else I'm going to have to sort out.'

They walked out of the salon. 'Have a word with Manius' woman, would you? Find out what she wants to happen to the murderers.'

As Petrus walked through the building, Tatius' wife, Camilla, approached him. She walked stiffly, as if in pain.

'Aurelius Petrus,' she said and moved a hand to push a lock of hair over her face, covering up a bruise on her cheek.

'Ma'am?'

'What's happening to my husband?'

'He's being detained in his room here at the house, pending the arrival of the Governor in a few days' time.'

'Can I see him?'

'No, you cannot. You should not even attempt to make any contact with him. That could result in him being taken to the cells, which would be a lot less,' he paused, searching for the right words, 'comfortable.'

'And what about me? And his children?'

'You must speak with Augustus Pollux about that. He is better placed than me to advise you.'

'He's the one who brought me here in the first place,' she murmured.

'Yes, Ma'am, and he will take care of you and the children.' Petrus bowed and left the frightened young woman alone.

XXIII

The cold wind pushed against Petrus' bare skin, numbing cheeks and lips as the senior officers waited for the men to arrive on the parade ground. Ruga began screaming orders at the soldiers who were restless and slow to stand to attention. A heavy silence settled on them as Pollux strode onto the stage.

'You'll all have heard that Tatius has been arrested in relation to Manius' murder. Cato, the former centurion, has also been detained in connection with this matter. Fabius Ruga will organise a guard for them. The rest of you should continue as normal. Try not to talk about it in the community,' he paused. 'Some time ago, Tatius ordered the removal of all families from the fort. I am rescinding that order. However, if you have a woman or family who you want to live in the fort, then you must first request permission from your centurion, who has the right to refuse them. Their decision will be based on security, as well as the number of people in the fort. There will be a weekly charge for family members staying in the fort. This charge will be deducted from your salaries. You will be held responsible for their behaviour and any crimes or misdemeanours committed by them will result in not only punishment for them but also for you as their guardian. Such punishments will range from beatings and deductions from salary to demotion and dismissal from the army.'

The men murmured their approval and one or two near the back of the parade ground cheered.

Petrus went to his office and sent for Balbus.

'Balbus, the Tribune would like to reward you for your hard work and persistence. You will be promoted to the most senior librarius' position. Ecdicius, the Signifer, has been punished for his failings and has been given a chance to redeem himself, as he was following the Prefect's orders. He will explain the duties to you and check on your work, as will I.' Petrus pushed a tablet across the table.

Balbus' mouth fell open in surprise as he stared at the orders detailing his new post.

'It is a big promotion. You are to move out of your contubernia's rooms immediately and take over Manius' rooms. All Manius' belongings are still there. They are now yours.'

'Thank you, Sir,' Balbus grinned.

'A new duty has been added. You are to check all the delivery records, just as you have been doing, but do them as they come in, not historically.'

Balbus nodded.

'Manius did not leave a will and his slave is now available for you to purchase from the army.'

Balbus raised an eyebrow. 'I don't have the finance for…'

Petrus waved his hand. 'If you want him, you can arrange for deductions from your pay. You'll be receiving a significant pay rise with your promotion.'

'Yes Sir, I want the slave.' Balbus' eyes were wide in excitement.

'Move to the rooms now and I'll get him sent to you this afternoon.' Petrus paused. 'It takes a while to get used to owning a slave, you know. You'll need to feed and clothe him and give him clear instructions.'

Balbus nodded.

'Treat him well, Balbus,' Petrus murmured softly as he watched the changing emotions on the man's face, pleasure and excitement mixed with worry.

Petrus pushed open the brothel's courtyard gate and strode past the slaves who were busy cleaning and washing. He knocked on the door to Caussa's room. She opened it and peered out. She smiled, a tired smile, as she beckoned him inside. One of the children snored softly from the bed. Petrus sat on a stool.

'The Prefect has denied forcing your husband to kill the librarius. The Governor is on his way here. There will be a trial and you'll be needed as a witness. You should stay here until after the trial. You'll be safe here inside these walls. I will come for you.'

She whispered, 'The Prefect is lying. What will happen to Cato? And us?'

Petrus shrugged. 'The punishment for murder may be up to the victim's family. It depends on what the Governor says.'

'And me and the children?'

'I will do my best to protect you.'

A look of fear crossed her face.

'I know you're scared, but if you flee, the Governor will send soldiers to look for you. You won't get far, especially with your two children. The best thing for you to do is to stay here and help the army.' Petrus said.

He watched her closely. Eventually, she nodded.

'Did you hear what happened to Lucullus' wife and children?'

She nodded and sighed. 'They are now servants in their own home. There are worse things.'

Petrus forced a smile. The small boy approached Petrus and put a tiny hand on his knee. He reached out to stroke the boy's head. He climbed onto Petrus' knee and leant against his chest.

Petrus breathed in the little boy smell that reminded him so much of his own son, Titus. He gave the boy a brief hug and patted his leg gently.

Caussa rose and lifted her son from Petrus' lap. 'Sorry, Sir. Of course, we will wait to hear from you.'

The sun's feeble rays had not yet warmed the street and his feet crunched on the frozen mud as he walked. The cool breeze tugged at his clothes and lifted his hair, chilling his scalp. He pulled up the hood on his cloak. Ruua's shop door stood open. Two women were chatting with the herbalist, one clutched a bunch of dried grasses in her hand. Ruua did not smile as he entered the shop. The two women hurried away.

'Greetings,' said Petrus.

'What brings you here?'

'I have news. We've arrested the men who murdered Manius.'

She went pale and her hands began to shake. She let go of the herbs she was holding, and they fell to the floor. She made no attempt to pick them up.

'What are you going to do with them?' she whispered.

'Roman law says we must take into account the wishes of the victim's family. I know you weren't formally married, but your opinion counts.'

'Show mercy, show mercy. They may have felt there was a good reason to kill him.' A tear rolled down her cheek.

Petrus raised an eyebrow in surprise and waited while the woman wept. A sudden noise behind him made him turn around.

'I heard you were here, sniffing around. What the fuck do you want now?!' roared Litorius as he strode in and went to his mother's side.

She stared at her son in silence, a look of horror on her face.

'Watch your mouth, or I'll arrest you,' snarled Petrus.

Ruua placed a shaking hand on her son's arm. 'He-he came to tell me they'd caught the men who murdered Manius.'

'They what?' Litorius clenched his fists.

'Caught the murderers. They confessed. I was asking your mother about punishment. She has a right to say what she thinks,' said Petrus.

'Bastards should be executed!' spat Litorius.

'Your mother favours mercy.'

Litorius turned to stare at his mother for a moment. Her lips trembled as she clung on to his arm. He shrugged her off, pushed past Petrus, and stormed out of the shop. Petrus caught sight of Tarpi staring out at him from behind some large sacks, her eyes wide in terror. He nodded to Ruua and left the shop. Behind him, he heard the girl's running feet and her mother's murmured reassurances.

Petrus pushed open the door to his home. Titus threw himself at his father. Petrus scooped him into his arms, hugged him close, and kissed his cheek. Titus laughed and pulled at his father's ears. Petrus put him down and he ran from the room, laughing. Petrus kissed Aurora who had Antigone suckling noisily at her breast. He poured two cups of ale from the pitcher in the corner of the room, handed one to his wife, and settled himself on a stool near the fire. His daughter belched quietly, and Aurora began stroking her back.

Petrus spoke. 'It's all over. Tatius wanted Manius to keep quiet when he found out about the grain thefts. Manius refused. Tatius offered to pay that drunkard Cato five hundred denarii to kill Manius and when Cato turned him down, he threatened him with banishment. Cato has confessed - he found Manius drunk in the street and was helped to carry him to the Mithraeum. He claims that he intended to go back for him but was too drunk and forgot all about it. Tatius has confessed that he told Cato to frighten Manius, not to kill him. He denies helping Cato with the murder. However, he can't account for his whereabouts at the time Manius went missing. Claims he was at the temple of Jupiter, but there are no witnesses to that.'

'What happens now?'

'The Governor will decide. There'll be a trial. I asked Manius' widow what she wanted to happen to the murderers, and she said, 'show them mercy.' I was quite surprised. Then her son came in and he said, 'Execute the bastards!' Quite a difference. There was no love lost between him and Manius.'

'Maybe Ruua just wants it all to be over with,' murmured Aurora.

'She's not the only one! I'm exhausted.'

Aurora pulled a basket towards her and lay her daughter down in it. She stepped towards Petrus, wrapping her arms around his shoulders and pulling his head in towards her chest. She breathed heavily and laid her cheek against the top of his head.

'Not too exhausted to take a woman with you into the fort yesterday, were you?' she whispered, moving slightly away and looking down at him.

'That woman was Caussa, Cato's wife. She was there to identify the man who paid Cato to kill Manius. I had to make sure no-one could see who she was when she came to the fort,' he sighed. 'Those bloody gatekeepers! Gossips! You don't really think I would take a woman into the fort, do you? Not when I've got you here?'

'No. Not really. It's just that someone mentioned it, that's all.'

'Some bitter old woman, I expect. Someone who's just jealous of you having such a handsome husband.' He grinned as he buried his face in her belly once more. 'I'm going to get some leave after the trial,' his voice was muffled against her smock.

'That's a sort of reward from Pollux. The Governor should be here in a couple of days.'

Aurora kissed him again and pulled him to his feet, wrapping her arms around him, and hugged him tightly. 'Why don't we practice ready for when you have several days or weeks of leave?'

She led him out of the kitchen towards their bedroom.

XXIV

Four days later…

Pollux made a brief address to the morning parade but did not dismiss the men. They stood shuffling their feet and murmuring in discontent. The beat of a drum thundered across the fort as the Governor strode onto the stage in his flowing purple robe, flanked by his bodyguards. Pollux stood aside. The men fell silent and stood to attention.

'Men of Banna Fort, as you know, two men were involved in the murder of your librarius, Manius. One is a retired centurion; the other is your Prefect, Silvius Tatius. There will be a trial here at the parade ground at the fifth hour of the day. Those of you without other duties can spectate,' announced the Governor.

Pollux stepped forward and dismissed the men. The Governor made his way to the praetorium. Pollux called the centurions to Tatius' office.

'I briefed the Governor when he arrived at my house last night. Petrus, bring Cato's wife to the fort, but keep her out of sight. She'll be called as a witness. Get a message to Manius' woman. She and her family have the right to be here if they wish,' said Pollux.

Petrus nodded.

Pollux said, 'Ruga, as the men have been told they can watch the trial, I want you and sixteen men to stand with the prisoners as guard. Cato is in a pathetic state, and I'm not worried about him, but Tatius may appeal to the Governor directly, or to the men. I don't know about their loyalties to him.'

Ruga raised an eyebrow and replied, 'He's not popular, especially after he banned the wives from the fort. I don't think there'll be a problem. At the end of the day, the men are soldiers and will take orders from the senior command, but I'll have some of my most trusted men to stand guard, just in case.'

'Very well. I expect all you centurions to be present for the trial and any immediate sentence.' Pollux pointed towards Roburius, Vegetinus and Ferullus. 'These three are having their pay cut in half for the next six months and they will not be allowed to leave the fort during that period except under my orders. They are being punished for their excessive gambling and bringing the army into disrepute. Rumours are even circulating in the vicus that they will act as debt collectors and hired muscle if you pay them enough!' He held up his hand to silence the three men who all began to speak. 'I don't care whether it's true or not. The point is the people of the vicus think you're no better than Cato. Go away, everyone! Now!'

Outside the office, the three centurions turned on Petrus.

'Thanks for that!' spat Roburius. 'You didn't need to tell them about us.'

'It's all over the vicus that you could be hired as debt collectors and you've all got a bad reputation for gambling and fighting. It's not a secret,' replied Petrus.

'Bastard!' muttered Ferullus under his breath as he walked away.

Vegetinus and Roburius followed him quietly.

Petrus made his way to the brothel. Caussa had big dark circles under her eyes.

'The Governor is here. He's holding a trial. Will you come to the fort to give evidence?' Petrus asked.

She nodded. 'I'll get one of the girls to mind the children.'

At the fort, Petrus ordered the gatekeepers to let her pass without giving her name.

'The Governor is here, Sir. We must take names for security,' said Rufus.

'This woman is a witness in the trial. Let her pass!'

The man looked as if he was about to refuse. Petrus felt Caussa tense beside him.

'Must I fetch the Governor?!' spat Petrus.

Rufus scribbled on his tablet '*Aurelius Petrus and a woman witness*' and held it out to Petrus. 'Please sign here, Sir, as a record. And use your seal.'

Petrus was secretly pleased that the gatekeeper was behaving so officiously, but he didn't let it show. At his office, he sent for Gauori to bring some watered-down wine.

'Caussa, you can wait here until the trial begins,' he indicated a seat near the window.

Gauori burst into the room with a pitcher and two cups. He paused in surprise when he saw Caussa.

'This woman will be a witness at the trial, Gauori. You must not tell anyone that you have seen her.' Petrus said.

Gauori nodded as he poured the wine.

'Gauori, I want you to go to the herbalist Ruua's place and tell her the trial is going ahead this morning, at the fifth hour of the day. She can come here with her family if she wants to see justice done.' He scribbled on a tablet, 'Give her this tablet. She probably can't read it, but it gives orders to the soldiers to allow her family into the fort today to attend the trial.' He handed it to Gauori who left the office and ran towards the gates.

Petrus began reviewing his reports into the investigation, making sure all points were covered. Caussa sat quietly, staring out of the window and occasionally sipping at the wine.

Petrus led Caussa to the parade ground and stood beside her

at the edge of the stage. She held her hood up so that it obscured her face. Small groups of soldiers stood around the parade ground, shuffling their feet, and holding quiet conversations. Petrus looked around, searching for Ruua. He could not see her, but thought he glimpsed Litorius hovering nearby.

Ruga marched Tatius across the ground and tied his bound hands to a post at the foot of the stage. Two soldiers supported Cato as he stumbled forward. They tied him to a second post. The Governor strode onto the stage and took a seat. Pollux stood at his side. Balbus sat nearby, clutching a stylus and some tablets, ready to make a record of the trial.

Pollux spoke. 'Silvius Tatius, you are charged with conspiracy to murder and the murder of Manius, a soldier of the Roman Army. How do you plead?'

'Not guilty to both charges,' Tatius stared defiantly at the Governor as he spoke.

Pollux turned towards Cato. 'Cato, you are charged with the murder of Manius. How do you plead?'

Cato raised his head. His eyes were bloodshot. 'Not guilty to murder. He, Tatius, forced me! He threatened me! I didn't mean him to die.'

Pollux nodded. 'You'll get your chance to explain.' He turned towards Balbus. 'Have you written that down?'

Balbus nodded, scribbling furiously on one of the tablets.

The watching soldiers moved closer to the stage. Ruga's men raised their swords and stepped forward to prevent them from approaching the prisoners.

Pollux turned towards Caussa, 'Step forward and take down your hood, so that we can see who you are.'

Caussa shuffled forward and slowly pulled her hood down.

'Identify yourself to the court,' Pollux's voice was harsh.

'I-I-I am Caussa, wife of Cato, mother of his children.'

'Do you swear before all the Gods and in the name of the Emperor Marcus Aurelius to tell the truth, the whole truth?'

'I swear.'

'I have a statement here recorded on a tablet. I'm going to ask you some questions about it.'

She nodded.

'Some weeks ago, a soldier visited your home to speak with your husband, didn't he?'

She nodded.

'I want you to tell us about that day. Speak slowly, as that man over there is recording what you say. I may ask you to pause, so that he can catch up,' Pollux said.

'An officer came to the house to speak with Cato. Cato was frightened of him,' she began.

'Why was he frightened?'

'I think it is because the officer was so senior. And it's never good news when the army arrives at your house, is it?' She blushed.

'Aurelius Petrus brought you to the fort a few days ago to see if you were able to recognise the officer, didn't he?'

'Yes. And I did recognise him.'

'Can you see that man here today?'

'It was him.' She raised her arm and pointed at Tatius.

Pollux smiled and nodded. 'Go on.'

'Cato asked me to listen in to the conversation from behind a door.'

'What did this man say to your husband?'

'He asked him to kill a man called Manius who worked at the fort. Said he'd give him five hundred denarii if he did so. Cato refused.'

'Then what did the officer say?'

'He said if Cato didn't do it, then he would make up some charges against him. Cato and the children would be stripped of their citizenship, and we would all be banished. He gave Cato one hundred denarii and said the remainder would be paid when the man was dead.'

'You wrote all this down, didn't you, on this tablet?' Pollux held up a tablet.

She nodded.

'Why did you do that?' Pollux asked.

'Cato told me to write it down, as a record of the conversation, and to sign and date it. He said we should keep it safe, in case he needed to defend himself in the future.'

'So, that's what you did. And you kept it safe for a day like today?'

'Yes, Sir.'

'Can you confirm that this is the tablet you wrote on? And this is your signature?' Pollux held the tablet towards her.

She peered at it and nodded, 'Yes, Sir.'

Pollux showed the tablet to Tatius who nodded and then to Cato who grinned. He passed the tablet to the Governor, who glanced at it and then gave it to Balbus.

'Why didn't Cato report this to the authorities?' Pollux asked.

She shrugged. 'I cannot speak for my husband. I do not know what was in his mind. But even if he had reported it, no-one would have believed him. He has a bad reputation, as a drunk and a gambler.'

'What did your husband do, then?'

'He just carried on, drinking and gambling.'

There were some sniggers from the men watching. Pollux raised a hand, and they fell quiet. 'When Manius' body was found. Did you discuss it with your husband?'

'He said he'd taken the man to the Mithraeum and had meant to go back for him, but he'd forgotten.'

'Did he tell you how he managed to take Manius to the temple? It's a long way.'

'No, just mumbled something about finding him in the street and then being helped to carry him to the temple.'

'Did he receive the remaining four hundred denarii from the army officer?'

'I don't know.'

'What will happen to you now? Now that your husband has

confessed.'

She turned to look at the Governor and dropped to her knees. Tears trickled down her cheeks. 'Please Sir, I beg you to show mercy on Cato's family.'

Petrus pulled her gently to her feet and kept hold of her arm as she sobbed.

'Cato. Do you want to question the witness?' asked Pollux.

Cato looked up and shook his head.

'Silvius Tatius, do you have any questions for her?' Pollux asked.

Tatius bowed awkwardly towards the Governor, bending his head down over his tied hands.

'Can I move to stand nearer the witness, so that I can address the court?' Tatius pulled at the ropes.

'You can stay where you are. Do you have any questions?' Pollux snapped.

'You say you saw me at your house and overheard me telling Cato to kill Manius?' Tatius said.

Caussa nodded.

'Speak, so that the whole court can hear you, woman!' Tatius shouted.

Caussa trembled, and Petrus moved closer to support her.

'Don't intimidate the witness, Tatius!' yelled Pollux.

Tatius took a deep breath. 'Can you speak up so that the court can hear you? Do you say you saw me at your house, telling Cato to kill Manius?'

'Yes, yes, I did. You paid him one hundred denarii and promised four hundred more when he'd done it.'

'You are lying! I came to your house and paid Cato fifty denarii to threaten Manius, to make sure he stayed in the fort and didn't get a message to the Tribune, didn't I?'

'No! No! That's not true!' Caussa raised her voice. 'You told him to kill Manius. You gave him one hundred denarii and said there would be four hundred more when the job was done. You said you'd raise charges against him and have us hounded out of the community if he didn't do as you'd asked!'

'It's in your interests to lie, isn't it?'

'No. No! I'm not lying.'

Tatius looked at the governor. 'It's in her interests to lie. If they can implicate me in the murder, then they hope that will lessen the sentence imposed on Cato. Particularly if the court believes, I forced him to do the killing. It's my word against hers. A common woman against a Prefect in the Roman army.'

The Governor nodded.

'Have you any further questions?' Pollux asked.

'No.'

'Cato, do you have any witnesses you would like to call to give evidence on your behalf?'

'No, Sir. You have heard from my wife; she is my witness. You have seen the tablet where she recorded the details of my meeting with him, with Tatius.' Cato shook as he spoke.

'Very well. Untie Cato and move him over here!' commanded Pollux, pointing to a spot in front of the stage.

The two soldiers untied him from the post and helped him to stagger forward. Beads of sweat dribbled down his face, despite the cold.

'Do you swear to tell the truth, the whole truth, before all the Gods and in the name of the Emperor Marcus Aurelius?' asked Pollux.

'I do.'

'Do you work in the vicus as a debt collector?'

'Yes, sometimes.'

'What does that involve? Does it involve violence?'

'Sometimes. I've got a bit of a reputation now, so usually threats are enough to get them to pay up.'

'A reputation, eh? So, if Tatius wanted someone threatened, or beaten, or even killed, he might think you were someone who could do that?'

Cato looked at Tatius, then back towards Pollux. 'I guess so.'

'Do you confirm the meeting your wife described took place between you and the Prefect?'

Cato stammered 'I... I do. He said he'd pay me five hundred denarii. W-when I said I wouldn't kill Manius, he threatened me, just as Caussa has said.' He wiped a sleeve across his sweaty forehead.

'How did you feel when he threatened you?'

'Trapped. I felt I had no choice.'

'You didn't act immediately though, did you?'

'No. I went drinking.'

'You drink most of the time, don't you?'

Cato nodded. 'Every day. I'm a free man.'

There were sniggers from the men watching.

'So why did you act against Manius on that particular night?'

'I just found him lying in the street on my way back home from the tavern. Must've seemed like a good opportunity to give him a scare, I suppose. I don't remember much about taking him to the Mithraeum, 'cept someone tall in a dark, hooded cloak was helping me, someone like him.' He nodded at the prefect who opened his mouth to protest.

Pollux raised a hand to silence Tatius.

'Are you sure it was the Prefect?'

Cato didn't answer.

'The two of you left him in the Mithraeum to die,' said Pollux.

'No! No! I meant to go back for him. I forgot.'

'You say that Tatius told you to kill him. Threatened you, forced you to murder an innocent man! What did you think would happen if you had remembered that he was in the pit, and you had released him? What would Tatius have done then? You wouldn't have done what he paid you for.'

Cato shrugged. 'I dunno. I can't say what Tatius would've done.'

'Do you expect the court,' Pollux waved his arms about, expansively, 'these spectators, to believe your story?'

'It's true! It's true!'

'I put it to you that following the threats made by Tatius, you grabbed Manius, who'd been drinking, drugged him and then took him to the Mithraeum. You placed him in the pit and covered it over. You took him to the Mithraeum to throw suspicion on all the worshippers who attend there. You never intended to go back for him.'

'No. No, I didn't. I was going to go back for him. I was, I was, I swear!' Cato wailed and began to sway from side to side. One of the soldiers steadied him.

'Did Tatius pay you the remaining four hundred denarii?'

'Yes, yes, he did. After the body was found.'

Pollux turned towards the Governor, 'I have no further questions, Sir.'

'Tatius? Do you have anything you wish to put to Cato?' The Governor asked.

'Yes. I do. Why are you lying about our meeting at your home? I offered you fifty denarii to frighten Manius, didn't I?' Tatius said.

'No! No! You gave me a hundred denarii and told me to kill the librarius. You promised four hundred more when I'd done it. You threatened my family, you bastard!' Cato screamed.

'You say a man helped you carry an unconscious Manius up to the Mithraeum?' Tatius continued.

'Yes.'

'Can you identify the man?'

'No, not exactly, but he was tall like you.'

'Not a firm identification, then!' spat Tatius. He turned to face the governor, 'I've nothing further.'

The Governor nodded, and Cato was taken back to the post and tied up.

'Tatius? Do you have any witnesses to give evidence on your behalf?' The Governor asked.

Tatius shook his head. The soldiers untied him and brought him to the front of the stage with his hands still bound.

'Do you swear before all the Gods and in the name of the Emperor Marcus Aurelius to tell the truth, the whole truth?' Pollux asked.

'I do,' Tatius inclined his body towards the Governor, but addressed the spectators. 'I am Silvius Tatius, Prefect at Banna fort.'

There was jeering from the men on the parade ground. 'Not for much longer!' shouted someone from the back of the crowd.

'Silence!' bellowed the Governor, 'Or I will have the area cleared.'

The men fell quiet.

'I did not kill Manius,' said Tatius.

Pollux nodded. 'So you say. What dealings did you have with him?'

'Not much, really. He was the senior librarius. His work should be monitored by the Signifer.'

'Manius came with Ecdicius, the Signifer, to tell you that Adrianus and Lucullus had been stealing from the army, didn't he?' Pollux asked.

'Yes.'

'What did you do then?'

'I told him I would deal with it.'

'Deal with it. What did you mean? Surely it would've been normal procedure to report the issue to me, the Tribune?'

'Yes, it would. But you were away. I wanted to resolve the issue myself before you arrived. I've had some problems here recently, and I needed to show my authority.'

'Were you afraid of being recalled to Rome in disgrace?'

There were titters from the spectators.

Titus looked around and then mumbled, 'Yes.'

'And did you make threats towards them?' Pollux asked.

'Er, no, not at that time.'

'Did you threaten Manius before he was killed?'

'No. I did not.'

'Tell the court about your visit to Cato's house, the one we've heard about earlier.'

'I visited him and gave him fifty denarii to threaten Manius. To make him shut up. It turned out Manius had already been threatened by Lucullus. I could've saved my money.'

The spectating men shouted and jeered.

'Silence!' bellowed the Governor.

The men immediately settled back down.

'You expect the court to believe that in order to maintain a façade of good management you paid a local drunk to threaten him?' Pollux sneered.

'Yes, yes, I do.'

'And having paid Cato to threaten Manius, did you resolve the issue of the thefts? Did you arrest Adrianus and Lucullus?' Pollux asked.

'Err, no, I did not.'

'So, you weren't sorting out the thefts at the fort, were you?'

Tatius did not reply.

'After Manius' death, Ecdicius told you to report the thefts to me, didn't he?' Pollux said.

'Yes, yes, he did.'

'Did you report them? Or did you threaten Ecdicius to keep him quiet?'

Tatius did not reply immediately.

'Answer the question!' Pollux bellowed.

'I didn't report them. I threatened Ecdicius, to keep him quiet,' Tatius' voice was barely above a whisper.

'You threatened to have his friend enslaved, didn't you?'

'Yes.'

'You're a liar, aren't you?'

'No. No. I'm not.'

'But you lied to me on three separate occasions concerning when you found out about the thefts, didn't you?'

'Yes, I was… was embarrassed. I tried to cover it up.'

There were mumblings from the spectators.

Pollux continued, 'You paid Cato to murder Manius in order to cover things up, didn't you?'

'No! No!'

'The night Manius went missing you were outside the fort. What were you doing?'

'I visited the brothel and then I went to the Temple of Jupiter.'

'We have verified your visit to the brothel. That's not in dispute. You've not provided any witnesses for your time at the temple. What were you doing there? You didn't return until almost daylight the following day.'

'I had a lot to pray about. I was petitioning Jupiter to bless my forthcoming marriage and to help me in my role as Prefect. As I've said, things have been difficult since… since those events months ago.' He paused and looked at his feet, then looked up again, staring straight at the Governor. 'I sacrificed a sheep, then I lay prostrate on the floor in front of the altar. I… I may have fallen asleep.'

'The priest was unable to confirm your presence in the temple. You're asking the court to believe you were there all night?'

'Yes, yes, I am. I swear on the lives of my children.'

Pollux raised his eyebrows and hissed, 'I put it to you, that you paid Cato a hundred denarii to kill Manius and promised a further four hundred denarii when it was done. Cato found Manius drunk in the street and saw that as an opportunity to get rid of him. You were in the vicus at the time and you both forced a sleeping drug down his throat, to keep him compliant. Then you took him to the temple and left him in the pit to die of thirst.'

'No. No. I swear.' Tatius began to struggle against the soldier holding him.

Two more soldiers grabbed Tatius and wrestled with him before dragging him back to the post and tying him up. This time he did not look up; he stared disconsolately at his feet.

Pollux turned to face the governor, 'To summarise, Sir. Cato is well-known in the vicus as a debt collector, someone not averse to using violence against people in return for payment. He states Tatius offered him five hundred denarii to kill Manius. He also states that he initially refused to do this and then Tatius threatened to bring charges against him, strip his family of citizenship and banish them. He states Tatius gave him a hundred denarii and promised the rest when Manius was dead. Cato has admitted to taking an unconscious Manius to the Mithraeum and leaving him there in the pit. He said he was helped to carry Manius by a tall man in a dark cloak whom he cannot identify. He claims he intended to go back for Manius but forgot about him, as he was drunk. After the body was found, Cato states Tatius gave him the remaining four hundred denarii. Cato's story is supported by his wife who has stated, under oath, that she overheard the Prefect offering her husband the money to kill Manius and the threats he made when her husband refused. She has no reason to lie. She cannot save her husband, who has already admitted to causing the death of Manius.

The Court contends that Cato was acting under threat from Tatius who had told him to kill Manius. He may well have intended to release the librarius, however, as he forgot about him, Manius died, of thirst, in a freezing cold pit in complete darkness. Cato must take responsibility for the man's death. The Governor should find him guilty of murder.

Tatius has been a weak and ineffective commander, one whose officers do not follow orders. He has admitted that he failed in his responsibility to effectively manage the fort's finances or conduct basic checks. One of the librarii had been conspiring with a merchant to steal grain from the army. The thefts were discovered by Manius who informed the Signifer and the prefect. Tatius wanted to save his reputation, but Manius was insistent that the thefts be reported to me, the Tribune. Tatius has admitted all this.

Facing ruin and an ignominious recall to Rome, he

needed to stop Manius from reaching me while he worked to cover up the thefts. He was outside the fort all night on Manius' last day. His claim to have been in the Temple of Jupiter all night is hardly credible and he cannot produce any witnesses to his being there. His version of the meeting with Cato is hardly believable, nor is his story of falling asleep in the Temple of Jupiter. Can we trust a man who, even on his own version of events, paid another man to beat up one of his own soldiers in order to cover up a crime that had occurred? A man who admits lying to me, the Tribune, on three separate occasions when I interviewed him.

I urge the Governor to find Tatius guilty of conspiracy to murder.'

Pollux took a seat at the side of the stage. The Governor sat with his hands on his knees, staring at the two men, who raised their heads to meet his gaze, Tatius once more defiant, Cato with tears running down his face.

Petrus could hear the blood rushing in his ears.

They waited.

The Governor whispered to Pollux who beckoned Aquilinus over and whispered to him. Aquilinus hurried away with six soldiers. The Governor settled back in his seat and closed his eyes.

The silence went on and on.

The watching soldiers remained frozen in place.

Aquilinus ran onto the parade ground. Behind him, the soldiers carried a yoke with a large black pot dangling from it. Smoke rose from the pot. They set it on the ground near Pollux.

The Governor sighed, 'Bring both men forward.'

The soldiers untied both men and brought them to stand in front of the stage. They kept a tight grip on their captives' arms. Two of the soldiers drew their swords.

The Governor spoke. 'The court finds the wife Caussa's evidence credible. She has no reason to lie. She has not sought to exonerate her husband from causing Manius' death, but to clarify what he did and why. I believe that Tatius forced Cato to kill Manius by threatening him and his family. He paid him five hundred denarii. So, he is guilty of conspiracy to murder. I cannot be sure it was Tatius who helped Cato carry Manius to the Temple, although it is highly likely. I believe that Cato, under threat from Tatius, decided to kill Manius, taking him to the temple and leaving him in the pit. Therefore, I find him guilty of murder.'

Nobody moved. Silence fell across the parade ground.

Pollux said, 'Silvius Tatius, do you wish to say anything to the court before it passes sentence?'

'I am a weak and foolish man. I beg the court for mercy.' Tatius did not look up as he spoke.

'Cato, do you have anything to say to the court?' said Pollux.

'I beg the court for mercy. I am a poor drunkard and I have made poor choices. Please show mercy to my family.' Cato fell to his knees, his hands clasped in front of him, his head bowed.

The Governor took a deep breath. 'The widow of the dead man has asked for leniency. Tatius, you have been found guilty of conspiracy to murder. You are a Prefect, son of a senatorial family. You will lose your citizenship and be enslaved. I will take you with me when I leave here, and you will be sold to the Gladiatorium in Londinium.'

Tatius cried out and began to struggle against the men holding him up. Aquilinus took something from the black pot, a branding iron. It glowed red hot. He stepped forward. He ripped open Tatius' robe, exposing his bare chest. Aquilinus pressed the brand against Tatius' bare skin. The thick stink of roasting flesh filled the air. Tatius screamed and collapsed, unconscious.

The watching soldiers were frozen in horror.

'Doesn't bode well for his life as a gladiator, does it? Can't take a bit of pain,' murmured Ruga under his breath.

'Cato is, was, a centurion,' said the Governor, 'He has sullied the reputation of the Roman Army and murdered a fellow soldier. The sentence is death. Effective immediately.'

Cato remained motionless. The two soldiers standing beside him stepped away. A third soldier drew his sword, raised it, and sliced through Cato's neck in one clean cut. Cato's headless corpse toppled forward; blood spurted from the neck in a red arc. The fingers of his left hand moved, scratching slowly at the earth. The severed head rolled forward and came to rest, facing the watching soldiers. The open eyes stared ahead.

Caussa moaned. Petrus put his arm around her and lowered her to the ground where she knelt and cried out in pain, rocking back and forth. She crawled across the ground and placed a hand on her husband's shoulder. His life blood soaked into her trousers as she wept.

'Take Tatius to the cells. He'll be kept there until the Governor is ready to leave. Petrus, inform Manius' family of the verdict and sentences. Take the woman home and deal with her the same way as Lucullus' wife,' said Pollux.

The Governor rose and walked off the stage, followed by Pollux. Aquilinus' men picked up Tatius' unconscious body and carried him towards the cells. Ruga dismissed the spectating soldiers, who walked away in shock, muttering amongst themselves. Petrus lifted Caussa to her feet and turned towards the fort gate. Behind them, soldiers carried Cato's body away and brushed sand over the bloodstained ground.

Petrus walked slowly alongside Caussa. They didn't speak. She wept silently. Her smock was soaked with blood and its metallic stink was all around them. Petrus winced as he heard men banging a stake into the ground outside the gate, knowing that Cato's head would be displayed there.

At the brothel, Sylva led them silently to her room.

'Take your children back to your house and pack your things.

Your house is now the property of the army and the new owner will be along soon. The Tribune has agreed that you can stay there with your family as a servant if you wish. You are not responsible for your husband's actions,' Petrus spoke gently.

Caussa raised her tear-stained face and whispered, 'Thank you.' She went into her room, closing the door behind her.

Her screams reached through the door and pierced his heart.

The sun's weak rays tickled his face as he passed through the empty streets. Word of the trial and sentences had spread quickly through the community. Even the tavern was quiet. He was relieved that the investigation was over, but shocked at the sentences meted out. The smell of burned flesh and memory of Cato's severed head brought tears to his eyes. He slowed his pace, allowing himself time to recover.

As he approached Ruua's shop, he heard raised voices. He recognised one of them as Litorius. He stepped into the shadow behind the shop door and listened.

Litorius said, 'They found them both guilty of murdering Manius. They executed Cato there and then. Tatius has been enslaved and will be taken to the Gladiatorium in Londinium, wherever that is. They won't be looking for anyone else. Tarpi has been avenged!'

Petrus could not make out Ruua's response. He waited a moment and then stepped into the shop. Ruua squealed in shock. Litorius whipped round to face Petrus, his face drained of colour. Tarpi screamed. She wriggled out of her mother's arms and ran out of the room.

'Why did your daughter need avenging?' asked Petrus, his hand on the hilt of his sword.

Ruua began to weep. 'Manius started visiting me after my husband died. He was kind and good with Tarpi. She was a toddler then. He played with her and showered her with toys. She would sit on his lap, and he'd tell her stories. Then… then…' she paused and wiped her nose on her sleeve, 'As she grew a bit older, she became frightened of him. She didn't sit with him anymore, always stayed near me and cried if he spoke to her. I... I couldn't watch her every minute.'

Petrus waited.

'I asked her what was wrong. She... she...' Ruua did not finish her words.

Litorius snarled, 'He raped her! He did it over and over! He-he'd done it before, to the children at the brothel. I challenged him. He said she wanted it. She was six years old! I didn't want him here after that, but he kept coming round. She,' he inclined his head in his mother's direction, 'relied on him for money, so he kept coming.'

Petrus felt sick. He relaxed his grip on the sword. Images of Manius raping Tarpi flashed through his mind. They were replaced by images of Manius raping his own daughter, Antigone. He took a few deep breaths. His heart thumped in his chest and his head began to ache.

'I tried to protect her. Never leaving them alone together. But sometimes ... I couldn't keep her with me every moment of the day,' wept Ruua.

'I had to protect Tarpi! That night, Ma gave him a sleeping draught, as she had been doing for weeks. She couldn't bear him near her. I stayed at the tavern where Cato was drinking. I gambled with him, and he was in debt to me by the end. As we walked home, we talked a lot. He told me about Tatius forcing him to kill Manius. I saw the opportunity. We came here and carried Manius up towards the Mithraeum. Cato wanted suspicion to fall on Tatius and the members of the cult. But Manius woke up when we were on the edge of town. He'd grown used to the sleeping drugs. He fought hard against us, nearly pulled my hair out!' he ran a hand through his straggly hair. 'Cato hit him on the head with a stone, knocked him out. Then the two of us carried him to the Mithraeum and put him in the pit. I clapped Cato on the back and told him he'd get the additional four hundred denarii. I knew Cato wouldn't give me up if he was caught and charged. Even if he remembered I'd helped him, Tatius had forced him to do it.'

Petrus was silent. He felt a great weight in his chest and a sharp pain in his head. Ruua looked from her son towards Petrus and then back again. Tears coursed down her cheeks.

'Manius was a man who abused children,' Petrus mumbled and put out a hand to steady himself against the wall.

Ruua nodded. 'I tried to protect her. I failed.'

They stood in silence.

'He deserved to die,' Petrus murmured to himself as he stared at Litorius. Petrus' mind was in turmoil. He took a step towards Litorius.

'Please!' begged Ruua.

Petrus' thoughts crystallised. He straightened up and looked at Ruua. 'I am here to inform you that Manius' murderers have been tried and sentenced. That is the end of the matter.'

Litorius opened his mouth to speak, then closed it again. He stepped towards Petrus his hands outstretched, the palms facing upwards, 'Thank you, Aurelius Petrus. I am in your debt.'

Petrus turned on his heel and left the shop. Behind him, Ruua sobbed quietly, and Litorius moved to comfort her.

Petrus made his way home. He needed to hold his family close. He would start his leave immediately.

Acknowledgements

Without the continuing help and support of my writing group 'Imaginary Friends' I would never have found Aurelius Petrus, or written about him. Their thoughtful comments and encouragement were invaluable. My husband, Phil, has continued to be a strong supporter of my work. Thanks go to all those at Northodox who believed in me and who have continued to work so hard to get it into print.

FIND US ON SOCIAL MEDIA

www.northodox.co.uk

f @northodoxpress

⊙ @northodoxpressofficial

▾ @northodoxpress

♪ @northodoxpress

🦋 @northodoxpress.bsky.social

⊛ www.northodox.co.uk

NORTHODOX PRESS

SUBMISSIONS

CONTEMPORARY
CRIME & THRILLER
FANTASY
LGBTQ+
ROMANCE
YOUNG ADULT
SCI-FI & HORROR
HISTORICAL
LITERARY

SUBMISSIONS@NORTHODOX.CO.UK

SUBMISSIONS

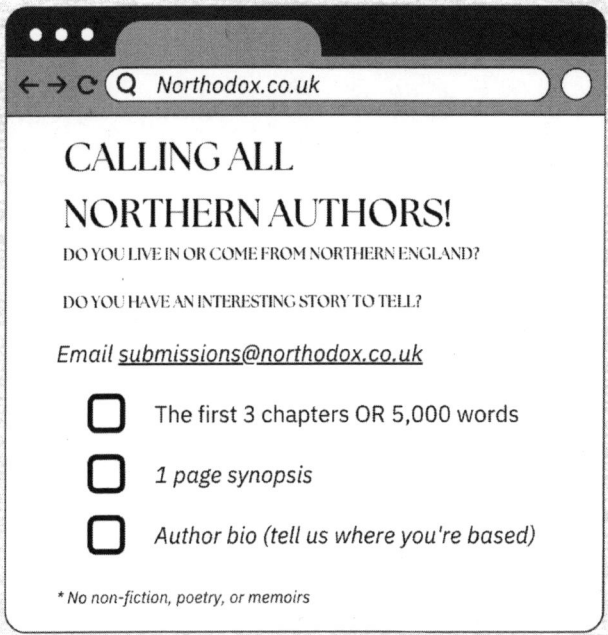

CALLING ALL NORTHERN AUTHORS!

DO YOU LIVE IN OR COME FROM NORTHERN ENGLAND?

DO YOU HAVE AN INTERESTING STORY TO TELL?

Email *submissions@northodox.co.uk*

- ☐ The first 3 chapters OR 5,000 words
- ☐ *1 page synopsis*
- ☐ *Author bio (tell us where you're based)*

* No non-fiction, poetry, or memoirs

SUBMISSIONS@NORTHODOX.CO.UK

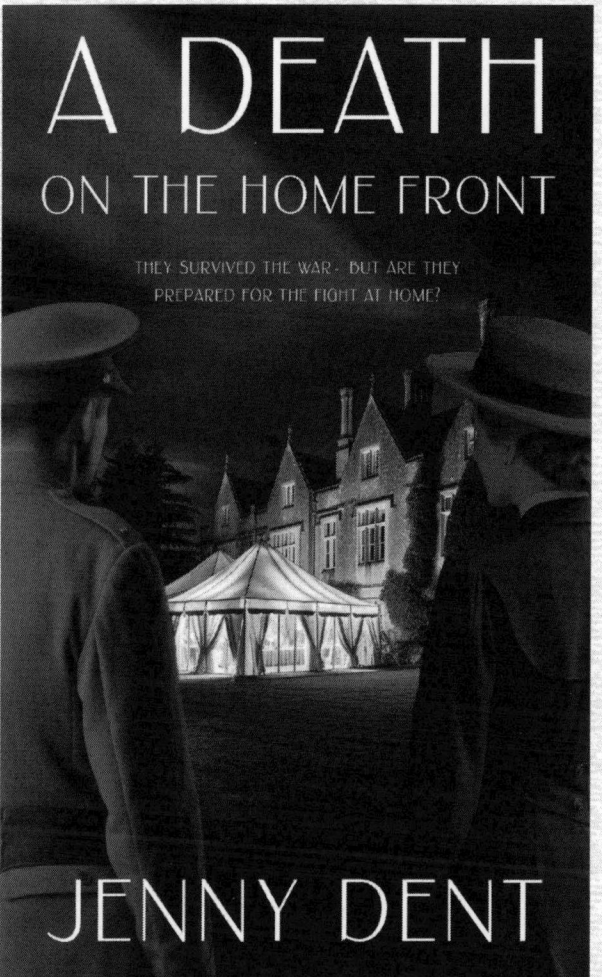

A DEATH
ON THE HOME FRONT

THEY SURVIVED THE WAR - BUT ARE THEY
PREPARED FOR THE FIGHT AT HOME?

JENNY DENT